CRASHING
down

To Niamh and Finn

KATE McCAFFREY

CRASHING *down*

 FREMANTLE PRESS

1

Lucy eyes with amusement the clothes strewn over the bed. They have to be the single ugliest collection of garments she has ever seen. The Thrift Shop Ball. The final social event before the beginning of the exam period. You had to buy your clothes from the Salvos — a far cry from the sheer extravagance of the School Ball earlier in the year, which saw thousands of dollars spent on dresses and H2 Hummers and ornate hairstyles. The Thrift Shop Ball was meant to be a statement. Lucy snorts — she knows everyone else regards it as just an opportunity to blow off steam and celebrate before the exams.

This is the last week of school, the mocks are two later, and then, after that, the big ones. The final exams. University entrance or — what? She can't even consider the possibility of not making it.

'Well?'

Lucy looks up as Georgia stands in the doorway. She is a sight. Green velvet mini over red paisley tights and knee-high brown boots.

'Beautiful,' Lucy says, laughing. 'Lydia?'

Lydia emerges from the bathroom in a floor-length blue chiffon gown with a huge diamanté brooch gathering the fabric under her breasts. The dress, which was probably the height of fashion in 1950, completely swamps Lydia's tiny frame. She looks like she is drowning in an ocean of fabric.

'Oh. My. God!' Lucy collapses on the bed in hysterics.

'What?' Lydia asks. 'Does it make my bum look big?'

'No,' Lucy says, 'but it makes your boobs look huge.' Lucy can't take her eyes off Lydia's sudden page-three-girl proportions.

Georgia reaches over and pokes one. 'Yeah, they're massive, Lyd.'

Lydia smirks. Georgia and Lucy exchange a look — they know that smirk. It's the one Lydia uses when she is feeling incredibly pleased with herself.

'Weeelll ...' Lydia drags the word out and turns to face the mirror, adjusting her enormous bosom as she speaks to their reflections. 'The dress was obviously too big.'

'Obviously,' Lucy and Georgia agree.

'And so I needed a little ...' — Lydia dips her hand into her cleavage and pushes her boobs up even higher — 'help.'

'Chicken fillets?' Lucy suggests.

'Ewww.' Lydia wrinkles up her nose. 'No, these.' She extracts a plastic insert from inside her bra.

'Chicken fillets,' Georgia confirms.

'What?' Lydia looks alarmed, she sniffs the plastic. 'Gross! Are these made from chicken?'

'No, Lydia.' Georgia sighs. 'That's what they're called. Could you have got them any bigger?'

'Nope.' Lydia puts the fake boob back in. 'Biggest they had. A double D. Why? Are they not big enough?'

'Seriously?' Lucy laughs. 'You look like a walking mammary gland.'

'Ewww,' Lydia says, 'what kind of animal is that?'

'Oh, Lydia!' Georgia sighs again, and then points

to the black pants-suit in Lucy's hands. 'You wearing that?'

'Yep.' Lucy holds it out in front. 'Finest PVC, circa 1981.'

'Catwoman, eat your heart out,' Georgia says. 'You're going to look hot.'

'I doubt it.' Lucy slides the tight vinyl up her legs.

'Wait till Carl sees you in that,' Lydia says. 'He may not make it to the dance.'

'Sure.' Lucy pulls the zip up her back. Does everyone think he's a sex addict? 'Man, it's tight.'

'Don't think you're going to hear any complaints from him.' Georgia raises her eyebrows. 'How come you can make some daggy old pants-suit look hot?'

Lucy hears his car, the rumbling throaty V8, from several blocks away, as he drives too fast, as usual, to her house. She opens the front door. It is raining heavily. Across the horizon are small flashes of light. The promised storm is heading their way. It could be a fierce night.

Carl is slouching against the portico, dressed in a blue velvet jacket and pink lace shirt. His tight polyester pants flare at the bottom. He offers her a corsage and gives his slow, lopsided smile. 'Cara mia,' he says, as he always does, 'you look beautiful. You could wear a garbage bag and still look as good.'

Lucy smiles at him as he pulls her close. 'And you look like a hot '70s porn star.'

He kisses her, far too deeply, and then holds her at arm's length to assess her closely again. 'Speaking of porn stars?' He raises his eyebrows.

'Stop it.' Lucy laughs lightly and pushes him gently in the chest. Sometimes he is too intense. 'Come on, I'll get the girls — we've got to go.'

2

The music is thumping as they walk up the steps to the school gym. Inside, lights are flashing and a machine sporadically spurts smoke into the air. Carl squeezes her hand as he sees his friends.

'I'm going over there. See you in a bit,' he says.

Everyone is colourfully and hideously dressed. Lucy, Georgia and Lydia spend the first half hour admiring their friends' outfits.

'Far cry from the real ball, hey?' Georgia says in Lucy's ear.

She nods. The ball had cost her over seven hundred dollars, and that was cheap by her friends' standards. 'White, middle-class extravagance,' her dad had said, coughing up half the money for her dress. 'It really is a crime.'

She'd tried not to feel guilty about it, but it was hard when your father was a perpetual human rights campaigner, with an overdeveloped sense of social justice. The Thrift Shop Ball had been Lucy's idea — to redeem herself. She'd been surprised by how enthusiastically everyone had embraced the idea.

The music is loud and everyone is moving on the dance floor.

At the first notes of a Miley Cyrus song, Lydia starts twerking. Quite a crowd gathers around her as she shakes and shimmies to the music. Lucy sees the first one fly and land on Isabelle Gordon's yellow platform boot. She starts laughing and grabs Georgia.

'Look,' she says, pointing to where the plastic blob sits like a jellyfish.

'Oh my God,' Georgia says laughing. 'Where's the other one?'

Lucy shrugs. Given Lydia's reduced bust, it is clear that the other one has migrated as well. Lydia keeps the twerk up. Everyone is clapping and cheering. Isabelle is still oblivious to the boob on her shoe. Lucy and Georgia are in hysterics and then the music ends.

A rather dishevelled Lydia approaches them, a smirk plastered across her face. 'Well, that showed them,' she says, adjusting her dress.

'Sure did,' Georgia agrees.

Lucy is laughing loudly now. 'Maybe more than you anticipated.'

The second chicken fillet is stuck to Lydia's beehive. Georgia sees it too and they clutch at each other for support.

'Whaaat?' Lydia's hand flies to her head. Her expression transforms into one of sheer horror as she touches the plastic. 'Oh my God!' She pulls it from her hair, her other hand automatically reaching inside her bra.

Georgia and Lucy can't speak.

'Where's the other one?' Lydia whispers.

Lucy points to where Isabelle is now chatting to JD, one of Carl's mates. For a fleeting second she wonders where Carl is.

Lydia sees her insert on the shoe. 'Shit,' she says, 'now what do I do? Oh man, why did she have to be talking to him?'

'Him?' Georgia says. 'JD? You got the hots for him, or something?'

'No,' Lydia says, pushing the plastic insert back into her bra and creating a bizarre lopsided effect. 'Don't be stupid. How do I get it back?'

'I don't know,' Lucy says. 'You don't want to make a boob of yourself.'

Georgia howls.

'Just act normal,' Georgia says, attempting solemnity, 'or they might think you're off your tits.'

'No, wait, Lydia.' Lucy feigns a straight face. 'You really do need to keep abreast of things.'

They laugh hysterically.

'You're not helping,' Lydia huffs and marches over to Isabelle.

Lucy and Georgia follow — this promises to be a fine Lydia moment.

'Excuse me,' Lydia says brightly, 'sorry to intrude.'

'Not at all.' JD is smiling.

'But I do believe that's mine.' Lydia points to Isabelle's shoe.

'What?' Isabelle looks down, horrified. 'What the hell is that?'

Lydia gracefully reaches down to pluck the boob off Isabelle's shoe, but she has to tug at it where the adhesive has stuck. 'Hmmm, sticky,' she says to no one in particular.

Georgia and Lucy howl loudly. JD glances over at them with an amused look on his face. Isabelle looks like she has smelled something foul.

'It's a chicken fillet,' Lydia says, straightening, 'although it's not really made from chicken. Thanks for minding it for me.' She pushes it back into her bra. 'Ta-ta.'

She walks towards Lucy and Georgia and grabs their arms. 'Oh my God, oh my God,' she whispers, dragging them to the toilets. 'I have never been so embarrassed in my whole life.'

After Lydia has composed herself, and Lucy and Georgia have used every boob joke they can think of, Lucy looks for Carl. Since arriving, she hasn't seen him once. She is surprised by the irritation that surges in her. He hadn't left her side at the real ball, attentive and interested, wanting to dance with her — every song. Now where is he?

And does she really care?

That last thought surprises her. She has to admit, she often finds him smothering, so why is she bothered by this neglect? She has had such fun tonight with her friends and it's only now that she's become aware of his absence. What is it that is annoying her here?

'Hey,' she says, finding him still in the corner with Big Al and Ben, 'want to dance?'

He's laughing at something Ben is saying and turns to her, wiping his eyes.

'What? Yeah, sorry. In a sec. You go ahead, we're just in the middle of something. I'll catch you in a bit.'

She frowns and shrugs. 'Sure. Fine.' And she walks off. A sudden wave of anger washes over her. What is the matter with him?

As the night progresses, she feels herself becoming more and more uptight. She tries to get back into the mood, but even Lydia's silly antics elicit only a hollow laugh from her. She can't help glancing Carl's way, watching how he sits in the corner with his mates. So blokey and cave-man like. They look like a bunch of stoners, laughing at each other's inane comments. Anger makes her want to stalk over there and demand his attention, but pride stops her. Suddenly she realises she is on the back foot, the power balance has shifted. He has it all.

Two hours to go and then their last school function is over. It can't end like this — so badly. And besides, she doesn't need the added drama of a complicated relationship now, when she's heading into her biggest challenge ever. She needs to talk to him.

'Hey,' she says brightly, 'want to go for a walk?'

He smiles at her and her heart lifts. As he grabs her hand, he does the most stupid thing. He turns to Big Al and pushes his own thumb into the middle of his forehead. She stiffens. They all laugh, their stupid stoner laugh. He grins at her, with bloodshot eyes. She tries not to scowl as she hears Big Al say, 'Totally pussy-whipped dude.'

It's windy outside as they walk along the deserted verandah. He puts his arm around her, but she is wooden in his embrace. That puerile behaviour he exhibits with his mates is a total turn-off. She feels so confused: one minute, smothered by him; the next, angry with him for neglecting her, for acting 'one of the boys'.

'What?' she says, suddenly realising he's talking.

'You haven't heard one word, have you?' He smiles at her and pushes her up against the wall. 'If it's not my conversation you're after, it must be my body.'

As his mouth descends on hers, she feels like she can't breathe. She feels owned. She pushes him off, more roughly than intended.

'What's the matter?' he asks.

She shrugs. She doesn't know what to say. Truthfully, she doesn't know what the matter is.

He watches her silently.

'What is it?' He grabs her arms, but his touch is too forceful.

She shakes him off. 'Nothing,' she says coldly, crossing her arms defiantly across her chest.

'Sure,' he says.

He's watching her intently. She finds it cloying. The silence stretches. He thrusts his hands in his pockets and takes a step backwards. The distance between them feels like it's growing.

'Lucy?' he says finally. 'Do you still love me?'

She can't look at him. She doesn't know the answer. Maybe she does love him. But what if she doesn't? The consequences of either response seem unfathomable. And anyway, is there even any point in talking to him when he is in this condition?

'I don't know.'

He puts his hands on her shoulders. She doesn't want to look up. But does.

'Well, then,' he says and his voice has an edge to it she hasn't heard before, 'I'll give you time to think about it.'

And then he turns to walk off.

'Wait, Carl,' she says, suddenly panicked, 'don't go.'

But he doesn't turn; he just lifts his hand to acknowledge he's heard her and then enters the school hall.

That gesture angers her again. She feels shaken. This wasn't meant to be happening. She sits on a bench, thinks she should cry. Did they just split up? She can't go back inside and face him until she can give him an answer. And she doesn't know what that is. She watches Carl emerge from the hall again, thinks he's coming back to talk to her, but then sees JD behind. They head off to the car park. *Where are they going?* He's supposed to be taking her home.

Lucy remains on the bench for another ten minutes.

She doesn't want to face Lydia and Georgia and tell them what's happened. *What did happen?* She shakes her head. But if she stays out here any longer, they'll come looking for her and then she'll have to explain. And she just can't. So she goes inside, puts a smile on her face and pretends she's having fun.

'Where's Carl?' Georgia asks after the last song has finished.

'And JD?' Lydia asks.

Lucy shrugs. 'Don't know.'

'You two had a fight?' Georgia asks.

'Carl's been acting like a bit of a weirdo tonight,' Lydia says. 'Not his usual charming self. Do you think they've been smoking weed?'

Lucy nods. It'd explain his behaviour.

'He's meant to be dropping us off,' Lydia frowns. 'Great. I don't want to walk in these stupid heels.'

'I'll call my dad,' Lucy says, feeling humiliated.

Lydia and Georgia know not to ask anything more.

3

It's dark.

The wind moans through the treetops. The rain has eased but has left large puddles along the sides of the road, their surfaces still rippling under the insistent breath of the wind. Boughs have broken off in the torrential downpour, and rivulets of sand have run from the soft edges of the road.

The car has stopped at the top of the hill. Its lights, like yellow eyes, cut through the blackness, reflecting off the glossy tarmac. Inside, Carl slaps the steering wheel hard. 'Shit!'

JD watches him, worried, and passes him the joint. In the darkness, the lit end glows a brighter red as Carl inhales deeply. The air thickens with the heavy smoke and sweet smell of weed. They sit in silence, passing the joint backwards and forwards.

'I can't believe her,' Carl spits furiously.

Instinctively, JD knows not to speak. He watches Carl's hands wringing the plastic steering wheel. He's never, in five years, ever seen Carl so mad. This is Carl the Ultimate Pacifist — the guy who'd risk his own safety to break up a fight. Outside the wind buffets the windows of the car.

'Turn the music up,' Carl says suddenly.

JD fiddles with the iPod and the sounds of reggae music fill the car. They sit silently, listening to the music and the next phase of the storm building outside. The engine is still running, and Carl's left hand grips the gear stick.

'Shit.'

'Lighten up, mate,' JD offers cautiously, as he flicks the butt out of his window. The rain has started up again and spits into the opening.

After a pause, Carl says, 'Yeah, you're right.'

JD feels an immediate lift in the tension.

'Hey,' Carl says loudly over the music, 'I feel the need ...'

'... the need for speed,' JD finishes.

Carl's foot stomps on the accelerator and the V8 roars into life. He revs it hard again. JD's hand automatically feels for his seatbelt clasp. Outside the sound of throbbing engine mixes with the howling wind.

Carl drops the handbrake and the clutch simultaneously and the V8 veers down the road. Rectangles of light from house windows and black silhouettes of trees rush past and then, suddenly, it's the end of the road. Carl pulls the wheel tightly right, but the tyres plane across the filmy surface. The wheels screech. The car spins. Drops from the bitumen into the soft shoulder. Its nose digs in and then it flips. JD automatically reaches for the dashboard as Carl grips the steering wheel tightly, his knuckles popping whitely. Crash! The back end of the car hits the road, the intrusion bars in the doors groaning metallically. JD's head whips forwards. Backwards. The momentum takes them over again. The iPod flies, then snaps back violently. The glove box spews its contents as the car flips again. And again. Finally, it rests on its roof. The wheels spinning.

In the heavy silence that follows, Bob Marley

warbles something about love. JD focuses on random words through his ringing ears: Able ... Cards ... Table ...

Along the street, more windows light up. Doors open. People run towards the yellow car.

JD is hanging upside down, suspended by his belt. He turns his head, but pain sears through his spine and into his ears. Carl is slumped sideways; blood trickles from his nose and ears. Reggae music thuds through the car.

A man shouts to JD through the crumpled and shattered window. 'Hey, you alright?'

JD tries to turn his head again. Each movement causes him to yelp with pain. 'I'm okay,' he croaks.

The man reaches through and turns the music off. The silence is loud. Then the rain comes again. Beating relentlessly against the undercarriage of the car.

'Ring my dad,' JD tries to say, but his throat is choking on sand. He whispers the numbers.

The man punches them into a mobile, while another calls triple zero. A floral breasted woman cries, 'Get them out. For the love of God, get them out.' But everyone ignores her.

Outside the car, JD hears voices and movement. How many people are there? How long will it take to rescue them? He turns his head again and feels the bones rubbing together, like unoiled cogs. The pain makes him stop. But he glances at Carl out of the corner of his eye. Carl, hanging from his seat, unmoving. The blood has trickled around the edge of his mouth and down the sides of his neck.

'Carl,' JD manages to whisper through the sand in his throat. 'Dude.'

Carl doesn't respond.

It feels like they've been hanging there an eternity. JD is aware of the sand down his back. It fills the console of the car, sand everywhere. It's like they've been buried alive. He feels panic rising in his throat. Carl still hasn't moved at all, and JD realises the truth: Carl is dead. And he is buried alive with him. He yanks at the clasp of his seatbelt, but pain electrifies his body. Then he notices the splintered bone poking through his ripped Levis — grotesque, obscene. And he can't feel it, can't feel a thing. He can't breathe and his heart is racing.

The same man from before appears at the

window. 'They're coming, mate,' he says. 'I can hear them.'

And JD hears them too, the sound of sirens. The high-pitched ambulance, the long warbling fire truck, the multi-toned police.

Within moments, it seems, they have set up high-powered spotlights around the car. The rain beats down mercilessly. Against the powerful lights, the raindrops glitter like small stars. JD fixes on their straight route to the ground while the car shakes and shrieks as the jaws-of-life slices it open.

A helmeted firefighter sticks his head through the new opening. 'What's your name?'

'Douglas,' JD whispers, 'Tan.'

'Right, Douglas, we'll have you out in a sec. How's your mate doing?'

'I don't know.' JD pauses to breathe. 'He's not moving, hasn't since we crashed. I don't know.'

'It's okay, mate. We'll have you both out in a jiffy.'

JD is strapped to a board, his neck secured by a brace and another strap. He hears someone shout, 'Spinal,' and it terrifies him. As they push him hurriedly to the ambulance, he searches out of the corner of his eye but can't see Carl.

'My friend?' he asks the ambulance officer, but she shakes her head grimly in the rain.

Then he hears Carl's dad. He's here. His voice is loud. As they push JD into the back of the ambulance JD hears him, his voice breaking. 'Carl, oh no ... Carl ... My son.'

4

Lucy has spent most of the night awake, alternating between sadness and anger. Now, in the yellowing light of morning, she gains perspective on what happened. It was everything suddenly becoming real that had tripped her out. School rushing to an abrupt end. Exams looming larger than life — carrying with them all her fears and insecurities. She'd been a little distracted lately; her Lit teacher had warned her to stay focused, with the mocks only two weeks away. She's worked so hard, has spent her whole life preparing for these exams, and she isn't going to let anything derail her. And her relationship with Carl, which at the beginning had been so easy, now seemed complicated. Okay,

maybe she had been a bit melodramatic last night —
a bit freaked out — but all he'd had to do was talk to
her. Allay her fears. All she had really wanted was
some words of comfort. He'd always been great at
talking her out of her anxiety. His whole approach
to life was to chill out. She knew he would make
her feel okay. Relax and not panic anymore. But he
hadn't. He'd embarrassed her in front of his mates
and then acted like a Neanderthal, groping her
against the wall.

As she showers and dresses for school, she
remembers when she'd first noticed that Carl liked
her. He'd hung out with the same group of mates for
as long as she could remember. Big Al — a flaming
redhead who towered above everyone in their year.
There was Ben, who always appeared so quiet but
had classic wit. And JD — probably Carl's best
friend, if guys even thought in those terms. JD was
smart and academic. He didn't really fit in with the
other guys, who were into their sports and not their
studies, but JD and Carl worked together at The
Cake Shop. An interest in weed and the FA Cup had
bonded them tightly. She'd always thought of them
as a group of jocks and stoners, had never really paid

any attention to them, until she'd gone to buy a cake for Georgia's birthday.

She stood at the counter and Carl emerged from the kitchen, wearing an apron covered in flour dust. He looked embarrassed when he saw her.

'Hey,' he said, 'how you doing?'

'Good.' She waved her hand in front of her face. The air-conditioning in the shop was broken. 'I'm hot.'

He smiled at her and it was the first time she'd ever really looked at him properly. 'I think you're totally hot,' he said.

She laughed out loud. She'd never expected something so forward from him. After that she always noticed him and realised he was watching her, too. There was a definite tension between them at school. Looks were passed, little comments made, an attraction developed.

Then one day when she was walking past their group, wearing an over-sized flower in her hair, Big Al shouted sarcastically, 'Hey, that's a nice big flower.'

She didn't pause in her stride, just kept walking,

and threw back over her shoulder, 'Yeah, I bet that's what people say about you, too.'

The entire group howled with laughter and Big Al went bright red.

Carl found her that afternoon at the bus bay.

'Want a lift?' he asked, pulling his yellow Ford against the kerb.

And she thought: why not? She jumped in his car and he roared off, leaving a trace of rubber on the road.

'Calm down, rev-head,' she warned.

And he laughed — he had a great laugh — and when he did his brown eyes sparkled. 'I blame you,' he said, 'you get all my engines revving.'

He asked her to the movies that night. She agreed; her own heart was hammering from being around him. He was so hot, and sweet. She'd felt nervous getting ready, but when she opened the door she could see that he liked what he saw. He didn't try and hide it — ever.

'Cara mia,' he said, 'you are so beautiful.'

Since then, it had been on.

The two of them don't really socialise at school

— he sits with his mates, and she with hers. But after school and on weekends they always hang out together. He's always so admiring, telling her how beautiful she is, listening intently to her stories. He's taken her places, bought her gifts. The attention was flattering, made her feel like the most desirable girl in the world. But lately she's been noticing more and more how little they have in common, and that attentiveness, once so attractive, has become smothering. She talks of her plans for uni — getting into Law — and travelling; he doesn't know what he wants to do, or where he is heading. In his typical way, he says he'll figure it out as he goes along. And that cavalier nature, once so appealing, has been slightly irritating.

'Lucy!' Mum calls from downstairs. 'You're going to be late!'

Lucy realises she's been sitting on the end of the bed, staring at her untied shoes. She gives herself a shake. She needs to take some action.

Last night had gone badly but she knows she needs to get her life back on track. Maybe she'd been a bit emotional. But he'd been such a jerk. Suddenly it's clear. It was the fear of being alone that had prevented her from saying the truth last night: that she didn't love him. And fear is not reason enough to stay with him.

It's over.

She talks to herself on the bus on the way to school. Sure, things are bad, but she can get through this. She knows she can. She knows what she wants.

When the bus pulls in to the school bay, she is still scared of what lies ahead. Can she really do it — face him and confirm what she couldn't tell him last night? *I don't love you. It's over*. But if she doesn't, what will happen? He is happy with this, plodding along together — no real direction or goal — rolling with it, probably forever. Forever. That's not the vision she has for her future. She has to do it — say those words to him. It's going to be hard to see the pain in his eyes, to listen to him plead his case — because she knows he will. But she has to be strong. She needs to think about the future, what she really wants out of life. Not his vision but hers. Any deviation from that would be a mistake.

5

Lucy makes her way through the other students heading for homeroom. It's hard to believe school is nearly finished. They have been such a solid group, the last two years bringing them together so tightly. Sharing exam pressure and socialising to let off steam has seen most of the bitchiness and cliques disappear. She loves school — the routine and the safety — but she's looking forward to a new life, too: university.

She needs to find Carl before homeroom. It seems like bad timing, but she tries to reason with the panic in her gut: it is better now than later. She heads for the Year 12 common room, an area with a small servery with an urn, coffee, milk — one of the privileges of sticking out high school. She knows she'll find him there. She enters the room but it's almost empty. She checks her watch. Last night's dance is no excuse; final assessments are due and everyone needs to be here today.

Big Al is heading her way. He doesn't smile when he sees her, but grimaces. Her stomach flips. He must know about last night. Carl must have told him.

'Lucy ...' He grabs her arm as if to restrain her.

'Get off,' she says, shaking his hand away. Al may be one of Carl's close mates, and angry with her, but she won't be manhandled by anyone.

'Sorry.' He drops his hand; automatically, his cheeks burn red.

She notices his reaction with surprise.

'Wait a sec.' He lifts his hand again, but then doesn't know what to do with it and leaves it hanging loosely in front of them.

'What?' she asks, suddenly scared. Something is terribly wrong.

'Last night, JD and Carl ...' He pauses and looks out the window.

She follows his gaze and there they are, all the Year 12s, gathered in small groups in the courtyard.

Watching their subdued movements, she knows their voices are low.

'What, Al?' She tries not to shout.

'An accident,' Al says softly. 'Carl smashed his car.'

She knows he's not lying by the look in his eyes and the tone of his voice, but despite herself she says, 'Very funny, Al.'

'It's no joke.' His hand reaches out again and stops mid-air. 'I went round to pick up JD for school this morning. His dad had just got back from the hospital. He's in intensive care. Broken neck.'

Broken neck. She's not sure what to do with this information. 'Carl?' she asks.

Al won't meet her eyes.

Her stomach gurgles. She presses against it to silence it.

'Coma,' Al says, really softly. 'He hasn't woken up since the crash.'

'Right.' She speaks so calmly it surprises her. 'Thanks.' And then, ignoring his bewildered look, she walks off to homeroom.

Around her the lower years are rushing through the halls. It must be after the second bell. She realises she can't hear properly. She feels like she's in a bubble and as she walks on, clutching her schoolbag over her shoulder, the bubble seems to shrink around her. Her ears feel blocked. She tries yawning to pop them, but it doesn't work. A boy from debating calls out to her.

'Hey, Lucy.' He waves.

'Hi ...' — and suddenly she has no idea what his name is, which is odd, as she's been third speaker to his first for three years now — '... there.' She finishes lamely, her voice sounding muted in her head.

He frowns and moves on.

She passes JD's homeroom. Normally he'd be at the back with Ben and Al. She sees most of the 12s are gathered around the teacher's desk. Sarah is crying, which makes Lucy feel angry — Sarah doesn't even know them. She feels a moment of confusion, not sure where to go. Homeroom was her destination, but she doesn't want to talk to anyone — certainly can't handle the details right now. Instead she slips up the walkway past administration and out into the car park.

His yellow Ford is noticeably absent. Her stomach groans again — she feels violently ill. She pulls out her mobile. The lack of messages from him last night had fuelled her anger even more, but now she knows why: he was trapped in a wreck, or in the back of an ambulance on the way to hospital.

It was her fault. The realisation causes her to gag. If she hadn't argued with him, he wouldn't have left the ball.

She hits her mum's number and it answers almost immediately.

'Just texting you,' her mum says. 'You alright?'

Her mum already knows. Lucy feels herself shaking her head. 'Yeah, but I want to come home.'

6

She's sitting under a tree, knees pulled up to her chest, waiting for her mum. All she can imagine is Carl and JD in the car. She cringes and tries to make the images disappear, but they won't. She imagines Carl and JD in hospital beds. A broken neck — that doesn't necessarily mean paralysis; she's sure she's heard of stories where people have broken their necks and totally recovered. And what's a coma anyway — isn't it just sleeping? Don't people usually wake after a little while? She remembers a TV show about a girl who was in a coma for twenty years and when she woke she still thought she was sixteen. But surely that's not normal?

'I can't think about this right now.' She realises

she's spoken aloud and looks around, embarrassed, but there is no one there.

She sees her mum's car coming up the road, jumps to her feet and brushes off her bum.

'Hi,' she says too-cheerily as she slips into the front seat. She pulls her belt on. 'Thanks.'

'Are you alright?' her mum asks, hand poised over the gear shift.

'Yeah.' Lucy shrugs. 'I just couldn't stay at school. How come you're not at the shop?'

'I called Suzie to cover for me. Aside from the morning delivery coming in, I've got all the table settings and bouquets ready to go for the Greenwood wedding. So not much else to do, really.'

Lucy knows this is a stretch of the truth. Her mum works long hours at her florist shop, which is why she is always in huge demand for big weddings and social events, sometimes booked over a year in advance.

'Carl's dad phoned me just before.' Her mum is watching for her reaction.

'Why?'

'He just got back from the hospital. No change — Carl is still in a coma.' Her mum looks so sad; Lucy knows how much she likes him. 'He wondered if anything happened last night, at the school dance.'

Lucy nods. 'Yeah. I kinda broke up with him.'

Her mum hasn't pried on the drive home, allowing Lucy to struggle privately with her feelings. Carl and JD. At home they sit in the kitchen.

'What else did he say?' Lucy asks. Her mum knows she means Carl's dad.

'Just that Carl physically looks good. No broken bones. Poor JD.' She shakes her head sadly. 'And he wondered if something had made Carl go off, drive like that.'

'Like what?'

'A hoon.' Her mum pushes a cup of tea towards her. 'The police have estimated his speed at 160 kilometres an hour going into a T-junction.'

Lucy sits still. That is so fast — what was he thinking? *That you couldn't say 'I love you',* the nasty voice in her head says. *This is your fault.* She shakes her head.

'What happened?' her mum asks eventually.

She shrugs. 'I don't know. I was a bit over it all, it was feeling too emotional and confusing. I didn't know what I wanted anymore.'

'He wants you to call him,' her mum says. 'Anytime.'

'Okay.' Lucy nods, but she can't face it — Carl's dad, his questions, his mantra: *My Carl has always been a good son and he will be a great man.* She knows he will be heartbroken. He'll want to know everything — every tiny detail — and she'll have to explain it a hundred times. She just can't do it now.

She goes to her study and looks at the mock exam timetable. Four days to go and then school is officially over, except for the mocks and then the finals. Everything is changing so quickly. She puts her head on the desk. There is no way she can concentrate. No way. All she sees is Carl and JD in hospital. The enormity of their injuries hits her — a broken neck, a coma. What if JD's a quadriplegic for the rest of his life? How will Carl handle that? What if Carl never wakes up? How will she handle that? What has she done?

7

The ringing phone jolts her awake, and she sits up.
The light outside has changed. She looks at the time
on her computer: 12.30. She's been asleep for nearly
three hours. She rubs her neck as her mum walks in
with the phone.

'Mr Kapuletti,' she says, handing it to her.

'Hi.' Lucy's mouth is dry.

'Lucy, what happened?' As usual, Mr Kapuletti is
straight to the point.

'I'm not sure — I wasn't there; I was at the dance.'
She adds, evasively, 'Carl left.'

'I know. But before. You were with Carl, yes?
Why did he leave?'

'He was ...' — she searches for the right words —

'a bit unhappy with me. We kinda had an argument.'

There is silence for the longest time. Lucy considers the phone may have gone dead. She pulls it away from her head and looks at it.

'Oh, mio dio,' Mr K cries into the phone as she puts it back against her ear. His words make her jump. Despite being a second-generation Australian, Mr K often falls into his wife's way of speaking when he's upset. 'I knew Carl wasn't so reckless as that. He was upset?'

'Yes,' Lucy says. 'I sort of broke up with him.'

Mr K is quiet. 'Why, Lucy? You love him, no?'

'No, I mean yes, I do, but ...' She shakes her head, flustered by her justifications, confused that she feels the need. This morning she had realised she didn't love Carl, was prepared to say it. Now it feels like a dirty secret that needs to remain hidden. 'It was complicated, Mr K. Look, I've got to go. Please call me when you hear something?'

'Yes, yes,' he says, hanging up.

She stares at the phone for the longest time. Mr K blamed her. Of course he did: it was her fault. But she shouldn't have to tell him everything.

Her mum is up the other end of the house, working on the GST payments. She looks up and smiles. 'Alright?'

'Can we talk?' Lucy says, sitting on a chair. She isn't sure what to say but needs to say something. 'I think it's my fault,' she blurts eventually, tears in her eyes.

'Oh, Luce.' Her mum shakes her head. 'It's not.'

'It is, Mum — I pushed him into leaving.' She wipes at her tears with the back of her hand. 'He's always been so nice to me. And I was so cold. He loves me so much and I ...' She doesn't know what to say now, because she doesn't want to admit the truth to anyone.

'He's such a nice boy,' her mum says.

'*A good son*,' Lucy corrects, and they both laugh at her imitation of Carl's dad.

'He is, Lucy, and your dad and I have always been happy about you being with him. You know, it's hard ...'

Her mum sounds wistful and Lucy knows this is one of those 'watching your kids grow up speeches', but for once it doesn't bother her.

'You want your kids to be happy. And there is so much bad stuff that can happen. Look at Emma —

she put us through the hoops. But she seems happy now. We just want you guys to have fun and be safe.'

Lucy nods. 'He just seems so intense sometimes. Like this is it — me and him forever. And I'm not ready for that.'

'It's okay,' her mum says. 'When he can, Carl will handle it — whatever it is you want to do. But don't beat yourself up about it now. Let's just see what happens.'

'Yeah,' she agrees.

'You're a clever girl, Lucy, you'll know what to do.'

And then Lucy can't say anything else at all. Clever is the last thing she feels.

8

She rings her dad later that night. Her parents had split up when she was twelve. It had been so hard not having Dad in the house, but he and her mum had maintained a strong friendship.

'We just didn't want to be together anymore,' her mum said when Lucy asked what went wrong. 'There was no one else, for either of us, and even though we were still friends we didn't feel the same way. Sometimes I think we could have stayed together for the sake of you girls. Maybe it would have helped Emma. But you've always been so level-headed, so pragmatic. I don't think anything could throw you.'

Lucy, totally thrown, waits for her dad to pick up.

'Hey, Rabbit,' he says, 'you okay?'

'Yeah, okay. Hey, Dad ... what do you know about comas?'

She listens to her dad, a mental health nurse but with training in all fields of nursing, explain the possible outcomes. 'A coma rarely lasts any longer than two to four weeks. The least amount of time a patient is unconscious lends itself to a better recovery.'

'Okay, so if he comes out soon he'll be okay. Like, no brain damage?' She can't believe she's considering this.

'Comas have so many variables, but the sooner he's out, the better his chances of returning to normal. Lucy, he'll be okay.'

'What about JD? His neck's broken.'

'That depends on spinal cord interference,' her dad says. 'If he has none, he'll be fine. If it's been damaged, the extent of paralysis will depend on where the break is.'

'So he could be in a wheelchair forever?' She can't bear the thought.

'It's possible — it'll depend. Rabbit, I'm sure they'll be okay. The human body has miraculous healing powers.'

She hangs up and thinks about what she knows,

realises she knows nothing. She feels tired, is dreading school tomorrow, but she has to go and face it.

Lucy chats to Lydia and Georgia on Facebook. She can't manage a real-time conversation, and things seem so much easier over the net.

Lydia says: Hey babe u ok?

Lucy says: Yep — it's all unreal.

Georgia says: Can't believe it either — was all anyone talked about. Why didn't you txt back?

Lucy: Sorry hon. Too stressed — didn't want to know the gory details.

Georgia: No one knew much at all — except Wayne — he was at the crash. Went on about it for hours.

Lucy: Finally a celeb hey?

Georgia: Yeah — to anyone who'd listen.

Lucy: Any goss about me?

Lydia: Some stuff said — but don't stress. Most people know Tasha and Taylor are full of shit.

Lucy: Those bitches — wot they sayin?

Georgia: Tell ya tomoz — but u know wot they're like — just wanna be centre of attention. Trying to blame u for it.

Lucy: It was my fault. We all know it.

Lydia: Don't hon — we'll talk abt it 2moz. Try and sleep.

Lucy: Ok c u then

Lydia: ☺

Georgia: xxx

She wants to go to sleep but is scared to, and clicks onto Skype. She realises she's been holding her breath as she sees her sister's face appear. Emma, thank God.

'Hey, kid.' Her sister looks dazed and confused. 'What's up?'

'Carl,' Lucy says, suddenly sobbing. 'He's in a coma.'

'What the fuck!' Her sister looks immediately straight, flicks her beaded plaits back in a chinkling fashion and comes in close to the camera.

'Oh, Em,' Lucy sobs, so relieved to be talking to her sister. 'It's a nightmare.'

They talk for more than two hours, making cups of tea and discussing everything that has been said and, more importantly, everything that hasn't. As she listens to her sister, Lucy starts to consider that maybe, just maybe, this isn't all her fault.

'How could you have known,' Emma says finally, 'that he would take off and drive like that? To be fair, you've told me before he's a bit of a rev-head. And at times a stoner.'

Lucy nods. 'I know. It's just ...'

'Bullshit, Luce,' Emma says. 'You couldn't have known. This isn't your fault. Don't get me wrong — I like the dude. True. He's okay. But he did this. Not you. It's fucked if you think that way.'

'I know.' Lucy starts to feel lighter. 'I miss you, Em.'

'One word, kid, and I'm on the next flight back. You tell me. I'm there.'

As much as she wants her sister now, she knows it's not going to change anything. She'll still be going through it. She'll need to talk to Em, but what is the difference doing it on Skype?

'Stay put,' Lucy says finally, 'wait for the SOS.'

'K.' Em yawns. 'I know it's late there but I've been pulling all-nighters. I'm kinda operating on your time.'

'Go to bed,' Lucy says, looking at her watch; it's just after 2 a.m. 'I'll talk to you soon.'

'Tomorrow, kid,' Emma says, signing off.

9

'Slow down, Carl!' she shouts. The wind is ripping through the car and they speed down the road.
He won't look at her. His eyes are fixed ahead and hooded, his mouth is set.

Suddenly he screams at her above the howling wind. 'What did you mean, Lucy? Do you love me or not? Which one is it?'

'Stop!' she screams, seeing the sign at the end of the road. 'Stop!'

The car flies through the air.

Lucy wakes up with a jolt, sweaty and shaken. She looks at the clock: 3.35 a.m. She groans and tries to go back to sleep. But sleep eludes her. Her mind is full of brutal images — warped and twisted metal, smoking tyres, hospital beds — and she tries to steady her thoughts, steer them back into safer waters. A simpler time. Their first date.

She'd never been on a proper date before. She'd never been interested in any of the boys at school — they'd all seemed so juvenile. Carl was different. Physically a man, not a boy. It made him seem so much more worldly than her.

She'd only ever kissed one boy — Peter Boyle, back in Year 10 — and that experience still made her cringe. So much tongue and clicking teeth and a desire to hold her breath until it was over. What if Carl wanted to kiss tonight? How would she handle that? She started to stress out and had to talk herself down.

In the car he hadn't even tried to touch her hand. So restrained, so gentlemanly. At the box office he pulled out his wallet automatically, dismissing her twenty with a wave. And then he grabbed her hand as they walked into the cinema. His touch was electric. She felt herself relax as the adverts began and he put an arm around her, dropping his hand over her shoulder. Classic move, she thought, waiting for him to pounce on her breast. But he hadn't, he'd just left his hand where it was.

It turned out to be the single most boring film she'd ever endured. To lighten the mood, she'd started making little comments, ad libbing what the actors were thinking.

'Just off the A list now. Career bombed,' she said as a new Hollywood star looked pensively into the distance.

Carl joined in, quipping about a sudden increase in Scientology numbers following this box office stinker, and then they had both cracked up laughing. The other patrons turned and glared and shushed them. It hadn't worked, and the last hour of the film flew with their ad-libs.

When he dropped her home, he kissed her goodnight. His lips, so soft and gentle, had her respond immediately — a swirling feeling in the bottom of her stomach. She pressed herself against him and he kissed her harder.

'Bella donna.' He pulled away and looked down at her. 'I have to go, before I can't.'

She nodded, flustered and excited by his touch.

'Okay.' She boldly kissed him one last time. 'See you later.'

　'You better believe it,' he said, reluctantly getting into his car and driving off.

She shakes her head at the memory, tears streaming down her face. Oh, Carl.

10

Lucy catches the bus to school. She hasn't had
her licence long and has been slowly building up
to driving to and from school, but now this whole
experience has shaken her confidence. Cautiously,
she enters the common room. It appears normal.
Sharon, not a close friend, rushes up to her.

'Lucy, are you okay?'

'Yeah, I'm fine,' she says, searching for Al or Ben.
'Just couldn't do yesterday.'

'No, of course not. It must be terrible. Your
boyfriend in hospital.'

Lucy smiles at Sharon and searches for Al. She
feels so bad about yesterday, needs to talk to him
today. She finds him by the urn.

'Hey, Al,' she says softly.

'Hey.' He looks up from his coffee and voices her exact thoughts. 'I feel real bad about yesterday, but someone had to tell you.'

'No.' She puts out a hand; he doesn't flinch. 'I'm so sorry. I think I was a bit shocked.'

'Yeah, we all were. JD is okay. Saw him last night — through the glass.'

'You saw him?' Lucy can't believe they've already been. She hadn't even asked Mr K when she could see Carl.

'Yeah, the nurse let us in to observation. Couldn't see much, mostly a white sheet. But we might be able to go later this week.'

'What about Carl?'

'Mr and Mrs K won't let anyone in yet. They're waiting for him to wake up.' Al shrugs. 'But what if he doesn't?'

'Don't, Al.' Lucy tries to sound confident. 'Dad says the outcome looks good.'

'Mate, I hope so. This is so unbelievable. I don't really know what to do with myself.'

'I know.' She nods; her stomach somersaults. She feels nauseous.

Lucy goes through the day in automatic mode. She sits in class, trying to listen, writing down tips for the exams, but the words are foreign on the page. The whole idea of cramming for exams just seems meaningless now. The issues Carl and JD are facing are too huge to handle — life and death issues. She warns herself against being melodramatic, but her mind keeps drifting back all the time to things beyond her control.

Her Lit teacher keeps her after class. 'Are you okay?' he asks.

She is sick of this question, even though she knows it's only because people care. But she's not the one in hospital.

'Yes, thanks,' she says.

Mr Cruz nods. 'I know exams probably seem trivial right now. And this couldn't have come at a worse time — although, whenever is there a good time for something like this?'

'True,' she says, nodding.

'I just wanted to reassure you your average will be safe. All assessments, with the exception of the mock, are in, and you are the highest achieving student. And even if you bomb in the mock' — Mr Cruz tries not to laugh — 'which is unlikely, I've spoken to the Deputy and the school will allow special consideration, at the discretion of the Head of English.'

'Which is you, Mr Cruz,' Lucy says, smiling at his gesture. This is no great surprise; she has been top in Lit for the last two years, and English the three before that. Still, it's a relief to know her average is safe. She wishes her Chemistry teacher was telling her this.

'Correct. And there is no way I'm going to let my top student bomb. If you need to talk, I'm always available.'

The day drags. The breaks are the worst. She wishes she could make herself invisible. She sees the other 12s are shattered by what's happened, but she doesn't want to talk about it. Ignoring things seems to be the best safety mechanism she has; her friends sense this and don't probe her for information. But at lunchtime she can't avoid Wayne, who is talking loudly and to anyone who'll listen.

'So I'm watching *Masterchef*. Couldn't believe all

youse guys would go to a lame school dance instead of watching the finale. Anyway, next thing I hear the squealing of tyres and brakes being applied mega hard.'

'Thought yesterday you said it was pissing down with rain?' someone says.

'Yeah, it was, but the noise from the car was so loud I could hear it over the top. Anyway ...' He waves his hand, annoyed by the interruption. 'There was this awesome crashing. Bang, bang, bang, bang. That car flipped six times, bonnet over boot.'

'The cops said three.' It was Al, sounding defensive.

'I don't know — it was a lot. So I run out and there it is, this mashed yellow Ford upside down. So I run towards it, with, like, all the neighbours from my street. I'm thinking, man, whoever is in there is bound to be dead after that, right? So I get there and Mr Wright is saying there is someone trapped in the car, calling out his phone number and saying *Ring my dad*. It was only later I found out it was JD.' Wayne sits back, as if pleased with his part in it.

'He was saying his number?' Lucy can't believe she's spoken, but is so shocked by Wayne's words.

JD knew to call out his number — as he was hanging upside down with a broken neck?

'Yeah, pretty cool, hey,' Wayne says, and he truly does sound admiring.

The others who've gathered nod and murmur in agreement.

JD had been in Lucy's classes since Year 8, when he arrived at the school from Sydney (via China, the red-necks always added). He was academic and dedicated, working harder than anyone, and always vying to beat Lucy as top English student. He never did — but he always challenged.

It was the English teacher who had coined his nickname. Mr Cruz was new that year and on his first day, reading out the roll, he'd called, 'Douglas'.

Everyone knew JD hated his name.

'Just Doug will do,' he'd said so politely.

And Mr Cruz had nodded, altered the roll and said, 'Well, Just Doug, do you mind if I call you JD for short?'

After that it'd stuck; in fact, no one called him Doug at all anymore, it was as if he'd always been two initials.

And now JD is a hero — the guy who'd kept his

head, even with a broken neck.

'I can't believe it,' Lucy says, aware everyone is now watching her. 'What about Carl?'

Wayne shrugs. 'I don't know,' he says sheepishly. 'At the time — I'm sorry, but I thought he was dead. In fact ...' — Wayne frowns, remembering the scene — 'it was raining real hard when they got him out and I didn't recognise him. It wasn't like he was mangled or nothing, it's just he looked so big and old. I swear I thought he was about twenty-five or something. I didn't even realise it was Carl and JD. They wouldn't let us get too close — the cops and stuff were there, cutting them out. It was pretty bad.'

Wayne stops speaking and puts his head down. Lucy can't tell if he's embarrassed or upset, and realises it's the latter when she sees him surreptitiously wipe his eyes.

The bell sounds for their last period and everyone moves more swiftly than usual.

Lucy is heading towards the car park to meet her mum, when Ben stops her.

'Hey, we're trying to get in to see JD when they'll let us. Do you want to come too?'

She nods gratefully. 'I would really like to come,' she says.

Ben pulls out his mobile. 'Gimme your number and I'll text you.'

Neither one acknowledges that, in all the time she and Carl have been going out, his friends have never contacted her.

11

That night Lucy texts Lydia and Georgia to say that
she won't be online. She can't think about anything,
not until she knows where things are with Carl
— and JD. She hopes it's soon. Lydia and Georgia
haven't probed her about what happened the night
of the ball. She is glad she didn't tell them the details
of her argument with Carl: that she hadn't been able
to answer his question. And neither does she want
to acknowledge to them that her plan yesterday had
been to split up with him for good. It makes her feel
so guilty, such a bitch.

She calls his parents and gets Mrs Kapuletti.

'Lucinda, cara mia,' Mrs K says. 'How are you?'

Unlike Mr K, who was born in Melbourne, Mrs K

came to Australia when she was twenty-one, a friend of the Kapuletti family and, from all photographic evidence, model material. Her English was good, although Mrs K would occasionally lapse into a hybrid of Aussie-Italian. Particularly when she was stressed.

'Okay. Any news?'

'He sleeps, like an angel,' Mrs K says. 'I worry. I hope his head is not changed.'

Lucy knows she's referring to brain damage, and hates this thought. 'It won't be, Mrs K — he'll be fine. Dad said so.'

'Your father, he is a knowledgeable and wise man, no? I put my faith in Jesus. He will watch my Carlo. He will bring him back, like before he was.' Mrs K sounds close to tears. Lucy wants to rush around there right now and comfort her.

She'd loved Carl's mother from the first day she'd been invited to their house. Mrs K had embraced her warmly. 'Lucinda,' she'd said, even though Lucy's name was just Lucy. 'She is very beautiful, Carlo. You look after this girl. Jes? You treat her like the princess.'

And he always had. Every month, flowers and a

card declaring his love.

Ever since, Mrs K had made a fuss of her, piling her plate with food, more food — her way of showing love. 'You eat, Lucinda. You eat like the sparrows.' Her back garden was a mix of vegetables, herbs and flowers, and she loved tending to her plants. 'It remind me of home,' she'd sometimes say rather wistfully.

Lucy clutches the phone, swallowing tears.

'Will you call me if — when — Carl wakes up?'

'As soon as he's opened brown eyes, I will call,' Mrs K promises before ringing off.

Lucy doesn't know what to do. She should study, but that seems impossible. Anyway, if she doesn't know her subjects now, she never will. She considers googling terms like *coma, broken neck*, but remembers the time she googled *stomach pain* and it came back with frightening results like bowel cancer, intestinal cancer, Crohn's disease. Despite this, she finds herself typing *prognosis for coma patients* into the search box. Better to be prepared for the worst.

12

Another sleepless night. Lucy stares at the ceiling, dry-eyed and remembering how it was with her and Carl. How exciting it was in the beginning. How it went from anticipation to something more.

One night after they'd been seeing each other for several weeks, they went out for dinner — not the usual all-you-can-eat places that most of her friends went to on dates but a real restaurant, with a menu and a wine list. She shook her head at his offer of alcohol; she didn't really drink and, besides, she was underage. He ordered a beer. It surprised her — being on P plates, he had a blood alcohol limit of zero — but she said nothing.

After dinner they went back to his house. His parents were already in bed. She was staying overnight in the spare room, as a group of them were heading to a music festival in the morning. He led her to the room and fussed around, making sure she had everything.

'Alright,' he said eventually, 'goodnight.'

'Goodnight,' she said from the bed, where she was nervously perched, sensing that something was about to happen. He leaned down and kissed her, the same deep and exciting kisses as before, and then dropped his hands to her breasts. She was excited, so she let him, but flinched in surprise as his hands slid her dress down and worked her bra off. But he continued to be gentle, although the intensity of his kisses increased. She lay back on the bed as he rested above her, feeling her body, kissing her face and neck.

'So beautiful,' he murmured against her skin. He was totally hard; she couldn't ignore it against her leg. Her dress was bunched around her waist, her bra off and all that was between them were her lace knickers and his Levis.

She felt his fingers under the elastic of her

knickers and tensed. He immediately stopped.
'Okay?' he asked, his dark brown eyes looking into
hers. She nodded, ignoring the confusion in her
head. Yes, she wanted this. But what if? What? Then
his fingers were touching her and she was telling
herself to relax.

'Show me,' he whispered into her hair. And
despite her embarrassment, she guided his hands
until he got it right.

Afterwards, he lay next to her, his erection still
visible through his jeans.

'Bedtime,' he said, kissing her again. She nodded,
almost surprised he hadn't wanted her to return the
favour, but relieved as well.

13

In the morning Lucy wakes to waves of nausea. She rushes to her toilet, heaves violently, then slumps, exhausted, against the toilet bowl. She wants to think it's something bad she's eaten, but she hasn't eaten much at all. A sudden thought occurs to her and it is terrifying.

At recess she is sitting outside the common room with Ben and Big Al. It's a beautiful day, warm and sunny. Lucy kicks her shoes off and lets the sun hit her legs.

'Mr Tan is coping pretty well with JD's condition,' Ben says. 'But he's really worried that JD is convinced Carl's dead, despite what everyone tells him.'

'Oh.' Lucy watches a line of ants, some carrying food pieces ten times their size. They are awesome to watch. 'Why?'

'At the crash he couldn't get Carl to speak. Didn't know he was just unconscious, I guess. Mr Tan says we can go Saturday afternoon — asked if you wanted to come too.'

'I've got work tonight and Saturday,' she says, evasively. She wants to see JD but is also scared.

'JD specifically asked for you,' Al says softly.

She wants to look away but knows how that will make her appear. Guilty.

'I finish at one.'

'I'll pick you up at two,' Al says finally.

At the end of lunchtime, she is confronted by Tasha and Taylor, two of the school skanks.

'Hey, how do *you* feel?' Tasha asks, and by the tone of her voice it's not out of concern.

'Yeah, not too bad,' Lucy says, walking on quickly. She's late for class. Her Chem teacher had kept her behind for a 'little chat'. That made all her teachers now.

The verandahs are deserted. Tasha and Taylor

have either been smoking or scoring a few bucks behind the gardener's shed, Lucy thinks meanly.

'If it were me, I'd be gutted having put my boyfriend and his best mate in hospital,' Taylor says snidely, looking at Tasha for support.

'Yeah, well, if you ever had a boyfriend, hospital would be a good place for him,' Lucy says angrily. 'Having CT scans to see if *he* has permanent brain damage.'

She pushes open the door to the library and sits at one of the computers. They're just a pair of bitches, she thinks to herself. But they've finally voiced what everyone is thinking, but no one will say. *This is your fault, Lucy. Look at what you've done.*

Unable to hold her fear in any longer, she leaves school without signing out.

Lucy searched each room when she arrived home early, but the house is empty.

She sits on the toilet lid and looks around the bathroom. She has known this room for twelve years. It's been white, off-white, beige, and is now yellow. The tiles have changed, too, from tiny ugly brown ones to these cream handmade tiles, *imported from Italy, darling,* her mum says, pretending to be pretentious. It's been Lucy's domain for the last five years, since Emma left to move in with Graham; later, after finding Graham in bed with her best friend, Emma had relocated to Europe. These days it's Lucy's towels and clothes on the floor. Her own makeup spread across the counter. Her own twenty-minute showers, with no one hammering on the door.

This is the room she'd spent over an hour in, for that first date with Carl. Changing her eye makeup — too heavy, then not heavy enough. Backcombing her hair — too high and eighties, then too flat. And twisting each way to see if her bum looked big in those jeans she wasn't sure of, but both Lydia and the saleslady said were flattering and totally hot. This is the toilet she spewed in the first time she'd had too much to drink at a party, only this year. This is the mirror in which she'd watched him watching her, the first time he ever saw her totally naked.

She shudders and her flesh prickles. She flips the box in her hand. What to do? *This* is a first she had never imagined.

She opens the box, surprised at her shaking fingers, and scans the instructions. It's straightforward. A no-brainer. She pulls out the first foil-clad stick. There are two — she hopes she doesn't have to use them both. She uncaps the plastic and holds it between her fingers. Lifts up the toilet lid, unzips her jeans, drops her knickers.

He had told her they would be safe. He knew what he was doing. She shakes her head. *Carl.* Maybe he had got careless. She'd known the first time he'd been unsure of how to put it on. But nothing had gone wrong that time, had it?

She pees on the stick. Feels the urine warm against her fingers. So gross. She tries to shake it off. After placing the stick on the foil wrapper — she doesn't want wee on her vanity — she washes her hands.

That white face in the mirror, wide-eyed — surely it can't be her.

'It'll be okay,' she tells her reflection. 'This won't happen to you. You'll be alright.'

She wishes she could blame him, be angry at his selfishness. But she knows that's not true. She'd been a willing participant. She eyes the stick warily. She can't see the control window. She feels ill. 'But,' she says, watching her reflection, 'it'll be good. So just look.'

She picks it up and stares at the window.

14

Lucy can't get away from her problems, because most of the late-night staff at Coles are from her school. At work that night, new rumours about the accident are circulating — the biggest one being that Carl was stoned. She prays this isn't true, despite his obvious stoner behaviour that night, but knows the hospital would have tested him for drugs. There are also whisperings about Lucy. She can't bear being the talk of the school — and now it's likely to get worse.

It panics her to let this new problem into her head, so she blocks that out too. She moves through the checkout area, acknowledging the regular shoppers with a false smile, helping the girls with transaction problems in a muted voice. She focuses on the task at hand, trying not to think about the other test — the confirmation one, the one she'd hoped not to need — that is hidden away in her bathroom cupboard. But her body is telling her as surely as any test. She shakes her head. *Don't. Don't think about it. Wait for Carl to wake up first.*

Finally her shift is over, four hours that felt like four days. She crosses the car park to her Honda — she'd made the decision not to let this accident shake her confidence, that now, more than ever, she needed to be able to drive. She slumps behind the steering wheel. Suddenly she feels so dreadfully alone. She can't talk to Lydia and Georgia for fear of blurting it all out. It's not that she doesn't trust them; it's having to say it and make it real — she refuses to give *it* a name. Not yet.

She should be concentrating on the road, but her thoughts keep wandering off track. She can't stop thinking about their first time. Where all of this began.

His parents were out, and despite the fact that it was only six in the evening, Carl's bedroom was dark, shrouded in its heavy curtains. He gently undressed her, kissing her and touching her — fulfilling the entire repertoire they had created over the months. She eased off his T-shirt and ran her hands over his taut chest — he was ripped, and the feeling of his muscles thrilled her. He unbuckled his belt and dropped his jeans. His eyes fixed firmly on hers. His erection stood straight through his underpants; she couldn't help but look. She'd felt it other times, even been brave enough to touch the skin; it had felt really weird. It didn't need much touching to spring into full life — it was always at some level of hardness. She had commented on that once, how he always seemed to have a hard-on, and he'd laughed. 'Only when I look at you, or think about you,' he'd said. But she'd never really seen it before outside his clothing.

He raised an eyebrow and she nodded. He slid his underpants down and stepped out of them, sliding into the narrow bed with her. She was surprised by the size of his penis. It was huge. And even though he started stroking her and kissing her, she couldn't help thinking that a thing that size was never going to fit into her. She remembered the first time she'd used a tampon and how difficult it had been to insert. This thing was longer and at least ten times wider. But he was gentle and slow, as always. Running his fingers over her, making her relax. All the while, she could feel his penis against her leg, throbbing like it had a life of its own.

'Shall we?' he asked finally. Her eyes were shut but she felt herself nodding. Why not? She felt him get out of the bed and took a peek. He was standing side-on to her, his massive boner like a flagpole in front of him, studying the condom. She watched him nervously as he fitted it on, taking his time and adjusting it, and then he was back in the bed with her. He lifted himself onto her, supporting most of his weight, and began kissing her. Then she felt it pushing against her. She tried to relax, but it didn't seem possible. The next minute the pushing gave way and she felt it sliding in. Not painfully but completely filling her. He gasped, and she turned her head away. Whatever sensation he was feeling, she knew it was different to hers. She felt invaded, and slightly clinical as she considered he was not only on top of her but also inside of her. The idea seemed suddenly ludicrous and she had to stifle a laugh. He began thrusting. That wasn't painful, either, but she wasn't sure what the effect was meant to be; it seemed a long way from the centre of her action. It was relatively quick and she knew it was about to happen. Two massive thrusts, a bit of groaning and then he sank down on her, still inside.

'I love you, Luce,' he said, kissing her.

'Love you too,' she said. It was actually done.

Afterwards, in the shower, she knew there was no going back to just holding hands.

15

It's the last real day of high school, even though there are still the exams to come. Lucy feels restless. Let down. This was never how she imagined her last day would feel. Other Year 12s are running around, signing school uniforms, but she just can't get into the frivolity of the day. There is a Carnivale on the oval — sumo wrestling, a dunk-the-teacher stand, music pumping — but she just wants to be out of there.

'I'm going, guys,' she tells Lydia and Georgia, who are standing in line for fairy floss.

'You okay, hon?' Georgia asks.

Lucy knows they have both accepted her distancing herself. They are far too good friends to push her on anything. But she is just unable to talk about that night, unable to face the reality in front of her.

She nods, despite the fact she is so not-okay. 'Just want to go home.'

'Sure.' Lydia hugs her. 'I'll call you later, babe.'

On the way home, she feels an eyelash away from hysteria. But she can't contain it any longer — if she does, she might burst. The idea makes her laugh — then it's problem solved, she thinks, as she knocks on her mum's office door. Lucy has noticed that since the crash her mum is working a lot more from home and leaving Suzie mostly in charge at the shop.

'Can I talk to you?' she asks, sitting.

'Everything okay?' Her mum puts down her pen. 'Have you heard something?'

'No, everything is the same. I need to tell you something. And I don't know how. I think you're going to be really disappointed in me.' Lucy feels the tears from the last week welling. She realises that, except with her sister, she hasn't actually cried; is there something wrong with her?

'You could never disappoint me,' her mum says.

'I'm so proud of you. Of everything you do.'

'Don't, Mum,' Lucy warns, her voice almost breaking. 'Let me tell you first.'

Her mum nods, but Lucy sees a new anxiety settle on her face.

'I don't know how to say it. So I'll just say it,' Lucy begins. 'I think I might be — well, I'm pretty sure I am — pregnant.' There, the words are out — but they still don't sound real. They sound dramatic and silly.

'Oh, God,' her mum says.

Lucy starts to cry, and the tears are fast, the sobs heavy.

'Lucy, don't.' But her mum is crying, too. 'It's okay. We'll be okay.'

Any other time, her mum's use of *we* would have caused Lucy to argue — *But it's not us, is it, Mum? It's me.* This time she takes comfort in it.

'I don't know what to do,' Lucy says into her mum's shirt. 'I've stuffed everything up, and I don't know what to do now.'

They sit for a while, consoling each other, and then her mum, as Lucy knew she would, swings into action.

'You did a test?' she asks, almost clinically.

'I did — but it was negative. I thought that was good. But nothing since. And my boobs are huge and they hurt. And I've been vomiting.'

'If you are, then how far along do you think you might be?' Her mum pulls out a calendar.

'Must be six weeks. I did the test yesterday, my period was then a week late.'

'Okay' — her mum makes some calculations — 'we should do another one.'

'Can you get a false negative?' Lucy feels totally despondent.

'I think so.' Her mum shrugs. 'I'm pretty sure you can't get a false positive, but the other, yes, I think it happens.'

They go to the bathroom and her mum waits outside the door. Lucy pulls out the remaining test. When she's finished, her mum comes in and sees it sitting on the foil wrapper on the vanity.

'I see you've done this before,' she says lightly.

'Only the once.' Lucy sits on the toilet lid, her eyes already puffy from crying. 'You must think I'm some huge slut.'

'No,' her mum says, grabbing her hand. 'I know you're not. Never think that. I did wonder if you and Carl were ...' She nods her head. 'But I didn't want to ask. I thought if you were, you'd be using protection.'

'We were, Mum,' Lucy says, suddenly glad to be telling someone. She hadn't even told Lydia any of this; Lydia had guessed they'd done it but Lucy hadn't gone into any details about her sex life. It was just too personal. 'We only did it a few times — five — but obviously something went wrong.'

'I wish ...' her mum says, and then shakes her head. 'Doesn't matter now. Okay, is it time?'

They both eye the pregnancy test warily.

'One more minute,' Lucy says, even though she knows it's time. But she wants one more minute of being a kid, talking to her mum like a kid, before everything changes forever. She looks away. The situation is surreal. 'I'd been thinking I should be more careful — go on the pill.'

Her mum frowns, thinking it through. 'So Carl doesn't know anything about this.'

'No. Although I'm pretty sure I know what he'd want if I was pregnant.'

'Marriage and babies?' her mum offers.

'Yeah — that's freaking me out too. I guess, I was feeling trapped and the idea of being with him forever was like a reality check. I knew I didn't want that future. But then he left and I didn't get to say any of that. And now ...' Lucy wipes her eyes. 'This sounds like an episode of *Offspring*.'

Her mum picks up the stick.

'Mum?' Lucy says, pleading.

Her mum drops her bottom lip. 'Positive.'

They talk into the early hours of the morning. And Lucy begins to feel lighter. She has options, there are choices she can make. She knew that, but to have them spelled out for her makes the future seem possibly brighter.

'The way I see it, there are three possible decisions. Keep it.' Her mum is ticking off her fingers. 'Never thought I'd be a granny at forty-four — but there you go. I'll help you financially, we'll look at school options later. I don't see any reason why you can't still go to uni — maybe a little later than expected. Adoption. There are plenty of childless couples desperate for a baby. A closed adoption, so that's it. Or abortion.'

Lucy bites her lip. 'I don't know — what's the right thing to do?'

'There's no right thing, babe. It's a matter of figuring out what's really best for you and the baby. Not Carl. You have to be the priority.'

'It's a baby,' Lucy says suddenly. 'I've been thinking of it as a pregnancy — but at the end there's a baby.' She feels foolish and naïve. Of course it's a baby. She'd only got as far as nausea and getting fat and everyone knowing and judging her. She hadn't considered nappies, sleepless nights, feeding, a baby seat in the back of her P-plate car. The birth. 'Oh, God.'

'Don't panic,' her mum says firmly. 'We can work this out. We need time. Dad will have some ideas.'

'No,' Lucy says, putting her hand on her mum's arm. 'Please don't tell him yet. I don't want him to think of me differently. I don't want not to be his Rabbit anymore.'

'You'll always be his Rabbit, even when you're grown up. That will never change.'

'Please, Mum.' Lucy's crying again. 'Please don't tell him yet.'

'Okay, we'll wait a while. We've got plenty of time.'

16

The phone rings at 6 a.m. It's Mrs Kapuletti.

'Lucinda! Carlo — he is awaken!'

'What?' she says, still wiping her face after her morning vomiting ritual. 'Carl? Is awake?'

'Yes, two hour ago. He awaken. Just like that. He speak — he is okay. He is fine. Carlo is awaken.'

'Can I see him?' she asks nervously.

'Yes, you come tonight. I call you later. I tell you where to come to.'

At work Lucy sends a bag of elastic bands to the office instead of hundred-dollar notes. When the office calls her, she panics, then finds the missing money in the elastic band compartment.

Al is coming to take her to see JD, and then later she'll see Carl. The prospect of finally seeing them both after nearly a week — although it's felt like a lifetime — terrifies her. She doesn't know what to expect.

Al pulls into her driveway at five to two, and she kisses her mum goodbye.

'See ya,' she says, like she's off to the beach, not to an intensive care unit.

'Okay, I'll be at the shop, but call me if you need me. Everything's done and Suzie can manage on her own. I have my phone on vibrate.' Her mum pats her pocket, making Lucy laugh. Her mum, for years the technophobe, now connected to her mobile day and night.

'You're not a teenager, Mum,' she calls, leaving the house.

It doesn't take long to get to the hospital, and the grounds are beautiful. Sunlight dapples the tree-lined walkways, heavy-headed hydrangeas bounce in the light breeze. In the hallway she is surprised by the smell, a slightly musty odour — more like an old people's home than a hospital.

Ben smells it, too. 'Lots of old people here,' he says. 'Rehabilitation unit, mostly for hips and stuff. JD's this way, he's still in the intensive care ward. They'll move him into a rehab room any day now.'

Outside a closed door sits Mr Tan. Lucy has never met him before, but he springs to his feet when he sees them approach.

'Alan, Ben, Lucy,' he says. Like JD, despite his very Asian appearance, he has a strong Australian accent.

'JD wants to see you, Lucy. Alone.' He gives her a small hug and she feels so tall next to him. 'He's asked not to wear his oxygen mask for the visit. He wants to talk.'

'Okay.' She smiles but is petrified.

She walks into another room, where a nurse sits in front of a computer, overlooking a glass window into the next room. Lucy glances at the window. Inside is a giant white-sheeted box. 'Through there?' she asks the nurse. The nurse nods and returns to her typing.

'Five minutes,' she says, without looking up. That suits Lucy fine.

Inside it's all white tiles and humming machines;

Lucy is reminded of that Monty Python skit, 'This is the machine that goes PING.' She rubs her hands nervously down her sides, realises she's holding her breath. It smells sterile in here.

She approaches the box cautiously. It's a bed, with some sort of contraption over it and a sheet over that. She spies JD's black hair poking out of one end and stands next to him, putting her face in the space above his. His face is white. There is a bandage taped to the left side of his head.

'Hi JD!' Her voice sounds overly bright and almost obscene in that room with the machine that sporadically pings. 'How are you?' She cringes immediately — what a stupid question to ask.

His eyes meet hers and he attempts a smile. 'Not too bad — aside from a broken neck.' He laughs but she can barely hear him.

She joins in, but her laugh is too loud. She realises his head is being held fixed by giant screws, with rods and elbows embedded in his skull.

'Honestly, JD, you okay?' she says softly.

'Yeah, the drugs round here are pretty good. I'm off my face most times. Have you seen Carl?' he whispers.

She shakes her head, and then feels embarrassed she has. 'No, not yet.'

'He's dead, isn't he?' There's a sudden harshness to JD's whisper. 'They keep saying he's not, but I saw him. He was dead.'

'No.' She raises her hand, even though he can't see it, and makes sure her face is over his. 'He's not, I promise,' she says hurriedly. 'He's been in a ... asleep. And he woke up this morning. I'm seeing him tonight.'

'Promise?' And he starts to cry.

'I promise, JD. Don't.'

But he won't stop crying. She panics and hits the bell.

The nurse runs in, checks him, calms him down. 'Time to go,' she says.

Lucy nods, mournful, and goes to leave but hears JD's weak voice.

'Lucy, wait.'

She walks back into his line of vision.

'Thanks for coming. Thanks. What happened isn't your fault.'

She nods, but it doesn't matter. His saying that means he knows it is. Carl must have been so mad — with her.

Al and Ben go in — so excited to finally see JD for real — and Lucy sits with Mr Tan.

'Mrs Tan is not coping well,' he tells her. 'She can't come, doesn't want to see JD like this. I try and encourage her but she is funny like that. Says she will wait until he's out of IC. In a proper room, she says.'

'How long do they think?' Lucy asks.

'Soon,' Mr Tan says. 'They'll move him and test him. I'm praying the break is clean and hasn't touched his spinal cord.'

'It won't have,' Lucy says firmly. 'JD will be okay.'

As she waits for the two boys to return, Lucy checks her phone outside. There are six missed calls — all from Mr Kapuletti. There is voicemail. She listens but can't understand what he's saying. She hits the button and calls his mobile.

'Lucy, we need you to come now,' Mr K shouts into the phone.

She pulls it away from her ear. 'What's happened?' she asks. She's scared.

'He's not himself. He's swearing at people and throwing things. He's not quite right in the head.

Please say you'll come now?'

'Yes,' she says, as tremors run through her body. 'I'll come now.'

Al drives her to the hospital. She's arranged for her mum to meet her in the foyer.

'Can we come up?' Al asks, not taking his eyes off the road. 'Did Mr K say?'

'He didn't. I didn't ask. He freaked me out,' Lucy says apologetically.

'Doesn't sound like Carl, man,' Ben offers from the back. 'That dude is the most non-violent guy I know. Bit of a pussy even.'

Ben's trying to lighten them up — but it's true what he says. Carl is gentle, kind; if he's acting aggressively, something must be wrong in his head. Lucy shivers violently. How will he react to her?

17

Lucy waits with Al and Ben in the foyer of the hospital. This one is different to JD's hospital. It's huge and busy. People coming and going. Some shuffle, others stride carrying flowers and gifts. Everyone hurrying about with heads filled with their own problems. No one knows her thoughts.

She watches the front doors, waiting for her mum. There is no way she is going up without her. Al and Ben sit in chairs, tapping their feet — not talking. Then the sliding doors open and her mum appears, slightly flustered.

'Hey,' she says, hugging Lucy.

Lucy looks at Ben and Al. 'Thanks guys.' She hugs them both. How close the three of them have become so quickly. Another bizarre turn.

'Anytime,' Al says.

'Text me,' Ben asks, 'after you see him?'

Lucy nods, grateful for their support.

Mum holds her hand as they ascend, and Lucy is glad for it. She wants to ask what will happen but knows this time her mum doesn't have the answer. They enter Level 6, as instructed by Mr K, and see him at the end of the hallway. Lucy grips her mum's hand tighter.

'Lucy, you're here,' he says loudly.

'I'm here,' she agrees.

'Carl is awake. But he's not right — he's not himself. I need to see if you can make a difference.'

'Okay,' she says, but wonders what she can do.

They walk down the corridor, past doors open on people in beds, looking up vacantly at TVs. An old man bending over, the back of his open gown exposing his hairy, saggy buttocks. Her mother squeezes her hand. Nurses push wheelchairs and IV drips. Up ahead a large tea trolley is parked outside a door. 624.

She breathes deeply. Carl is awake, she reminds

herself, and talking. He is not right? What exactly is wrong with him? What if he gets angry with her?

Suddenly a loud shattering noise. A cup has smashed on the floor. Lucy looks at her mother wide-eyed, unconsciously squeezing her hand again. Her mother gives her a small smile. They step into the doorway; the curtain in front of them is closed.

'I'm so sorry. So sorry.' It's Mrs K's voice. 'My Carlo, he normally the good boy.'

'It's okay,' an unfamiliar voice says.

'Okay?' Carl's voice, but deeper. 'I'd say that's as far from okay as you can get. Isn't it your job to collect cups and wash them, not smash them? Can't see your boss thinking that's okay.'

Lucy frowns. The tone is snide, hateful.

'Here!' Carl shouts so loudly that Lucy jumps. 'You forgot this!'

A saucer hurtles into the curtain in front of them and clatters to the floor, unbroken but chipped. An orderly bends down to pick up the saucer, as he opens the curtain. Seeing them standing there, he says casually, 'Common in head injury,' by way of explanation. 'The aggression and violence.'

Lucy looks past him to where Carl lies on the

bed. He is stretched out, propped up, glaring towards her. She freezes. It looks so much like him, but so much unlike him. The difference is disturbing and disconcerting. It's like she's seeing a copy of Carl, with a few tiny variations. His face is white, yet grey. His eyes are open, but she can't see his eyes properly. The entire socket is black, making him look alien, foreign. Eyeball-less. Like a face without eyes. His mouth is a thin, mean line. Then it drops open, as though someone has shot him with 100 volts of electricity.

Lucy stares at him. Carl, but not Carl. He smiles. A sly, wolfish grin.

'Hey,' he says, super casual, like he's trying to chat her up. But his voice is deep and gravelly. Nothing is right about him. 'Long time, hey?'

Lucy nods. Even though it's only been five days since the crash, it's felt like years to her.

Mrs K is nodding and gently weeping. 'My Carlo,' she says, patting his arm.

He flinches and glares at her, sending death rays through her with his eyes.

Lucy takes a step backwards.

'Here,' he says, nodding towards the seat next

to the bed, 'sit down.' It's an order, and Lucy is too scared to refuse. She moves towards the bed.

A sickening unwashed odour comes from him. She wrinkles her nose and then tries to pretend she didn't. She tries breathing through her mouth. Despite the leather cuffs restraining the full extent of his movement, he is still able to pick up her hand and crush it in his. His hand is filthy; there is black dirt under his fingernails and in the webbing between his fingers.

'So whatcha been doing?' Again, that very casual voice that sounds nothing like Carl.

So many thoughts rush through her head, but she dismisses each one. Telling him how frightened she is, how worried about him and JD she's been, and now the pregnancy — all seem totally wrong. She shrugs.

The bones in her hand are rubbing together painfully. That eyeless face is watching her. He is freaking her out.

'I went to work,' she says, although her mouth is suddenly dry and her tongue feels three times its normal size.

'Yeah?' He leans closer.

The smell of rotting meat is overpowering. A wave of nausea rushes through her.

'Where do you work, then?'

She frowns at his question, which immediately elicits the same response from him. Even his frown is menacing. She struggles to breathe normally. 'Coles,' she says. She's been working there for a couple of years — every Thursday night and Saturday morning since she was fifteen. He has even picked her up from there.

'Serious?' With just one word he sounds so disappointed in her, and releases his grip for a minute. 'What happened to all your plans?'

'Plans?' She looks at her mother and Mrs K. They smile encouragingly.

'We go for coffee,' Mrs K interjects, seemingly happy that Carl knows who Lucy is, 'leave you lovebirds.'

Her mum gives her the *are you alright?* look and Lucy nods, despite feeling the polar opposite of alright. She watches them leave, wishes she was leaving with them.

'Thank fuck they've gone,' Carl mutters, grabbing her hand again. 'I'm sick of them spying on me. So what happened, then?'

Lucy thinks quickly — what happened? That night? He doesn't remember? 'What?'

'Your plans. You always said back when we were in high school that you were going to go to uni — become a ...' — he pauses and frowns — 'a something. What happened? How come you ended up working at Coles?'

'Oh.' She realises there is a lot wrong with him, aside from the black eyes. 'I work there part-time.'

He smiles, that strange secretive smile. 'So uni, then?'

'No.' She wiggles her fingers, the tips of which she thinks are turning blue. 'I'm in high school, doing Year 12.'

'What!' he shouts and she jumps. 'Why? What happened to you? You were, like, the smartest girl in school. Why are you repeating?'

'I'm not.' Lucy has a blinding headache. 'I'm still doing it.'

He shakes his head, the information bothering him, but Lucy sees he can't figure out why.

A nurse puts her head around the curtain. 'Hello,' she calls cheerily, pulling a trolley behind her. 'Just need to do some obs.'

Carl tenses and tightens his grip on Lucy's hand. 'What the fuck do you want?' he snaps at the nurse.

'Hey Carl, settle down.' She puts a hand on his wrist. 'I'm Petra, just need to take your temperature and stuff.'

'Nurse, hey?' he says triumphantly. 'So this *is* a hospital.' He looks at Lucy, nodding.

She doesn't know what to say.

'Do you know what day it is today?' Petra asks, as she fiddles with a machine.

Carl ignores her and turns towards Lucy. 'My fucking eyes are killing me. What have they done to me?' he whispers.

'Do you know where you are?' Petra asks, shaking a thermometer.

'*Do you know where you are?*' Carl mimics her nastily. 'No, I don't, you stupid bitch. But I bet you fucking do. Get away.' He shakes his head from side to side and grits his teeth. 'I'd stick that thermometer in your eye if you weren't wearing glasses. And my hands weren't tied.'

'Calm down, now.' The nurse tries to soothe him.

'Fuck off, you fat slut!' he screams at her.

Lucy recoils. 'Carl!'

'What?' He looks at her, confused.

'Don't be so horrible.' Lucy feels close to tears. She watches Petra, who remains unfazed, pack the trolley.

'Sorry,' Carl says churlishly. 'You're not really fat. More like pear-shaped.'

'Carl!' Lucy says again.

'What?' He frowns. 'Look, it worked. She's gone. So where were we? Tell me about yourself, then.' There it is again, that slightly sleazy tone. 'Where do you live, what do you do?' He glares and drops her hand. 'Who are you with now? That guy? Did you get married?'

'What?' She rubs her hands together, trying to get the circulation moving again. 'Married?' She wishes she could laugh — she's in *The Twilight Zone*.

'To that guy?' He spits as he speaks. She feels it on her face but is too scared to wipe it away.

'What guy?'

'You know.' He turns from her. There is dirt all through his hair; the white pillow beneath his head is filthy.

Nausea rises in Lucy again. Everything is

overpowering — the sight, the smell, the weirdness.

'That guy you dumped me for.'

'Carl.' She reaches over to touch his hand, but she's scared of what he might do. Her hand hovers in the air between them. 'I never dumped you.' And once the words are out, she immediately regrets them. They had almost broken up, hadn't they? It was nearly all over that night, wasn't it?

He turns to face her and his black eyes glisten. He's crying, she thinks. In their fourteen months together, she'd never seen him cry. *Real wogs don't cry*, he'd say when she sat there, weeping over *The Notebook*.

'Are you sure?' He frowns and grabs her hand again. 'Where have you been, then? How come I ...' He trails off and looks around furtively. His eyes fix on the smoke detector above them. 'Why am I here? Do you know? What have I done? What do they want from me?'

'You're in a hospital, Carl,' Lucy whispers, engulfed by his paranoia.

'Yes!' He nods triumphantly. 'I figured. I think they keep experimenting on me. I'm not sure why. It was a total relief to see you. I figured you'd got word and come here to get me out. You have, haven't you?' He drops her hand again. 'You're not one of them, are you?' He pushes himself back against the headboard. 'How do I know if I can trust her?' he asks, as if to someone else in the room.

'Carl!' She is horrified. What has happened to his brain? Who is he? Who is he talking to? 'You had an accident. You're here to get better.'

'Sure, yeah.' His eyes narrow suspiciously. 'Get me a drink?'

She leaps to her feet, relieved to get out. 'No probs. Back in a minute.' She pushes open the curtain.

'Hey,' he shouts. She flinches, ready to duck. 'Make sure you do.'

'Do what?' she says, steadying herself against the curtain.

'Come back in a minute.' He looks at an imaginary watch. 'I'm timing you.'

She tries to laugh, but is frightened it will come out as a sob.

18

Lucy walks unsteadily down the hallway. Is this permanent? Is this how he will stay? She rubs her hand over her stomach. Her awareness of how serious everything has suddenly become makes her want to swoon. It sounds so romantic — swooning — but there is nothing romantic here; it's dirty and sad and totally wrong. She sees her mum in the lounge area at the end of the corridor, listening to Mrs K, who is gesticulating wildly. As she gets closer, she notices they've both been crying. There's a pile of tissues between them and their eyes are red-rimmed.

'Hey,' her mum says. 'Okay?'

Lucy shrugs and slides into the chair. *Make it all go away*, she wants to say. This is a nightmare. 'Yeah.

Nah.' She shrugs again and blinks; she doesn't want to cry.

'But he knows you. No?' Mrs K says. 'He sees you. I see his face. It changed. He knows you, Lucinda.'

Lucy shakes her head. 'He does know me,' she says, 'but something's wrong.'

'Wrong?' her mum asks. 'What do you mean?'

'He's totally paranoid. He thinks there's some type of conspiracy, or something. He thinks he's a prisoner. He thinks ...' — she recalls as much of the conversation as she can — 'that years have gone by. That this is, like, in the future.'

'Oh dear,' her mum says. 'What did he say to you? Did he get angry?'

'No.' She retells as much as she can remember, each word giving the weirdness an odd reality. 'He didn't get mad. He got sad. He cried.'

'No. Not my Carlo.' Mrs K allows the never-ending tears to roll. 'My boy never cries.'

'Well, he did.' Lucy looks up as Mr K approaches.

'Carl remembers you?' he asks.

'Yeah, he remembers me, but he's pretty confused.'

'He remembers you. That's the important thing.'

Mr K looks elated. 'The doctors said he might not remember anyone again. But if he remembers you, that's good. It means he can get better now. Thank God. I'll go to him.'

Lucy nods; she feels exhausted.

She goes to the coffee shop and grabs a water for Carl and a latte for herself. As she nears Carl's room, she hears loud voices. Not again, she thinks. She approaches the curtain cautiously and pulls it back. Mr Kapuletti is seated next to the bed, looking up at Carl who is glowering at him. The hard, eyeless face boring holes into Mr K. Lucy grips the curtain.

'Carl, Lucy *has* been to see you.' Mr K sounds imploring.

'I've told you already. I don't know why you tell me the same things all the time. She hasn't been in. I haven't seen her for ages.' Carl spits the words at his father.

'Mother Mary,' Mr K says. 'We may have to let them test your head.'

'What!' Carl roars and makes to launch at his father, but he is restrained by the leather straps. 'You tell your God-bothering friends, Father, that you won't touch my head. One opportunity and I'll take the lot of you down.'

He glances over to where Lucy hovers in the doorway. 'Lucy!' His tone is immediately softer. 'There you are. I was just talking to the Father about you. Been a long time, hey?' That sleazy tone is back.

Lucy finds herself nodding.

Carl looks at his dad. 'Go on, then, Father. Fuck off. Mother is waiting for you. Go bore her.'

Lucy's hand flies to her mouth. She watches Mr K rise like a broken man from the chair. He touches her elbow as he passes, his face a crumpled mass of misery. From the bed Carl growls like a dog, like he was growling when she first arrived, and it makes her nervous. He's so unpredictable. So volatile. She sits next to him.

'Where have you been?' he asks, his tone soft, almost sulking. 'I've been waiting and waiting. That fucking priest won't leave me alone. I can't stand this place.' He glances at the ceiling, blinking tears.

'What priest?' His tears are more upsetting than his rages. This is not her Carl — this is someone completely different.

'The bald dude.' Carl points at the doorway. 'The one who just left.'

'That's your dad!' Lucy says in horror. 'Don't you recognise him?'

'My dad?' Carl frowns, his black eyes searching her face. 'Thought he looked familiar. Thought I'd seen him before. But it's this place. They're messing with my head. He told me they were. Why would my dad say that?'

He looks so confused. Lucy can't bear it.

'Carl, you've had an accident. You've hit your head pretty badly. They're trying to fix it. You keep forgetting things.' Lucy takes his hand gently, noticing where the leather strap has bitten into his skin. 'You look really tired.'

'I am,' he agrees. 'I've been here so long. Nothing changes. The interrogations are the worst. The questions they ask me. It's relentless and I don't know what they want. I thought for a while it was you they were after. But you're here. So it can't be.' He is starting to ramble and whisper, glancing around.

'Carl,' Lucy begins, but he interrupts her.

'Shhhh,' he says, 'someone's coming. I need a knife — something.'

'Carl!' Lucy shouts. 'You're safe, you don't need anything.'

He narrows his eyes at her. 'That's easy for you to say,' he hisses, 'you're not being held prisoner.' He looks around wildly. 'Pass me that pen, my stupid hand won't pick it up.'

'No,' Lucy says firmly, despite her terror. What is the right thing to say to him? What will or won't tip him over the edge? She breathes a sigh of relief as she sees Mrs K in the doorway.

'Who are you?' Carl asks, narrowing his eyes again. 'You look familiar. Are you an actress?'

'Carlo?' She shakes her head at Lucy. 'Oh, mio dio,' she says, rushing at him.

'Who the hell are you?' He pushes her away with his shoulder. 'Stop crying and kissing me.'

Mrs K dissolves. 'I get sister. I get father,' she says, rushing off.

Carl turns to Lucy. 'Great. More nuns and a priest. What is this place — a seminary? You told me that dude wasn't a priest.'

'He's not,' Lucy says, overwhelmed by the display in front of her. Carl's parents hover in the doorway, and she looks at them for help. What is she meant to do?

'Carl,' Mr K says softly, 'you know me. No?'

'Not sure, mate,' Carl says angrily. 'Is that a trick

question? Are you asking me if I know you — or telling me I don't?' Carl seems to find this funny and starts laughing loudly, but just as quickly stops. 'What's wrong with you lot — someone remove your funny bones?' This also seems to strike him as particularly funny. 'For Christ's sake, why don't you all just fuck off,' he snaps, irritated.

'You no speak in front of your mother like that,' Mrs K says, wringing her hands.

Carl straightens at her words and leans forward. 'You know, I've been meaning to ask,' he says casually, 'that old Immaculate Conception thing — it was a scam, wasn't it? You just came up with the greatest lie ever to excuse yourself for bonking some other bloke. Did they ever let on to old Joseph that you'd deceived him with the Almighty's spawn? Or did you always get away with it? The Catholics swallowed it whole, didn't they? Pray to you and all. Even though you're no more than a garden-variety slut.' He looks pretty pleased with this logic.

'Oh, mio dio — my Carlo, my good boy. He's like a devil,' Mrs K wails.

'I'll get someone,' Mr K says, running out of the room.

'What for?' Carl shouts after him. 'An exorcism? Fuck!' He looks at Lucy with panic in his eyes. 'Don't let them touch me,' he whispers.

'Carl.' She wants to touch his hand but is frightened of him. 'They're trying to help you.'

The doctor strides into Carl's room and takes the chart from its holder. 'Hey Carl, how are you?'

'I don't like your smile. You look like a rat,' Carl says, turning away.

The doctor pulls a torch out of his pocket — it's a little like a pen — and points it in Carl's eyes.

'Hey!' Carl shouts so violently that Lucy jumps. 'You trying to blind me?' The next minute Carl pulls a rolled-up newspaper from under the sheets and, limited by the restraints, awkwardly wields it in front of him. The torch flies across the room and hits the wall with a shattering noise.

'Hey,' the doctor says, putting his hands up in surrender, 'steady on. Just want to test a few things.'

'Like what?' Carl snarls, letting the doctor get closer, then hits him hard with the paper. The doctor tries to cover his face, but Carl gets in a few blows. If it wasn't so terrifying, it would be laughable, Lucy thinks.

Orderlies in dark blue arrive.

'Soldiers!' Carl shouts, thrashing wildly.

One grabs him from the other side, as the doctor jabs him with a needle.

'Poison!' Carl screams and then relaxes back against the bed.

Mrs K sobs loudly. The doctor looks at her. 'It's okay,' he says reassuringly. 'This is quite normal.'

Normal? Lucy thinks. How is any of this normal?

Carl sleeps for a while, and they sit in silence. He is perfectly still but for the rise and fall of his chest.

'He's a lot calmer now,' Mr K says weakly.

Lucy nods, still reeling from the shock of it all. 'Yeah, nothing a dose of muscle relaxant can't fix.'

Her mum lifts an eyebrow at her.

Mr K laughs lightly, but the laughter sounds forced.

There is a knock at the door: Carl's Aunty Adele. Lucy smiles at her.

'Hi,' Aunty Adele says. 'How is he? Mama wants to come, but after what you say about the aggression, I tell her to wait. I see him first?' She embraces her sister. 'How are you?'

'Surviving.' Mrs K teeters on the edge of tears. 'So much not like my Carlo.'

'He needs a good wash,' Adele says, looking at him and wrinkling her nose.

'They bathe him in bed,' Mrs K says, 'while he is sleeping. Now, when he's awakened they can put him in the shower.'

Carl stirs. 'Hey,' he says, trying to lift himself up. 'Where am I?'

Adele rushes to Carl's side and puts her hand on his. 'How are you?'

He watches her guardedly. 'Okay.' He frowns, looking at her hand on his.

'Do you know who I am, Carl?' Adele asks sadly.

Carl shifts uncomfortably. Looks at Lucy. Looks at his mother. Looks back at Adele. 'Yeah,' he says slowly, 'I think I do. You might be my sister. But ...' — he pauses, examining her face — 'I'm not sure if you're the older one or the younger one.'

'Carlo!' Mrs K grasps her hands together, as if in prayer. 'You have no sister. She is your zia. Carlo, you don't remember your zia?'

Carl looks at his mother. In front of Lucy's eyes, he seems to turn greyer. 'Are you my mum? You could be. You remind me of her. Maybe a bit fatter.'

Mrs K clutches her hands to her breast. 'Cara mia, when will it end?'

'Look, Carl.' Adele has picked up a get well card and reads aloud: *'Thinking of you. Get well soon. Bill and Angela.* Isn't that nice of them.' She places it back on the shelf.

Carl looks at her angrily. 'I want everyone to get out except for Angela,' he snarls suddenly. The venom is vicious. Mrs K and Adele recoil.

'Who?' Lucy asks.

Carl doesn't look at her. His black eyes are fixed on his aunt. 'Everyone out!' he roars. 'Except her.' He thrusts his thumb in Lucy's direction.

Lucy's mum gives her a worried look, but Lucy nods bravely.

Mrs K doesn't know what to do. She bustles about, fussing over the cards and flowers. Adele grabs her worrying hands and stills them.

'C'mon, sorella. Later.' She looks over her shoulder at her nephew. She's trying to be casual, but Lucy sees how upset and shaken she is.

Lucy looks at Carl. Maybe he doesn't know who I am, she thinks suddenly. 'Do you know my name?'

He laughs abruptly. 'Yeah.'

'What is it?' she asks softly, wondering about the extent of his memory loss.

'Lucy.' He squeezes her hand so strongly she thinks he's fractured a bone.

'Why did you call me Angela?' She frowns.

He leans closer, his black eyes glinting, and drops his voice conspiratorially. 'I didn't think you'd told them your name. I didn't want to dump you in the shit.' He winks at her and taps the side of his head. 'Up here for thinking.'

19

It's dark outside. Their headlights cover the distances between the evenly spaced streetlights, illuminating the glistening black tarmac. Lucy looks at the houses as the car passes, rectangles of yellow light in the blackness. She wonders if that night was like this one. Did he have a moment of clarity when he realised they were going to crash? When he knew the car had taken control and his hands on the wheel, his foot on the pedal, were useless? Was he scared when they were airborne? Did he consider what would happen next? Was he panicking as the car flipped? Did he cry? And when they came to rest on the roof and JD was screaming his phone number, what had they heard, all those people inside their houses, in front of their 65-inch LCDs, watching the latest release on Foxtel? The screech of brakes? The sound of the car wiping out the fence? And what sound does a half-tonne car make as it flies through the air, flipping and hitting the ground several times? How loud were the crashes, the shattering windows, the splintering metal? What did the people inside their homes say to each other? *Did you hear that? That sounds terrible? Someone's in trouble?* What did they think when they ran to the car, its wheels still spinning: hoons, stolen car, car chase? And the man who called Mr Tan — did he wonder what it would be like to receive the very same call?

'You okay?' her mum asks, watching her profile.

Lucy shrugs. 'Yeah. Nah. Thinking.'

'What do you want to do now?' her mum says.

'About what?' She laughs loudly. 'There are so many things that need doing.' But breaking up with Carl just came off the priority list. What kind of heartless bitch would she be if she did that?

'Tomorrow,' her mum says, squeezing her hand. 'Let's use the AA adage: take each day one at a time. What do you want to do tomorrow?'

'Come back,' Lucy says, sighing. 'I have to.'

'Okay, I'll bring you,' her mum says, nodding. 'And you don't have to.'

'Of course I do.' She looks out the window, thinking.

She lies in her bed, reliving the events of the day. Carl — but not Carl. How are you supposed to feel when your boyfriend wakes up from a coma and now seems like a complete stranger? When you are pregnant to a man who doesn't seem to exist anymore. When you remember the fourteen months you spent together and realise that the relationship was not what you wanted? She tries to pinpoint when it happened, when the shift came.

They were out in the city, the usual — a movie and a restaurant. And it was in the restaurant that she realised this was all they did. All they ever did. Go to the movies and dinner, having polite conversation. She had looked at her hand, the small gold ring he had given her for their six-month anniversary. It had come in a blue Tiffany box. And she'd feigned excitement when she opened it. It was so not her. A small love heart ring — and she hated mainstream jewellery. But he had been so excited to give it to her, so she wore it dutifully every day, denying it was a symbol of their difference. But that night she couldn't deny it any longer.

He wasn't interested in culture and the arts; she wasn't interested in the FA Cup and weed. They didn't agree on refugees — they were 'queue jumpers', as far as he was concerned, whereas she'd argue vehemently that they were human beings in need of help. He believed global warming was a hoax, while she was concerned that there was no Planet B, only this one, and the threat to it was real. As for the treatment of Indigenous Australians, he called them 'dole bludgers' when she argued for their right to the land and some form of compensation. They disagreed on religion — he was a devout Catholic, but not so devout that he would forgo sex before marriage. Their politics were opposite ends of the spectrum, as was even their taste in furniture and design. She remembered clearly the feeling that had engulfed her, which could be summed up in three single-syllable words. *This is it.* This was all it would ever be. And a vision of the future: the pair of them in a similar restaurant — him balding and her (hopefully not) fatter, looking at each other with nothing to say.

Lucy wanted to travel and study. She wanted to explore the world she lived in. She wanted to meet other people. She wanted to meet other boys. Not necessarily for sex — she wasn't that much of a fan — but for meaningful conversations. She didn't want to be stuck in Perth forever, in a four by two, a theatre room with surround sound and an alfresco area with an outdoor kitchen. She didn't want barbecues every Sunday with Big Al, Ben and JD, or even just Lydia and Georgia. She certainly didn't want the sum total of her existence to be movies and restaurants every weekend. And as she watched him across the candle's dancing flame that night, she knew that was what he would be happy settling for. She didn't want to be a settler; she wanted to be a pioneer. And at that point, her brain shifted.

We need to talk, she messages Lydia and Georgia on Facebook that night.

Immediately Lydia, who is electronically attached, types back *When hon? You okay?*

All good.

Simultaneously, Georgia types, *When?*

Tomoz. She sends this message to both and sits back, staring at the screen. What is she going to tell them? Or how much isn't she?

20

They meet at Dome in Mullaloo. A girl from school
brings their order to the table.

'Sorry,' she says, slopping coffee into the saucer.
'I'll be back in a sec.' She returns with serviettes
and proceeds to mop up the coffee. The trio wait
in silence. 'Hey,' she says before she tucks the table
number into the back of her apron. 'I was really
sorry to hear about your boyfriend.' She is looking at
Lucy. 'Hope he and his mate will be okay.'

Such kindness from a total stranger surprises
Lucy and she fights back tears.

'I think he will be,' she manages eventually.

'How are you?' Georgia asks, stirring her skinny
chai latte, as the waitress leaves. 'How are they?'

'Okay.' Lucy stares into her own latte. 'Carl is weird — head injury weird.' She goes on to tell them about yesterday.

'In restraints?' Lydia can't get past that one detail. 'What does that mean?'

'He's tied down,' Georgia says. 'Means they think he's dangerous.' She looks at Lucy. 'Is he?'

'He's definitely different,' she says and recounts the things he's said, the conspiracies, the madness.

'Shit.' Lydia sucks her spoon. 'What a nut job.'

'There's more.' All of a sudden Lucy feels she's swallowed truth serum. *Tell them everything*, it demands. 'Actually, it's even weirder.'

'How?' Lydia looks across at the park and the Indian Ocean beyond, crashing mercilessly against the sand dunes. 'What a cute dog.' She points to the golden coloured spoodle. 'A cockerpoo.'

'A spoodle,' Georgia corrects, not taking her eyes off Lucy. 'How weirder?'

'I'm pregnant,' Lucy says flatly.

'Pregnant!' they both shout.

Lydia's eyes widen. 'A baby! Will you name it Lydia?'

'If it's a boy, that would seem cruel,' Lucy states.

Lydia doesn't get it. 'A baby!' she says again. 'We can dress her up. Play with her. Oh my God.' Her eyes widen in alarm.

Now, Lucy thinks, the reality is setting in.

'You have to push it out your virginia.'

'It's *vagina*, Lydia,' Georgia corrects. 'What are you going to do?' She reaches across and grabs Lucy's hand. 'What do you want to do?'

'I don't know.' Lucy feels exhausted. 'I think I need to tell Carl, but it's bad timing right now. Or, I go ahead and never tell him.'

'Go ahead?' Georgia asks.

'Yeah. He never needs to know. He's got a lot to deal with. Once he finds out about JD. Then there'll be a court case.'

'Why?' Lydia asks.

'Dangerous driving. Liability,' Georgia says. 'What you're saying is that you'd only not tell him if you were getting rid of it.'

'Yeah.' Lucy nods.

'Getting rid of what?' Lydia asks.

'The baby.' Georgia's eyes have never left Lucy's.

'Oh, the baby — it'll be so cute.' Lydia twirls her glass. 'Hey!' Her eyes widen. 'Maybe you could be on a documentary — you know, *Teen Mom* or something. We could be on it, too. As your BFFs.'

Lucy shakes her head. She loves Lydia, but she is so off the planet sometimes. 'I don't think I can do it,' she says slowly. 'Have it.'

'What?' Lydia looks bewildered. 'You don't mean you'd get rid of it, like in ...' Her words drift. As she realises the enormity of the situation, Lucy sees her shudder.

'Whatever you want, we'll be here,' Georgia says. 'But you need to think this one out. It's Carl's baby, too — doesn't he have a right to decide as well?'

Lydia nods fiercely. 'Georgia's right, it's his baby, too. He should be part of it — whether he's a nut job or not.'

A right to decide? Lucy bristles at the idea. Why should he have a right to decide? When did she become someone's property? 'No.' She shakes her head certainly. 'I don't think so. It's my body. My life. Carl doesn't have a say.'

But Lydia is looking angry. 'But it's a baby — and half his, too. He needs to have a say.'

'What?' Lucy can't believe this is coming from one of her best friends.

'It's half his,' Lydia insists. 'Why do you get to make the decision? What if he wants it? What if he says he'll look after it?'

'Lydia!' Lucy shouts. She feels ill, the coffee bringing her nausea on. 'It's my body! When did I become a baby-making factory? When did other people have the right to decide what happens to my body?'

'I'd suggest when you had unprotected sex,' Lydia says.

And, hurtful as those words are, Lucy knows Lydia doesn't mean to be spiteful.

'Hey.' Georgia puts a hand on each of their arms. 'Don't. We're best friends. Let's not fight. Lydia, you sound so judgemental.'

'I'm not.' Lydia frowns. She's upset by the conversation and Lucy sees she doesn't know why. 'I'm not judgemental. But how come you get all the rights? Why doesn't Carl have any? If you wanted the baby, he'd have to accept it and become a father whether he wanted to or not.'

'True.' Lucy nods. For once, Lydia has a point that no one else has thought of.

'So why can't he be part of the decision, too?' she says.

'Because if he wants it, what's he going to do? Force Lucy into having it?' Georgia says. 'How can anyone do that?'

'Maybe legally.' Lydia shrugs. 'Maybe he can make you have it?'

Lucy and Georgia laugh. 'Imagine that,' Lucy says. 'Gilead.'

'Gilly-who?' Lydia says, frowning.

'From *The Handmaid's Tale*,' Georgia says, 'a book we're studying in Lit, where all the women are the property of all the men. That makes you Ofcarl.'

Lucy shudders. 'What a hideous concept.' Then she shrugs. 'I don't know what to do.'

'I think you have to tell him,' Georgia says, 'and figure it out from there.'

'But you know what he'll say.' Lucy's had the conversation with him a hundred times in her head. *'Let's get married. We can live with my parents. You can eventually go back to school. I'll help.'* The image makes her nauseous. She certainly knows she doesn't want that. 'I don't want to do it.'

'What?' Lydia asks. 'You don't want to tell him? I think Georgia's right. You have to tell him.'

'No, I don't mean that.' Lucy sighs and looks at

her watch. 'I've got to get going in a sec. But look, I don't want to have it. I'm sure of that.'

'So quickly?' Lydia says.

'She's had a while to think it through,' Georgia says, and then turns to Lucy. 'But are you sure you've had long enough?'

Lucy blinks the tears. 'The longer I wait, the more it becomes a person.'

'It's a person already,' Lydia says.

Lucy shakes her head, thinks of her Biology classes. 'It's not, it's just a bunch of cells. It can't exist without me. It's like a parasite.'

'Gross.' Lydia shakes her head. 'Like a giant tapeworm. I was watching that show *Embarrassing Illnesses* and this dude had this massive tapeworm in him. When they got it out, it was like a hundred metres long.'

'I don't think so,' Georgia says.

'Ten metres, then,' Lydia says.

Georgia still looks sceptical. 'Unlikely.'

'Well, I don't know, but it was massive. Disgusting. Blah.' Lydia looks at Lucy. 'I don't mean your baby is like a tapeworm or anything.'

'It's not a baby,' Lucy says. She can't allow herself

to think of it like that. If she did, how could she even consider abortion? Be clinical, detached, she tells herself. Remember it's just a mass of cells, still dividing and unable to exist in its own right. It's like a tumour.

'So when does it become a baby, then?' Lydia says. 'If it's not when you get pregnant, when is it?'

'I don't know.' Lucy needs to talk to Dad; he'll have all the clinical information she needs. But to tell him? It's almost as bad as the idea of telling Carl. 'I guess when it's viable.'

'Viable? What does that mean?'

'When it's able to exist outside of me — without me giving it life.'

'So one second before it's viable means it's not a baby and the next second it is?' Lydia grapples with the concept.

'Yes.' Lucy nods.

'But when is that? Is it the same for all babies?' Lydia says.

'I guess not. I don't know.'

'Seems a bit random,' Lydia says.

Lucy has to agree. When does an embryo become a foetus, become a baby? When does life begin? And if so, when is there ever a time when someone can take that life away? It's doing her head in. She can't think anymore.

She looks at her watch. 'Gotta go.'

Both Georgia and Lydia embrace her. 'Call. Text. Anytime,' Georgia says.

'Me too,' Lydia says. 'Love ya, babe.'

'I know,' Lucy says. 'See ya.'

She gets to her car and heads to the freeway. She can't stop thinking about the conversation. When is it a person? When does life begin?

21

It doesn't take long to get to the hospital and Lucy parks the car and heads into the lobby. She stops at the gift shop, looks at all the magazines, buys a packet of gum. There's a rack of get well cards, and she picks up one. It seems so inappropriate — *get well*. He's not exactly sick. *Get better* would have had more meaning. *Get normal. Get real.* She realises that she's procrastinating. She glances around at the baby clothes, the stuffed toys, the mobiles, the booties. They are so small. She holds a crocheted sock in her hand — so tiny — then puts it gently back on the shelf and heads for the elevator.

'Hey,' she says as she enters Carl's room. He's lying on the bed, staring at her, the white sheet pulled up to his chin. 'How you doin' today?' She sits in the chair next to his bed. 'You look tired. Sleep well?'

He doesn't reply. His mouth is set in a straight line. He narrows his eyes and looks aggressive.

'Carl.' Lucy shifts in the chair. She suddenly feels way too close to him. The vibe she's getting from him is really violent. 'What's the matter?'

'You!' he spits. 'I know all about you. What you've done. What you're up to. Everything. EVERYTHING!'

She leaps from the chair and puts as much space between them as she can. How can he know? She thinks quickly. There are only three people who do and none of them would tell him. She watches him in horror, glad he is still restrained. He looks maniacal — like Jack Nicholson in *The Shining*.

'What are you talking about?'

'I heard them.' He's venomous. 'Last night, talking. About you.'

'Heard who?'

'My parents. My dad.' He shakes his head at the memory. 'He said how you were going out all the time. That you were only with me out of pity. That you were seeing other guys.'

Lucy doesn't know whether to be relieved or annoyed. *As if!* When did she have the time, or the inclination? She wants to tell him that if she wasn't here, she'd be home studying for exams, not off with some fictitious boyfriend and having a rollicking time. 'I don't think so,' she says.

'WHAT?' he roars at her. Spittle flies from his mouth. 'Are you calling me a LIAR?'

'No.' She edges towards the door. He is mental. Psychotic. 'I just don't think they'd say that. They know I'm not going out. I was at school every day until you woke up. Now I'm here. I think you misheard them, or maybe you dreamed it.'

All of a sudden he deflates. Right in front of her, he loses all puff and steam and collapses down against the pillows. He turns his face away.

'I don't know what to think.' He sounds like he's crying. 'I can't tell what really happened. I don't get what's going on. One minute I think something, and then the next minute I'm told something else, and I don't know what's real. You're real, though? Aren't you?' He turns to face her, cheeks streaked with tears.

'Yes.' She wants to move towards him but is

scared he might turn violent again.

'Why did you tell me I was in a hospital in Melbourne?' he asks.

'I didn't,' she says.

'You did.' His voice becomes strident again. 'Why would I make that up?'

She is worn down. 'I don't know, but you have to believe me. I'm not lying to you. You are at Sir Charles Gairdner Hospital and have been here for seven days. Five in a coma. You were in a car crash.'

'Oh.' He looks puzzled. 'A car crash? Why didn't anyone say?'

'I've told you before. We all have.'

'Was there anyone in the car with me?' he asks suddenly.

She hesitates, unsure whether to tell him or not. What if he can't handle the news? What if it tips him over the edge? She wants to wait and ask his father or a doctor before she does. 'I don't know.'

He sighs and looks relieved. 'That's okay, then. Cos if there was, you'd know.' He indicates the chair. 'Come on, sit down. Why the face? You look sad.'

She worries about her lie, what he'll say when he finds out the truth, but then realises he'll have probably already forgotten it.

There's a knock at the door.

'Hello.' It's Big Al and Ben.

'Hey.' Lucy leaps from the chair. 'Come in, guys.'

'Hey, bro.' Al comes close. 'So good to finally see you. How you doin'?'

'Alright.' Carl is surly again. He has pushed himself back up against the headboard. 'What do you want?'

'Nothing.' Ben looks a bit embarrassed. 'We just came to see how you are.'

'Who told you I was sick?' Carl's tone is suspicious again.

'A little bird.' Big Al laughs.

'Yeah,' Carl snarls, 'then that bird should be hunted down and shot. Say something and get out.'

'Carl!' Lucy says, but Ben and Al just shrug.

'No worries, bro, get better.'

'Catch ya soon.'

They wave at Lucy and leave.

'Carl.' She turns on him. 'Why would you be like that? They're your friends.'

'Are they?' He rubs his face against the pillow. 'I thought they were Jehovah's Witnesses.'

'That's Al and Ben,' Lucy says.

'Oh, right.' He looks really tired. 'Thought they looked familiar.' His eyes start drooping. Within minutes he's asleep.

Lucy looks out the window and then decides to go for a walk while he sleeps.

It's beautiful outside. It's spring, the days are still cool, but the light is bright and the air fresh. She wanders along the gardens. What to do? What to do? It's all she can think about. She was almost going to tell him about the pregnancy, but now, after that violent reaction, she thinks she'll wait. She has calculated she is six and a half weeks pregnant, which means, according to her Google search, she has another three and a half until she will no longer be allowed a medical abortion. And that seems like the best option. A few pills (she thinks) and job done. But if she leaves it longer, it will be surgical. An abortion clinic. She hates that idea. She needs to talk to Dad. Has to. He knows all this stuff. She'll just have to face his disappointment.

She looks at her watch. Fifteen minutes. She should head back. It's all so majorly depressing. Carl.

The pregnancy. Poor JD. Exams. While she is here, she can't study and the mocks are soon. It's been her whole life, getting the score to get into uni — train to become a lawyer. But, she reasons with herself, it's not over yet. She needs an 80 ATAR for a basic Bachelor's degree. She's sitting on 97 now — surely she'll be okay? She wanders back to the hospital.

Mr K is heading for the elevator as she arrives.

'Lucy.' He grabs her and kisses both sides of her face. 'How is Carl today? Better?'

'Yeah. Nah.' She hesitates. 'He got a bit mad, but then sleepy. I think he's okay.'

'Look at these.' Mr K hands her his camera. 'I've just come from the wrecker's yard.'

She scrolls through the photos. Carl's car is mangled. The roof on the passenger side is totally flattened; the car looks like it's wearing a hat at a rakish angle. The entire front is stoved in. The back seat is obliterated. That Carl and JD even came out alive amazes her.

'I stopped in to see Douglas earlier,' Mr K says as they enter the elevator. 'He's a strong boy. But he was crying over Carl. I told him Carl will be fine. Soon. That you're making him better.'

She raises her eyebrow at this. She's no neurosurgeon, and Carl's problems are huge. 'Don't you think Carl might need some extra help?'

Mr K nods. 'Yes, I've discussed it with the doctors. They're assigning a psych to him.'

They stand in silence as the elevator ascends.

'I'm so sad for Douglas,' Mr K says eventually. 'He's such a good person.'

Lucy nods. He is. Carl is. She isn't so bad herself. So why are they up to their necks (so to speak) in shit?

She follows Mr K into the room. Carl is awake.

'Carl,' his father says, going immediately to his side.

Carl flinches but stares at Lucy, his black eyes boring into her. 'So you decided to come back?'

'I went for a walk. You were asleep,' she says, crossing her arms over her stomach.

'Yeah, three weeks ago. Long fucking walk,' he snarls.

'Carl,' his dad says. 'Be nice.'

'Why?' Carl snaps. 'Why be nice when my wife is slutting around with other men? Flaunting it in my face. While I'm sick here in bed.' He pauses and frowns. 'Why am I sick? What's wrong with me?'

Lucy looks at Mr K; he is ashen. The fact that Carl has already forgotten he was in a car crash washes over Lucy easily, but the mention of her being his wife freaks her out.

'You've been in a car accident,' Mr K says. 'You banged your head up. But you are going to be okay.'

'Oh.' He looks at Lucy. 'Why didn't you tell me?'

She sighs — this is like *Groundhog Day*. 'I did, you've forgotten.'

'Was anyone else in the car?' He sounds like a little boy. 'Was I driving?'

Lucy looks at Mr K and raises her eyebrow. 'Yes, Carl, you were driving. Douglas was in the car.'

'Douglas?' Carl looks at Lucy. 'Who's he?'

'JD,' she says.

'JD?' Carl looks puzzled. 'That Asian kid?'

'Yes,' Lucy says. She is exceptionally tired.

'Is he okay?'

Carl sounds concerned, and for some reason it lifts her spirits. She looks at Mr K.

'He is okay. He will be okay,' Mr K says.

'Can I see him?' Carl asks.

'Soon.' Mr K pats his restrained hand.

'Why not now?' Carl whips his head around. 'Where is he?'

'Not here,' Mr K says. 'He's in another hospital.'

'Why?' And Carl now sounds suspicious.

'Broken bones,' Lucy says, 'different hospital. That's why.'

'Okay.'

He sounds relieved, but Lucy's not sure why.

22

She watches her dad across the kitchen bench.
He's chopping vegetables, making his famous nasi
goreng. She's always loved these evenings with her
dad, just the two of them, spending time together,
talking. He's always been a great listener and is
never judgemental. So why do the words she wants
to speak remain lodged in the back of her throat?
She knows he'll be disappointed, but it'll be fleeting
— he'll be more concerned. He'll want to fix the
problem. *Tell him,* she instructs her vocal chords, *tell
him now.*

'So Dad ...' She tries for jovial.

'Rabbit.' He looks up from his chopping board.

The word knifes her. Rabbit. He's called her that

since she can remember. She doesn't know why. She doesn't have buckteeth, or floppy ears — she's never even had a fondness for carrots. But that was what he always called her. And she wants to stay his Rabbit.

She thinks quickly. 'So Lydia ...'

'Little Lydia — what's she done now?' Dad is already laughing. He loves Lydia, accepts she's not the smartest kid in the world, but has always defended her big heart.

'She learns the word *procrastinate*.' It's easy to come up with a Lydia story; the girl excels in all things silly. 'And she uses it as much as possible.'

'And probably out of context,' her dad says.

'Totally,' Lucy agrees. 'So she's upstairs at home, studying. Her mum, downstairs, texts her: *What are you doing?*'

'Her mum texts her from within the house?' Dad is still laughing and he looks so young. So handsome. Sometimes Lucy wonders why it didn't work out between her parents — after seventeen years. But, as both of them tell her, seventeen years is a long time and people change. They both did — *evolved separately* is how they explained it.

'Yeah — refuses to come upstairs because she's fed up with Lydia asking her to get things. So anyway, Lydia gets this text and replies: *Homework. Well, I'm meant to be but I'm procrastinating.* And get this ...' —Lucy is now laughing — 'auto correct changes it to *masturbating*!'

Her dad roars with laughter, puts his knife down and hangs on to the benchtop. 'No way.'

'Yes!' Lucy is laughing hysterically, recalling Lydia's face as she retold the story. 'Of course, Lyd doesn't see it. She's sitting at her computer when the door opens and her mum comes in, head swinging around, looking.'

'Wait — what?' Her dad is gasping for air. 'She thinks her daughter is masturbating and rushes in?'

'Exactly what I said.'

'Isn't that when you call out loudly — or in Lydia's mum's case, text — *Taking the dog for a walk*?'

'True.' Lucy nods. 'Lyd reckons she thought she was up to mischief.'

'Masturbating mischief!'

'Reckons she thought Lyd was sexting — and sent it to her by mistake.'

Neither of them can stop laughing.

After a while, her dad resumes chopping. 'That sexting stuff is serious,' he says. 'Young girls sending naked images of themselves to their boyfriends, well, once they're out there, they're irretrievable.' He doesn't look up.

'I don't do that sort of thing, Dad. Carl's not into that. But ...' Her courage deserts her again.

'What?' He looks up and puts the knife down, sensing something serious. 'What is it?'

How many ways can you say it? How do you soften the blow? How do you prepare your dad for the hardest thing you've ever had to tell him?

'I'm pregnant,' she finally blurts.

He nods. Eyes never leaving her face. 'Right. Okay. Right.' He turns and washes his hands.

Procrastinating, Lucy thinks.

'What do you want to do?' he asks, coming around the bench and sitting on the stool next to her.

She bursts into tears.

He puts his arms around her. 'Shhh, Rabbit. Don't. Let your old dad help you here.'

'Dad.' She sobs into his shirt. She loves this man so much. And he hasn't shown anger or disappointment. Just his total love. It kills her. 'I don't know what to do.'

'What does Mum say?' he asks, knowing Mum knows already, and not mad or upset.

'Whatever I want.' Lucy looks for a tissue, can't see one, uses her sleeve.

'Me too,' Dad says. 'Come on, Rabbit, let's figure it out.'

They talk late into the night. Dad discusses all the options with her. He is in favour of an abortion. 'Your life, Lucy, it will become something unimaginable. Eighteen with a tiny baby. And what about Carl? You'll be connected to him for the rest of your life. You've got uni, travel, and going out with friends, being young. Having a baby takes all that away.'

'A baby, Dad.' Lucy wipes her tears with the kitchen towel Dad found when he couldn't bear seeing her use her sleeve.

'It's not yet.' Dad shakes his head, pours his third whisky.

She notes this — as stoic as he is presenting, he's shaken. Her dad is not a big drinker.

'Let's look at the facts.'

She nods eagerly. Facts are what she needs.

Knowledge is power, her dad always says. Give her the power. 'When does life begin?' she asks.

'That's the wrong question.' Her dad sips his whisky. 'Most people — pro-life and pro-choice — would agree that life begins at conception. When the sperm fertilises the egg, this "zygote" now has life. The true question is: when does personhood begin? A fertilised egg has the ability to turn into a person — but, for a myriad of reasons, that may or may not happen. We are talking about when it is a person.'

'When?'

'Let's take it back a few steps. All ova are considered "human"; they contain human DNA. Yet a woman — unless fertilisation happens — sheds one a month, and this isn't cause for concern. A man produces millions of sperm a day also containing human DNA; most are lost, very few fertilise an egg. Again, no real cause for concern. But once an egg is fertilised, people agree it is now a life, but this is where it gets complicated. If a woman has an IUD, that doesn't prevent fertilisation, it prevents implantation. Most women with IUDs can expel fertilised eggs if conception takes place — again, no cause for concern. IUDs are not under scrutiny by the pro-lifers. And if a fertilised egg is a person, with all the rights that a person is entitled to, then a woman who miscarries could be charged with murder. So "personhood" must be defined the same way "death" is.'

'What do you mean?'

'When we declare someone dead, it is due to a lack of brain activity. The brain has flatlined. By this definition, the uniqueness of humans is the developed brain — that allows for an awareness of its surroundings, the ability to feel pain, that sort of thing. It's not until the fifth month that this development takes place, in a primitive neurological way. So, applying the same logic as "death of a person", then "life of a person" begins around twenty to twenty-two weeks.'

'About five months?'

'Correct.'

'That's a bit of space to think,' Lucy says. 'But I guess the sooner the better?'

'Yes, but it gives you the chance to consider all the options. Adoption is a consideration — but of course the pregnancy and birth may be difficult.'

'And then there is a baby out there in the world.

My baby.' Lucy shrugs. 'That sounds so selfish and horrible, doesn't it? It's all about me. What I want. How it will affect my life in the future. I don't like the idea of my baby growing up without me in its life, so I'm thinking about ending its life. I'm some sort of monster.' She starts crying again.

'Hang on,' her dad says, putting a hand on her leg. 'It *is* about you. It's your life and the decision you make fundamentally affects you more than anyone else. If we use the logic that it's not a person yet, then we are not ending a life. Just the potential for one.'

'Sounds like semantics.' Lucy wipes her eyes.

'Philosophy and law are both based on semantics.' After a pause, Dad says, 'And there is the other option.'

'Having it?'

'Yes. What do you think about that?'

She exhales loudly. To become a mother — could she do it? She's only just turned seventeen; what does she know about raising a child? What does she know about teaching someone how to become a person? She's barely qualified. And the resources? How would she afford a baby? Would she have to go to work? Would she have to give up on the idea of uni?

'It's unimaginable,' she says finally, realising that everything is leading her to one solution. An abortion. The thought makes her feel sick. How can that be a solution? She sighs and looks down. 'What's the right choice?'

'It may not even be about the right choice, Rabbit; it may come down to the least worst one,' her dad says finally. 'A decision of this nature isn't going to be easy, but we will get through it together. You, me and Mum. Have you thought about telling Emma?'

'Yes.' She nods. 'But I wanted to tell you first.'

'And Carl? With his violence and aggression, he might not handle the news,' Dad says.

'I was going to tell him today. But you're right, he's in such a bad place — I don't know what the right thing to do is. There are so many decisions to make and all of them feel wrong.'

'It's not a great situation,' her dad concedes. 'You don't have to tell him.'

'I thought about that, too — but that seems so wrong. Even though he can't make me have it — and

I know he'll want to do that. At least, the Carl before the accident would have wanted that — who knows what this one will want? He might surprise me and ask me not to have it.'

'And if he does?' her dad asks.

'I guess I'd feel better, knowing that we were both in agreement. And that he knew. It feels deceitful, doing it without his knowledge.'

'Okay,' her dad nods. 'Have you heard of RU486?'

'The abortion pill?' Lucy asks. 'Is it better than the surgical option?' She shudders; both options are hideous.

'I think so,' her dad says. 'It creates a type of miscarriage, cramping and bleeding, like a heavy period. The surgical procedure requires anaesthetic — a twilight one, but in a clinic. This way it can be done at home, or here. Whatever you want.'

'I don't want any of this,' Lucy says.

'I wish I could make that an option, but I can't,' her dad says sadly. 'It's late, let's talk about it tomorrow.'

When she wakes in the morning, she feels more convinced that a medical abortion is the least worst option. Her dad is making coffee when she walks into the kitchen. He nods at the machine.

'Yes, please.' She sits on the stool and gets straight to the point. 'I think I want the drug.'

He nods. 'Do you want me to ring around?'

'Yes.'

And suddenly there it is. A decision.

23

She can't bear to go to the hospital first thing in the morning. She needs some space. She needs a chance to consolidate everything in her head before she tells Carl.

She phones Mr K and says she'll be in later if she can.

He doesn't sound happy. 'Carl needs you.'

'I know, but there are things that I have to do. I'll try and come this evening.'

'I'll tell Carl you'll come later.'

She doesn't want to argue and so she says goodbye and hangs up. Now what to do? She needs to talk to her sister, but it's about midnight there.

She'll have to wait until later. She organises to meet Lydia and Georgia.

'I'm not having it,' she tells them as they sit on the grassed area overlooking the ocean. The wind is strong and flings sharp needles of sand at them.

'Ouch, I just got bitten by something,' Lydia says, rubbing her face.

'It's sand, Lydia,' Georgia says.

'Sand can bite?' Lydia says.

Georgia doesn't even bother to reply. She looks at Lucy. 'You've made a decision?'

'Yes.' Lucy tells them the logic that her dad applied to the situation, and both girls nod in agreement.

'What about Carl?' Lydia says.

'I'll tell him before I do it. You're right: he should know.'

Lydia persists. 'But what if he wants it?'

Lucy shrugs. It seems heartless and cruel, but it's really too bad. It's not his decision and, besides, she thinks angrily, if he'd read the instructions he'd know how to put a condom on properly. She shakes her head — blaming him isn't going to make things better.

'It's not his decision.'

'But ...' Lydia begins.

Georgia holds her hand up. 'Lydia, Lucy has made a choice and we have to respect it. If you badger her with your ideas you'll undermine her, and she'll feel judged. It's not fair.'

Lydia shrugs. 'Thought I was playing devil's avocado.'

'It's *advocate*,' Georgia says.

'Whatever.' Lydia rubs her face again. 'I won't say another thing. Man, that sand bite is bad.'

'I'll see him this evening,' Lucy tells them. 'And then I'll do it and this mess will be over.'

'We're here for you,' Georgia says. 'Let me know what I can do.'

'And me,' Lydia adds.

'Thanks, guys.'

24

When Lucy gets home she logs on to Skype. Her sister answers just before it rings out. She's been sleeping, her hair is a mess and she hasn't taken off her makeup.

'Big night?' Lucy says.

'Yeah — drank way too much. Feel pretty average. How's Carl? Mum said he was pretty messed up.'

Lucy spends the next fifteen minutes outlining what's been happening.

'Man, that is screwed up. You okay?'

Lucy shakes her head. 'There's more.'

'Really?'

'I'm pregnant.' She watches her sister's mouth drop open.

'No way.'

Lucy nods. 'Wish I wasn't, but there you go.'

'Shit, when is it due?'

'I don't know.' Lucy realises that during all these conversations she's never considered its due date — only how many weeks it is now. *That's because you've always considered an abortion as the number one choice*, she thinks. How telling.

'I'm about six and a half weeks or so,' she says.

Her sister quickly calculates. 'About May next year — a couple of months before you're eighteen. Guess your eighteenth will be a bit different.'

And Lucy realises with horror: her sister thinks she is going ahead with it.

'I'm not having it,' she says.

Emma's mouth drops open again. 'Are you for serious?'

Lucy nods. She can't believe this — never expected it. She thought her sister would force her into an abortion, whether she wanted one or not.

'What does Dad think?'

'He says to do whatever I choose. My decision. He's pro-choice.'

'No, Lucy,' Emma's voice is sad. 'You'd kill your baby?'

'It's not a baby,' Lucy says. Tears well up in her throat again. 'It's not a person until it has brain activity.'

'Oh, Lucy.' Emma sighs and has tears in her own eyes. 'That's just Dad Logic. His way of constructing the facts to suit an outcome.'

Lucy recoils at Emma's words. 'Dad's made sense of plenty of messes you've been in,' she snaps, thinking of the time Emma had gone to Graham's place and hidden prawns in the curtain rod. 'The smell will drive him bonkers,' she'd said madly at the time — and then had a nervous breakdown. Dad had counselled her through it all — made her see that she'd been driven to uncharacteristic behaviour by Graham's betrayal, that she wasn't a deranged lunatic. And wasn't it Dad who had coughed up for her airline ticket so she could travel and *find herself*? If this is who she'd found, Lucy wishes she'd lose her. She wants *her* Emma back. 'I thought you'd support me,' she says sadly.

'I do support you'— Emma leans in closer to the camera — 'but I don't support your decision. I love you, Luce, but what you're talking about is murder.'

Lucy shakes her head. Such emotionally charged

words — *murder*, *baby*, the two collide.

'Why can't you have it?' Emma says desperately.

'Because ...' Lucy pauses. 'I don't want it. I don't want to be a mother. I want to be a teenager. I want to finish school. Have a life — go to uni.' There, said out loud again it still sounds awful.

'Sounds selfish, doesn't it?' Emma says gently.

Lucy nods. But that's the big dilemma. What real reason does she have? And aren't the reasons she does have real enough?

'You wouldn't be doing it alone,' Emma says. 'I'll come back and help you. Mum and Dad will, too. We'll get through it, make it work.'

As much as Lucy knows Emma means what she says, the undeniable truth is that the responsibility will ultimately be all hers. And Carl's. Carl. She shudders.

'I don't want to be with Carl anymore. And as soon as he's better, or well enough to handle the truth, I'm breaking up with him.' Lucy suddenly blurts the truth she's been keeping to herself. That wasn't something she'd really thought about saying — but there it was. Lurking in the recesses of her mind, all this time — affecting her thinking about the pregnancy. 'I don't want to have his baby and raise it as a single parent. I don't want that life.'

Emma purses her lips thoughtfully. 'I hear what you're saying. But heaps of people do it every day of the week. Look at Aunty Liv — she did it.'

'Look at Aunty Liv,' Lucy agrees, 'she's a case in point.' Aunty Liv had had a child when she was seventeen and single. She never said who the father was. She raised Jonas as best she could but struggled with money — state housing, poor areas. Sure, they managed, and Jonas was a nice kid, but he hung out with a rough crowd and drove Aunty Liv demented with worry. And Aunty Liv would often comment on how she wished she'd done things, gone places — but had to work a day job and a night shift to make ends meet. That was exactly the future that terrified Lucy.

'She's not a bad example,' Emma says. 'Look at the bond, the friendship between them. Look at Jonas — he wouldn't exist, wouldn't have a life at all, if she'd done what you're thinking of.'

'I know, Emma. Please stop.' More messages, more thoughts, more opinions. She feels hammered. 'I've got to go. I have to see Carl.'

'Okay.' Emma reaches up and touches the screen.

'I love you, Luce. You know that. I am here for you and I'll fly back on the next plane if you need me. I just don't want you to make a dreadful mistake.'

Lucy reaches out too, so their fingertips are virtually touching.

'That seems like the only outcome,' she says. 'Every choice looks like a dreadful mistake.'

'Please, please, give this more thought,' Emma begs her.

Lucy nods. 'Gotta go. Love you.'

She watches her sister wave as she logs off.

For a moment, she stares at the screensaver. Her conviction wavering again. *What to do? What to do?* She looks at her watch. Carl now.

Wearily she drags herself out the door.

25

Carl is propped up in bed against the pillows while a nurse takes his blood pressure.

'So, how about it?' he asks the nurse.

Lucy frowns as the nurse — Molly, her name tag reads — turns red and shuffles things on the cart, obviously uncomfortable, wanting to leave. But Carl is tethered to the blood pressure monitor, which is wheezing and tightening as it inflates.

'C'mon.' He waves a hand, and Lucy notices the leather restraints have been removed. 'You chicks do it all the time. I've seen the movies.'

Lucy can't believe what she is hearing — he sounds like he is propositioning the nurse. That sleazy tone, this different persona. Her stomach drops radically.

Molly writes quickly in her notebook, then leans across to unfasten the Velcro strap on the monitor's armband. Carl grasps Molly's breast, and at the same time he pulls the sheet down, exposing his hard penis. Lucy gasps in horror.

'Suck it,' he snarls. 'You know you want it.'

Molly hits a panic button and in seconds an orderly runs through the door. Lucy shrinks into the wall. It's horrific. Unbelievable. So not Carl. Who is this deranged sexual predator?

The orderly is very matter-of-fact. He grabs hold of Carl as he tries to leap from the bed and instantly gets the restraints on him. Carl snaps and snarls like a vicious dog, hurling abuse and obscenities. Molly returns with a doctor, who quickly jabs Carl with a syringe. Carl abuses him but mid-sentence his jaw slackens and his head falls to one side. Lucy leans against the wall, shaking.

'Common in head injury.' The doctor trots out the line Lucy's already heard from countless mouths. 'Should only be temporary.'

'Should?' Lucy manages, taking the glass of water Molly has offered. She smiles weakly at the nurse. Wishes she could apologise. *Sorry about my boyfriend. That was a bit awkward, hey!*

'Yes,' the doctor says, 'most of these responses diminish over time. Some may linger. He may exhibit personality traits that were not evident before. Brain damage can do that.'

Lucy stared. 'So Carl could stay a violent, sleazy perv?'

'Look, it's unlikely. A trace of it may remain. Depends. Can't see into the future. Got to do my rounds. And you should go home. That tranquilliser would knock out a horse. He'll sleep until morning.'

Lucy feels relief. Dodged another bullet. Another day. She looks at Carl sleeping — still so handsome — and realises that he is clean. They must have let him shower. She wonders what he dreams about.

26

'Hi, Carl.' A doctor peers around the curtain. 'How are you?'

'Fine.' He looks at her suspiciously. 'What do you want?'

'Just a chat.' She points to her name tag. 'I'm Dr Field. Shall we talk about what happened yesterday?'

'What happened yesterday?' he snaps.

'With the nurse, Molly?'

'I have absolutely no idea what you are talking about.' Carl stares at the doctor angrily.

'An unwanted sexual advance?' the doctor says.

'Ha! Unlikely,' Carl sneers. 'My sexual advances are never unwanted. She must be a lesbian.'

'So you do remember?' the doctor probes.

Carl frowns, this time genuinely thinking. 'Do you know what? I think I do.'

'Can you tell me what happened?'

'Yes.' Carl seems excited to be able to recall something. He straightens in the bed. 'They had been torturing me for a bit. You know, the usual stuff that goes on in here — sleep deprivation, that kind of shit — so I was pretty whacked out, and she offered to give me a shower.' He nods and looks at the doctor. 'I know, right? Pretty forward stuff. I didn't even know the chick. So she undoes the restraints and I think it's my chance to run for it, so I make to go, but I think they've been poisoning me because my legs won't work and I end up spewing. Everywhere.' He folds his arms across his chest.

'What happened next?' the doctor asks gently.

'She gets one of the guards in to carry me to the shower and they put me in this white plastic chair — exactly like the ones Nonna had in her garden.' He pauses and frowns again. 'She was the best cook, my nonna, she'd make cannoli with the creamiest custard. She'd fill me up with food, and pastries, and chocolates, and then she'd warn me, "Carlo, your tits will fall out." It was years before I knew that my tits were my teeth. The woman was a nut. But I loved her. My nonna ...' He sighs and tears well in his eyes. 'Nonna. I don't know when she died. I don't even know if I saw her before then.'

'Carl,' the doctor says, flicking through her notes, 'I don't believe she is dead.'

'Yeah.' Carl looks at her again. 'You sure? But Nonno is. Yeah, he died all of a sudden. I was only ten.'

'Your long-term memories are very clear,' the doctor says, making notes.

Carl looks triumphant. 'Despite the testing and experimenting, I've still got full control.'

'So, you still believe that this is a conspiracy of some kind? Do you still hear voices?'

'What voices?' Carl looks around suspiciously. 'Who told you about that? Was it the religious order?'

'There is no religious order,' the doctor says.

'You would say that,' Carl says. 'You're one of them.'

'Carl, I'm going to come in daily, for chats,' the doctor says. 'Your paranoia will decrease and there are good indicators that your memory is not permanently damaged. I think it's a matter of time.'

'Sure, whatever.' Carl crosses his arms. 'And anyway, to answer your original question — she wanted it.'

'Who wanted what?' the doctor asks.

'And I'm the one with memory problems? Ha!' Carl snorts. 'Molly, that nurse, she wanted me. She asked me to have a shower with her, and then I guess she went a bit cold. Cock tease, I'd say.'

'Okay, Carl.' The doctor stands up. 'I'll see you tomorrow.'

27

Lucy sits at her desk and stares at the pile of books in front of her. Each reprieve from being with Carl allows her more time to study. But she just can't focus. How is she meant to remember constitutional law, the philosophy of the surrealists, French verbs and quotations from *Frankenstein*? Her mind constantly drifts back to Carl, JD and the pregnancy. And all she is aware of is time. Everything is a countdown. The exams are looming — she panics, so unprepared. She feels like the White Rabbit from *Alice in Wonderland*: 'I'm late. I'm late.' And that makes her aware of her other deadline. She is running out of time for a medical abortion — the days click over so quickly. Each day making it less likely, more unreliable. And then what? A surgical procedure, at a clinic.

But she can't do anything yet. Can't go ahead with this until Carl knows. She has it firmly in her head that he must know before she does it. He can't change her decision, but in all this wrongness, telling him seems right. Both of her parents have offered to go with her, to support her when she tells him, but she's refused. She has to do this on her own. To show him that this is her decision alone. Every time she goes to the hospital she thinks she'll tell him. But every time there's another eruption.

So she waits. But as she does, time is running out.

28

'Can I talk to you outside?' Mr K nods to the doorway.

Lucy glances at Carl. He's fallen asleep, as he tends to do. She often wonders how much sleep one person can handle. She follows Mr K into the hallway.

'What's up?' she asks nervously. There is no way he could know anything.

'We've had to get a psych involved,' Mr K says. 'She says that he's still struggling with some aspects of reality. Like the whole conspiracy thing. She says he sees you as an ally.'

'Right.' Lucy nods. 'What do you want me to do?'

'Nothing, really.' Mr K wipes a hand over his

face. 'She wants to speak to you, though, get a bit of a picture from you.'

'Okay,' Lucy says. 'When?'

'Now,' Mr K says. 'Is that okay?'

Lucy taps on the door and a woman looks up from her papers. 'Hi, Lucy.' She beckons. 'Come in. Thanks for seeing me. I'm Dr Field, but you can call me Nicky, if you like.'

'Sure.' Lucy rubs a hand over her stomach, decidedly nervous.

'I've been talking to Carl,' Nicky says. 'He has memories that he's able to retrieve, which is good, and I'm sure the paranoia will diminish. I just wanted to help you deal with him.'

'Help me how?'

'Strategies. You're his strongest support, at this stage. He told me he trusts you.' Nicky skims the notes in front of her. 'It's a good thing; you can help him understand the situation.'

'How?' Lucy asks. 'I'm not sure what the right thing to say is.'

'The truth,' the doctor says. 'It's repetitive, I know. But you just have to keep telling him that he's in hospital. That he was in an accident. He'll gradually believe it.'

'Okay,' Lucy says. It makes her feel so weary.

'And you?' the doctor says gently. 'Are you okay? Can you handle this? Do you need someone to talk to as well?'

'No, I'm good,' Lucy says, getting up to go. 'I can handle it.'

Suddenly it feels like she's never told a bigger lie in her life. But what other option is there?

29

Every day it's more of the same. She spends the majority of the day with Carl, leaving around two, to either attempt study or, on Thursday, go to work. Work has never been more appealing, a respite. Lucy thinks she sees minor improvements in Carl's memory. It's hard to believe it's not yet been two weeks since he crashed the car, when it feels like forever. He's keen to reminisce, but even these memories he thinks are from years ago — friends from school, his parents. His short-term memory seems to be the biggest problem. But she has to hold on to the fact that there *are* improvements. In fact, she thinks he might be ready to hear the news. He was relaxed and happy this morning before he went to sleep; when he wakes, she'll tell him.

She looks up from the *NW* as he opens his eyes and looks around, disoriented. She knows what he's about to say: the same thing he says every time he wakes up.

'Hey, where am I?' he asks, reaching for her hand.

'Hospital.' Lucy tries not to sound weary, but she has never said that word so many times as she has over the past week.

'Why?' He tries to lift his hand and realises it's restrained. He looks at the cuffs with interest. 'What are they doing to me?'

'Helping you get better,' Lucy says. 'You were in an accident.'

'Oh, right.' He looks confused. 'I had a strange dream.'

'Really?' She leans closer. This is the first time he's recalled a dream. 'What was it about?'

'The cops were chasing me,' he says slowly. 'I was in a high-speed chase. They came after me with their blue lights flashing, their siren wailing at me to stop. But there was no way I was pulling over. They looked weird — like in those movies where one minute they're normal and the next they have yellow eyes with black slits. Freaked me out. So I drove fast.'

'Oh,' she says. 'What happened?'

'Dunno.' He laughs. 'I woke up and it was all a dream.' He frowns at her. 'Or maybe I'm still asleep. This place is weird.' He looks around curiously. 'Hey,' he says loudly, making Lucy jump again. 'What's happened to my mates?'

'Your mates?' she says.

'Yeah, how come if I'm sick no one comes to see me.' He sounds petulant.

'They have been in,' Lucy says, 'several times. You're not sick, you've been in an accident.'

'Right.' Carl watches her. 'Was it that guy Big Red?'

'Big Al.'

'Yeah, him.' Carl nods to himself. 'What about that Asian kid?'

'JD,' Lucy says, feeling nervous at the mention of his name. She hates having to talk about him, still unsure how much information is too much.

'Yeah.' He nods again. 'The smartest kid in the world. I think we worked together.'

'You did,' Lucy says. This is a new recollection.

'In a cake shop,' Carl says. 'Do you know that kid made a special cake for one of his friends, marked it not for sale, and someone else sold it to a customer? Didn't know it was full of weed. Wiped out an entire fiftieth birthday party — they were all puking and tripping out. I think someone got the sack. What happened to that Asian kid?'

'His name is JD, Carl.' Lucy tries not to be annoyed.

'Has he been in?' Carl frowns.

'No,' Lucy says, 'he hasn't.' To her relief, he seems to lose interest in the question.

A nurse comes in with a trolley. 'Obs,' she says cheerily. She fixes the armband around his arm, letting it inflate, and puts a thermometer in his mouth.

He rattles it around angrily with his teeth, as his fingers tap out his displeasure on the blankets.

'So,' the nurse says, 'do you know where you are?'

Carl grips the thermometer between his teeth. 'Do you know where *you* are?' he snaps.

Lucy places a hand on his arm.

'I don't know,' he sighs wearily. 'Lord something, something or other.'

The nurse nods. 'Sir Charles Gairdner. Do you know what the day is?'

Carl exhales loudly. 'What do I look like? A fucking calendar? No. I don't.'

'Okay,' the nurse says, writing in her book. 'All good.' She smiles at Lucy and packs up the trolley.

Lucy waits for her to leave. 'Carl,' she says softly, 'you don't have to be so rude to them.'

He rolls on to his side, as best as he can in his restraints. 'I'm so sick of this shit. It's all the time. Poking, prodding, questions.'

'They're just trying to help.'

Lucy feels close to tears. One step forward and then a rapid leap backwards. It is relentless. How can she possibly tell him she's pregnant when he gets upset about what day it is? He's not ready, and neither is she.

30

She hates the drive. Every day, getting up and dressed, sitting in the same traffic, going to the same room, to sit in the same chair and answer the same questions. The irony of it strikes her hard. Wasn't this the underlying fear? A life of sameness? And here she is, bang in the middle of it. Each day almost an exact replica of the one before. Meanwhile, things change around her and behind her and inside her. Time is moving on and leaving her in a bubble. A time warp.

She clears her head. Revises the same words she has thought every day over the last week. Should the opportunity arise, she'll tell him today. It has to be done. She steels herself. Today, she'll do it. She grits her teeth as she strides purposefully across the car park to the sliding doors of the hospital.

'Hey there.' He gives her his best smile. 'What's up?'

'Not a lot.' She sinks into the chair next to him. 'What about you?'

'The usual.' He grins at her. 'Thermometers, questions — that kind of thing. I'm getting better at the answers, though.'

'Yeah? What do you mean?' Lucy frowns.

'I remember the answers,' he says. He looks pretty pleased with himself. 'I've been checking my phone to see what day it is — and then I tell them. I still don't get why it's that important.'

Lucy is about to say something, but doesn't.

'And you didn't notice,' he says.

'Notice what?'

'This.' He holds his hands up in the air. They are uncuffed, the straps are gone. 'So, looks like they might release me from this shithole soon.'

'Really?' She sits up.

Carl nods, pleased. 'Yeah, the doctor — you know, the one who looks a bit like a rat?'

She nods her head. 'Dr Wiseman.'

'Yeah, him — reckon he might be just that.'

Lucy laughs at his joke.

'He says maybe by the end of the week, if I keep going this way. Not sure what that means, but hell, I'll do anything.'

'You're so much better,' she agrees, taking his hand. 'More like your old self.'

'Yeah.' He nods. 'Hey, what happened to me?'

She frowns again. 'You had a car accident.'

'I know that. But ...'

He drops his voice, and Lucy sees he's still not convinced the room isn't bugged.

'I don't remember where I was, or what happened.'

She looks unsure for a minute and then she tells him what happened, as much as she can remember from Wayne's story.

He looks shocked. 'Is it wrecked? My beautiful car — I paid three and a half grand for that baby.'

She nods. 'Totalled.'

'Fuck.' He sits for a minute in silence. 'No insurance. What a dick. Dad kept telling me to get it. Now I've got nothing.'

'At least JD is okay,' she says eventually.

'Why? What do you mean? What's wrong with him?'

She is quiet for the longest time. He has obviously forgotten JD was with him. 'He's in hospital, too,' she says eventually.

Carl recoils. 'Fuck. Where is he?' And his voice sounds really angry. He swings his legs out of bed; they move effortlessly, but he looks a bit light-headed by the motion.

She flinches. 'Wait.' She puts a hand on his arm. 'He's not here.'

'Why not?' he barks.

'Calm down.'

Carl sits back in the bed.

'He's in a different hospital,' she says.

'Why isn't he here too? We could've shared a room. Man, that would've made things so much better. Having him here would've been awesome.'

'He's in rehab,' she says, when he's settled back against the pillows.

'True story?' Carl starts laughing. 'Little JD, the druggie. Man, he likes a bit of weed — but rehab?'

'No.' Lucy's not laughing; she's trying not to cry.

'What is it, babe,' he says, holding her hand. 'Tell me.'

'Broken neck,' she whispers. 'He's in traction. He

has a broken neck.'

'How did that happen?' he asks. 'My mate has a broken neck and no one bothered to tell me? I should be visiting him, not lying around in bed.'

'In the car crash,' she says softly. 'His neck, arm and both legs got broken.'

Carl sits silently, trying to put the bits together. 'Why?'

'When the car flipped. Several times. He got all broken up.'

'His car flipped?'

She shakes her head. 'No — your car.'

He looks like a cartoon character. *Ka-pow!* She watches him fearfully. She had been dreading this conversation, too, unsure how it might affect him.

'Carl,' she says softly.

He won't look at her, keeps his head turned away.

'He's alright.'

'Alright?' Carl snaps. 'I've broken my best mate's neck and he's alright?'

'Yes,' she whispers. She can't bear it, his pain and confusion, and now she sees his guilt. 'I'll get Dr Field. Maybe you need to talk to her.'

Carl keeps his face turned away.

31

'How come you're not at the hospital?' Georgia asks. 'Or at work?'

They're at their usual table at the coffee shop. The day, although sunny, has a cold edge to it. It feels like the weather is about to change. Lucy shivers.

'Did you get a day off?'

Lucy shakes her head. 'From work, yes. I was way too tired to put up with stupid customer complaints. But Carl, no. I went in this morning. I told him that JD was in the car and had a broken neck, and he took it pretty badly. So I got his psych and left.'

'Yeah,' Lydia says, 'imagine how you'd feel, knowing you nearly killed someone.'

'I think I have a fair idea,' Lucy says grimly. She stares out at the ocean. All the while she is dealing with Carl and his issues, she is trying to shelve her own.

'Luce,' Georgia says, touching her hand. 'Don't be like that.'

Lucy shrugs. 'He says they'll let him out soon.'

'Awesome,' Lydia says.

Lucy shrugs again. 'I'm not sure. Yeah, it will make Mr and Mrs K happy, and it'll be great not to have to do the hour and a half round trip, but I don't know. He doesn't seem ready to me.'

'Well, there's nothing you can do about that,' Georgia says.

'I know, I can't seem to do anything. I haven't even had a chance to study properly and exams are next week.' Panic rises. What's the worst that can happen? *You fail*, the mean voice in her head reminds her. She can't fail — miss her chance for uni — because if she does, then what was all this for?

'My tutor says you have to work out a timetable and stick to it,' Lydia suggests helpfully. 'You know, focus on one subject at a time.'

Lucy laughs wistfully. 'I wish that was all I had to

focus on. I need to tell him about the pregnancy, but the effect the news about JD had on him scares me.'

'Maybe best you do it before he leaves hospital,' Georgia suggests.

'Yeah,' Lydia agrees, 'that way they can tie him up again, if he goes psycho.'

'Lydia!' Georgia shouts.

'What?' Lydia frowns into her latte.

'It's a good point,' Lucy says and Lydia looks grateful. 'I'm so scared of how he'll respond if I do it after he's discharged. You're right.'

Lucy grits her teeth, demands her brain get it together. Tomorrow is the day. Tomorrow she'll tell him. No excuses.

32

The next day there is a massive change in the weather. The days of sunshine suddenly give way to an unseasonally cold and blustery day.

Lucy shuts her computer down. Revision for Biology complete. Cursory at best. It's her first exam next week. She's got one ready, via last-minute cramming — five to go.

On the drive to the hospital, she formulates the conversation. The same one she's planned fifty-nine times already. It must be perfect now. The only thing she can't be sure of is his response. She was always good as third chair in debating, based on her ability to counter an argument on the spot; now she has to rely on that skill.

It's a bit of a shock when she gets to his room and finds him out of his bed and seated in the chair next to it. In jeans and a T-shirt.

'Wow,' she says as she walks in.

'Not bad, hey?' He stands rather unsteadily. 'Watch this.' And he shuffles, like a geriatric, towards her.

'Steady,' she says, holding out her arms as though he's a toddler taking first steps. 'Don't overdo it.'

He grabs her, but his hold is weak and she feels him shaking. 'Fast track to home,' he says, his breathing heavy.

'Easy.' She holds his arm and helps him back to the chair.

She sits on the bed. *Now what?* She wants to tell him — the words are ready to burst out of her. *But what if this is the wrong time? When is it not going to be the wrong time?* She argues with herself.

'Hey,' he says. 'What's up? You're quiet.'

'What?' She's brought back from her thoughts and looks at him, watching her. The black eyes have lightened; now the sockets have taken on a yellowish hue, and the whites of his eyes are coming back, crazing the dark brown like haphazard pavers. It still gives him a weird look, but he is starting to look more like himself.

'What are you thinking about?' He grabs hold of her hand and pulls her near.

The words are there, waiting to be said. She opens her mouth. He smiles at her. She snaps it shut. Can't say it. Too scared.

'Let's get out of here. Look.' She points out the window; the sky has cleared. 'Let's go for a walk.'

'A walk?' He looks doubtful.

'I'll walk and you can sit.' She jumps to her feet, desperate to get out of the room. 'I'll get a wheelchair.'

The nurse tells her no more than fifteen minutes, but agrees it's a good idea to go out for fresh air. 'Do him good,' she says. 'Poor love's been cooped up in here so long. He's so lucky to have you.' She pats Lucy's arm. 'You've barely left his side.'

Lucy comes back with the chair. 'Come on,' she says, helping him into it. 'Now hang on.' She pushes the chair to the hallway and they wait for the elevator.

'Where are we going?' he says to the space in front of him.

'Just into the gardens,' Lucy says to the back of

'Just into the gardens,' Lucy says to the back of his head. 'Change of scenery.'

It's cool outside and she shivers slightly, pushing him along the footpath to a small garden. The air holds the scent of this morning's rain. She breathes in deeply. Can she do it? Tell him now?

The young guy from Level 5 is sitting on the bench, having a cigarette, as she rounds the corner.

'Hi,' he says guiltily, dropping it and squashing it with his slipper. 'Busted.'

'Nigel!' Lucy says. 'Smoking! And you only had surgery yesterday.'

'I know,' he says sheepishly, 'but I figure with all the drugs I'm on, how can this hurt? I'm giving up as soon as I'm out of here.'

She nods.

Carl has straightened in the chair. She pushes him near the bench and sits down next to Nigel.

'This is Carl. Nigel.'

'Hey,' Nigel says. 'How you doin'? Heard a lot about you.'

Carl sneers. 'Have you, now? I haven't heard anything about you. What does that mean, then?'

'Carl!' Lucy hasn't seen this hostility in him for a while. She thought it had gone but remembers the doctor telling her that aspects could linger. He had never been suspicious or jealous before — was this going to be part of his new personality?

'Well, your little friend here seems to know a lot about me,' Carl spits nastily. 'So I guess you two must spend a fair bit of time together.'

She shakes her head and looks at Nigel apologetically. She's run into Nigel in the garden a handful of times when she's escaped Carl's room to breathe, and they've had a few chats. 'I'm sorry,' she says.

Nigel rises. 'No worries,' he says. 'I gotta go anyway — my girlfriend's up there waiting for me.'

'Okay,' she says, watching him shuffle off. She can't look at Carl.

'Dickhead,' he says angrily.

She grabs hold of the wheelchair's handles and starts pushing him back towards the building. She can't speak. She's mad, and sad. Every time he appears to be normal, he does something else, something random and hostile. Will he ever be normal again?

Back in the room, she helps him into the chair.

Looks at her watch deliberately and sighs.

'What's up?' he says, the episode in the garden already forgotten.

'Nothing. I've got to go in a minute.'

'Why?' He looks sad.

'Exams,' she says. She can't make eye contact with him. He disturbs her so much. 'I need to study.'

'No, you don't.' He grabs her hands and pulls her on to his lap. 'You're too smart for study. You don't need it at all.'

He kisses her and it's hard and frantic. She feels waves of revulsion, wants to pull back, but he is holding her tightly. She feels like gagging.

'So ...' She manages to get her face away and breathes. 'I've got to get going.'

'Fine,' he says sulkily. 'Go, then. Make sure you stop in and see your little friend, too.'

She shakes her head, totally fed up. His memory has improved, although his temper hasn't. 'See you tomorrow.'

He looks at the wall. 'Yeah, fine.'

She hovers in the doorway. She doesn't want to leave like this, on bad terms — look what happened last time. It's hard not to feel superstitious. 'Sorry, I've got a lot on my mind.' She takes a step towards him.

'Like what?'

He looks so bewildered and confused, it breaks her heart. She sits on the bed and holds his hand.

'Lots.' She shrugs. 'Exams, your accident — other things.'

He nods. 'What other things?'

Here it is — an open invitation. *Just do it.*

'I'm pregnant.' There, done. Said. Out there. *Now what?*

'Really?' His face breaks into the biggest smile.

Part of her strength and resolve withers. *Fight it,* she tells herself.

'Is it mine?' He frowns.

'Of course.' She doesn't mean to snap.

'Oh, wow!' He laughs loudly. 'I'm going to be a father!'

He grabs her other hand and tries to pull her closer. She fights the nausea. *This is what you expected,* she reminds herself. But that other slim option — that he might be horrified, might instantly declare *I don't want to be a father* — has disappeared. Dust.

'No.' She shakes her head.

His eyebrows meet in the middle.

'I'm not having it.'

'What?' Angry.

She pulls her hands away and covers her stomach.

'What do you mean?'

'I'm not having it,' she says, shaking her head as if that will change his opinion. 'I'm going to have an abortion.' There, she's said that word now, too.

'No!' he shouts, trying to rise.

She sits still. *Don't back down, physically or mentally.*

'You can't do that!'

'Yes, I can.' She doesn't want to cry. *Remember the script, think on your feet.* 'I don't want to be a mother. I don't want to give up my life. I'm not having it.'

'What about me?' He sounds so plaintive, she could cry. 'What about our discussions?'

'What discussions, Carl?' She shakes her head at him.

'Before, before I got sick.' He waves his hand around wildly. 'After we got married, we talked about having children. We wanted ...' He is shouting and shaking his head at her.

She watches him, horrified. 'That never happened,' she says softly. It kills her to see him like this, so confused, so different. 'We never got married.'

'It did. We did. I remember it clearly. At Trigg. The dress. All of it.' He is pushing his fists into his eyes. 'I remember it. I do.'

'No, Carl.' She wishes she could pick up his hand but knows she can't. 'It's not real.'

His face is buried in his hands, his back trembling. 'But I want this baby. What about me?' he mumbles.

'I've thought about you. About everything. About this,' she says gently. 'You couldn't do it, either. You need time to get better and this wouldn't help you. We're not ready. And it wouldn't be fair on anyone. On me. On you. Our parents. The baby.' There, she's said another key word.

'No.' He looks up, tears in his eyes. 'Don't do this.'

'I have to.' She gets up. Has to move away from him. His presence is overwhelming her. She needs to stay in control. *My body. My choice. My decision.* 'Don't think I've come to this easily. I've thought about every option. And this is the least worst for us all.'

He turns his face away. 'And so it doesn't matter what I want?'

'Of course it matters,' she says, crying. 'But it doesn't count. I have to do this.'

He cradles his head in his hands again. He won't look at her.

'You should leave,' he suddenly snaps. 'I can't bear to look at you. I've got a massive headache. You make me sick. Get out!'

'Okay.'

She walks slowly to the door. A small part of her wants to stop. She looks at him in the chair, holding his head as though it's about to fall apart. *Go back*, the voice in her head says, *put your arms around him, tell him it'll all be okay.* But at what cost?

She shakes her head sadly and leaves. This is the best decision she can make.

33

Carl rages. He wants to pace the room, smash things, but he is too weak. His weakness sickens him. He punches Lucy's number on his phone, listens to it ring out several times, then it goes straight to message bank. She's turned it off. Which infuriates him even more. He feels desperate, has nowhere to go. His head pounds.

'Hi.' Dr Field walks into the room. 'Nice to see you out of bed. Hey' — she notices his white face and streaming eyes — 'what's happened?'

'Lucy.' Carl chokes on her name. 'I can't believe it. I can't believe her. I never imagined she would betray me like this. She has never ever made me so mad. So angry I could do something bad.' The rage washes over him as he sits on the chair and looks at the bed where she sat.

'What's happened?' the doctor asks again.

'She's pregnant,' Carl says, 'with my baby. And she's not having it.' He starts to sob.

'Have you thought this through?' the doctor says. She starts jotting notes. 'You've only just heard the news. Have you had time to really consider the ramifications? This is a huge issue.'

'What?' he snarls. 'What are the ramifications? It's my baby. My baby. And she just gets to chuck it away? I want my baby.' He pushes his fists into his eyes.

'Are you okay, Carl?' the doctor asks.

'I've got a fucking massive headache,' he moans.

'I'll get you something, but first you need to calm down.'

'I'll have it,' he says eventually, 'even if she doesn't want it. I'll have it and raise it on my own.'

'Okay,' the doctor says. 'This is certainly something we can discuss. The logistics of it all. But Carl, you have to remember, this is her body. Ultimately her choice.'

The doctor's words don't sit well with him. He

rages again. 'It's my baby — did I make that clear? I want my baby!'

'Calm down,' the doctor says.

Carl sits in the chair and breathes deeply. 'If she doesn't want it, why can't I look after it?' He looks at the doctor. 'I can get a job, live with my parents. Look after it.'

'It's a huge commitment, Carl,' Dr Field says. 'The financial responsibility — let alone the emotional and physical. Just you, totally responsible for another human being.'

'People do it all the time. Why can't I?' He groans and grabs at his head again. 'Fuck, the light is blinding me. I need to shut my eyes.'

'I'll get you something,' the doctor says, reaching over to buzz for the nurse.

34

Lucy has to sit in the car park for fifteen minutes. She can't drive, she's crying so hard. It's so unfair. Everything. To both of them. She doesn't want him to feel like this after everything he's been through, and is still going through. But what's she to do? Offer herself up as the sacrificial lamb to make him better? Then what would become of her? Her identity, her sense of self? No. She won't do it. She can't. None of this is fair — but this is what's on offer. *Deal with it.*

Her phone is going mad, alternating between text messages and phone calls. She looks at the screen: all are from Carl. Panicking, desperate to stop her, or angry and aggressive — perhaps more abuse? She turns her phone off and drives to her dad's.

He's in the study writing a report when she lets herself in.

'Hey,' she calls, but her voice is small and wan.

'Rabbit?' he calls back. 'Through here.'

She walks into the study.

His hair is dishevelled and he has glasses perched on the end of his nose. 'First sign of ageing,' he said when he got them. 'Damn body.'

'They look hot,' she'd said. And they did — made him look like a sexy professor; she could imagine the nurses (male as well as female) falling over him at work.

'Okay?' He takes the glasses off. 'What now?'

'I told him.' Lucy dissolves into tears again. 'It was as bad as expected. He wants it. Got mad. Ordered me out.'

'Okay.' Dad gathers her in his arms. 'It'll be okay. Let's talk.'

In the kitchen, he puts the kettle on and they talk through the time line. Looking at the dates, they agree she's best to wait until after the mock exams next week — there is still time for the chemical abortion.

She shivers at the words. She is really going to go ahead with it.

She shivers at the words. She is really going to go ahead with it.

'After the exams, we'll go see Janice. I've told her already. It's not an issue. You'll stay here with me, and we'll get through it.'

Lucy nods. Despite the weight of the decision, she senses a lightening in the burden. She has made a plan. She'll get through it.

Dad makes dinner, but Lucy can't eat. She feels sick to her stomach. And whenever she thinks of her stomach, she has visions of what is developing inside her body. She tries to blank the imagery — but it's so powerful. Blobs, shapes of amoeba, curled up jellybean foetuses dance through her mind. *Stop thinking,* she orders her brain. But she can't.

She has a restless night, worrying about Carl in the hospital. Tempted to call, but terrified to speak to him. She considers ringing his parents, but then she'll have to tell them about the pregnancy. She shivers. She'll wait it out a bit longer.

35

In the morning, rain thunders down, an unexpected spring storm. It's grey and dreary. Exactly like me, Lucy thinks, drinking tea with her dad.

There's a loud knock at the door. They look at each other. Lucy's first thought is that it's Carl. He's come for her.

'I'll go.' Her dad gets up.

She listens to him open the door. Hears a voice. Sounds like Mum. Dad's voice. Slow. Punctuated. Grim. Fear clutches her stomach. Something really bad is happening. She feels herself panicking. Rises.

When both her parents walk into the room, she notes their identically pale faces. Mum's been crying. Dad has that tremble in his chin he gets when he's trying not to cry. Lucy fears she might vomit.

'Lucy ...' Mum comes towards her, hands outstretched.

'What?' she whispers. *What now? How can anything get worse?* But she knows it is about to. Knows it already has.

Her mum sits next to her, hand on her knee. 'It's Carl,' she says. She bites her lip. 'Oh God. He's dead.'

'Why?' Lucy asks stupidly, realising the question is *How?*

'Aneurysm,' her dad says, on the other side of her. 'Probably caused by the accident, possibly hereditary — apparently, his grandfather died from one. But it can be an after-effect of head trauma too.'

Carl's dead. New words that don't sound real even when said out loud.

'Carl's dead? He can't be. I was just there yesterday. I was just talking to him. He was fine. He was mad.' Her voice is rising with each new note of hysteria.

'Yes.' Her mum is in tears. 'Oh, baby.'

'Mum ...' Lucy disintegrates. No control. 'This can't be real. Can't be really happening. Can it?'

No one speaks, and a horrible truth hits her. 'I killed him.'

'No, Rabbit.' Dad is quick — too quick. Lucy knows he's already gone there in his head. So she must have.

'Can shock do it?' she demands.

'No.' Dad is vehement, but for once Lucy is unsure whether he's being totally honest. 'There is little that can be done for a massive bleed like Carl's. They were aware there was a bulging vessel — were monitoring it — had him scheduled for a scan tomorrow. These things lurk and sometimes do nothing. But his head was traumatised; your words didn't do it. His actions did. His genes did. This is not your fault.'

'It's really *Offspring* now, hey, Mum?' Lucy feels hysterical. Someone give her the script — tell her what's about to happen next, please. No more surprises. She doesn't know what to do. She rises. Then sits. Looks at her mum and dad, and realises with horror they don't know what to do, either. She stands and walks to the window, looks out. Where can she go? How can she escape? How can he be dead?

Carl.

Oh, Carl.

36

'I left at three-ish,' she tells Lydia and Georgia.
They've come over straight away after her dad called
them. 'He was so angry. He kept calling me. I turned
my phone off.' She feels such a bitch.

'What happened?' Lydia asks. 'Do you know?'

Lucy wipes her red nose with another tissue.
There is a mountain of them next to her.

'The psych had been in. Given him some sort
of sedative. Apparently, he was really tripping out.
He was asleep when his parents arrived. Woke up
complaining of a massive headache. Refused to let
them call the nurse. Wanted to talk first. Told them
about the ...' — Lucy pauses and swallows hard —
'pregnancy.'

'You told him?' Lydia asks. 'What did he say?'

'That he wanted it. And he got mad. Told me to get out. Said then he had a headache.'

'What did his mum and dad say about it?' Georgia asks.

'I don't know — Mrs K didn't tell mum. Carl's dead. I guess there's nothing else to think about. Oh, poor Mrs K.' Lucy grabs more tissues.

'She'll be devo,' Lydia agrees. 'Her only child.'

'Lydia!' Georgia snaps. 'Don't.'

'Don't what?' Lydia's tear-streaked face crumples with worry. 'Oh, right. I'm sorry, Luce. I don't think. Ever.'

'It's okay.' Lucy sniffs; she feels full of mucus. 'His headache was really bad. So bad they called the nurses. Everyone freaked out. There was a dodgy vessel in his head. He was scheduled for a scan tomorrow and they were going to decide whether he needed surgery. I didn't know — no one told me. The doctors rushed him to theatre, but it was too late.'

'Too late?' Lydia says. 'When you're in a hospital?'

'Yeah.'

Lucy feels incapable of speaking. Speaking means

thinking. And thinking requires imagery. She can't bear the images. Rushing him through the hospital as a massive blood vessel erupted in his head. Killing him instantly. Before he even hit the theatre doors. There was no saving him. He was gone.

'I can't believe it,' she says. 'Everything is so fucked up. I could top myself.'

'You're not serious, are you?' Georgia grabs her hands. 'Look at me. You don't really mean that, do you?'

Lucy shakes her head. 'No. I don't. I don't mean it. I'd never do that.'

'Promise me,' Georgia says sternly.

'I promise. I'm sorry. I shouldn't have said it. I'm just overwhelmed,' Lucy says.

Lydia and Georgia stay the night — despite the fact that they should be studying for exams.

Exams.

Lucy can't sleep. She understands now what Pink Floyd meant by *comfortably numb*. As numb as this means feeling nothing. Her mind has left her body and is pursuing all different lines of thought. And her body sits there, gestating. She looks around the lounge room. Lydia is like a coiled cat in the armchair and Georgia is stretched out on a mattress on the floor.

Lucy gets off the couch and goes into her dad's kitchen. She turns on the tap for a glass of water, which she drinks slowly. Sees Dad in the darkened window.

'Can't sleep?' he says. 'Milo?'

She nods and sits on the stool. 'Exams next week. Can you believe it? It's one thing after another.'

'Forget about it. You don't have to sit them,' Dad says, boiling the kettle. 'I haven't had a chance to tell you, but Mr Cruz rang earlier. They're waiving them. Curriculum Council will give you special consideration for the finals in a month, too.'

Lucy exhales. 'What does that mean?' She doesn't have to sit exams? The idea had never occurred to her.

'If you're not fit to sit them in a month, they'll work out an ATAR based on your academic record. They have special conditions for circumstances like these.'

'Okay.' Lucy nods. 'That's a relief. There's no way I could do them.'

'I know. No one would expect it of you.' Dad passes her the Milo. 'How do you feel?'

'Bizarre.' Lucy shrugs. 'I don't know — scared.'

'Scared?'

'Of what could happen next.' Lucy's tears come back. 'Just when you think nothing worse could happen, it does. I don't understand why. Is this karma? Is it because I'm planning on getting rid of a baby? Am I being punished?' She feels hysterical.

'No.' Dad puts his arms around her. 'Shhh, it's not karma. It's not divine intervention. It's life, that's all. And sometimes it sucks.'

'I'm so tired, Dad,' she muffles into his chest.

'Me too,' he says. 'Come on, I'll tuck you in.'

37

When Lucy wakes the next morning, she's confused. Something monumental has happened, but there's a gap in her memory. *Like Carl's*, she thinks. *Carl*. She puts her hands to her mouth. Carl is dead.

She finds her dad downstairs on the phone. He hangs up and looks really worried. *I knew it, knew there would be something worse,* Lucy thinks. Panic sets in again.

'What is it now?' Her hands are shaking.

'The Kapulettis are coming over,' he says, his mouth turned down.

'Why?' She feels an edge of hysteria. Are they going to blame her? She upset Carl and he died. Are they coming to point the finger?

'They said they wanted to talk.' Dad frowns and Lucy knows he's worried. 'I'll see where Mum is.'

Lydia and Georgia leave; they have a study group that afternoon.

'You're so lucky,' Lydia says, hugging her. 'I wish I could get out of exams, too.'

'Lydia!' Georgia chastises. 'Lucy would rather sit the exams than go through this shit.'

'Yeah, I know, sorry,' Lydia mumbles. 'I didn't mean that.'

'I know.' Lucy hugs them both.

'Love you,' they both say as they leave.

Lucy is indescribably nervous. She listens to her parents talking in the other room, bolstered by their presence and unwavering support. She feels lucky when she thinks of them. Things could be worse; at least she's not alone.

The sound of the Kapulettis' Alfa makes bile rise in her throat. There's no food in her stomach — she gags at the sight and smell of food. She might be pregnant but she knows she's losing weight from every part of her except her massive boobs.

She hears Carl's parents come in, Dad offering

coffee. The whirr and grind of the machine. *Be brave.*
She walks into the room.

Carl's parents are devastated. They sit slumped
and broken in the armchairs.

Lucy bursts into tears and runs to Mrs K. 'I'm so
sorry' is all she can say.

'I know, cara mia.' Mrs K strokes her head. She
smells like basil. 'I know. My heart is broken in three.'

'Lucy ...' Mr K holds his arms open. He is
weeping, too. 'You loved Carl. You did everything
you could to help him. We know.'

It takes a while to pull away from Mr K, his hold
is so tight. But eventually she does and sits next to
her mum, who strokes her hair. Tissues are passed
around like a plate of biscuits.

'Carlo tell us of the baby,' Mrs K says. Her voice
wavers. 'He tells us he want baby. You don't want
baby, Lucinda.'

Lucy nods. What is there to say?

'We say no to Carlo. A baby born out of wedlock
is bastardo. He was so angry. He said his head hurts.
I want to call nurse. He says no. He says he marries
you, Lucinda — so no bastardo. We say you are too
young to have babies. He says too late. He wants

his baby. We know it is not right not to have God's baby, but we say no to him.' Mrs K pulls out an embroidered handkerchief and wipes her eyes. 'We told him he must listen to what you want, Lucinda. He cannot make decision.' Mrs K can't speak anymore — she is wracked with sobs.

'Carl was so angry with us. Screaming. Swearing. His head was hurting so much. He kept grabbing it.' Mr K holds his own head. 'I said I'd call a nurse. And then he grabbed me. He tried to stop me. He was so angry.' Mr K shows his wrist, where a bruise circles it like a bracelet. 'He was so strong. And then he just stopped. Let go of my hand. Collapsed.'

Mr K weeps loudly. Mum gets up and puts an arm around him.

'We called the nurses. We called the doctors. They came. But it was too late. Carl died. There, in front of our eyes. My son.'

'My son,' Mrs K wails, echoing.

The room is so thick with emotion, it is hard to breathe. Lucy buries her face in her dad's chest. She wants to muffle the words. Doesn't want to hear anymore. Especially when she hears what Mrs K says next.

'Now our Carlo gone. Sleeping with the angels. He such a good son. And you have his baby. Lucinda, cara mia la bella. You need to have his baby. For us. For our Carlo. So he live on.'

38

Lucy sits in her bedroom at Mum's. She'd had to leave Dad's, with the Kapulettis still there. She couldn't bear their pain. The pleading with her to save their grandchild. She blinks back tears. She'd heard Dad rationalising the decision with them. She knew he'd put forward her case better than she could. She feels so guilty, so responsible and yet also so irresponsible.

Light plays across the wall — she's left the window and blinds open slightly. She remembers Carl coming in through that window. How some nights, he'd jog through the streets to her house. He'd tap, and she'd open the window. In the beginning, it was just to be together, listening to music and talking. But more recently he'd just come over wanting sex. She squeezes her eyes shut tightly. If she'd said no, she wouldn't be in this mess. Maybe some of it — maybe Carl would still have crashed the car. Maybe not. Who knows? In some parallel universe, is a non-pregnant Lucy getting up to sit her next exam? Is Carl alive? Is JD walking around unharmed? She wants to blame Carl — make him responsible. But the debater in her won't allow that when she knows she wanted it too. But they'd only done it five times. Five times! It was so unfair. What about Cheryl Hicks, the skank? She boffed everyone and never got pregnant. But then maybe she knew what she was doing. Was on the pill. Why hadn't she, Lucy, gone on the pill?

Her computer makes a noise. Someone is Skyping her. Emma.

'Hey,' she says, seeing her sister's face appear.

'Luce ...' Her sister has been crying. 'I'm so sorry.'

'I know,' Lucy says, and immediately their last conversation is forgotten. She talks to Emma for nearly an hour about Carl and what happened.

'I owe you an apology,' Emma says eventually.

'It's all good,' Lucy says — she doesn't want to revisit the last chat.

'It's not,' Emma says, shaking her head. 'There's

something I have to tell you.'

'What?' Lucy frowns, wipes her nose, so red and raw.

'I was pregnant, too,' Emma says.

'What!' Lucy is poleaxed. 'When?'

'When I was with Graham.'

'Why didn't you tell me?' Lucy feels betrayed. She thought they'd shared everything.

'I wanted the baby, but Graham didn't. He wanted me to have an abortion.' Emma shakes her head.

'What happened?' Lucy says. 'Who knew?'

'Mum and Dad.' Emma is crying again. 'Don't be upset, I begged them not to tell you. I didn't want you to know. I was ashamed. I got the pills and lost the baby. It was awful, Luce. I hated myself. But he was going to leave me if I had it. And I wanted him so much.'

'Oh, Emma.' Lucy touches the screen.

Her sister does the same.

'Afterwards I was so low. So depressed. I thought all the time about this baby. I was a murderer. I hated myself. I hated Graham more.'

'But you stayed with him,' Lucy says.

'I had to.' Emma shrugs. 'I'd given up my baby for

him. I had to make it work. But then I caught him in bed with Susan and that was it. I realised I was wasting my time. My life. Dad bought me the ticket, sent me here.'

'Are you okay?' Lucy asks, incredulous.

'Every day I get better. And when you told me you were pregnant, I was frightened for you — that you would experience exactly the same feelings. Depression is such a bitch. But I was wrong to impose my views on you. Our situations are totally different. I completely understand why you have to do it. And it will be so different for you. You're so much more level than me. So much cooler. Calmer.'

They talk for a while longer and then sign off. Emma promises to call the next day.

Lucy walks down the stairs. Her sister had an abortion. Now she understands Emma's response, everything she'd said, and about Dad. More information to process in a brain that feels like it's about to explode. The thought immediately makes her cringe and grasp the railing for support. Carl is dead!

Her mum sees her and rushes towards her.

'Lucy, Lucy,' she says, gathering her in her arms. 'It'll be alright.'

They sit on the steps, hugging each other tightly.

'How, Mum?' Lucy sniffles. 'How is any of this going to be alright?'

Her mum has no reply.

Later that day her dad turns up.

'How did it end up?' Lucy asks, referring to the Kapulettis' visit.

Dad shrugs. 'Not good. Morella is grief-stricken — can't see that her thinking is totally irrational. Thinks that this is God's plan. To take Carl and replace him with another child. Antonio seemed to agree with most of what I said, but at this point I think he wants to go along with Morella.'

'What now?' Lucy asks.

'Sleep, Rabbit. I've brought you some medicine. And right now that's what you need. A really good sleep.'

She looks at the pills, considers fleetingly what they might do to the baby.

Her dad, as if reading her thoughts, nods. 'It's okay.'

She swallows them and tries to rid the voice that whispers *What does it matter anyway?*

39

Lucy looks at the clock: it's just after 9 a.m. She's been asleep for nearly thirty-six hours. She has woken several times, got up to go to the toilet, had a few glasses of water, but felt so groggy, wasted. She thinks she should feel better now, yet she's still exhausted.

She moves down the stairs.

'Hi,' she calls out to her mum in the kitchen.

'You okay?' Mum appears in the doorway. 'Dad's just left.'

'Dad stayed the night?' Another bizarre twist.

'On the couch, the last two nights,' her mum says. 'He wanted to be here if you woke up and couldn't cope.' She sounds like a naughty teenager explaining her actions. 'You were pretty zonked. Feeling better?'

Lucy nods. Everything is still upside down, and almost laughable. 'I'm hungry,' she says, surprised.

'Good,' her mum says, smiling. 'I'll make you something.'

'Nah, I'm good. Think I'll just have some cereal.'

There's a knock at the door. Her mum passes her in the hallway as Lucy heads for the kitchen.

'I'll get it,' she says cheerily, but there's worry on her face. Why wouldn't there be? Every time there's a knock or a phone call, they brace themselves.

Well, Lucy thinks, what else can possibly happen? *Serve it to me, universe. Hit me with your best shot.*

She's pouring cornflakes into a bowl. 'Who was it?' she asks her mother.

'Oh.' Her mum is white and pulling out her mobile from her hip pocket. In her other hand is a folded pile of papers. 'It was a process server.'

'A what?' Lucy eyes the cornflakes warily — her stomach is flipping out.

'A process server — works for a lawyer. They've just served papers on me as your legal guardian.' Mum is hitting a contact. It's Dad.

'Who has?' Lucy says, knowing straightaway the answer.

'The Kapulettis.'

'What for?' Lucy's mind has leapt ahead — but it can't be right. There's no way.

'To stop the abortion.' Mum holds the phone to her ear. 'They've taken out a legal injunction against you.'

The universe aces it.

40

Lucy stares out the window as they head into the city. Dad has called a lawyer and they are meeting him in fifteen minutes. Legal action — it's all they've got. Or not having the abortion. But that isn't the issue right now. The issue is bigger than her. How can the Kapulettis force her into having a baby? How can anyone demand that of a person? The arguments are endless.

And while they argue, the foetus grows. How long can they prevent her? What if the action takes long enough that it's too late for an abortion even if she wins? And then they've won. Then she's been forced into having a baby she doesn't want. Then she's lost rights over her body — her life. It's difficult to control the panic.

'Pull over!' she shouts to Dad.

He's just pulled into the emergency lane on the freeway and she's got the door open as vomit hits the bitumen. Gross, she thinks heaving again. *This can't be good for me or a baby. I'm a wreck.*

'Firstly, I want to assure you that this is an unwinnable case for the Kapulettis,' William Paterson says, pouring them all water.

'Why is it even getting a hearing, then?' Lucy's dad asks. There's an edge of anger in his voice.

'Their lawyer, Richmond Monte, is worse than an ambulance chaser.' Paterson pauses. 'He is what I refer to as a coffin chaser.' He looks over at Lucy. 'I'm sorry for having to say that, but you need to know that not many lawyers would take on a case like this. It's unscrupulous. Preying on the grief-stricken and wealthy. The only one who will win here is Monte.'

'So, again, why is this even going before a judge?' Dad asks.

'Monte has put us in to ethically shaky territory,' Paterson says. 'Many men have tried to prevent a partner — or ex, as is usually the case — from having an abortion, but no court has ever ruled in their favour. I have case law going back thirty-odd years showing how a "potential" father's rights are denied in favour of the mother's wishes. On those grounds, if Carl were alive he'd have no legal basis whatsoever to mount this case.'

'Phew.' Lucy's mother's relief is audible. 'That's the main issue, then.'

'Well, yes — but unfortunately, it's not that clear-cut. The case law I've referred to has been about the father's rights. But Monte has referred to other aspects of case law.'

'Such as?' Lucy's dad asks.

'They are arguing for grandparents' rights. It's new, and doubtful at best — but we have to have a hearing in court.'

'What does it mean?' Lucy says finally. 'What can they do?'

'Nothing yet, except delay the abortion,' Paterson says. 'The courts will rush things through, given the nature of the case, but it may take a couple of days — a week at most.'

'But what is their claim based on?' Mum asks.

'Ownership of sperm ... legal heir ... fatherhood.

I have to tell you, Monte is throwing everything at us.' Paterson sips his water. 'Because it's a novel, unprecedented submission, in the interests of procedural fairness, Judge Lund wants to hear it. But we are preparing.'

'What's their case?' Dad asks.

'In a nutshell, they are trying to exercise two rights — that of parent and grandparent. Neither has ever been recognised by the courts, but they have this — and it muddies the waters.' Paterson holds a piece of paper in his hand. 'It's Carl's final wishes.'

'And they are?' Dad asks.

'To exercise his right as a father — to keep the baby.'

'But you told us that none of these "father injunctions" have ever won in court,' her mum says. 'Why is this any different?'

'It's not,' Paterson concedes, 'but Monte is arguing that it is. This piece of paper establishes Carl wanted children — in particular, *that* child.' He nods his head towards Lucy. 'He told his doctor and she wrote down his wishes.'

'Right,' Dad says, 'I think I know where this is headed. They are using an argument that would be applied if Carl had frozen sperm?'

'In the first instance, yes.' Paterson nods. 'A precedent has been set that posthumous retrieval is acceptable if there has ever been a manifestation of intent on the part of the deceased to procreate after death.'

'What does Carl say?' Dad asks. Paterson reads from the paper.

'Carl has expressed his intention to pursue the pregnancy and birth of his unborn child. If Lucy Wishart decides not to continue the pregnancy, he will use a lawyer to prevent this. If she proceeds with the pregnancy, he will raise and parent the child with no financial nor emotional input from her.'

Lucy can't breathe. Carl's final words are so final. They're hard to disregard.

'Where did that come from?' Dad asks.

'Carl's psychiatrist,' Paterson says. 'She has included her case notes as well. While Carl was demonstrating some extremes of behaviour, she has noted that she discussed all the logistical possibilities with him and he understood them. It is clear, from this, that Carl's intention was to challenge you legally, Lucy, had he not passed away.'

'But it wouldn't have been successful,' Mum says. 'That's what you indicated.'

'True,' Paterson says, 'but because that was Carl's intention, and they have it in writing, that's where this case becomes unprecedented.'

'And the doctor's findings are admissible in a court of law?' Mum asks incredulously, 'given Carl's physical and emotional state?'

'I'm not saying they would hold up under scrutiny if this was a court case,' Paterson says, 'but they are enough to get the Kapulettis a hearing. And that's all Monte really cares for.'

'And then there's the final twist in the tale. The court needs to decide whether sperm is property. If so, the Kapulettis are heir to that property. That also then allows for another argument, which does have precedents set in court: following conception, a child is considered "rightful heir" of the deceased father. They are arguing that they are the owners of Carl's property — his sperm. And as that sperm is part of a fertilised egg, it is now "his rightful heir" and therefore if you, Lucy, go ahead with an abortion, you are destroying Carl's property, the Kapulettis' inheritance, and the "rightful heir" of anything else belonging to Carl.'

'Seems a bit of a stretch,' Mum says.

'It is,' Paterson agrees. 'It's quite convoluted. But all unprecedented cases are — and then they set precedents that define law. The Kapulettis' lawyer has combined many different aspects of law just to build a case.'

'What happens next?' Lucy asks.

'The hearing,' Paterson says.

41

She was walking through Kings Park, holding Carl's
hand. It was a beautiful day. The sky cloudless, a
clear translucent blue. Below them the Swan River
was streaked with trails of white as speedboats jetted
across its glassy surface. Peaceful and tranquil. She felt
his hand, twice the size of hers, enveloping her own.
He squeezed it. She squeezed back. They didn't look
at each other; there was no need to. They stopped at
the War Memorial and read the names. He looked for
Kapuletti, she for Wishart. There was one. A Corporal
James Wishart. She traced the name with her fingers.
Who were you? she wondered. What happened? Did
you die in the trenches? Running across the muddied
fields like a lamb to the slaughter? Did you survive

battle and then get hit by a car — or fall off a train on your way home — a decorated soldier? Carl came up behind her and wrapped his six foot four body around her. In terms of the space they occupied on this earth, he took up more than twice her allotment.

'Hey,' he said, and she turned to face him. His face was a patchwork of emotion. Sadness, fear, thoughtfulness, wonder. 'You okay?'

'Yeah.' She slid her arm through his. 'All good.'

'I love you, Luce,' he said.

Lucy stares at her computer screen, the Facebook page — RIP Carlo Kapuletti. The comments and pictures make it difficult to breathe. Her recollections are endless. She keeps thinking about him, when things were good between them.

Carl loved her so much. She remembers how much. And now he is dead. It's unfathomable — how can he be dead? How? Her Carl. Her lovely kind and gentle Carl. These memories of him are real; the hospital Carl, an aberration. Dead. No. She holds her stomach — the last vestiges of him. His baby.

'Oh Carl.' She sobs loudly. 'It's not fair. So, so not fair.'

The case is scheduled to be heard before a judge in four days — a rushed case, as Paterson predicted. Lucy can't sleep. Or think. Or really do anything at all but think about Carl. This isn't a break-up, this is final. He's dead. She'll never see him again, hold his hand, kiss him, feel his love. He's gone. She can't wrap her head around it. When was he ever a bad boyfriend? A bad person? Never. He was loving and kind. And loved her so much. Sometimes too much — but that was who he was. And now he's no more. She can't understand it.

She hasn't heard or seen the Kapulettis since they issued the injunction against her. She doesn't want to feel angry towards them, but it's difficult not to. They are trying to control her — force her into doing something they want. *And what if?* What if the Kapulettis win and she's forced to continue the pregnancy, and then forced to hand the baby over? It seems like fiction — or another episode of *Offspring*, she wryly thinks.

42

The house is an imposing white mansion, at least three storeys high, and set in lavish green gardens behind wrought iron gates. It reeks of opulence and wealth. Lucy is surprised — she had no idea. *They must be loaded,* she thinks as she rings the doorbell. Inside she hears voices, the slam of a door and footsteps. The front door opens.

'Hey, beautiful girl,' Mr Tan says hugging her. 'Good to see you. How are you?'

'Surviving,' she says, fighting back the tears.

'True story,' Mr Tan says. 'Aren't we all. Except ...' And his face crumples.

'Don't,' Lucy says.

'I know.' He nods and his eyes are glistening. 'I

watch JD — I think how lucky he is, how lucky I am. I think of Carl, his parents. It makes me shudder. There but for the grace of God ...'

He steps back and Lucy enters the house.

'How's JD?' she asks, gathering her composure and following him down the hallway. The house smells of ginger and coriander. The walls are lined with artwork. The pictures are bright swirls of colour, abstract and beautiful in feeling. The interior is light and airy.

Mrs Tan comes down the hallway.

'This is Anh,' Mr Tan says.

'Lucy.' Mrs Tan opens her arms and hugs her tightly. 'Thank you for everything you've done. These have been such trying times for all of us.'

Lucy pulls back and shakes her head. 'I've really not done anything.'

'You have,' Mrs Tan says; she has tears in her eyes. 'You've been there for JD and the boys and poor, poor Carl. Oh dear.' Mrs Tan wipes her eyes with a tissue.

'Through here,' Mr Tan points, also overcome with emotion.

They walk into a large family room of vaulted ceilings and huge Palladian-style windows. On a green leather couch sits JD, surrounded by a new metal contraption — both legs in casts, jutting in front of him like the legs of a shop mannequin.

'So now you can ask him yourself,' Mr Tan says, smiling. 'We got him back yesterday.'

'Hi.' JD looks over without turning his head.

Lucy sees new screws are embedded in his skull, holding it firm. 'Hey,' she says, sitting opposite him. 'Home, hey?'

'Yeah.' He tries not to cry. 'I can't believe it.'

'Me neither.' Lucy is holding back her own tears. 'It's unreal.'

'I just thought, after all this time, he was okay,' JD says. 'I can't believe I'm alive and he's not. I never even got to see him after ...'

'I know,' Lucy says, but she realises she doesn't know. What can she know?

'I feel so bad,' JD says.

'You can't.' She shakes her head. 'None of this is your fault. You're a victim, too — look at you.'

'I wish it was me,' JD says softly. 'I rolled the joint, thought it would chill him out. I gave it to him — I shouldn't have.'

'You can't think like that,' she says. 'Carl wouldn't

have wanted it.' And as she says it, she knows it's true. He wouldn't have.

'He was my best friend,' JD says finally, allowing the tears to fall.

'I know,' Lucy cries. 'He loved you.'

There's a knock at the door and Big Al and Ben arrive, carrying a slab.

'Hey.' Ben leans down to kiss her. 'How are you?'

'Terrible,' she says. 'You?'

'Same.' Ben opens a beer. 'Want one?'

'No thanks, I'm driving,' she says.

JD indicates no with his unbroken arm. 'Too many meds. Off my face anyway.'

'Here's to JD,' Al says, raising a beer, 'and our mate Carl.'

'JD and Carl,' they all say. Lucy and JD clink glasses of water together.

'Funeral tomorrow,' Big Al says. 'Ben is delivering the eulogy. If that's okay, Lucy?'

She nods. She doesn't even know if she's welcome at the funeral. But how can she not go? And do these guys know about the injunction? The pregnancy?

'Do you want to say something tomorrow?' Ben asks.

She shakes her head. What would she say? What if she broke down? She can't cry in front of everyone — but not to say anything seems as damning, like she couldn't give a shit. She wishes she could stand tall and proud and deliver something in an even voice — but what? An apology? Carl is never going to hear it. And what would she be apologising for? That she got pregnant? That he is dead? That she feels guilty? She clutches her stomach. Too hard, too hard.

'I'm not sure.' Her voice wavers. 'I don't know.'

'It's okay,' Ben says. 'I'm not sure I can, either. I can't believe we are doing this. My mate's funeral. Fuck.' He turns away.

'I wish I could come,' JD says eventually. He is quiet for a bit. 'I guess from the beginning I thought he was dead. I never believed anyone when they said he was alive. Except you, Lucy, when you came to see me. But I guess I was so used to the idea that when it happened, it didn't really surprise me. It's just now — here, it becomes real. I can't believe it. And I can't be there.'

'We'll live stream it, mate,' Al says in a thick voice. 'His family in Italy want to see it.'

They sit in silence.

Lucy starts to panic. What if the Kapulettis shout at her? Prevent her from coming in? Why did she have to think of that? Now it's all she can think of.

'Mr and Mrs K aren't speaking to me,' she says softly.

'Why?' JD asks, and the looks of surprise on the others' faces confirm they have no idea about the pregnancy or the injunction.

'I think they blame me.'

'Shit, mate. No.' Al puts an arm around her. 'No one does. It's not your fault.'

She shrugs. 'Do you think I should go tomorrow?'

'Yes,' they all say in unison. 'For sure.'

Ben offers to pick her up. She shakes her head. 'Thanks, but my parents will take me.'

She picks up her bag. 'Gotta go.' She feels like she might vomit again.

'See you tomorrow,' Ben calls as Mr Tan walks her to the door.

'See ya then,' she calls back.

'Stay strong,' Mr Tan says, hugging her.

'I'm trying to.' She fights more tears.

'No.' He squeezes her hard. 'You don't have to try — you are.'

43

Lucy looks at herself in the mirror. She feels terrible, yet she glows. That's a weird feeling and a strange term, but she does. Her skin literally shimmers with life. The saddest and cruellest twist of all. Life is brimming inside her while Carl lies dead. Life brims inside her and all she wants to do is end it. She is going to Carl's funeral. The final farewell. She sits on the edge of her bed and cries again. So many tears. They never seem to end.

It's a warm day and she finally settles on the dress she wore to the school ball. It's strapless, long and flowing, blue silk with an overlay of velvet-style lace. Carl had loved it — they had been so happy then, so together. It seems like the right choice.

'Ready?' her mum calls.

'No.' She twists up another section of her hair and glances again at her reflection. *When will I ever be ready for this?* 'Yes, coming.' She turns off the bathroom light.

Downstairs Mum and Dad are talking softly.

'Okay, Rabbit?' Dad says, seeing her. 'You look beautiful.'

'Thanks,' Lucy says, 'I feel awful.'

But she won't let the tears escape now. She's had her cry. *Be strong — be tough — stand tall.*

The drive to the cemetery is long. They haven't joined the cavalcade from the funeral parlour — Lucy couldn't bear it. When they arrive, the coffin is already being lifted from the hearse. The vision of it almost stills her heart. Inside that box is Carl. And he is dead. She shakes the tears and thoughts away.

'Okay?' Mum says, grabbing her hand as they walk inside.

Lucy nods. She's glad she's worn waterproof mascara — then chastises herself for being so shallow. *Who on Earth thinks of that, at a time like this?*

Ben and Al are pallbearers. Al is struggling. He

can lift the coffin easily, single-handedly even, but his face is grief and tears and sadness.

The room is already full. The benches occupied. And people stand at the back against the windows. There must be more than four hundred people. Through the masses she sees the Kapulettis at the front, heads bowed and sobbing. Behind them, family members Lucy has met over the last year or so. Before them, a slideshow of Carl plays — as a baby, a toddler, first day of kindy, school, winning fairest and best, a random birthday party. The photos chronologically display his growth and development until she recognises her Carl. Long and lean. Teeth too big. Then handsome and kind. Hot as — even her granny had thought so. 'A movie star's looks,' she'd whispered to Lucy when he went into the next room. The next photo jolts her. It's the two of them at the school ball. Then at the Swan River. All the ones that follow are of him and her.

She looks away. People are turning to see if she's here. She's been spotted.

Al and Ben and the other pallbearers bring the coffin in, and Uncle Benito stands and takes the mike.

'Carlo was a beautiful boy,' Benito says. His voice wavers slightly but he regains control. 'A kind and caring lad. A footballer — not the Aussie kind, the real kind. Not a great scholar, but a hard worker.'

Benito talks but Lucy can't bear his words — they make it all real. He is talking about Carl when he was alive — because he is now dead. She tries not to listen. Looks at the slideshow. Thinks better of it and starts planning essay responses to the Lit paper, should she sit the exams.

A cousin stands and talks about Carl's youth. Sprinklers and dams and growing up together. The bucolic, idyllic days of childhood. More music, more images on the slideshow. Then Ben — his eulogy. Lucy hears nothing.

Finally, when Ben finishes, he asks the crowd, 'Is there anyone here who would like to say something?' And he hasn't even finished when Lucy realises she is heading down the aisle towards him.

'Lucy.' Ben smiles and steps back from the mike.

Lucy can't believe she is doing this. What her brain is saying her body is ignoring. She reaches the podium and looks at the faces and then speaks. Her voice is clear and even. She avoids eye contact with anyone.

'I'd like to recite a poem,' she begins:

To laugh is to risk appearing the fool.

To weep is to risk being called sentimental.

To reach out to another is to risk involvement.

To expose feelings is to risk showing your true self.

To place your ideas and your dreams before the crowd is
to risk being called naive.

To love is to risk not being loved in return.

To live is to risk dying.

To hope is to risk despair.

And to try is to risk failure.

But risks must be taken, because the greatest risk in
life is to risk nothing.

The person who risks nothing, does nothing, has nothing,
is nothing, and becomes nothing.

He may avoid suffering and sorrow, but he simply cannot
learn, and feel, and change, and grow, and love,
and live.

Chained by his certitudes, he is a slave, he's forfeited his
freedom.

Only the person who risks is truly free.

She doesn't make eye contact with anyone and returns to the back of the room. She knows that poem off by heart; she'd once recited it to Carl and his eyes had lit up, impressed by her.

'That poem is about you,' he'd said, grabbing her around the waist. 'You're a risk taker and a free spirit.'

But the truth was, it was really about him.

The tension is broken by Ben, who gets up again and delivers a funny story. Then another from Al. More pictures. Some music and then someone hits the button and the coffin descends. Benito says, 'Please meet us in the foyer for coffee and refreshments.' And the Kapulettis leave the room. Lucy feels Mrs K watching her on the way out.

'You did real good,' Lydia says, grabbing her hand.

'You were so strong,' Georgia agrees.

'Wake?' Lydia asks.

Lucy shakes her head. 'I can't. I'm going home.'

She looks at Mum and Dad. Both have been crying and they nod in agreement. Tomorrow is the hearing.

44

Lucy watches the judge. The Kapulettis' lawyer
has laid out the case, exactly as Paterson explained.
Paterson refutes the points, drawing on previous
case law to support his claims. The hearing takes an
hour and a half. The judge calls for a recess.

In the coffee shop, Mrs K keeps looking her way.
Her lawyer seems to be telling her not to.

Finally Paterson gets word that the judge is back.
'It's time,' he says, wiping his mouth with a napkin.

On the way out, Mrs K happens to be behind her.
'Lucinda,' she whispers.

Lucy turns. Mrs K's youthful beauty is shattered
— she is haggard, destroyed.

'We love you, Lucinda. But that is our grandchild,

no? Our last part of Carlo. Please, I beg you!'

Lucy reaches out to touch her but Paterson intercepts the move and hustles her away. All Lucy sees is their overwhelming sadness.

The courtroom is silent as the judge begins.

'The first question is whether this plaintiff has a right at all. The foetus cannot, in Australian law, have a right of its own, at least until it is born and has a separate existence from its mother. That permeates the whole of the civil law of this country.'

Lucy feels her mother squeeze her hand.

'For a long time there was great controversy over whether, after birth, a child could have a right of action in respect of prenatal injury. The Law Commission considered that, but it was universally accepted, and has since been legally accepted, that in order to have a right, the foetus must be born and be a child. From conception, the child may have succession rights by what has been called a "fictional construction", but the child must subsequently be born alive.'

Lucy glances at her parents. Dad is nodding. Mum is squeezing.

Mr and Mrs K are devastated. Lucy looks away.

'Prior to this case, the courts have only heard from husbands issuing injunctions against wives. I considered these. In these instances, the father's case must therefore depend upon a right which he has himself. I would say a word about the illegitimate father and I call him such as he is not authorised by law, at this stage. It seems to me that in this country, the illegitimate father can have no rights whatsoever except those given to him by statute.'

Lucy shakes her head. She is losing the thread — she doesn't understand — but her lawyer seems to and is nodding in agreement.

'So these plaintiffs must, in my opinion, bring their case, if they can, squarely within the framework of the fact that they have a husband's rights. Which this case does not allow. The husband, if you will, is now deceased and so the case does not rest with him. The law is that the court cannot and would not seek to enforce or restrain, by injunction, matrimonial obligations, if they be obligations, such as sexual intercourse or contraception. No court would ever grant an injunction to stop sterilisation or vasectomy. Personal family relationships in marriage cannot be enforced by the order of a court.

'I ask the question, "If an injunction were ordered, what could be the remedy?" and I do not think I need say any more than that no judge could even consider sending a husband or wife to prison for breaking such an order. That, of itself, seems to me to cover the application here; a husband, or party acting for the husband as in this case, cannot by law stop his wife by injunction from having what is now accepted to be a lawful abortion within the terms of the *Abortion Act 1967.'*

At this point, the judge pauses for what seems to Lucy the longest time. And with each lengthening pause, she starts to feel nervous.

'However ...' he begins, and for the first time that innocent word, which she uses frequently to link paragraphs in Lit essays, takes on a menacing dimension. This *however* reeks of possibilities she hasn't wanted to entertain.

'... this case offers up new facets of law never discussed before. And the plaintiff has referred to a Canadian case, *Yaakov vs State,* where the courts found in favour of the plaintiff. To summarise: in this case, the courts heard that the parents of the

deceased wished to utilise frozen sperm and had,
in writing, Yaakov's wishes to become a parent —
after his death. Unusual, indeed, but in its rights the
State found reason to grant the bereaved parents the
right to utilise the sperm — to create a grandchild
and legacy to Yaakov. In the matter before us, the
deceased has also made clear, via his doctor's written
account, his wishes to be a father and create a legacy.
I found, however ...'

At this point, the judge pulls off his glasses and
wipes his eyes. His use of *however* has changed in
tone. Once resetting the glasses on the bridge of his
nose, he continues.

'... that it would be a folly to pursue this idea
here. Yaakov's sperm had not fertilised an egg. It
was not in the process of conception. And while
the argument rages about when life begins — or
personhood — the law finds a foetus has no legal
rights. Under that law, I'm compelled to dismiss
the plaintiffs' first claim. On the second, about
inheritance, to grant that would be to override the
mother's choices, which the law so far has indicated
are the primary consideration. On those grounds,
I dismiss that claim, as well. Which leaves us only

with an injunction against a woman to abort.'

Dad sighs loudly. Lucy glances at him. She is holding her breath.

Paterson winks at her — *in the bag*. She feels her mother's hand clutched in her own. Too tightly. She releases her grip.

'I will look at the *Abortion Act 1967* very briefly. It provides by section 1: (1) ... a person shall not be guilty of an offence under the law relating to abortion when a pregnancy is terminated by a registered medical practitioner if two registered medical practitioners are of the opinion, formed in good faith — (*a*) that the continuance of the pregnancy would involve risk ... of injury to the physical or mental health of the pregnant woman ... (2) In determining whether the continuance of a pregnancy would involve such risk of injury to health as is mentioned in paragraph (*a*) of subsection (1) of this section, accounts may be taken of the pregnant woman's actual or reasonably foreseeable environment.

'Two doctors have given a certificate. It is not and cannot be suggested that the certificate was given in other than good faith and it seems to me that there is the end of the matter in Australian law. The *Abortion Act 1967* gives no right to a father to be consulted in respect of a termination of a pregnancy. The husband, or any party operating for him, therefore, in my view, has no legal right enforceable in law or in equity to stop his wife having this abortion or to stop the doctors from carrying out the abortion. And so my findings are to dismiss the case in its entirety.'

Lucy looks at her parents. Dad covers his face briefly. Mum kisses her. Paterson looks jubilant. Next to them, the Kapulettis don't move or speak. Both sit with heads bowed, as if in prayer.

We've won, Lucy thinks, but at what cost? What have we actually won?

As they leave the courtroom, Lucy glances towards the Kapulettis. They are both weeping. With the judge's ruling goes all hope of Carl living on — in his baby, her baby. She can't look away, and Mrs K senses it — turning her eyes on Lucy. Their grandchild is now at Lucy's mercy.

She looks away quickly.

45

Lucy paces her bedroom at Dad's. She is consumed by choice. It devours her. What to do? What to do?

The hearing has annihilated her. If it had been successful, it could have stripped from her the right to make decisions about her body. What was that all about? What world did she live in where people could set the law onto you to stop you doing something to your own body? Your *own* body? Mr K smoked way too many cigars; could Lucy ever take out an injunction to stop that? And Mrs K cooked with too much salt, potentially thickening the arteries of those who ate her food; again, would an injunction be possible? It riles her. How dare they? How dare anyone claim rights over her body? She can't even believe it went to court. That she had to face a judge and defend her right to exercise her freedom of choice.

But on the other hand, this is the only grandchild the Kapulettis will ever have. And Lucy is the only one who can decide whether it reaches that potential or not.

She shakes her head. What is she to do? Her heart says no. Having a baby, at this point in her life, would be devastating. It would be the end of Lucy. But the other option means the end of Carl. And making a decision she's not sure she can live with for the rest of her life. What is the answer? No one can tell her: it always comes back to her choice.

A decision has to be made.

Dad watches her. 'Are you sure this is what you want to do?'

She nods, but is unsure still. 'Yes. I have to. I think.'

'Okay, but I'm concerned that it might be too late.'

She nods again. With every day, every crisis, every drama, her preferred option has been slipping away.

Dad gets on the phone. Their fears are confirmed.

'Janice says we are past the date for a medical abortion. Now it's surgical.'

Lucy nods. Devastated. It's bad enough to have had to come to this conclusion twice — but to have to go to a clinic, through a surgical procedure ...

She remembers the film *Juno*, what the protester said outside the abortion clinic: *Your baby has fingernails*. Will there be protesters there? Will they say the same things? Will she be able to go through with it? She knows she must.

'Let's do it.'

46

When The Day arrives, Lucy hasn't slept. She knows she is probably the unhealthiest she has ever been. She's hoping that today will end this, but worries it might generate a new set of anxieties.

She dresses like she is going out with her girlfriends and even puts on makeup. Looks at herself in the mirror. Assesses the fact that the person she sees before her is about to terminate a baby. *Not a baby*, the reflection says. *A possible baby.* Not real, not yet.

'Who are you?' she says aloud to her reflection. 'I don't know you at all.'

'Hey,' Mum says as Lucy finally comes downstairs to the kitchen. 'Okay?'

'Yep. All good. Ready?'

Dad has the keys in his hand. 'Good to go. Listen, Rabbit, there may be protesters there. When we get close, I want you to duck down.'

Lucy frowns. 'Will they attack me?'

'No.' Dad looks over the car's headrest at her. 'They wave placards and try and guilt you out of your freedom when you're probably at your most fragile. It's like emotional terrorism — they should be stopped.'

They drive in silence, and in that silence Lucy multi-tasks, gestating and prevaricating. The gestating she cannot control — her body continues with its relentless cell division. The prevaricating she can — *distract, delay, don't consider*. That's what she tells her mind — which somehow has a mind of its own and won't listen to her.

Her mobile beeps and for a second she thinks it could be Carl. But of course it's not. He'll never text her again.

Emma. She opens the message.

Thinking of you kiddo. Love you. Call me when you can.

She smiles to herself, relieved she has the unconditional support of those she loves the most.

Dad turns into the next street. 'Okay, duck down,' he says.

Mum smiles and grabs her hand. 'Don't look at them.'

Lucy nods and guiltily slides down, but as she does she is filled with anger. Why should she? Why are they allowed to demonstrate their freedom and she's not? This is bullshit. So she sits up.

There are three women holding placards. Do they really believe their demonstrating will sway people whose lives they know nothing about? *Do you know I'm seventeen, that my boyfriend is dead? Do you know how difficult this decision was to make? Do you feel your opinions are so much more important than mine? That you have a right to enforce them? When I would never do that to you?* These thoughts make Lucy straighten and make eye contact. The placards read: 'Does your baby have a name?' and 'The Australian Law Court Supports Abortion'. And there are graphic images of dismembered babies, a comparison being made with the shallow graves of Jews during the Holocaust.

Lucy maintains eye contact. One of the women, a round-faced, pleasant-looking woman, gives her a small smile. It is a smile of total sadness. It communicates her desire to stop Lucy. *Please don't do this, give your baby a chance.* Lucy feels deeply ashamed. She wants to look away. But anger collides with her shame. They pass close and she shakes her head at the woman resentfully. No, she will not back down. They don't know her; they don't know her life. They can have as many babies as they want and Lucy will never protest. No.

But as Dad parks the car, Lucy realises she is trembling uncontrollably. And she has searing pain in her stomach and lower back.

'Okay?' Dad says, turning off the engine.

'I feel really sick,' Lucy says, wanting to double over, the pain is so intense.

'More than nerves?' Mum opens the door.

'These are so bad.' She has to haul herself out of the car. Wishes she could crawl in on hands and knees but compromises with a hunched-over shuffle.

Dad puts a hand under her elbow. 'How bad? On a scale of one to ten?'

'Five,' she lies. It's really fifteen, but she doesn't

want to worry him.

This pain is monster.

The clinic is an old house that's been converted. It still looks like a house. Where the reception desk is, covered by a plastic shield protecting the women behind, Lucy sees the original ornate fireplace against the wall — this must have been the lounge room. She wonders what the shield is for. Someone demanding an abortion? And then realises it's probably the opposite — anti-abortionists. Extreme people go to extreme lengths. She starts to feel really nervous. What if protesters break in and shoot them all? Pro-lifers killing people? That has to be the greatest oxymoron ever.

There's a row of chairs, and another waiting room off to the side. Lucy sits and watches. A young girl is called into a small room. There are very few men here. Most of the women have come with a female friend. The woman next to Lucy is talking to another woman beside her.

'So it's my second time. Hubby in for a misdemeanour — at least two years. And I go, can't do it alone. Got two under two — a third will be unaffordable and, like, well, too much. He goes, yeah babe, your decision. So here I am. It's not so bad. Okay. Over and done. Nothing to it.'

'Yeah,' the other woman agrees.

The conversation panics Lucy. After a while, do you become immune to the gravity of the situation? If you do it once, do you find it easy to keep doing it?

The young girl emerges from the room after about fifteen minutes. Her eyes are red. She shakes her head at the receptionist and leaves through the front door, despite the fact that they have all entered through the back door. Outside there is a cheer from the protesting women. A baby saved.

Lucy starts to shake. This is too much. She has searing pain. She catches her breath, doubles over.

'Okay?' Mum asks.

'No, the pain is so bad.' Lucy looks around. 'Where's the toilet?'

She sees a sign and shuffles to it. In the cubicle she drops her knickers — there's a stain of blood. Suddenly she's burning up and wants to strip off her clothes. Doubles over. Hears her ears ring. Panics she might be about to faint. She pushes her hands against the cubicle walls and breathes deeply. *Okay,*

okay, she tells herself. A smear of pink when she wipes herself with toilet tissue.

'Okay?' her mum asks again when she returns to her seat.

'There's blood,' Lucy says, catching her breath.

A woman comes out from behind the counter and indicates for Lucy to go into a room for her counselling session. Her mum and dad stand up, but the woman says, 'She has to do this part alone.'

Dad nods. 'You okay?'

The pain has subsided somewhat. Lucy grimaces. 'Yes, why can't you come in?'

'Routine,' the woman says. 'The counsellor likes to speak to you alone, free from any other influences or opinions.'

The irony strikes her and she laughs out loud. 'My decision counts here? My right to choose what I want to do with my body?'

'Of course.' The woman shows her into the room. 'Your decision is the only one that counts here.'

'Hi, Lucy. I'm Denise.' The counsellor, a short, stocky woman with wiry hair, grasps her hand firmly. 'How are you doing?' Despite her brusqueness, there is a softness to her.

'Okay. I was in a bit of pain before. Mum thought nerves, but there was a spot of blood.'

'Oh.' Denise frowns. 'Mid-cycle bleeding often happens during the course of a pregnancy.' She consults her notes. 'This would be about day thirteen in your cycle. The pain bothers me, though.'

'It's not so bad, a niggle now,' Lucy says.

'Okay, well, tell me if it increases. Now, let's talk about the termination. You'll go through for a couple of tests — blood, ultrasound — and after that you'll go under a light anaesthetic, a twilight one. It will make you drowsy, but you'll still be conscious. The doctor will basically insert a cannula and vacuum aspirate the contents of the uterus. Most women say it is painless, a bit like menstrual cramping, at worst.'

Lucy nods. It sounds so clinical — *vacuum aspirate the contents*. She notes they never refer to it as a baby, a foetus, even. It is merely *contents*.

'Let's discuss your decision,' Denise says.

Lucy shrugs. 'It wasn't an easy one.'

Denise nods. 'Of course. It never is. I see from the notes the father is deceased.'

Lucy catches her breath; the stabbing sensation is back. 'Car accident — caused a brain aneurysm.'

Saying those words doesn't make it feel real. Over the last few weeks, she's had to deal with Carl's death, the court case, and now this. She realises that she is still completely numb — but not comfortably now.

'I'm going to recommend you have follow-up counselling,' Denise says, 'not just to deal with the emotions following the procedure. There is a whole raft of emotions that you will experience to do with his death, too.'

Lucy nods. 'Dad already has me scheduled.' She laughs at her choice of words. 'I don't mean scheduled to be committed to a mental ward — I mean scheduled for counselling. He's a mental health nurse.'

Denise smiles. 'How fortuitous. How do you feel about your decision?'

Lucy grimaces. The pain is building again. This time it is more of a hollow ache. Like a slow throbbing. 'Unsure, but sure. It's hard. But I'm sure this is what I should do. Not necessarily right, but the best option. I can't do it alone. I can't deal with Carl's death and grow a baby. I think the reality of it might break me.' She gasps.

Denise rises. 'The pain is back?'

Lucy nods. It's increasing. Seems to hit a high note and then subside. It feels like — and this fills her with fear — what she imagined contractions would feel like.

'It's coming in waves.' She bends over, feels a leaking. 'I think I'm bleeding.'

'I'll get the doctor.' Denise goes out.

Dad and Mum rush in.

'Hey, Rabbit,' Dad says, 'what's happening?'

'Lots of pain. I think I'm bleeding.'

'Looks like the decision has been made for you,' he says, watching the door for the doctor. 'I think you're miscarrying.'

They take her through the waiting rooms to a consultation room. It's sterile, like a doctor's office, in contrast to the waiting rooms, which were like sitting in a stranger's house.

The nurse hands her a gown. 'Take off your underwear and lie on the bed.'

The bleeding has increased. And the pain keeps ebbing and flowing.

'I'm Dr Gregory,' the doctor says, smiling at her. 'You're presenting with signs of miscarriage.'

Lucy looks at her dad and fights tears. He has tears, too, and squeezes her hand.

'You wouldn't be the first,' Dr Gregory says. 'This sometimes happens. I'm going to check for a heartbeat.' He applies a clear gel and runs a scanner over her abdomen. There is no sound but for the gurgling noises in her stomach. 'No heartbeat,' he says.

Lucy feels an overwhelming sadness. It surprises her. 'None?' she asks.

He shakes his head. 'I'll do a quick exam.'

It's the most uncomfortable feeling. Lucy lies with her legs bent as the doctor inserts a gloved finger. She cringes, and tears escape.

'Okay?' Dad is holding her hand.

She feels humiliated and degraded. She nods.

'The cervix is dilating,' the doctor says. 'This is a miscarriage.'

'Oh.' Lucy shuts her eyes as the pain courses through her again. 'What will happen?'

'Your body is doing everything to expel the contents. In a matter of hours, I would suggest, this will be complete. Because you are here, you can stay — or, if you prefer, go home. I see no reason for it to be complicated. It's all pretty textbook. If the miscarriage turns out to be incomplete, I'd ask you to return to your GP for a D and C. Otherwise, it will pass naturally.'

'What's that?' Lucy looks at her dad.

'A dilation and curettage — they open up the cervix and scrape the uterine lining to remove anything that might be left behind,' he says. 'Don't worry about that, though, the doctor says it's textbook.'

'Why is this happening?' Lucy says. 'Is it because I was going to have an abortion?'

The doctor shrugs. 'No one knows why miscarriages occur. There is no definitive research to suggest stress is a cause; however, we see a lot of stressed women miscarry. If stress is a factor, you would certainly be in the high-risk category, with everything you've gone through.'

'We'll go home,' Dad says. 'I'll monitor the situation.'

Lucy nods. She wants to get the hell out of the clinic. She just wants to be at Dad's — he'll take care of her. 'Let's go.'

The bleeding and cramping increase.

'All natural,' Dad says.

He makes her chicken soup and tea. She is constantly up and down to the toilet. Monitoring the blood loss, changing the pads. It's disgusting, she thinks. But there is a weird sense of relief that washes over her. It was never going to happen. She was never going to have a baby. Despite the fact that she'd made the decision, and was there to do it, the onus has been taken away. Right to the last minute, she wasn't sure of her conviction. And now she'll never know. Never have to know.

It takes three hours for the cramping to subside. The blood loss is quite heavy.

'It may continue for a few days,' her dad says, reassuring her. 'No tampons, only pads.'

'What happens next?' Lucy says.

'I think in a week we'll do another pregnancy test. Confirm this is over. And then move forward.'

She nods. 'Okay.'

Moving forward seems like a terrific option — but can she really? Can she leave this wreckage behind? Move on. Forget Carl, this pregnancy — everything that has shaped her over the last few months. But she doesn't want it to define her. And so, to the future.

There's the prospect of really dealing with Carl's death — she knows she hasn't had the opportunity to truly grieve for him, knows that in the coming weeks and months it may become difficult. But she has Dad and Mum and Emma, Lydia and Georgia. People who will listen. People who will support her. And in spite of the horror that lies behind her, and the uncertainty in front, she feels reassured knowing they are there.

47

'It's over,' she tells Lydia and Georgia. 'Finished yesterday. Dad says another pregnancy test next week and that's it.'

'Awesome,' Lydia says. 'You get what you want but don't have to feel bad about it.'

'Lydia!' Georgia says. 'That's awful!'

'Whaaat?' Lydia moans. 'What did I say?'

'Just stop it.' Georgia frowns and dismisses her.

'To be fair,' Lucy says, 'she's right.'

'I am?'

'It's true,' Lucy says. 'No one ever knows what they will do until they have to do it. People can bang on about what they think they'll do — and with conviction — but no one ever really knows. I never thought I'd get pregnant. And I always thought that if the unthinkable happened, I'd get an abortion. Straight up. No hesitation. No doubts. But it wasn't as easy as that. There is this huge conflict, and you just can't know what you'll do until you face it.'

'Yeah.' Lydia nods in agreement, though it's apparent she's not convinced that that was what she said.

'I will never know whether I could have gone through with it, despite actually being in the clinic.'

'Then that *is* awesome,' Georgia says.

'Yes and no,' Lucy says. 'I didn't want to continue the pregnancy, but when I was there and the protesters waved pictures at me, I started to get nervous. Rethink what I was doing — whether I could actually do it. I hadn't got to the point of no return, which I guess is the anaesthetic. I could still back out. And that scares me the most.'

'Why?' And Georgia is more puzzled than Lydia.

'Because if the decision hadn't been taken away from me, I may not have done it, and I'd still be pregnant now. Even though I so desperately didn't want to be pregnant, I'm not convinced I could have had the abortion. So Lyd is right — I get what I want with a dose of reduced guilt.'

'That's okay, but,' Georgia says.

'I guess, but it doesn't eliminate the guilt,' Lucy says. 'I guess nothing will.'

'What's happening with exams?' Georgia changes the subject.

'Special consideration,' Lucy says. 'Mum's been on the phone to the Curriculum Council and they're prepared to waive the exams and give me an ATAR based on my current record.'

'That's awesome,' Lydia says.

'Sure.' Lucy sighs. She can't escape the images of Carl and JD. And the jellybean foetus, the bulging artery — she can't get her head away from them.

'It's awful, Luce,' Georgia says. 'Nothing will make what you've been through any better. But at least you don't have to go through the exams now.'

'I know.' And now she can't restrain the tears. 'But I keep feeling like I'm cheating. It's another thing I'll never know — if I could have done it. Passed the exams with the ATAR I wanted.' She feels hysterical. 'It's like I can't finish anything — I can't know what it's like to win.'

'Or lose,' Lydia says. 'Why should you have to do

it? Why? You've always been a perfect student. To sit them and not get your best would be totally unfair.'

'Lyd's got a point,' Georgia agrees. 'Why do you have to prove it now? You've proven it for years. You need to be a bit nicer to yourself.'

Lucy nods — she's supported by their words — but they don't know what it feels like. No one else does.

She thinks of Atticus Finch's words in *To Kill a Mockingbird*: 'You never really understand a person until you consider things from his point of view — until you climb into his skin and walk around in it.' If there is one thing she has learned, it's that there is no such thing as black and white, only shades in between. Perhaps this is what it means when you turn grey as you get older — less convinced and more unsure.

48

It's Graduation Night, the last school function they'll attend before WACE exams and the Awards Night. It's so hard to believe. Then, after the exams, Leavers.

Lucy wasn't going to go to Leavers, even though halfway through the year they had booked a chalet down in Dunsborough. After everything she had gone through, it seemed inappropriate. How could she go out and have a jolly-up when Carl was dead? But both her parents had strongly encouraged her to go.

They had all laughed at the positions they'd assumed.

'Who would ever think a parent would be coercing their kid into Leavers?' Mum said.

Dad nodded. 'It's a strange situation — but fits

perfectly with the last year. You need to go, Rabbit.'

'Dad! You've always been strongly against it. You said, and I quote, "It's nonsense as a rite of passage. Society shouldn't encourage it. We need to find other ways to celebrate".'

'All true,' her dad agreed. 'However, one needs to be flexible in one's opinions. And if experience dictates anything at all, it's to learn from it, embrace change and anticipate the unexpected.'

'You need to be a part of things,' Mum said. 'This is why you endured all you did — to be a kid, to live your life. You have to go.'

'Okay.' Lucy put her hands up in surrender. 'If you insist, I will. I wouldn't want to be grounded for not going to Leavers.'

She rang to tell Lydia that she was back in, would be making the trek to Dunsborough, and that she'd be designated driver for the week.

'As if you weren't going, right,' Lydia said.

'I just thought it might be a bit soon to be doing stuff like that.'

'Stuff like what? Living?' Lydia said. 'Carl would've wanted you to get on with your life.'

But that has been part of the problem: Lucy isn't

sure he would have. She hates thinking about how miserable she made Carl before he died. She is glad she has her first psych session tomorrow. She needs it, before all this thinking sends her mad.

The idea of returning to school, to that same hall that housed the Thrift Shop Ball, makes Lucy anxious. But this is it.

They pull in to the car park. Already school looks different — this place she attended nearly every day for five years. She holds her parents' hands as they walk up the steps. She feels like she's steeling herself. The gym is decorated with flowers and balloons. A PowerPoint presentation plays behind the podium, showing snapshots of the last five years: the ball, the river cruise, assemblies, camps. Most parents sit in their seats, watching.

The graduates aren't paying any attention — they are hugging each other as though they haven't seen each other for years, when in fact it's only been weeks. The girls are dressed in short summery dresses in bold colours and swirling prints, most tottering about on four-inch heels. The boys look casual in open-necked shirts and long pants.

Lucy sees Big Al and Ben leaning against a wall, talking to someone seated — she can't see who it is. And she has a sudden pain in her heart. Carl is not here. And he'll never be anywhere ever again. He is gone. The reality is forceful. Al glances over, and his face breaks into a smile when he sees her. He waves her over. Her parents nod for her to go and socialise, as they take their seats in the audience.

'Hey.' Al reaches down to give her a hug. Where Carl was huge in comparison to her, Big Al is a man mountain. 'Look who's here.' And when he steps aside, Lucy sees who they are talking to — it's JD. He's sitting on a chair and his head is haloed in a new metal contraption that holds his neck still. He is pale and thin, but he smiles when he sees her.

'Lucy.' He offers a bandaged hand.

She grabs it gratefully. 'How are you?'

'Great. Good. How are you?'

'Not too bad. Getting around, as much as they'll let me.' He nods towards his parents, who sit holding hands, watching him cautiously. 'I'm in portable traction now.'

'Hi.' Lucy waves and goes over to the Tans. She hugs Mrs Tan and then Mr Tan.

'How are you, beautiful girl?' Mr Tan says.

'Still here,' she says lightly.

'Me too,' Mr Tan says so sadly, 'and life goes on, despite everything.'

'I know.' Lucy takes a step back. Mr Tan's guilt is palpable — but then, she guesses there are many of them who feel guilty, not just her. The Tans, for rejoicing in JD's survival; Big Al, who plays *what if* all the time; Ben, co-pilot to Al's guilt trip; her parents, for their relief that things have worked out — no, are turning out — the best way for Lucy. The only people not wracked with guilt, but consumed with grief, are the Kapulettis.

As if on cue, Lucy sees them enter the hall. She feels herself wilt. She expected them, but didn't. Tonight Carl would have graduated — of course they would come. What else do they have to do with their lives now?

'Antonio and Morella,' Mr Tan says, seeing them. He grabs Lucy's arm. 'Stay with me. I'll talk.'

Again, she feels grateful for support, people rallying around to shield her from any anger or blame. But she didn't really do anything wrong. *Did she?* If so many people feel the need to protect her, then maybe she did. Her muscles tense as the Kapulettis approach.

'Relax,' Mr Tan says, feeling it too. 'It'll be cool.' He releases her arm to embrace first Mr K and then Mrs K, who clings to him tightly. 'How are you?'

'It is so hard. Just to put one foot in front of left one,' Mrs K says, wiping her eyes. 'Too not believing.'

Lucy finds she has retreated behind Mr Tan, but Mr K puts out his hand.

'Lucy, cara mia,' he says softly.

She wants to weep, but won't. *Stay strong, like at Carl's funeral.*

She finds herself in his cigar-scented embrace. 'How we have missed you.'

She relaxes, feels forgiven, looks over his shoulder at Mrs K, but recoils. Mrs K is looking at her with pure hatred. Lucy flinches. She wants to say something but can't, her vocal cords paralysed.

'Morella,' Mr K says, looking at his wife, 'it's time to forgive. Nothing can change what has been done. We love her.'

Mrs K bristles — won't break eye contact with Lucy.

She speaks to her husband. 'That girl, she kill

my Carlo. She not want his baby. She make his head hurt. She make his baby die. I never forgiving her. May she burn.' And to everyone's horror, she spits on the floor and walks off to sit in the rows near the front.

Lucy is trembling. 'I'm so sorry,' she says, eventually giving way to the tears. She understands the attack. Of course Mrs K would hate her, blame her. It is her fault.

'Don't be sorry,' Mr K says. 'I spoke to the priest. He told me this is God's way. No one can take from the Earth but Him. He has a greater purpose for Carl. Carl is now an angel. Morella will see. She is a loyal and faithful servant. When God tells her, she will understand. In time.'

Lucy nods. Mr Tan has his arm around her again, holding her up against the attack. Lucy is shaking. Now everyone knows about the pregnancy, the baby. She looks at Mr Tan fearfully. What will he think of her?

'You know what?' he says, like he hasn't heard any of the words. 'Shit happens.'

She wants to smile, is frightened of crying, but then laughs lightly. And so does Mr Tan.

'Time to celebrate,' he says. 'Go talk to your friends. Don't let an old man like me monopolise you.'

Lucy slides into the vacant chair next to JD. 'So how are you, really?' she asks.

'Weird,' he says. 'Saw the funeral on live stream — you did well. I wanted to be there, but no way would they let me out. It's been an effort to get this far.' He shrugs.

Lucy nods. It's the first time she has stood in this hall since the night of the accident — the night Carl left the ball and didn't come back. It was confronting to walk through those doors, remembering how last time she passed through them she was furious with him for leaving her and formulating the big break-up speech in her head. One she never had to deliver.

'It's like being numb. Like having thoughts but not feeling them. Like I've been decapitated.' Her hand flies to her mouth in horror when she realises what she's said. 'Oh, JD, I'm so sorry. That was such a Lydia thing to say'

He laughs. 'Don't be. I'm lucky I wasn't. If that car seat hadn't broken, I might well have lost my head. Where is Lydia anyway?' JD asks. 'Wouldn't saying hi. Haven't seen her since hospital.'

'She came to the hospital?' Lucy frowns. 'She never said.'

He gives a limited shrug. 'Came a lot.'

Lucy smiles. She'd always known Lydia had a crush on JD — but to visit him and not say? Sneaky little cow.

'What's happening for you with the exams?' Lucy says, knowing the great importance they have for him. He has worked harder than anyone else to get into uni.

'Got a scholarship,' he says proudly. 'Based on my average.'

'Awesome! You deserve it. Well done. Engineering?'

'As planned,' JD says. 'I'm inscrutable. Must be the Chinese in me.'

'You're Vietnamese,' Lucy says.

'Whatever — still an Asian.' He winks at her. 'What about you?'

'I'll get a score from Curriculum Council,' she says. 'Hopefully enough to get me in.'

'It will be, if it's your average,' JD says.

'Oh,' she says as she gets up to leave, 'you need

to know I will have beaten you again, despite everything.'

'How?'

'Lit — Highest Achieving Student.' She points at herself.

'You were always going to be,' JD says. 'Poor Asian kid never stood a chance.'

She laughs. 'Poor Asian! Give it a rest.' She sees a peacock parade of her friends. 'I'll go get Lydia.'

'Oh my God,' Lydia says, 'you look so beautiful.' She wraps her arms around Lucy and hugs her tightly.

'So do you,' Lucy says.

'You're so thin,' Georgia says, 'but totally hot.'

Lucy nods — she is the thinnest she's been since she was twelve. After the miscarriage, it took a few weeks for her boobs to understand, but eventually they reverted to their normal size. The rest of her body was thinner than ever. None of her clothes fit, which was ironic, given she'd recently been pregnant.

'Pumped,' Lydia shouts loudly and everyone laughs.

'JD's looking for you,' Lucy says.

'Really?' Lydia's eyes widen. 'Where is he? Is he here?' She sounds so excited and then tries to tone it down. 'I mean, I didn't know he'd be here. Didn't that kid break his neck or something?'

Lucy laughs at her transparency. 'Yeah — he's over there, waiting for you to visit him.'

Lydia pushes her hair back and starts to head over.

Lucy shouts after her, 'Like you did in hospital!' She's sure she sees Lydia teeter slightly on her heels.

The lights dim and soft music plays. The principal, Mr Criddle, takes to the stage and speaks into the mike, asking everyone to take their seats. Lucy sits between her mum and dad. Over the aisle are the Kapulettis. Mrs K stares blankly ahead.

Mr Criddle begins. 'Welcome to the Graduating 12s of McCauley High. It gives me great pleasure to present them to you in alphabetical order. Andy Andrews.'

As Andy steps on to the stage, a school photo from Year 1 flashes up on the screen, followed by his Year 12 picture. The difference is phenomenal — he has gone from a freckly, toothless cherub to a lean and angular ranga. The crowd laughs; some of the and angular ranga. The crowd laughs; some of the parents *awwwww* in unison.

Name after name, face after face, then 'Carl Kapuletti' and on the slide are the two pictures of Carl. There is a murmur in the crowd. Lucy looks down, feels most eyes on her. Mr K steps on to the stage, shakes the principal's hand as Mr Criddle goes in for a hug — awkward moment — then he steps off, holding Carl's certificate in his hand, tears glistening in his eyes.

Mr Criddle continues calling names: '... and JD — Douglas — Tan.'

Ben walks on to the stage. He says something to the principal, who nods, and Ben steps up to the mike. Everyone looks around in surprise. What is Ben doing?

'I just want to take a minute to acknowledge our mate JD,' Ben says, gesturing towards where JD sits in the front row, harnessed into his metal frame. 'It's been a tough year for us all. Carl is no longer here. And the only way this situation could've been any worse is if this little guy hadn't pulled through, too. But he did. And I want to ask for a minute of silence to acknowledge Carl and JD and the time we've all gone through.'

Most people bow their heads. Lucy stares at her shoes. It had to be said. The elephant in the room had to be acknowledged.

Ben breaks the silence. 'Before I go, can I just share with you something JD told me when he was in rehab? He told me to appreciate the little things in life. That you have no idea how hard it is to take a piss when you've got a broken neck and someone holding a bottle.'

Everyone erupts in laughter. Ben has successfully eased the tension. He returns to his seat, only to bob up three people later to collect his own certificate. The principal won't let him speak again — instead, hurries him off the stage.

And finally her name is called: 'Lucy Wishart.' She gets up, smiles at Mum and Dad, passes in front of JD, who makes to touch her arm, and on to the stage. Now every single pair of eyes in the room is on her (with the exception of the Physics teacher, Mr Sims, who has nodded off) and she feels nervous. She's not sure what to expect — loud boos, rotten tomatoes? Instead she gets applause — as loud as anyone else's, maybe even louder — and then she hears a *woohoo*. It's her mum. She glances at them. Dad is frowning at Mum for misbehaving; Mum is giving her *WTF* look and laughing. Lucy shakes the principal's hand and steps down.

High school complete. It is actually, finally and totally over.

49

Over the next four weeks, everyone is studying for the exams. Lucy monitors their progress on Facebook. Study sessions at the local library, pictures of books scattered on the floor and captions that read 'The Ultimate Torture — thanks, Curriculum Council.' It's hard not to feel left out, despite knowing there was no way she could have crammed, and retained, any knowledge. She feels ripped off — but also liberated.

She is glad she has her twice-weekly sessions with Diane. She goes on her own — drives the thirty minutes to her office in Subiaco and reads five-year-old magazines as she waits. The sessions are painful, teary and traumatic and then, slowly, cathartic and calming. She talks; Diane listens and then offers her thoughts.

'What you've endured is a lifetime of emotional trauma crammed into a few months. You need to take credit for the strength you have. And utilise the support that is offered. You had to make certain decisions — you did, whether they were fulfilled or not. You have to take courage in your convictions and accept that we can't control everything in life, only those things within our control. At the end of the day, do you consider you would have done anything differently?'

Lucy frowns. What would she have done differently? Had she known Carl would leave and smash the car, she would never have fought with him. Had she known telling him about the baby might have precipitated high blood pressure, bursting an artery, she would not have told him. Had she known the Kapulettis would seek a legal injunction, she wouldn't have revealed the pregnancy at all. But at the time she hadn't known the outcomes — and, as Diane said, those outcomes were beyond her control.

'No,' she says finally, and then pauses. 'Yes.

There is one thing I would change: my part in the contraception.'

'How?'

'I wouldn't have left it up to him. I would have made sure that even though we were using condoms, I was on the pill — or an IUD. I would have taken my own steps to prevent the pregnancy.'

'Would you have abstained from sex — now, in retrospect?'

Lucy thinks this through. She and Carl had been seeing each other for months before he even remotely started pressuring her to take it further. And *pressuring* made it sound so heavy-handed. It wasn't. It was just that they were both seventeen, both virgins, and in a relationship that seemed solid. The pressure was driven from desire, not force. It was that little bit further each time. She had wanted it, too. He wanted it so much — they both acknowledged that — but in the back of her mind was always the fear of pregnancy. *So why didn't she go on the pill?* Embarrassment? Acknowledgement that she was now 'sexually active', as the Health Ed teacher put it? It all seemed so awkward. But given the circumstances that followed, she'd face that embarrassment and awkwardness in a heartbeat if it meant never having to go through what she had — telling her parents, friends, Carl, his parents, doctors, lawyers, judges, abortionists.

'No,' she says eventually. 'I think what we did was okay. It's what we didn't do that was the problem.'

'What about in the future?'

'Who knows?' Lucy says. 'If you mean with a new boyfriend, that's just not something I can even consider at the moment. But I know I'll never put myself in that position again.'

'Leavers soon?'

'Next week. Exams are finished. Everyone is pumped. I feel a bit out of the loop. I don't have the same experiences to share. I'm kinda worried I don't belong.'

'But you do,' Diane says firmly. 'Your phone beeps every minute to say you have a text as you sit here. You're on Facebook and Messenger every night. You do still belong.'

'I guess,' Lucy says, considering it. In all this time, her friends, especially Carl's, have never forgotten her. Never left her out.

'Enjoy it. I'll see you for a catch-up when you get

back. But I don't think you're going to need me much more. I think you've figured it out.'

Those words cause an element of panic in Lucy. 'But what if I do need you?'

'Then you come in, but I don't think you will have to,' Diane says. 'People tell you it takes x amount of time to grieve for this or that — it's not true. It takes you as long as it takes you. And that is not to be judged or assessed.'

'Thank you,' Lucy says, rising. 'This has been so helpful.'

'You'll be okay,' Diane says, hugging her.

50

Lydia's pink Barina flies into the driveway. Lucy peers out of her window. Lydia is in a hurry, she thinks, watching her leap from the car, catch her skirt in the door and then fumble with her keys to unlock it and detangle herself. She's comical to watch and Lucy holds on to the edge of the window, laughing. Lydia runs up the driveway and Lucy hears her enter the house.

'Hello,' she calls.

'In my room.' Lucy folds the last of her clothes into a bag. Packed and ready to load.

'Oh my God.' Lydia barrels through the doorway. 'You're not going to believe what I've done!' She's out of breath, her cheeks are pink and she is in true

Lydia panic mode.

'Give it a go,' Lucy says, amused. There is nothing in this world Lydia could do that she wouldn't believe.

'Oh my God.' Lydia is flapping her hands around and walking in circles. 'Oh my God.'

'Go on,' Lucy says, 'spit it.'

'You may not know this' — Lydia averts her eyes to the ceiling — 'but I visited JD in hospital.'

'Yes.' Lucy nods.

'And then after the graduation, he, well, then, he well ...' Her hands are flapping madly.

'Asked you out?' Lucy offers.

'Yes. Oh my God, I need to sit down.' She plonks herself on the edge of the bed. 'I am the stupidest person in the whole world.'

'Probably not the *whole* world.' Lucy laughs.

'Shut up, listen. Have you ever been to his house before?'

'The Taj Mahal?' Lucy says, thinking of the pre-funeral conference there.

'I don't know its name, but it's, like, the biggest house in the whole world.' Lydia slows down.

'Yep, it's huge,' Lucy agrees.

'Anyway, I go there yesterday for this date. Because JD can't go out, right?'

'Yesterday!' Lucy says. 'And you wait all this time to tell me?'

'I couldn't tell anyone.' Lydia starts flapping her hands again. She pauses and breathes deeply. 'So I get there and it's this huge lunch. Like, heaps of his relos from China who are over at the moment.'

'Vietnam,' Lucy says.

'Whatever.' Lydia puts a hand to her cheek. 'Oh my God, I'm so friggin' hot. I think I might die.'

'Keep going,' Lucy says.

'So, like, I'm out in the garden and I'm talking to JD and it's, like, a hundred degrees, so I'm drinking heaps of water. And then I'm busting for the loo and I ask him where it is.' Lydia presses both her hands to her cheeks. 'So he says upstairs on the left. So I go up and find the room and I go in and lock the door, but there's no toilet — just a sink attached to the wall and a mirror and towels, right?'

'Right.'

'So I think, this isn't the toilet, and then I hear them calling that lunch is ready. And I'm still bursting for a wee, and then I think, maybe this *is* a toilet and this is how the Chinese go.'

'Vietnamese,' Lucy says, starting to laugh — she knows exactly where this is going now.

'So I think, okay, and I drop my knickers, climb up on to this sink thing and pee.'

'Oh my God.' Lucy can't stop laughing. 'You peed in their sink?'

'Shut up.' Lydia is flapping her hands wildly again. 'It gets worse. I'm perched there, peeing, and it's, like, total relief. You know, when you think you might pee your pants and then you make it in time? But then the next minute I hear this horrible creaking noise and the whole sink starts to wobble. And the next minute the friggin' thing breaks away from the wall and I'm thrown across the room.'

Lucy is hysterical now; in fact, she thinks she might pee *her* pants.

'So the bloody pipes explode, there's water spraying all over the place, and I'm almost unconscious where I've smacked my head into the wall.' Lydia rubs a lump on the side of her head. 'Then it gets worse.'

'How?' Lucy says, catching her breath. 'How could it get any worse?'

'I'm really groggy, can't sit up. There's a friggin' hammering on the door — they must have heard the noise. And then the bloody door bursts open. And there is Mr Tan and Mrs Tan and behind them some friggin' uncle and JD's little grandma.' Lydia looks like she might cry.

'Oh, Lydia.' Lucy tries to stop laughing. 'What did they say?'

'Nothing. They all just looked at me. I don't know what was worse. That I'd broken their sink, or that Mrs Tan knew I was peeing in it. Or ...' And Lydia waves her hands again frantically. 'That Mr Tan saw my virginia.'

'Oh, Lydia.' Lucy bites her lip, tries not to laugh, but can't help it. She explodes into peals of laughter. And Lydia does, too. They hang on to each other, gasping for air. 'Too funny,' Lucy says finally, wiping her tears away.

'How can I ever show my face there again?' Lydia says.

'It's not your face I'd be worried about showing.'

'Stoopppp,' Lydia whines. 'It's not funny.'

'Oh, come on, it is.' Lucy grabs her arm. 'Look, it'll be forgotten in a while.'

'How long do you think?' Lydia says, as they carry the bags down to the car.

'I dunno. Five years would be my guess. Or when the Tans move out.'

Georgia arrives and starts putting her stuff in the car.

'Awesome,' she says. 'I'm so excited. Leavers, finally! Where are we meeting the boys?'

'At the servo,' Lucy says.

'Boys?' Lydia looks horrified. 'Who? What boys?'

'Al and Ben,' Lucy says. 'And Mr Tan is bringing JD down for a couple of days. He's meeting us there, too.' She bites back her smile.

'Mr Tan!' Lydia shouts.

'Better get it over and done with, Lyd,' Lucy says.

'What are you two talking about?' Georgia says, frowning. 'Hey, Lyd, how did the date go?'

'Oh, Georgia!' Lydia grabs her arm and takes her over to the shade of a tree and starts retelling the story.

Lucy heads over to her parents. 'Back next Monday,' she says, hugging her mum. 'We've got enough food to feed a small African village — if they could survive on Doritos and Tiny Teddies.'

'Drive carefully and text on the way,' Mum says. 'I don't mean text while driving. I mean ...'

'I know, Mum.'

'Don't forget to stop and have a break from driving,' Dad says, hugging her hard.

'Have fun,' Mum says.

'An adventure,' Dad says.

'Yeah.' Lucy smiles at them both. *How weird is this?* She is going off for a week to have fun. After the last few months, it seems incomprehensible.

'Be careful,' Dad says.

'I will. Don't worry.'

'We will,' Mum says. 'It's part of the job description.'

'I'll be fine.'

Georgia is clinging on to Lydia, laughing so hard she can barely stand.

'Another Lydia story?' Dad says, nodding at them as they approach.

'Yep. Tell you when I get back. Funniest one ever.'

She gets in the car and starts the engine. 'Right.' She looks at Lydia and Georgia. 'Ready?'

'Totally,' Georgia says. 'Turn up the tunes.'

Lucy plugs the iPod in and cranks up the volume.

'Let's do it,' she says as they pull out of the driveway and head down the road.

the end

Notes

WACE — Western Australian Certificate of Education
ATAR — Australian Tertiary Admission Rank

The authorship of the poem Lucy recites, page 243, is disputed.

Quote page 272 from *To Kill a Mockingbird* by Harper Lee (first published 1960).

Acknowledgements

As always I'd like to thank my family, friends and my colleagues at Sacred Heart College who allow me to bore them tirelessly with my characters' latest high jinks. Thanks particularly to Mum, Jane, Savannah and Lou (always my first readers) and Willow, for putting up with egg and chips. Thank you to my team of lawyers, particularly Aunty Joy and my cousin Sophie, your input was greatly appreciated. Cate Sutherland and Amanda Curtin, thank you for helping turn a rather shoddy manuscript into something well-polished; your professional eyes never let me get away with anything (and while I curse you at the time, I am eternally grateful!) Thank you Lydia Binky Boo and Georgia, for providing me the inspiration to write two of my most favourite characters, and a shout-out to my girl band, who always remain supportive. And finally, thank you dear reader, by doing what you do, you allow me to do what I love.

Kate McCaffrey

Kate grew up in Perth's northern suburbs. She has a degree in English and Art and a diploma in Education.

Kate is the author of three other award-winning novels for young adults: *Destroying Avalon* (2006), winner of the WAYRBA Avis Page Award for older readers and the Western Australian Premier's Book Award for Young Adults; *In Ecstasy* (2008), winner of the Australian Family Therapists' Award for Children's Literature; and *Beautiful Monster* (2010), named a 2011 White Raven, selected from newly published books from around the world as especially noteworthy by the International Youth Library in Munich, Germany.

You can find more information about
Kate and her work at
katemccaffrey.wordpress.com

More great reads ...
fremantlepress.com.au

First published 2014 by
FREMANTLE PRESS
25 Quarry Street, Fremantle, Western Australia 6160
www.fremantlepress.com.au

Edited by Amanda Curtin.
Cover designed by Ally Crimp.
Front cover photograph by Aleshyn Andrei.
Printed by Everbest Printing Company, China.

National Library of Australia
Cataloguing-in-publication data

McCaffrey, Kate, 1970– .
Crashing down.

ISBN: 978 1922089 85 4 (pbk.)

A823.4

Publication of this title was assisted by the Commonwealth Government
through the Australia Council, its arts funding and advisory body.

Fremantle Press is supported by the State Government
through the Department of Culture and the Arts.

Government of **Western Australia**
Department of **Culture and the Arts**

At Thy Call
We Did Not Falter

At Thy Call
We Did Not Falter

Clive Holt

ZEBRA

Published by Zebra Press
an imprint of Struik Publishers
(a division of New Holland Publishing (South Africa) (Pty) Ltd)
PO Box 1144, Cape Town, 8000
New Holland Publishing is a member of Johnnic Communications Ltd

www.zebrapress.co.za

First published in Australia by Paradigm Media Trust in 2004
New edition published in South Africa by Zebra Press in 2005

1 3 5 7 9 10 8 6 4 2

Publication © Zebra Press 2005
Text © Clive Holt 2004

Cover design: Interlusion Productions

PHOTOGRAPHIC ACKNOWLEDGEMENTS
Certain images contained in this book are from sources other than the author. Where
images have been used from other sources, this has been done with the permission
of the copyright holders, as follows: Sentinel Projects (owned by Barry Fowler),
M. Davies and Stephen Addison

PUBLISHING MANAGER: Marlene Fryer
MANAGING EDITOR: Robert Plummer
EDITOR: Marléne Burger
PROOFREADER: Ronel Richter-Herbert
TEXT DESIGNER: Natascha Adendorff
TYPESETTER: Monique van den Berg
PRODUCTION MANAGER: Valerie Kömmer

Set in 10.5 pt on 14 pt Minion

Reproduction by Hirt & Carter (Cape) (Pty) Ltd
Printed and bound by Paarl Print, Oosterland Street, Paarl, South Africa

ISBN 1 77007 117 2

At thy call we shall not falter,
Firm and steadfast we shall stand,
At thy will to live or perish,
Oh South Africa, dear land.

– Extract from *The Call of South Africa*, the official English version of the national anthem from 1960, when the country became a republic under the National Party, which governed it from 1948 to 1994

Contents

Foreword

WHEN CLIVE FIRST MENTIONED that he wanted to write a book about his time as a conscripted soldier in the Angolan War, my reaction was one of trepidation and despair. During the 10 years of our marriage, I have known Clive intimately and he had confided in me some of his deepest and darkest war experiences. My recollection of those shared moments was of a young man who had suffered immensely and still had not dealt with the many painful and traumatic events he had known in Angola, to say nothing of the post-war challenges he faced.

I studied psychology as part of my degree and realised that facing your demons was a good healing process. However, two years ago, I strongly believed that Clive was not yet ready to do so. I also thought that his book would be a bitter and angry account of the events, people and organisations he 'blamed' for some of his shortfalls in personality and relationships.

Yet once Clive began discussing the format of the book and the way he wanted to present the facts, it became apparent that the numerous personal development courses he had attended and the reading he had so diligently done over the years would be utilised in a positive manner. Clive has amazed me with the way that he has applied his knowledge of all that he has learnt in terms of how not to become a victim of circumstance. The result is a book that is an inspiration to those who have been through any trauma in their lives (no matter how big or small) and an example of how anyone can overcome the effects of post-traumatic stress disorder (PTSD).

By writing this book in an easy style that allows readers to follow his experiences on a day-to-day basis and sharing his ability to overcome the effects that they had on his life, Clive has embraced and extended his role as a husband, father and now positive role model. He has grown and learnt a great deal in the process, and I believe that anyone who reads his story will learn and grow a great deal too, and endorse my admiration for his positive and personal approach.

ALISON HOLT
Speech pathologist, BA (SP & H Th) WITS; and wife
Kalgoorlie, Australia
2004

Acknowledgments

WHILE THIS IS ESSENTIALLY a personal account of the Angolan War as I experienced it, I have cross-referenced my information with other books and information sources in a bid to ensure the highest possible level of accuracy with regards to points of historical importance, such as official facts, figures, battle statistics and dates.

One such book is Helmoed-Romer Heitman's *War in Angola – The Final South African Phase.* I highly recommend it to anyone interested in learning more about this war from a historical or tactical perspective. Another book that I found useful is *The Buffalo Soldiers* by Colonel Jan Breytenbach, a story of South Africa's elite 32 Battalion, which played a major role in most cross-border operations in Angola.

Sentinel Projects is a website owned by Barry Fowler, a clinical psychologist and member of the team sent to debrief returning troops at the end of the war. Barry has collected personal accounts and photographs of the war from guys who were involved and published them on his website. Many of the photographs in this book have been used with Barry's permission, with copyright being retained by *Sentinel Projects.* The loss of quality in some photographs is due to the fact that they were taken by soldiers who had smuggled small instamatic cameras into the war zone – we were not supposed to have cameras there.

Former brother-in-arms and now friend, Hein Groenewald, kindly agreed to be interviewed for a particular section of the book. I know it was not easy for Hein to relive the events he spoke about, so I really appreciate his effort and contribution.

This book is dedicated to honour, respect and gratitude: to honour those who made the supreme sacrifice in the defence of their country, family and beliefs; to respect those who performed their patriotic duty without question, receiving no support or recognition from those who deliberately placed them in harm's way; to thank those who have supported me through the challenges of writing it, particularly my devoted wife, Alison.

CLIVE HOLT
Kalgoorlie, Australia
2004

Introduction

FOR THOSE WHO GREW up in South Africa during the 1970s
and 1980s, national military service was simply a way of life
that seemed to have always been there. Few ever questioned why
conscription was necessary or how it had come to form part of
society. We just knew and accepted that, as white males living in
South Africa, we had to do two years of 'army' at some stage. Those
who wished to further their studies immediately after leaving school
had the option of deferring their national service until after they
had graduated, but, at that point, they too would be called upon to
serve their country.

However, most, myself included, felt it preferable to do national
service immediately after school and get it over with before choosing
a career path. After all, it was only two years – what could be so
hard about that? It wasn't as though South Africa was actually at
war with anyone, and, by all accounts, army life was the realisation
of many a young boy's dream – you got to wear a real uniform and
use real guns. It was also seen as a way of achieving superior physical
fitness levels and a key element in the transition from boyhood
to manhood. While there was the real possibility of being posted
to The Border and having to do patrols to keep undesirables out,
the prospect of actually having to go to war never entered into
the equation.

The term 'border' refers to the frontier between Angola and
South West Africa (now Namibia), and border duty was generally

seen as a way of getting paid more money and drinking more beer. This may have been true for about 99 per cent of the guys, but the other 1 per cent actually got to see combat, were placed in harm's way, and had to kill or be killed.

But that would never happen to me, I thought. After all, there were units such as Special Forces, and surely they would be the ones who would have to deal with such situations? Besides, as far as I was concerned, there was no serious enemy at that stage for us to go and fight. No one could have imagined sending a conventional force hundreds of kilometres into a foreign country, with the express purpose of clashing with another army – especially not the Cuban army.

Conscription by ballot was introduced for white South African men by the ruling National Party in 1957, which effectively transformed the old Union Defence Force into the Afrikaner-dominated South African Defence Force. Over the next 15 years or so, the ballot system was scrapped and national service became compulsory – initially for nine months, then a year, and finally, for a two-year stretch. Thereafter, as members of the Citizen Force, we were subject to mandatory call-ups for up to three months at a time when the military situation dictated. Employers were obliged to hold jobs open for 'campers' and make up the difference between their civilian and military pay. Deferments were granted in only the most exigent circumstances.

The primary justification for conscription of white men was to protect the Afrikaner nation (and nationalist government) against the large black majority. The implementation of various nationalist policies, including apartheid, led to increased protest action by the black population, spearheaded by the African National Congress (ANC) and Pan-Africanist Congress (PAC), culminating in their eventual banning in 1960 and forcing the liberation movements to go underground.

The banned activists sought refuge in neighbouring African states that were sympathetic to their cause and offered support to the anti-apartheid movement. The reality of the situation was that these sympathetic neighbours enjoyed the backing of communist regimes such as Russia and Cuba – and, since the South African government was totally opposed to communism, the die had been cast for the inevitable outcome: conflict.

By the mid-70s, Unita was the official rebel movement opposed to the MPLA government in Angola, which was supported by Cuba and Russia in a bid to expand communism in southern Africa. It was widely believed that the Cuban leader, Fidel Castro, was intent on gaining control of the strategic Cape sea route, and in order to do this, he would need a platform from which to launch an attack on South Africa. Castro's support for parties such as the ANC and South West African People's Organisation (Swapo), which was also banned by the South African government, meant that he already had people supporting his cause in both South West Africa and South Africa. If he could get his forces across the border and into South West Africa, he would have a solid base from which to operate and launch his assault.

The South African government's decision to intervene in the Angolan conflict in support of Unita was based on the rationale that if Jonas Savimbi's forces gained control of the provinces immediately adjacent to the border, the Cuban threat to both South West Africa and, ultimately, South Africa itself, would be minimised. The Angolan army (Fapla), along with elements of the Cuban army, had been massing near the town of Cuito Cuanavale in preparation for a massive final onslaught against Unita. This action was interpreted by the South African government as aggressive, resulting in its decision to intervene in August 1987.

The clandestine nature of this intervention was primarily

due to the South African government's already poor image on the international stage – an image based on a poor human rights record through the implementation of apartheid policies and the banning of black liberation movements. The government had been under increasing international pressure to clean up its act, and the decision to invade a neighbouring country, albeit in a supportive role, would not have scored too many points with the international community.

The information blackout surrounding these operations did not stop with the media. It was also imposed on the troops involved and extended to their families. Troops sent into Angola were not privy to any of the big-picture information as to why they were going or whom they would be fighting against. In most cases, they were told that they would be going to the border for a 'bush-orientation' phase, only to find themselves crossing into Angola within hours of landing at Rundu airbase in the Caprivi. Family members were neither informed of their location nor of the fact that they would be participating in what was probably South Africa's largest and most significant military operation since the Second World War.

The lack of official information at the time compounded the issues faced by the soldiers on their return. The South African public had no real knowledge of what transpired in Angola, and when returning servicemen spoke to friends and family about the brutality of this war, very few people could comprehend what they had endured, or grasp the enormity of the war and the impact it had – and would continue to have – on their lives.

As the South African combat death toll rose, though, the public began demanding answers. The SADF finally had to admit that it was still involved in Angola, but played down its role as 'minor'. In most cases, casualty reports carried by the media consisted only

Map not to scale

of the names of soldiers who had died 'in the operational area'. However, what the average South African understood by 'the operational area' was a swathe of land south of the border between Angola and South West Africa, not foreign soil hundreds of kilometres inside Angola. It was some time after the war that the first few books containing details of these operations began to shed light on how and where that war was waged, but, even then, the publications were written from an orthodox military perspective and dealt essentially with the tactical components of the war. I fear many people have still not been told the truth about what really happened in Angola.

But the mere fact that this type of information is now publicly available justifies that what I had been involved in had, in fact, been quite a big deal, and that the difficulties I had in dealing with these experiences were entirely normal for someone who had been in combat. It is a great relief for me to know that the truth is becoming known – it is almost like having proof that all those things we did *really happened*. I had not imagined them or been spouting bullshit on the odd occasion that I tried to tell people about what had happened in Angola. I eventually just stopped talking about it for many years, because I could see the disbelief in people's eyes. 'This all sounds too far-fetched to be true, he's just making it up' was the message I could read on their faces while attempting to recount some of the incidents. I can't blame people for being sceptical or downright disbelieving; there was so little independent information available to back up what I said, and yes, it did sound too far-fetched to be true (the SADF would never have done *that*).

The Angolan War has been widely referred to and documented by historians and military writers as one of the most significant events in African history. While this is undoubtedly true, and conjecture persists as to who had actually 'won' the war, the effect this war had – and still does have in many cases – on those who fought in it has not yet been fully explored or placed into context.

It has taken me the best part of 15 years to get my own manuscript to this stage, mainly because I did not know how to tell my story. The one thing I did not want to produce was yet another historical account of the Angolan War. Rather, I felt the need to look at it from the personal perspective of the troops involved – those young men who fought in the trenches and, in many instances, bled and died on a foreign battlefield while their loved ones at home had no idea where they were or what they were doing.

This book is based on the day-by-day diary that I kept during my operational deployment in Angola, and it is my intention to take you, the reader, inside the gun turret of a Ratel armoured assault vehicle and have you experience the intensity of the battles we fought and the extreme conditions we lived under for months at a time, not knowing when or even if we would ever see our families again. You will also have the opportunity of getting up close and personal with some of the soldiers involved in this conflict, most of whom were around the age of 19 at the time. They were your sons, brothers, friends, colleagues and neighbours, a bunch of ordinary guys who were thrust into a life-and-death situation without knowing what they were getting into, or being afforded the freedom of choice prior to becoming involved in something that would change their lives forever and haunt many for years to come.

I will also look at some of the challenges faced by many of these young war veterans, myself included, when they tried to fit back into a normal society once the war was over and come to terms with what they had been through, done and witnessed. The impression I got was that the SADF had not previously experienced a war of this magnitude and, as such, had no idea how to deal with demobilised servicemen; so they opted to sweep the problem under the rug in the hope that it would just go away. It did not.

Throughout the book, I have included many extracts from my original Angola diary. Some of the language, terminology and slang used in these passages may not be grammatically correct, but they are an honest reflection of the way most 19-year-olds spoke at the time. I have transcribed these passages verbatim, as I believe they accurately mirror the way many of us felt as events unfolded, and highlight the transformation from civilian schoolboy to combat soldier. If this offends anyone in any way, this was not my intention; I am merely telling the true story as it happened and was recorded from my perspective.

This is an actual account of what happened on the ground during my time in the Angolan War. I have pulled no punches and describe events the way they occurred, and in graphic detail, where necessary. This may reopen some painful memories for people who were directly or indirectly involved in the war, so unless you are prepared to deal with the whole truth, stop reading now or proceed with caution.

While the book focuses largely on the actions of my own unit, 61 Mechanised Infantry Battalion, this should in no way be construed as intending to detract from the contribution of other units involved, such as 4 SA Infantry Battalion (4 SAI), 32 Battalion, various artillery elements and the SA Air Force. But those stories will need to be told by the members who were there.

It should be borne in mind that South Africa's military involvement in Angola dates back to 1975, in the form of Operation Savannah and other campaigns. While each of these operations played a significant role in the 14-year war, I don't discuss them in this book. My first-hand knowledge is limited to the latter stages of the war, and information on what transpired prior to that period is available elsewhere to those who seek it.

In August 1987, a small South African force entered the south-eastern corner of Angola. Their task was to support Unita's defence of its bases against an imminent large-scale offensive by Fapla, heavily supported by Cuban surrogates, and equipped with the latest Russian weaponry and equipment. The Angolan forces were massing at the town of Cuito Cuanavale, and comprised of five brigades, totalling around 12 000 troops. Additional shipments of T-55 and T-62 tanks arrived from Russia, along with new MiG 21 and 23 fighter aircraft, numerous combat and assault helicopters, and SAM ground-to-air missile systems. This brought the total strength of the Angolan force to approximately 500 tanks, 80 fighter aircraft, 120 helicopters and a healthy contingent of armoured infantry combat vehicles.

Adding support to this formidable force was an artillery component consisting of long- and medium-range guns, as well as multiple rocket launchers, known as Stalin Organs. Fapla's ground-to-air defence revolved around the ZU-23-4, a quadruple 23mm gun system capable of firing between 800 and 1 000 armour-piercing and high-explosive rounds per minute out of each of its four barrels. These guns were mounted on an amphibious vehicle chassis and could be easily moved around. They were later used with deadly effect to deliver direct fire on the South African forces and were probably more feared than the artillery.

The force that entered Angola in 1987 under the code name Operation Modular had as its objective nothing less than to halt the Fapla advance southwards towards the South West African border. This was effectively achieved on 3 October, when Fapla's 47 Brigade was destroyed at the Lomba River. The South African government decided to extend the operation in order to prevent the threat of new Fapla attacks in 1988. The original assault force consisted primarily of conscripts who were due to be discharged in December 1987, so it became necessary to rotate the manpower by bringing in new troops to continue the operation.

And that was where I entered the picture, as a member of 61 Mechanised Infantry Battalion.

On 13 December 1987, Operation Modular segued into Operation Hooper, which is the main focus of my tale. Modular and Hooper ultimately culminated in the Battle of Cuito Cuanavale, described by General Magnus Malan, South Africa's defence minister at the time, as 'one of two highlights' of his military career.[1] He continued:

> To have been part of the Cuito Cuanavale battle – the biggest, the greatest battle to have been fought in the history of South Africa – where we had a limited number of 3 000 troops and lost 31, and the enemy lost between 7 000 and 10 000 – and I'm not even talking about wounded – where they lost sophisticated equipment worth $1 billion. That was tremendous. I doubt whether the South Africans of today realise that. And I'll tell you why: because we could not keep the press informed of the battle. There was a lot of pressure from the United Nations, specifically, telling us 'Get out of Angola.'

---

1 Interview in the *Sunday Times*, cited in *Focus on South Africa*, March/April 1993, p. 9.

1

Firm and Steadfast
We Did Stand

REGARDLESS OF WHERE AND how we live, we are continually governed by at least one set of rules in order to maintain social harmony and permit people to live and function with a certain degree of freedom and independence. In most societies, these rules have a religious basis and are aimed at teaching us right from wrong, thus instilling a sense of moral values in each and every individual. If correctly taught, our moral values equip us with a conscience that guides us to make appropriate choices and decisions as we move from our formative years into adulthood.

In South Africa during the 1980s, the norm was that, by the time you left school, usually at the age of 18, you had sufficient grounding in terms of the rules of society and the moral values behind them to go out into the wide world and make your mark as an adult. If you were a white male, there was just one other little thing you had to do in order to attain adult status – national service.

This was where the whole 'rules' thing became somewhat blurred. I had spent the first 18 years of my life learning and applying a certain set of rules to everything I did, said and thought. Would I now have to change some of those rules? Apparently not. According to the information I had been given regarding my two-year stint in the South African Defence Force (SADF), I would still be living within my learnt paradigm, although there might be times when

I would have to bend or adapt the rules slightly to get through the physical and mental demands of military training. The general consensus was that the next two years would teach valuable skills, leadership and maturity. 'What could be so wrong with that?' I thought. There was, however, one small yet vital piece of information left out of this scenario – I would have to go to war! Not just patrol a border and keep enemies out of South Africa, but actually go into a foreign country as the aggressor and fight against a vastly larger army of Angolans and Cubans armed with sophisticated Russian equipment. This would certainly require a 'new' set of rules by which to live, and it did.

Part of my purpose with this book is to illustrate how we had been brought up and taught to live by a certain set of rules, then were suddenly told to forget what we had learnt over the past 18 years and apply a new set of rules. This would not be too challenging if the new paradigm was similar to the old, but it was not. The new rules we were given were, in most cases, totally opposite to what we had been taught. And, to confuse things even more, after two years of living by these new rules, we were told to go home and to please revert back to our original set of rules and live a normal life, without any assistance whatsoever from the SADF. It came down to the fact that we had given the SADF two years of our lives, placing our bodies on the line in many instances, and, once it was all over, we no longer existed or served any purpose.

One of the basic biblical commandments is 'Thou Shalt Not Kill', so how do people cope when they are told that for the next two years it is quite all right to kill, but thereafter they must again observe the original commandment?

Welcome to another world – a parallel world that existed unbeknown to all but those who dared to step into it and partake of the pain it had to offer. The majority of us were around 19 years old at the time, and less than 12 months before would have been sitting behind a school desk writing final exams and enthusiastically looking forward to a future full of promise with unlimited potential. The people you will meet in this book are real people: not fictitious characters, but real people who, in most cases, could have been your friends at school or just the average boy next door in your neighbourhood. Most had no intention of becoming soldiers, or veterans for that matter. The word 'veteran' always conjured up a mental image of some 'old' guys who had fought in one of the world wars or Vietnam. In my wildest dreams, I could never have imagined that I would become a war veteran at the age of 19.

As for post-traumatic stress disorder (PTSD), well, this was something I had only ever heard about through watching movies about the Vietnam War, and, as far as I was concerned, it only affected the guys who had fought in Vietnam. Little did I know that I would be affected by this condition as a result of serving my country with pride and patriotism. And the thing that really irked me was the total lack of support offered by the SADF once the war was over – we were told that what we had done, seen and been a part of was 'nothing special', and that we should just go home and get on with our lives. In fact, when we were sent home (after a group debriefing session lasting approximately 30 minutes), the message from our senior officers was something to the effect that most guys who do national service would have done what we had done, so we shouldn't think we were anything special, or go home and speak shit about it to our families and friends. Needless to say, I had some difficulties adjusting to normal civilian life, and began to doubt myself in terms of my ability to cope with what 'most other guys' had been through. I thought that I was somehow weaker and inferior because I was having these difficulties, while everyone else around me seemed to be coping just fine.

It wasn't until recently that I decided to revisit this chapter of my life in a bid to put these ghosts to rest once and for all and get on with my life. In the process, I discovered some startling – if not shocking – facts, which led me to write this book.

My first step was to dig out the diary I had kept throughout my time in Angola. That led me to an Internet quest to locate someone with whom I had served and subsequently lost contact with. It was through the Internet that I located the extract from the interview with General Magnus Malan and suddenly realised that what I had experienced was by no means 'normal' for most national servicemen, but rather a story that warranted telling. Some of the interesting and official facts about the final stages of the Angolan War, which took place during 1987 and 1988, are the following:

- On 9 November 1987, a South African tank destroyed the first enemy tank since World War II.
- The Battle of Cuito Cuanavale (part of Operation Hooper) was fought by approximately 3 000 South African troops against an estimated combined Angolan–Cuban force of 25 000.
- South African combat losses (deaths) as a result of Operations Modular, Hooper, Packer, Displace and the Calueque Dam incident totalled 44, while the Angolan–Cuban fatalities were a staggering 4 768 (these are official figures released by the SADF – some estimates are as high as 7 000).

The specific period that I deal with runs from August 1987 to July 1988, when the SADF conducted numerous offensive operations in Angola against combined Cuban, Soviet and Angolan forces. The rationale behind these operations was essentially to minimise any potential communist threat along the South West Africa–Angola border and prevent communist-backed forces from spilling over into South Africa.

Operations Modular, Hooper, Packer and Displace all took place in the south-eastern corner of Angola in the Cuando Cubango province, culminating in the Battle of Cuito Cuanavale on 25 February and 1 March 1988 at the town of Cuito Cuanavale, approximately 600km inside Angola. The fighting then moved west into the Cunene province, with the final battle taking place at Calueque Dam on 26 and 27 June 1988, when a ceasefire was finally negotiated to facilitate implementation of United Nations Resolution 435 – the structured withdrawal of all external forces, South African and Cuban, from Angola.

Official SADF figures put the size of the South African force in Angola at 'never more than 3 000 troops', of which an overwhelming majority would have been conscripted national servicemen or Citizen Force 'campers' (men who had already completed their national service and were required to attend military camps once a year until age 55). They had no choice regarding their involvement in these campaigns. The prevailing levels of secrecy enforced by the National Party government of the day ensured that very little information surrounding these events ever made it into the public arena. While these operations were in progress, the South African government vehemently denied any involvement in Angola. It was only on 29 June 1988, after the Calueque Dam incident in which 12 South African soldiers were killed made the front page of major newspapers, that the South African government finally admitted to extensive involvement in Angola.

I was one of those conscript servicemen who served in Angola, and while the story you are about to read is based on my personal diary, I have made every effort to ensure the highest level of accuracy possible when it comes to points of historical importance, such as dates, times and battle details. The major battles that I will be focusing on are as follows:

- Attack on Fapla's 21 Brigade – 13 January 1988.
- Attack on Fapla's 59 Brigade – 14 February 1988.
- The first Battle of Cuito Cuanavale – 25 February 1988.
- The second Battle of Cuito Cuanavale – 1 March 1988.
- The Calueque Dam bombing – 26 and 27 June 1988.

The nature of these battles was decidedly different from most previous SADF incursions into Angola, as they involved massive assaults on fortified enemy positions with the sole purpose of destroying as many as possible and forcing the survivors to flee. In most cases, the battles would last for the best part of an entire day, with long hours being spent getting into position and preparing for the attack. The fact that we were the aggressors in a foreign country meant that we did not enjoy the benefit of air support and came under continual bombardment on a daily basis from Russian-made and Cuban-piloted MiG 21 and MiG 23 fighter aircraft. Add to this the fact that we were hopelessly outnumbered by the Cuban–Angolan forces and far away from our logistical bases, and it made for an uphill battle all the way.

I was a member of a unit known as 61 Mechanised Infantry Battalion (61 Mech) under the command of Commandant (lieutenant colonel) Mike Muller. Our training had equipped us to effectively deal with the threat of conventional warfare involving armoured assault vehicles, tanks and artillery. Our primary function in Angola was simple: Destroy all enemy positions south of Cuito Cuanavale (five brigades in total) and drive any survivors back across the Cuito River.

Perhaps the best way to describe 61 Mech and its function within the SADF is to share with you a piece written by journalist Clyde Russell to mark the 10th anniversary of the unit's founding in 1988, under the heading 'Fighting Force – 61 Mech Bn Gp':

61 Mechanised Battalion Group is probably the only unit in the SADF that has been publicly praised by the Cubans. At the recent peace negotiations, a member of the Cuban delegation said that the guys of 61 Mech were 'really professional'. This compliment probably stems from the fact that in the last 18 months, the combined Cuban and Fapla forces received a bloody nose from this unit.

61 Mech was established in 1978 as Battle Group Juliet ... in order to counter any conventional attack from Angola. The unit took part in Operation Reindeer which destroyed the Swapo base, Vietnam. On 2 January 1979 the unit was established as 61 Mech and since then the unit has grown in strength and successes.

The unit is a fully operational fighting group. In fact, it is possibly the only unit of its type in the SADF. It has the capability to counter any threat of a conventional nature against SWA. The impressive factor is that the Group's strength is mobile to strike anywhere it is needed.

In the last eighteen months the unit has added to its already enviable operational record. As part of a task force in Operations Modular, Hooper, Exite and Hilti, 95 enemy tanks were destroyed. Approximately 7 000 Fapla and Cuban soldiers were killed. The OC of the unit, Cmdt Mike Muller, ascribes the successes to superior training, careful planning, good leadership and high morale. Morale is especially important, as a guy with low morale does not have much will to fight. For that reason, Cmdt Muller looks after his men, and the pride all the members of 61 Mech have in their unit has to be seen to be believed. The unit really does manage the man and not the number.

61 Mech is always where the action is. It has taken part in all the major operations, including Smokeshell, Protea, Daisy,

Askari, Modular and Hooper. The unit is also now 10 years old, and its achievements are nothing short of phenomenal. The confidence of the local population in the unit was illustrated by the unit being awarded the freedom of Tsumeb.

As far as Swapo and Fapla are concerned, 61 Mech is the poisoned arrowhead of the SADF. The unit has never been defeated and the price of this has been the death of only a few in action. However the cost for the enemy has been infinitely higher. As Col E van Lill, a former OC of 61 Mech remarked, 'If you were in 61 Mech, you were there.'

Standing face to face with the dark side of man, and realising that you are part of it, is an experience not easily forgotten, and one that nobody should ever have to endure. I hope that this book can be not only a story of war, but also a story of triumph in overcoming the effects of these traumatic experiences and drawing positive strengths from a particularly negative situation. Who knows, it may even help other veterans (and their families) to deal with these experiences in a positive manner and move forward with pride. Being able to understand the mental processes associated with conditions such as PTSD – and traumatic experiences in general – is a powerful step in learning how to deal with these events and regain control of our lives.

While I make no claims that the coping strategies discussed in this book are guaranteed to bring success, I have done a lot of research into this field and feel it pertinent to share this information with others who may have experienced or are still experiencing trauma. The coping strategies are ones that I found to be effective, but they might not be equally effective for others. It is a start, though.

2

From Schoolyard to Battlefield

D URING THE 1980s, national service in South Africa consisted of a two-year period during which conscripts received basic military training, followed by advanced instruction that prepared them for deployment in various fields. These ranged from patrolling black urban townships, wracked by anti-apartheid violence at the time, to a stint on the border between South West Africa and Angola.

In what was generally known as the 'operational area' across the breadth of what is now northern Namibia, patrols centred largely on the prevention of cross-border incursions by small groups of Swapo terrorists based in Angola and other neighbouring countries. The prospect of becoming involved in a full-scale war in another country did not really exist at that stage.

The first three months of national service consisted of basic training – or 'basics', as it was commonly known – and was designed to equip the new recruits with all the essential soldiering skills, including superior fitness levels, understanding and handling of weapons, communications abilities, camouflage techniques and various other combat skills.

During this phase, candidates were selected for participation in the junior leaders' programme, where they would essentially be trained to become officers or non-commissioned officers over an approximate nine-month time frame. Those not selected for junior leadership training would proceed to second-phase training, which covered specialised areas such as driving, gunnery, signals and a host of other functions. By the end of the first year of national service, recruits would be sufficiently qualified and able to apply their skills in the field as part of a functional military unit. Approximately half of the candidates completing the junior leadership programme would be assigned to take command of newly formed platoons and companies, while the rest would assume the roles of instructors for the following batch of recruits.

I had been called up to do my national service at 1 South African Infantry Battalion (1 SAI) in Bloemfontein, and arrived there at the beginning of 1987. This unit was rather unique in that it was the only one in the country to specialise in mechanised infantry training. We would receive the same training as any other infantry-man, but with the inclusion of an additional advanced training phase to enable the smooth transition from regular infantry (foot soldiers) to mechanised infantry. Mechanised infantry essentially takes all the standard functions of an infantry unit and mobilises them by placing troops in armoured personnel carriers and assault vehicles. The benefit of a mechanised infantry unit is that it is a highly mobile strike force, capable of delivering immense firepower, while at the same time being able to deal with the threat of enemy tanks, armour and artillery.

National servicemen who completed their training at 1 SAI were generally posted to one of two units, either 4 SAI (based at Middelburg, about 200km north-east of Johannesburg) or 61 Mechanised Infantry Battalion (based on the border in South West Africa). The prevailing mindset was that your second year of national service would be a lot less demanding than the first, consisting primarily of various patrols and training exercises. You would also get to see your family on a more regular basis.

The major benefit of being posted to 61 Mech was that, due to its location in the operational area, you would be entitled to what was known as 'danger pay', about an extra R120 a month over and above the average troop's pay of about R200 a month. The downside to this was that you might actually have to deal with the odd terrorist incursion or attack from time to time.

I had set very definite personal goals in terms of achieving some form of rank through participation in the junior leaders' programme. I wanted to become an officer in the South African army and enjoy all the benefits associated with this position of authority (and the increased pay). Unfortunately, these plans became somewhat derailed about two days prior to final selection for the programme when I suffered an asthma attack during a punitive training exercise known as an '*Opfok*'. Directly translated, this means to 'fuck up', and that was exactly what it was designed to do by pushing body and mind to the limit – and beyond. The underlying rationale to this kind of activity (administered at the sole discretion of your instructors) was that it would both enhance physical fitness levels and build up team spirit and morale within the platoon. It was also common knowledge that these types of exercises were designed to break new recruits down to nothing, enabling the army to then mould them into soldiers.

The net result of my asthma was a medical reclassification that placed certain limitations on the type of activities I was permitted to perform (such as route marches and strenuous physical training), and meant that I would not be permitted to participate in the junior leaders' programme. Besides this being a major disappointment, I soon discovered that having anything less than a 100 per cent medical classification meant that, in the eyes of most permanent force staff, your social standing was considered not much higher than that of a doormat (unfortunately, enemy bombs and bullets were unable to distinguish between medical classifications – everyone was an equal target).

This meant that I would have to wait until completion of the basic training phase in order to reassess my options and select another training course that I would be allowed to complete within the constraints of my medical classification. I managed to get onto the Regimental Non-commissioned Officers (RNCO) course, and, in spite of the fact that this would probably see me spending a large portion of my remaining service performing administrative functions, it seemed like the best available option at the time in terms of achieving a rank. The other thought I had was that I might even be able to get a transfer closer to home, since I was essentially no longer viewed by the army as 'fighting fit'.

The RNCO course was almost finished, with one exam to go, when one Sunday afternoon in July I was called down to the duty room by the lieutenant on duty. When I arrived, he informed me that I had a phone call, and I remember noticing that he looked quite concerned. It was practically unheard of for anyone to be allowed to receive a phone call during training, so I knew that something was wrong. My suspicions were confirmed when I heard my brother Gary's voice on the other end of the line, telling me that my father had suffered a heart attack while holidaying at the coast.

Gary said: 'Dad had a heart attack, but he is in hospital and he is fine, so don't worry. Can you get here as soon as possible?' Dad was in hospital in the Eastern Cape town of Grahamstown, approximately 800km away from the military base where I was stationed, and since I had no car at that stage, it meant having to hitchhike all the way. The lieutenant signed an emergency leave form and arranged for someone to drop me on the highway, with strict instructions to contact my company commander as soon as I arrived in Grahamstown.

It was a long night, and I managed to catch about three different lifts, finally arriving at the hospital at around 07h00 the following morning. The ward sister walked up to me and pleasantly asked if she could help.

'Yes, I am here to see Mr Holt,' I said. She then asked if I was a relative, to which I replied, 'Yes, he's my father.' Her facial expression changed the instant I said that, and she took me by the arm and said, 'Come and sit down in my office.'

I will never forget her words as she told me: 'Your father took a bad turn early this morning and suffered another massive heart attack. I am afraid he didn't make it.'

I was probably in a state of shock at the time. All I remember is a sense of total numbness all over my body and not knowing what to do or where to turn. The beach cottage where my family had been holidaying was about an hour's drive from the hospital, and I had to phone them to tell them that I had arrived, so that someone could come and fetch me. I went and sat in the car park and waited for my brother to arrive. The sense of helplessness and solitude was overwhelming.

I shared a very close relationship with my father and would always go to him for guidance and help; now he was gone and I didn't even get to see him one last time or say goodbye. I was still in a state of disbelief when I arrived at the beach cottage, but on seeing my mother's face and hugging her tightly for what seemed like an eternity, it hit me that this was very real and not just a bad dream. I had a sinking feeling, followed by a sense of total emptiness and loss.

Still in my army uniform, I went for a walk along the beach with my brother. We both just sat there for some time, silent, staring out at the ocean and trying to come to grips with what had just happened. I knew that the family would need to pull together and support each other through this time of tragedy, but I also knew that I would not be there to help them, as I would have to return to my unit. I phoned my company commander and he granted me seven days of compassionate leave to travel to Johannesburg, bury my father and return to base.

Not long after getting back to base, we were told we would be participating in an official army exercise code-named *Sweepslag* (Lash) at the Army Battle School at Lohatla, a seemingly endless tract of bush near a town called Kimberley in the Northern Cape. This effectively meant that the entire unit would pack up all its equipment, vehicles and weapons and set up a temporary tented base at Lohatla for the duration of the exercise. I was informed that my company would work predominantly from tactical headquarters, to ensure that all logistical and administrative requirements were met in terms of weapons, ammunition, food, communication equipment, fuel and vehicles – more of a support role than actual combat. In a way I was looking forward to this, as it would give me an opportunity to leave the base for a while and do something different.

During this exercise, I became quite friendly with a guy called Donald, who drove one of the ammunition trucks. His function was to ferry supplies and ammunition from the base to the main force in the field, and I would often go with him on these trips to spend some time in the field and catch up with my buddies. It was during this time that I learnt how to drive one of these trucks (unofficially, of course). The exercise involved simulated, coordinated assaults on 'enemy' positions, and incorporated all the elements necessary for conducting what is known as conventional warfare – artillery, tanks, infantry Ratels, mortar Ratels and anti-tank Ratels. It was an enormous exercise, and I could not help wondering why the army was going to such lengths for what seemed like nothing more than a routine training exercise.

We had been told that the manoeuvres would last until about the middle of November 1987, when we would return to our permanent base in Bloemfontein and then go home on leave (or 'pass', as we knew it). It was some time towards the middle of October that I became aware of some subtle changes around the place. There suddenly seemed to be a sense of urgency among the permanent force staff, and it was not long before rumours began to surface and do the rounds. One of the rules in the army is not to listen to rumours, but I think we were all guilty of breaking this one occasionally.

The particular rumour doing the rounds was that something 'big' was happening in Angola that involved our 1 SAI predecessors from the previous year's national service intake, and would probably have some bearing on us in the near future. But no one had any idea of the magnitude of what lay ahead. The rumours continued to circulate, getting juicier all the time, and then something significant happened. We were told that the completion date for the exercise had been moved forward, and everything would be completed by the end of October. The initial response among the guys was very positive, as this meant we would be going home on pass sooner than expected.

Over the next couple of weeks there was a marked increase in the intensity of training. Even the headquarters staff were ordered to take an active part in the various exercises and become competent with battle procedures (medical classifications did not seem to be relevant now). We were spending more time in the bush, and there was a very definite sense of urgency about everything that we did. Basic battle drills and procedures were being done over and over, with the instructors demanding an almost perfect level of execution. The exercise culminated in a well-orchestrated night attack, which was apparently satisfactorily carried out, and then we received orders to break down camp and prepare to head back to base. We did, indeed, return to base, and although I can't remember exactly what date we went on pass, I was fortunate enough to spend my 19th birthday at home with my family.

Little did I know that, five days later, I would be crossing the Angolan border and embarking on a guided tour of hell.

When I returned to base after my brief visit home, the sense of urgency among the permanent force staff had, if anything, increased. There was a definite buzz in the company HQ, and I had to make sure that everybody's personal details were up to date and correct, particularly next-of-kin details, as well as determine exactly how many guys were in each platoon. Then, without warning, one of the other HQ guys came running into my office and said we all had to report to the parade ground immediately! Once assembled, we were told that we would be divided up and posted out to either 4 SAI or 61 Mech, HQ staff included.

There were three HQ staff, and one of the guys, Jacques, wanted to be posted to 4 SAI as he had family in Middelburg, where the unit was based. The other guy wanted to remain at 1 SAI, and I did not particularly care where I went. I figured that spending the remainder of my national service in the admin office at 61 Mech would give me some time to get to grips with my father's death – not to mention that I would qualify for danger pay. By that stage my enthusiasm to become a 'real' soldier in the SADF had waned totally, and I merely wanted to get the next year over and done with as soon as possible. So it was decided. Jacques would go to 4 SAI and Jaco would remain at 1 SAI. I would go to 61 Mech, in the operational area, and the rest of my service would be a breeze. I could not have been more wrong.

We were dismissed from the parade ground and told to go

and pack our bags, as we would be leaving soon. The remaining 14 months of national service would be spent at our respective units, so we had to ensure that we packed all of our belongings and left nothing behind – including any civilian items that we had brought back with us from pass. We had to ensure that we had full kit (rifle, rucksack, sleeping bag, groundsheet, raincoat, battle jackets, spare magazines, helmet, etc.) and that all of our equipment was fully functional. I was attached to Oscar Company, which comprised of two mortar platoons, two anti-tank platoons and two assault pioneer platoons. We were told that we would be flown to an air force base in South West Africa and then transported by road to our new permanent base, 61 Mechanised Infantry Battalion, where we would receive our new Ratels and other vehicles and commence with 'bush orientation'. We left Bloemfontein on 19 November 1987, and would not see civilisation or South Africa again for the next four months.

'Who left the fucking oven door open?' one of the guys in front of me said as we stepped out of the aircraft on landing. The blast of hot air coming in through the aircraft door was a result of the 42°C heat outside. It was the first thing to strike me as I stepped onto the ground. The other notable thing was how many of the troops were wearing sunglasses to combat the glare coming off the vast expanse of white sand all around us.

The flight from Bloemfontein had lasted a couple of hours and, although it was not the most comfortable experience, it was one of the rare opportunities we had to relax without some corporal or sergeant bellowing in our ears and hurling their unique brands of abuse at us. The respite was short-lived, though. No sooner had our boots hit the ground than I could hear the sergeant's voice ordering us to get our *balsakke* (kitbags, literally translated as 'ball bags') and other equipment out of the aircraft and onto a waiting truck – your rifle stayed with you at all times, and this had been drummed into us during our training. 'Your rifle is your wife,' they used to tell us, 'she never leaves your side.'

Like cattle bound for the abattoir, we were herded onto the trucks and told to find a place to sit (a full *balsak* actually makes quite a comfortable seat on the back of a truck). Once again it was the old 'hurry-up-and-wait' syndrome we had all become accustomed to over the past year of training – everything is urgent and you have to rush to get there, but when you arrive, you end up waiting around for something to happen. So there we were, uncomfortably squashed onto the back of a truck and sitting in the blistering African sun at Rundu airbase (located in the extreme north-eastern corner of SWA), waiting to be transported to our new border base camp at 61 Mech. But something was not right. What were we doing at Rundu, when 61 Mech lay a few hundred kilometres to the west? By that stage I was becoming quite suspicious that something strange was going on. This was confirmed when the truck convoy left Rundu and turned east, when it should have headed west. Something was amiss.

After bouncing through the bush on the back of the truck for a few kilometres, I noticed a very large river ahead of us. We were heading straight for the water and, thanks to my school geography lessons, I realised that this was the river that formed the border between SWA and Angola. We were about to cross the Kavango River and enter Angola. I remember mentioning this to my sergeant, who just smiled and said, 'Yes, I know.' As if this shock was not big enough, I noticed a black man standing on the other side of the river holding a Russian-made AK47 assault rifle. He wore a green uniform, unlike any issued to the SADF or SWA Territorial Force (SWATF), and I immediately thought he must be a 'terrorist'. There was a bridge across the river, but it was not a permanent structure – it was one of those 'portable' bridges (pontoon bridge) erected by military field engineers.

The sergeant informed me that the soldier on the other side of the river was from Unita, and that we would be working closely with Jonas Savimbi's troops in Angola. I was pretty taken aback by all of this, as I'm sure many of the other guys were too. An uncomfortable silence descended on us as we crossed the bridge and entered a foreign land. There was a sense of sheer disbelief that we had been misled and deceived in such a way. I remembered that a few guys had not returned after our last pass and had been listed as absent without leave (AWOL), and I wondered if they had perhaps known something that the rest of us did not.

We moved into a temporary base camp just across the border, where we would spend the next two weeks living in tents and acclimatising to the harsh weather conditions. So the army had not lied totally. We would be doing bush orientation for two weeks – they had just neglected to mention why we were doing it and where we would be spending the next four months. The heat was extreme and unlike anything we were accustomed to, so it would take some time for everybody to get used to the conditions. As for the flies, they were plentiful and a real nuisance. We also had our first encounters with a rather nasty creature known as a 'piss moth', a very large moth that would settle on the inside of the tent roof and, if disturbed, fly around while spraying a liquid substance that would form burn-like blisters wherever it made contact with your skin. Definitely not a pleasant creature.

We did not do much in terms of physical exercise or training during this period, but we did spend a lot of time walking around in the bush and getting used to the look and feel of the terrain. It was also an opportunity to run through more kit and equipment checks and ensure that everything was fully functional. I think by this stage most of us had realised what lay ahead, and training drills were taken very seriously.

On 28 November, we drove back to Rundu and boarded an aircraft for a night flight to Mavinga, a town situated a couple of hundred kilometres inside Angola, which had previously been the scene of fierce fighting as the South African and Unita troops had driven back Fapla forces. It also housed the only serviceable airstrip that was not threatened by the Angolan Air Force. Mavinga was like a temporary logistics base from which all operations inside Angola were launched. The flight was made in total darkness and it was raining quite heavily when we arrived. Conversation on the aeroplane was limited, and I think the reality of our situation was beginning to sink in. We were going to war.

After landing, it was straight onto trucks again and we proceeded to move a few kilometres into the bush. I couldn't help but think that it reminded me of scenes from one of those Vietnam War movies; the climate was hot, wet and tropical, the vegetation was like a jungle. After driving slowly for about 10km we got off the trucks and were told to find a place to sleep, not too far away from where we had disembarked. It was raining heavily and everything was soaking wet. I erected a small shelter by tying my poncho between some trees and propping it up in the middle with a stick. A crude shelter like that is only big enough for one person and not the most effective in the world, but it does keep most of the rain off you. I lay down and tried to get some sleep.

When morning came, it was like waking up in another world. The bush was dense and silent, the climate oppressive and the flies overwhelming. It had stopped raining, so I set about sorting out my kit and drying everything out. Donald had erected his shelter close to mine, and we decided to join our groundsheets and ponchos together and make one big shelter that we could share, which was a bit more spacious and effective against the rain. I went over to where Lieutenant Strydom, our company commander, was camped so I could receive orders and perform whatever my role was in this new and unforgiving environment.

Administrative personnel were generally seen as pen-pushing office clerks who spent their entire national service behind a desk, but here there was not a desk in sight. The lieutenant informed me that I would be based with him in the command vehicle and, until we received our vehicles, there was not much to do other than ensure that everyone was present and accounted for.

When I got back to the shelter, I could not believe what I saw. There was Donald, kneeling down, with the barrel of his rifle in his mouth! My first instinct was to take the rifle away from him, which I did, and then to remove the loaded magazine. I tried to find out what was going on, and he told me that he just could not handle this and 'wanted out'. It was my duty, as a non-commissioned officer, to report this incident to an officer. I also felt that it would be better to get Donald out there and then, as there was no telling what he might do when things heated up, as they undoubtedly would before too long. I made the report and Donald was put on the next aeroplane out of Mavinga. This campaign was effectively only one day old, and already things were starting to get a bit hairy.

DIARY ENTRY

29/11/87
Everything is drying out, flies are even worse than before. Had incident with Donald putting rifle into his mouth and saying he was going to blow his brains out, took rifle off him and reported incident to Lt. Donald flew out.

When I look back at everything now, there are times that I can't help but wish it had been me leaving that day, but that was not to be. I think by that stage we were beginning to accept that there was a shitty job to do and that someone had to do it – and we were the ones sent to do it. Call it patriotic pride or whatever, some age-old emotions were definitely starting to stir in these young men destined for battle.

The next day, we took delivery of our vehicles from the outgoing troops who had completed Operation Modular and were preparing to be discharged at the end of their two years of national service. I was looking forward to finally getting into a vehicle, but nothing could have prepared me for the sight that greeted us when we went to sign for the vehicles. Carrying full kit and still adjusting to walking in the thick sand, we were greeted by a phalanx of the wildest, dirtiest-looking people I had ever seen. These guys had not shaved for months, and it looked as though they had not been near water for as long. They were wearing filthy overalls and their hair was long. They clapped and cheered as we walked through their ranks to our 'new' Ratel. I thought to myself, 'These guys look like animals, what the hell have they been doing up there?' As for the Ratel, there was no doubt that it had been through some serious shit over the past few months. It was pretty battered and quite a few things needed fixing before we could even think about taking it into a combat situation.

The next few days would be spent taking ammunition stock, assessing vehicle damage and driving the vehicles into Mavinga for the necessary repair work to be carried out. There were limited maintenance facilities at Mavinga, so we could send only a few vehicles at a time, until all had been repaired. I would occupy the gunner's position in the turret next to Lieutenant Strydom. This meant having to take a crash course in signals and gunnery, which

I did over the next few days. The rest of the crew consisted of Scott, the signals guy in charge of communications, and Robbertse, the driver. Lieutenant Strydom was a likeable and easy-going fellow and we got on well together. Scott was a laid-back character with sharp wit and an often dry sense of humour. He was good fun to be around and we shared many light-hearted moments, all in the name of preserving our sanity. However, Robbertse and I obviously had some kind of personality clash that no one could quite put a finger on – we just could not seem to agree on anything or be in the same space without bumping heads over something. My primary function involved liaison between the platoon and our support echelon, under the command of Sergeant McDonald, to ensure that the main force had all the necessary resources, ammunition and supplies to sustain itself on a daily basis.

Diary entry

30/11/87
Signed over vehicles and ammunition from outgoing troops. Moved slightly higher up North and set up temporary shelter.

6/12/87
Stock-taking of ammunition, tested weapons for working order, checked over vehicles and reported all repairable damage. Had first bath in a river, good to be clean again.

7 and 8/12/87
Took vehicle to Unita base (formerly a village) for major over-haul and repairs. Slept in Unita base and tried to communicate with Unita soldiers. They only speak what sounds like a mixture of Portuguese and Spanish. Managed to trade cigarettes and pieces of ratpacks. Ratpacks are starting to take their toll on

stomach now, wish I could get hold of some fresh meat and a few cold 'Charles Glass' [colloquial term for Castle Lager, a South African beer]. The houses and buildings here have all had the shit shot out of them; this could have been a nice little village at some stage. All the houses are built in a Spanish villa style (or what's left of them anyway). The countryside in general resembles a tropical rainforest, especially since it is the rainy season now. This country is beautiful, pity about the circumstances.

With all the repairs complete and weapons functional, it was time to start moving up towards Cuito Cuanavale, or 'the front' as it was known. Cuito was where we would do most of the fighting and, from all accounts, there had already been some heavy battles in the area. Our radio call sign for the command Ratel was Six-Zero, and we would now have to stay in constant radio contact with battle group commander Commandant Mike Muller, whose official call sign was Zero, though he later personalised it to 'Mike Mike', with the word 'Mike' being radio alphabet for the letter M.

The move northwards would also bring us within range of the Russian-made MiG 21 and MiG 23 fighter aircraft, so we would have to be even more alert from there on in. When MiGs were in the air, a general radio broadcast went out from Zero to all other command vehicles, which in turn would have to relay it to the platoons on their internal radio frequency. The warning call for MiGs was Victor-Victor, two words that we would hear at least once a day, every day, for the next four months. The call sign was derived from the Afrikaans term *vyandelike vliegtuig*, meaning enemy aircraft, and since radio alphabet for the letter V is Victor, the warning call was Victor-Victor.

The problem with enemy aircraft was that, as soon as they were reported as being in the air, all vehicles had to leave the tracks and seek shelter in the bush. This manoeuvre was known as 'fishbone', meaning that vehicles would leave the tracks in an alternating left–right pattern, resembling the skeleton of a fish. Once under some form of shelter, usually a tree, the entire vehicle had to be camouflaged with the aid of a net (known as a 'cammo-net'), carried on top of the vehicle. Each vehicle had its own net, which was rolled up in a way that allowed it to be unfurled quickly in the event of an aircraft warning. Although I realise this was a very necessary step in ensuring our force remained undetected, it was also extremely irritating having to perform it so often.

DIARY ENTRY

9/12/87

Left Mavinga at 05h00 on the way up to Cuito Cuanavale (the 'Hot Spot'). Encountered first Victor-Victor at 09h30 and took cover-up measures. Still quite a distance from Lomba, last stop before Cuito. Enemy intercepted our radio comms, hassled with constant VV threats, cammoed until earliest possible movement time of 16h30. For the first time now I'm seeing the reality of the enemy threat and their seriousness, and, by the same token, ours too. There is an uncomfortable tension in the crew, covered up by light humour most of the time, but in the times of silence the tension and sense of anticipation are so that you can almost reach out and touch it.

The flies are getting worse as we get closer to the front, it is said that the reason for this is the plentiful supply of corpses and rotting flesh left behind by the Faplas as they have been driven back. I'll have to wait and see it to believe it.

Time for coffee. Sitting around waiting for something to

happen is the worst part, one starts to think of home and loved ones – they say you should not do that, as it can cause you to lose your fighting edge.

10/12/87

Stopped for the first time since last night. Got out and grabbed some 'kaffir oranges' [a local hard-shelled fruit that contained pieces of grey fruit which tasted exactly like an orange] for breakfast. We are having coffee now and waiting for the tiffies to repair a log vehicle. We aren't too far from Cuito Cuanavale and apparently there is a minefield to be crossed on the way, hope all goes well.

At the moment I'm just feeling bloody exhausted and not really thinking of what lies ahead (maybe it's just as well). The entire crew is starting to show signs of bossies; myself included ('I am sailing'). The tiffies took their sweet time about the job and now we've lost radio contact with the rest of the force. We managed to close the gap and regain radio contact just in time to hear a VV warning (the usual crap – fishbone & cammo). After about 10 minutes we threw caution to the wind and decided together to make use of the air warning delay and catch up with the main force. All went well, luckily. We've now pulled into a closed laager formation about 10km from the front line and should be moving in tonight. Did final pre-battle procedures, i.e. clean the Browning [machine gun], get ammo into the turret and check radio comms.

My mind, in its tired state, has been wandering back to Civvie Street today, strange thoughts and very cold feelings. Civvie Street is a good few thousand km away and what's quite strange is that I don't feel like I have any ties to it at all. I'm beginning to feel like part of the bush and civilian life seems out of my grasp and understanding at the moment. Civvie life seems all too petty and shallow; they don't appreciate life, they just accept it. Life takes on a whole new meaning when you could lose it at any moment; I mean, think of the pressure of having your life threatened 24 hours a day, 7 days a week? (Crack!!!) To think that these words I'm writing now could be my last – quite something to try and accept; that's why we just laugh it off with silly humour and madness (bossies). An over-serious attitude will kill you.

3

Hostile Intent

W E WERE GETTING QUITE close to the front and it was becoming more and more apparent that it would not be long before we encountered some hostile direct fire from the enemy. There were more frequent air raid warnings, and although we had not yet seen a MiG, this would all change very soon. We were actually starting to get used to bush life: long periods between bathing, no shaving, living on ratpacks, and the fact that going to the toilet required little more than a shovel and a few pieces of toilet paper (and preferably a shady tree). Sleeping arrangements usually involved digging a shallow trench and placing your groundsheet or poncho in it, with your sleeping bag on top. When it rained, there was the option of sleeping under or inside the Ratel, but neither was particularly comfortable.

Our rifles were also permanently loaded and you did not dare go anywhere without your weapon – not even to the toilet. I think this was probably when most of us started to make the transition to bush life and accept that this would be the way we would live for a while, though we generally believed it would only be a few more weeks before we returned to base, maybe even in time for Christmas! But this operation would be plagued by endless delays. I now know that these were necessary and probably played a vital role in ensuring that the death toll on our side was not significantly higher. At the time, however, the information we were receiving from the commanders was still somewhat unclear, and resulted in a lot of driving around and manoeuvring into different positions. It seemed that the primary goal was to avoid detection by the enemy and remain concealed as far as possible, while the senior officers continued with their planning.

It was more frustrating than anything else, as we had no idea what was going on or how long we would have to be in that hellhole. We did not know what was going on at the tactical HQ in terms of the 'big-picture' stuff – all we could do was wait for an order to come through, react to it and then wait again. There was also no way of telling when we would actually go into combat, and, as a result, we had to be in a permanent state of readiness, 24 hours a day, so as to react at the drop of a hat.

This certainly added to the levels of tension and stress, which were becoming more evident. I remember quite clearly being extremely pissed off with a particular lieutenant, an arrogant prick who bore a striking likeness to a frog, when he decided to relieve me of my last two litres of water – at a time when we had run out of fresh water – while I was sleeping one night. I actually wanted to shoot him. There were also other little internal skirmishes breaking out among the troops, but I suppose this was only to be expected. Realistically, here was a bunch of guys from different walks of life, living in each other's faces for a prolonged period of time and under highly stressful conditions – at some point, something had to give.

Another factor highlighting this newfound level of constant alertness was the necessity to stand guard every night. This involved the establishment of a guard post (or 'listening post', as it was known) about 50 to 100m away from where the vehicles were parked. The guys at the listening post were generally rotated every two to four hours, and it was their job to pick up any strange noises and report these (by radio) back to the guard commander, stationed at the platoon command vehicle. The guard commander would have to relay any reports of strange sounds/movement/lights back to the force commander's vehicle. Being guard commander meant that you would stand a six-hour shift, either from 18h00 to midnight or from midnight to 06h00, and be responsible for waking up the next watch, escorting the members to the listening post and ensuring that the rotations ran smoothly. This became one of my functions and, while it generally went without a hitch, there were some occasions when things got pretty tense.

One such incident involved my old school friend, Layton, who was at the listening post on this particular night. I was guard commander and it was standard practice to do radio tests every so often to ensure that everything was still fine and the radio batteries were functioning correctly. Layton was one of those people who manage to find humour in any situation and was generally regarded as the 'class clown' – he always had a joke to share and could brighten up any situation.

I am uncertain of the exact time when this incident occurred, but it was fairly late at night when Layton radioed through to me to say that he could see some lights in the nearby bush. At first I thought he was joking and just trying to liven up a boring guard stint, but then I noticed something different about his voice; it sounded unsteady, and I knew that something was going on out there. Layton said that there were lights moving around in the bush and it looked as though they were heading straight for our positions. I immediately woke the lieutenant and asked him to come and listen. I also radioed the battalion commander to find out if we had any vehicles in the area – the answer was negative.

By now there were a few people around the radio and Layton was still reporting these strange lights coming closer and closer all the time. His voice was a lot shakier and I could tell that he was really worried. By this stage, half the battalion was awake and wondering what the hell was going on. We were prepared, but we had no idea what for. The situation went on for about an hour until the lights changed direction and moved off. We were all very relieved – probably none more so than Layton.

At first light we sent a small party out to have a look at the area where the lights had been seen. To this day there are differing opinions as to what was going on. The general consensus was that it was a Fapla reconnaissance patrol sent out to locate our positions, but this was later dismissed by some of the senior officers, who said it was South African forces. Sergeant McDonald found some tracks that convinced him it was a Fapla patrol, and the fact remains that if it was indeed South African troops, why did nobody know who they were or that they were so close to us?

DIARY ENTRY

11/12/87

Last night I nearly shat my pants; while lying on the top of the Ratel a signal flare went up quite close to us. About 3 minutes later, 2 helicopters came with a shit-speed just over the treetops (that's where I nearly shat myself). I think (hope) they were ours, but I'm not certain. At the moment we are under VV delay again.

Well, I've just seen my first MiG, a damn nice plane, but not friendly. He bombed our artillery (about 4km away) with a 'Fiver' but apparently he missed – Pilot Platneus!

It is actually quite frightening when you hear that bastard going over, you don't know if he's seen you or not. After his second turn I must admit that I was about ready to head for the foxhole and my legs were trembling. To be honest, I haven't experienced this kind of fear before; this was the first time my legs actually trembled and I started sweating through fear.

12/12/87

Last night was another long night; we drove right through the night and right through an artillery offensive. My nerves are on edge after a night of having bombs hurled directly over my head – and the noise of each shot shakes you incredibly (G5). We have taken up positions only a few km from the front line and our next movement should be an offensive on Cuito Cuanavale. The G5s have started up again, they are now directly behind us and the earth literally shakes with every shot. We are making really sure that we have sufficient bomb shelter after hearing that 'Fiver' drop in this area yesterday. Well, there's nothing to do for now but to lie low and wait for orders to attack. I think I'll check the Browning one more time, clean & oil her and make sure there's a couple of thousand rounds in the turret with me.

I still can't really grasp that this is war – it's for real, however; it is becoming more apparent as my nerves are getting more on edge each day. I suppose when that first bomb falls within a few hundred metres, everyone will be shaken into the reality of the situation. It sounds cold, but I am trying not to think of home at the moment, because here you have to be alert all the time, no time for wandering thoughts. This is where men start to pray again. About 22 tanks pulled in last night and have taken up positions about 4km behind us – looks like there's going to be a rumble in the jungle before very long.

I've just been informed that we are going in for an attack tonight. In case something happens, just remember, I love you Mom.

13/12/87

We were scheduled for an attack early this morning, but it had to be called off due to Recce personnel within the enemy lines. We've moved into a new position and are awaiting orders – attack should take place on Tuesday.

I've been temporarily relieved of my position in the gun turret by something I call 'The Frog'. He no longer has a place since his Ratel rolled and is currently US [unserviceable]. He is a windgat [arrogant] little bastard whom I don't like one little bit. We got new orders this evening and it seems that we will be locating enemy positions for the next couple of days before hitting them. Our water tanks have just run dry, shit!

14/12/87

No water. I awoke and located my last 2 litres of water which I had stashed – the bottle was empty and all my suspicion points towards the Frog. I'm seriously considering putting a bullet in him and if he screws me one more time, I'll bloody do it! He must not try and push his weight around out here, I've got too much ammo and my mind is not exactly in a very healthy state, especially after going for a day without water. By the end of today our crew might be one less – what a pity!

Last night, Scott and I spent a few hours packing our webbing in case the Ratel takes a direct hit. Fully packed, between us we have got 800 R4 rounds, 5 HE grenades, 8 smoke grenades, 4 signal flares, 4 ratpacks, 4 litres of water (provided we get water), 200 chlorine tabs, 4 bandages, a compass, binoculars, a groundsheet and my ammo vest. If we have to make a duck we'll be well prepared.

We got some fresh meat and a few beers when we pulled into the laager and because of the MiGs, we had difficulty making a fire to braai [barbeque] the meat. I ate mine raw; it's actually bloody nice, it's got a lot more flavour than cooked meat. Our water tanks were also refilled and now we have water again. I've just heard that while driving last night, we got horribly lost and noticed some lights just on the other side of the Chambinga River. Nobody knew what they were and only after checking on our map did we realise that we were within 1km of the Fapla

66th brigade (enemy, 800 strong). There was also an extra set of lights behind our convoy which turned out to be a Fapla recon vehicle sent in to have a look. Last night was quite a narrow escape; I think we were bloody lucky they didn't decide to attack.

15/12/87

The same old crap, changing positions and setting up new ones. The MiGs came in early this morning (4 of them) and bombed only a couple of kms behind us. They are a bloody nuisance. At the moment we are awaiting orders for a possible attack tonight; I hope so because the constant moving around and avoiding detection is getting boring, I think it's about time for some action and a bit of blood to flow. It's hard to believe that Christmas is only 10 days away; it's no big deal because time has no meaning out here, just the difference between day and night means that we no longer have to shit for the MiGs and the artillery and most of the flies are gone; but then it's the turn of the mosquitoes and piss moths.

At last, a positive sign. Four of our Mirages came over at tree-top height and went in and bombed the shit out of someone near Cuito Cuanavale. I think their target was the Cuito Bridge to cut off the supply link of the Fapla troops. We've set our observation post overlooking the 25th brigade and it shouldn't be long now till we hit them with everything we've got.

16/12/87

OPs [forward observers] are reporting all movement, mortars took up new positions within striking distance, and hopefully we'll take them tonight. So far the MiGs haven't bothered us today; I think they're a bit scared after yesterday's Mirage attack – yellow bastards!

It is 23h30 and we have just completed our first attack and I think some people are bleeding – good!

17/12/87

We've moved to a new position and should be refilling tonight. Shit, we're under mortar fire, 120mm I think, it is 10h30 and I'm going to take cover.

The D30s joined in for a while, but it wasn't long before our G5s dropped a few big ones on them and wiped them out. Those bastards managed to drop bombs all around us, but were unable to score any direct hits – Gunner Platneus!

It is now about 15h00 and we've moved out of cover. The G5s have started firing again, this time on the Cuito Bridge; good luck guys. It is quite frightening hearing bombs explode a few hundred metres away and knowing they are meant for you – although we seem to be getting used to it now and also the degree of inaccuracy of the Platneus troops. I should be going out into the OP for the next attack which will probably be quite soon.

At last, it looks like SA has woken up; 2 Mirages have just streaked over the top of the trees towards 25th brigade. We heard the commotion from here as they made their strike. 25th brigade should be even more reduced after that. Platneus is bleeding, good! (Better him than me.)

18/12/87

In general a very quiet day. Did a bit of trading with the Unitas, my Portuguese is improving. Settled down for a braai with some fresh meat.

19/12/87

On the move again and none too soon. We are about 5km from last night's positions and are sitting under cover watching the MiGs bomb our previous positions (sorry Platneus, but we will always be one step ahead of you). Just sitting here listening to some music, I realise it's been 2 weeks since any of us took a bath. A man starts to develop a kind of smell that blends in with the bush after a while. Deodorant is a forgotten civvie luxury, it's hard to believe one can actually live in these conditions and get so used to it that you actually just accept it and it becomes like a new way of life. We ran through a full attack drill this afternoon and it makes me think it won't be long before something interesting happens.

20/12/87
Set up alongside the Cuito River and spent the morning swimming and washing. The water is crystal clear and you can literally swim with the fish. The fish here are in abundance, a fisherman's paradise – big buggers. It's hard to believe that just a few km upstream, this very same river is going to be the scene of one very big and bloody battle – it is the dividing line between us and the Fapla forces.

We watched some of our bombs falling behind a piece of high ground on the other side of the river – we are close enough to see the smoke and dust from the explosions. There have been more enemy bombs falling around us today, but they are still way off course. Well, all I can say at the moment is that it's good to be clean again and put on some clean clothes.

21–22/12/87
We've been waiting for diesel to refill with and otherwise just parking off getting bored. There has been artillery fire landing near us for both days, but nothing too close for comfort yet. There is wind of a big attack planned for the 24th (on the 21st brigade) and then hopefully something on the 25th as well. Just think about killing people on Christmas Day!

23–24/12/87
Moved down south to the Lomba River in order to join up with the rest of the force. The plan is to move the entire force up

and then attack from a flank. The prospect of going home soon looks a bit more likely. I think we will probably be withdrawing after the big attack, but it will have to be a really big one. We've got a vegspan [combat team] covering the Cuito River, which will be the only way out for Fapla if they run – if all goes as planned, we should take out most of them, hope it happens soon. Well it looks like we'll be spending Christmas in our current positions. I'm hoping to score a bottle of Captain Morgan [rum] and spend the day in oblivion – try to forget about what I'm missing out on back home.

25/12/87
Christmas Day – big deal, just another day – the sun comes up, the sun goes down. We've just heard, from the horse's mouth, that at 18h00 we start moving towards Cuito. The climax of the operation will start on the 27th & 28th and we hope to have cleared up by the 5th of January and then get the hell out of here. It's about bloody time we started doing something. I can't help thinking of home today. Merry Christmas Mom and Gary; I hope you're coping OK. Sorry I can't be there to give you support, but I'm there in thought.

I have just had the best news ever. The Frog has departed and vacated my seat in the gun turret, and I'll be able to shoot the shit out of those bastards in the attack!

26/12/87
We drove through an old Fapla camp this morning and found a complete skeleton. The guys wanted to mount the skull on the front of the Ratel, but the Lt cracked and said it would be a bad omen and bring us bad luck. Shit, I'm burning up with fever and have been since last night. There's some kind of bite on my arm, swollen and with a big hole in the middle – reckon I've either got tick-bite fever or malaria, how shit.

28/12/87

D-Day has been shifted to the 30th and we should be positioned on the edge of a shona waiting for Platneus to come running across and then we'll open up on them. My fever seems to have broken and I'm feeling a bit better. There was one shrapnel wound that came in last night, not too serious, but it just shows the bombs are getting closer all the time. Change of plans, going in for attack now, 12h00, will elaborate later.

We moved into an ambush position in front of the artillery as there was a Fapla battalion moving in for an attack. At about 21h00 we heard that a 400-strong infantry group was coming directly towards us – they must have stopped, because we haven't made contact with them yet. It looks like D-Day plans might have to wait, thanks to these bastards. Anyway, it shouldn't be long before we make contact with them.

29/12/87

The most frightening day of my life. We found out early that the Fapla battalion had advanced to within two kilometres from us and just as we got ready to attack, the MiGs came over and their bombing was on target this time. We spent a couple of hours pinned down in our foxholes with helmets on, just listening to the bombs exploding around us and praying that they would not make a direct hit – and they didn't, but the Fapla battalion started hitting us with rocket fire and pinned us down again. When we finally managed to advance, the Faplas had already begun the retreat. We drove them a good 10km back, and then they broke up and ran for it. We've come back into our original positions for the night and just heard that our 90s [Ratel 90] took out a few of those bastards.

We are spending the night here on our own, as the rest of the company is going to help with a contact in the west. We spent the whole night on guard, rifles ready and with instructions to shoot first and ask questions later, as the Faplas would probably try to infiltrate our position and gain some territory. Well, at the end of the day, all I can say is that we reached our goal for today in driving them back and I'm not ashamed to say that today I really was scared in that foxhole. Today made everybody realise what real war is all about. After the bombing and successful defence of our positions, there seemed to be quite a good spirit among the guys, I just hope it stays that way.

30/12/87
Spent the day resting and only got bothered twice by the MiGs. I took a walk over to where the G5s were firing and had a shot with one of them – Wow! What a gun! Hopefully the bomb killed some of those bastards!

31/12/87
Another day of sitting around waiting and doing bugger-all.

01/01/88
New Year's Day – big deal. There was a brigade attack launched at midnight by all of our long-range weapons, Fapla started off the New Year with a big bang! We are changing positions again this morning to avoid the MiGs as they will be looking for the guns that fired last night.

4

Playing by Different Rules

NEW YEAR'S DAY MARKED an important point in the operation. Morale was very low and we were all beginning to wonder what we were actually doing there. Besides the limited attack on 16 December, which was only on a 'possible' enemy position, all we seemed to have done during our six weeks in Angola was drive around and act as target practice for Fapla. The general feeling was that we had sacrificed Christmas and New Year (potentially with our families) to act as cannon fodder without really being able to fight back.

There was a lot of aggression and resentment building up and it needed to be channelled somewhere. Compounding this issue were the propaganda pamphlets distributed by Fapla in an attempt to demoralise us. I must confess that the first time I saw them, they did have some effect. There were four different pamphlets that had been dropped randomly out of aircraft in various areas. All carried the same message: 'Desert or Surrender'. The spelling and grammar were poor, but the point was made by the use of extremely graphic images of South African soldiers who had been killed in previous operations in Angola. The enemy was saying that, unless we deserted or surrendered, we would end up like the men in the pictures: dead.

The initial shock factor soon passed, however, and I believe these pamphlets actually did more to fuel the burning anger inside us than to deter us. Anyhow, even if someone did want to desert, we were hundreds of kilometres inside a foreign country and certainly not about to walk back to South Africa. At one stage, some of the senior officers told us to stop collecting the pamphlets, until someone remarked that they were printed on recycled paper that felt really soft, almost like … that's right, toilet paper! Fapla's propaganda efforts had helped us out in terms of 'essential supplies', and the notion of literally wiping your arse on the enemy's propaganda message was quite appealing.

The SADF, meanwhile, was waging its own brand of psychological warfare by deploying 'Ground Shout' teams. Most of us knew about these teams at the time, but did not fully understand how they operated or what their purpose was. It was only in later years, after reading a piece written by a member of one such team, that I fully understood what had gone on.

We heard that they would move around on the opposite side of a river near a Fapla brigade and cut down trees in order to create the impression that they were building a bridge for an attack force to cross the water. They would also play music over loudspeakers just prior to an artillery attack, which would send the Fapla troops scurrying for their bunkers. The first few times, there really would be an artillery attack after the music, but then they would just play the music for a period, thus lulling Fapla into a false sense of security, so that they started ignoring the music and carried on with their normal activities. Then a sudden attack would catch them unawares and above ground, resulting in high numbers of casualties. The propaganda teams did not actually cut down any trees, but played recordings of chainsaws and other equipment over the loudspeaker system to create the bridge-building illusion.

There was also another element at play among the SADF troops, a phenomenon affectionately known as NAFI, an acronym for No Ambition and Fuck-all Inspiration. This was evident in the general manner of the troops and the way they spoke and conducted themselves. A common expression was 'I feel fuck-all', and in most cases, this was absolutely true; we did not have much feeling towards anything or anyone. All we wanted was to get this operation over with and get out of there – but not before killing a few of the enemy.

It was almost as if a kind of bloodlust had built up, and nobody seemed to have any fear of killing – or dying, for that matter. We had been there long enough and had come under fire just about every day without sustaining any serious casualties, so why couldn't we just go in and have a crack at these guys? I think we were probably erring very close to the 'bullet-proof' stage and had no fear of the enemy – they had pretty much thrown everything at us (or so we thought) and not so much as even dented anything. Unfortunately, we would crash back down to earth with a bang before too long.

Diary entry

04/01/88
No entries until now, because I was totally out of it with some kind of virus that I picked up. All that happened was that the MiGs gave us a hard time with constant bombing raids – the bombs were falling all around us and they scored a direct hit on one of our water trucks, without casualty though. They have already been over this morning at 06h00, and will probably be back before too long. These are days of lying low in the foxholes and praying hard. My fever is finally broken and I'm feeling a bit better this morning. I've been having weird dreams about Civvie Street and I am not sure I'll be able to adapt again, and that worries me.

Newsflash: the Cuito Bridge has been blown up, a great turning point in this war, as it cuts off all supplies to the brigades lying east of Cuito River and now they are sitting ducks. It's just a matter of time now. They can't swim through the river due to crocodiles, and every time they move down to get drinking water, the G5s bombard them while playing music to them. There were another 184 enemy fatalities reported yesterday by our forward observers.

05/01/88
Dug ourselves solidly into new positions. When standing in the bunker, I can't touch the ground level! NAFI emerged as king of the day, with lots of negative feelings among the guys. Layton and I are well on our way to becoming basket cases of bush madness and bomb madness (bossies!). We get together on a daily basis and speak the biggest load of shit imaginable for as long as possible – it helps to escape the shittiness of this war. It may sound stupid, but it gives you something else to think about and keeps your mind active and occupied for a while.

06/01/88
We changed positions again last night and I was woken up with a 'Condition Red' on the radio (meaning that the MiGs are close, have acquired a target and are coming in for a strike). There were no foxholes yet, so we all jumped into the Ratel. The bastards came close enough for the explosions to shake the Ratel. Anyway, the foxhole has been dug, about 2m deep, and he can come back and try again. This time I'm ready!

Some of the guys have moved up to the river where the Faplas are sitting on the other side. They are busy with some psychological action where they cut down trees and make noises like they are building a bridge to cross over and attack Fapla. They then play some music over loudspeakers and then fire in some G5 bombs. After shooting, they play more music, sounds like lots of drums or something.

We have just been told to construct proper bunkers instead of just digging foxholes, because the MiGs have got a new bomb called a 'cluster bomb'. Clusters are big bombs containing a lot of small bombs (like hand grenades) and explode above the ground, scattering all the small bombs all over the place and causing some serious damage. Our bunker is now just over 2m deep with about half a ton of sand and logs on top of it making a roof – once again we've got the preparation to give the MiGs a big toffee!

07/01/88
Operation 'Balbak' continues [directly translated means 'ball bake' and refers to lying around and baking your balls in the sun while waiting for something to happen].

08/01/88
Awoke at 01h00 with orders to move out, join up with Bravo Company and locate an advancing Fapla battalion. Everything was looking good and at about 06h55 the front Ratels reported seeing fresh tracks. We armed our weapons and got ready. At 07h00, two foot soldiers were spotted and one of the Ratels began to close in on them. A troop-carrying vehicle emerged from the bush line and Captain Terblanche made the announcement we had all been waiting for: 'Contact, left, 9-o-clock!' The entire force swung to the left and I had my gun sights dead on target. We all anxiously awaited the order to fire, but it never came, as the other soldiers identified themselves as Unita troops (they nearly saw their arses). Anyway, we carried on with our search, but to no avail. We got a bit of flak from the MiGs and the Stalin Organs [multiple rocket launchers], but nothing too serious.

09/01/88

Spent the day quite peacefully and carried on with refilling vehicles etc.

10/01/88

Moved into new positions and there is talk of D-Day being just around the corner. They are just waiting for decent cloud cover and a moonless night.

We have just been attacked by what we think is the MiG 29. They came in just over the trees and from a sitting position in my foxhole, I saw them diving in directly towards me. Those few seconds felt like a lifetime and I went totally lame and thought that this was the end. My thoughts went back to that scene in 'The Wall'[1] and I was just in too much of a state of shock to even start praying. That was a vision and sound that is going to stay in my memory for a hell of a long time.

At the moment it is only 13h30, so they still have the whole day to try again. Their bombs fell just behind us this time and now I'm really starting to doubt whether I'll come out of here alive. They must have seen us on that last run, and now it's just a matter of time before they come in for another strike. I am beginning to understand the true meaning of the words 'fear' and 'pressure'.

Thank God, the weather has come up and there was quite a violent electric storm, which lasted for the rest of the daylight hours. Tomorrow is another day though.

11/01/88

Spent the day lying low under some rocket fire, no casualties or damage though. We started the D-Day form-up late in the afternoon and joined up with the rest of our guys, forming a

---

1   Alan Parker's 1982 film *Pink Floyd The Wall*, which tells of a rock star's descent into madness in the midst of his physical and social isolation from everyone around him.

powerful strike force. The MiGs must try some low-flying stunts again and they'll shit – we've now got 6 anti-aircraft guns along with 6 Stinger crews [ground-to-air missiles]. We drove through the night and formed a laager in the early hours of the morning.

12/01/88

We're lying low and just waiting. The D-Day march has officially begun and the attack was postponed by 24 hours this morning due to a break in the weather and clear skies. It's about 5 o'clock now and the clouds seem to be building up into a thick, low bank – if it's like this tomorrow, then we'll be going in for sure. The actual 'destroy' part of our attack is expected to last no more than 48 hours, but I can say now, those 48 hours will be the longest in our lives. During the attack we will not be allowed to leave our vehicles, even if we are attacked by MiGs. It's going to be hard times, but the adrenalin is running high and everybody now just wants blood – after all, these bastards owe us a Christmas and New Year with our families. They're going to pay dearly!!

4 SAI will head up the main attack on 21st brigade and we'll be placed in a cut-off position waiting for Fapla's retreat and preventing other brigades from joining in to help; sitting on top of a hill, we'll be able to pick them off at will, these communist bastards!

13/01/88 (D-DAY !!!)

We moved out at around 12h00 and proceeded to our positions. Made contact at about 15h00 with 2 BTRs and some ground troops – neutralised them with a 90mm bombardment – bodies lying all over the place. We went on and took up our position on high ground where I went into an OP in a tree with binoculars and a radio. I had an excellent view of the battle. The tanks came up as expected to help out with the

21st and our 90s spoke hard and proud; 2 tanks shot out within 10 minutes and a BTR exploded and its ammo went off for the rest of the night. Oom [uncle] Gert was driving past the wreck when a rocket went off and took out his left front wheel.

14/01/88

The attack continued and the MiGs started coming in low, but each time they came in, our artillery put white phos over the 25th brigade and they ended up bombing their own guys. One MiG came streaking over our heads and then we heard anti-aircraft fire go up after it and a few minutes later it came back over our heads; only this time it sounded more like a lawnmower than a MiG. The pilot bailed and the MiG went down! Early in the afternoon we spotted 4 vehicles moving across the shona, one of which looked like a tank, and reported it. The mortars came into action and put some bombs in among them. The troops bailed and headed into the bush line, some of them peeling off their clothing as they ran, possibly because of the white phos.[2] As we were getting ready to pull back, a Unita battalion that was with us made contact about 300m in front of us. We could see the Faplas running across the shona 'kaalgat' [naked] and dropping like flies as they ran. We came into action again and dropped 4 more bombs slap in the middle of them. We could actually see the bastards scatter and fall as the bombs went off – each bomb taking about 20 of them with it. We continued our pull-back and drove through the night to a refill point. While leaving the contact area, I saw three bodies on the ground. One had a tree fallen on his head, another had been shot to pieces and the third one had

---

2   This incident was mentioned in *War in Angola – The Final South African Phase*, Heitman, p. 210, where the reason for the troops discarding their clothing was linked to a pamphlet, supposedly distributed by Unita, in which Fapla soldiers were urged to remove their clothing as a sign of wanting to surrender. This information was not available at the time of the incident.

been driven over by a tank and cut clean in half. The bodies were all bloated and a bloody mess. The flies were taking full advantage too.

On the way we came under BM-21 rocket fire. The bloody things fell about 100m to the left of our Ratel, and, as I put my hand up to close the hatch, it was just about ripped off by the shockwaves from the explosions.

15/01/88
Now in a laager waiting to refill, probably going in for another attack on another target soon.

16–19/01/88
Refilled with water, food and ammo. Next attack should be tomorrow.

It was round about this point that my writing efforts slowed considerably, with the exception of recording contact reports and 'scorecards' after each battle. At first I put this down to a lack of new information to write about. We were doing the same sort of movements that we had been doing prior to the last attack: avoiding detection, ducking and diving from the MiGs on a daily basis, taking cover from artillery fire, checking and preparing equipment, and generally getting sick of being in Angola.

Upon later reflection though, I realised that it was much more than this. I was shocked and appalled by what I had witnessed and been a part of in the first attack. There was a distinct lack of respect for the dead, and we would actually laugh and joke about the bodies we saw lying around. Taking this one step further were the guys who went in pursuit of souvenirs and mementos of the war to take home. Cuban-made camouflage uniforms, worn by Fapla, became a sought after possession. It was a challenge to see if you could collect enough pieces to make up a complete uniform. Boots probably held the highest value, as they usually had to be removed from dead bodies. Jackets, shirts and caps were generally easier to come by, but trousers were pretty scarce, too, and in many instances were acquired at the same time as boots.

As Unita troops were usually tasked with the mopping up operations following a battle, they had the best access to these items and would generally salvage whatever they felt they could use in terms of clothing and equipment. This soon resulted in a primitive bartering system that saw us trade items of clothing with each other in order to try to obtain that seemingly elusive prize of a complete set of Fapla camouflage uniform. The other challenge was to get hold of a complete set of the Angolan currency notes, the Kwanza, which, although totally worthless in monetary terms, made for a nice little souvenir.

There we were, supposedly civilised, God-fearing young men, engaging in possibly the most disrespectful and barbaric acts imaginable – collecting the possessions of the dead for little more than our own amusement. I think we did it more as a way of staying sane and blocking out the brutal reality and gravity of the situation we found ourselves in, but it was also a way of numbing our senses to the trauma of having to deal with dead and disfigured bodies for the first time in our lives (for most of us, anyway). I suppose the underlying rationale was that if we could become desensitised and accustomed to dealing with violent death, we would somehow cope better with our situation and surroundings. And what better way to become accustomed to death than by touching and facing it head on? It became more of a game than anything else, and I think that for many of us it was the only way we could mask our true feelings about the brutality of the situation in which we found ourselves. To this day, I still feel sick inside when I recall some of the sights I saw in Angola.

Certain people were better at this 'game' than others and would stop at nothing to get what they wanted. One troop, who shall remain nameless, but who was also the main instigator behind wanting to hang the skull up on the front of the Ratel, came to me with a pair of Cuban boots after the attack on 21 Brigade on 13 and 14 January. He told me that he had originally given them to his lieutenant, but then the lieutenant asked him where he got them from, and he said he had taken them off a dead body. The lieutenant did not keep the boots. But I did. By the time we finally left Angola, I not only had a full set of Kwanzas, but my uniform collection was complete: a cap, shirt, jacket, trousers, boots and even a groundsheet. This is not something that I am particularly proud of today, but it does give an accurate reflection of the mental state we must have been in at the time to engage in such acts without any emotion whatsoever. In many ways, I likened our situation to the one described in the book *Lord of the Flies*, where normal people can be transformed into primitive and barbaric animals when placed in a different environment or subjected to a different set of rules.

The other factor influencing my writing was that I had now witnessed people dying and played an active role in the destruction of life. This gets back to the whole 'changing-of-the-rules' thing that I spoke about at the beginning of the book. These were definitely not the rules that I had been raised by. I was still struggling to come to terms with my own father's death, yet here I was involved in the taking of other lives in an extremely violent manner. The confusion this created within me was easily overcome at the time by believing in a simple creed: It was either him or me.

This somehow justified and made it easier to accept and continue numbly doing whatever I was told to do, without question or judgement.

5

My Bloody Valentine

After the attack on 21 Brigade, we soon settled back into our normal routine of preparing for the next attack, only to have it delayed for one or other reason. This usually had to do with weather conditions or the lack of serviceable vehicles and equipment. Due to the air supremacy of the MiGs and the threat they posed, it was generally better to launch an attack when there was overhead cloud cover to hinder the pilot's vision. If they decided to fly in below the clouds, they risked being taken out by anti-aircraft fire or ground-to-air missiles. The attack on 21 Brigade had been fairly easy and we had not encountered any stiff resistance from Fapla, nor did we have any serious injuries to South African troops, which is probably what contributed to the kind of blasé attitude towards this war that was beginning to creep in.

We laughed and joked about the last attack, and in some dark way were actually looking forward to the next one – Fapla was a walkover and this was going to be a breeze. Bearing in mind that this operation was our first real war experience, and that it was nothing like the movies, I'm not surprised that we felt the way we did. However, there was one threat that was always in the back of our minds, but never really spoken about: chemical weapons – gas!

When we signed over our vehicles from the outgoing troops, I noticed that the package included gas masks. This was really a preventative measure, as it was believed that Fapla (or the Cubans) were in possession of chemical weapons such as mustard gas or other nerve agents, but nobody had actually used the gas masks yet. The chemical weapons training we received was for use in the seemingly unlikely event of a gas attack launched by the enemy. The drill was pretty standard.

In the event of a gas attack being detected, a general warning – 'Gas! Gas! Gas!' – would be issued over the command net on the radio. Troops had to react immediately by placing their ponchos over their heads to protect their bodies, then don the gas masks, making sure they were tightly sealed to their faces, then pull the poncho hoods over their heads. We would then proceed to a designated area where some kind of big shower would be set up, strip naked and go through the shower ensuring that we washed ourselves thoroughly before coming out at the other side. Everything that had been exposed to the gas (clothing, equipment, vehicles) would effectively remain outside the shower and simply be abandoned – we were to literally just walk away from everything, even the clothing we were wearing at the time. We would occasionally practise these drills (just up to the poncho and mask stage) in order to stay sharp and up to speed with the procedure, but I don't think anyone really believed it would ever happen.

I'm not sure how the subject arose, but one day, while sitting around and chatting about nothing in particular, somebody brought up the subject of gas and asked: 'What will you do if you've been hit by gas and know you are going to die?' Well, this was certainly not appropriate dinner table conversation, but it did open up a whole new area of personal dilemma. The information we had been given was that if you did get hit by gas, a slow and extremely painful death was an absolute certainty – a lot like when a person is exposed to radiation. Layton, as usual, was part of this conversation and it lasted for most of the day, with all kinds of morbid scenarios being explored in graphic detail. The final conclusion: We would all write a letter saying that, in the event of becoming contaminated with gas, we gave permission to our friends to shoot us – and the letter had to be signed, witnessed and carried with us at all times. It was almost like signing your own death warrant. I don't think anyone actually wrote the letter, but it was always at the back of my mind. Once again, this illustrates the frame of mind we were in at the time and the type of behaviour that had become normal and acceptable under the circumstances.

Almost a month had passed since the attack on 21 Brigade, and we knew that our next target had been identified as 59 Brigade, which was significantly stronger than 21, but we did not know exactly when the attack would take place. It was in the last few days leading up to this attack that I became acutely aware of my intuition – you know, that little voice inside all of us that warns us about something (also called a 'gut feeling') and which, in most cases, we tend to ignore. I had often experienced this feeling during my life, but never as strongly as this. It was so powerful that I even wrote about it in my diary.

DIARY ENTRY

10/02/88
We have been lying low until now and planning a 'big' one. We should move in tonight, if the weather holds. We picked up 2 Fapla Recces today, so it looks like we'll be moving just in time. The MiGs have still been pretty regular, although they have not made any direct hits yet.

Layton got his ticket out of here today; the poor bastard has some kind of liver infection and will be heading out on the next chopper. I'm actually worried about this next attack, because Fapla have got some new 23mils [ZU-23-4 anti-aircraft gun], each gun has 4 barrels with about 1 200 rpm/pb [rounds per minute, per barrel]. These bloody things go in one side of a Ratel and out the other, taking with it anyone who's in its way! The plan is to attack the remaining brigades and then move on and take Tumpo – a bit ambitious with the small force we have. I don't want to become negative, but I don't feel good about this one – there's a voice inside my head saying that we've bitten off more than we can chew this time. I hope to God we all make it out of this one alive, but I have my doubts.

12/02/88
Attack delayed until better weather comes in. My bad feeling was reinforced last night by a really shitty dream that, no matter which way I interpret it, the message is the same: my time is up.

13/02/88
It looks like tomorrow is the big day and I still have that horrible feeling inside me. Church parade will be held tonight, which is a sure sign of us going in. Going in is a definite, but coming out is where the question mark lies. The threat of mustard gas is much greater now and I'm really not looking forward to this attack. In my dream the other night I saw Dad, and he took a firm grip on my arm and said, 'Get ready, we're going now.' Maybe it's time for me to go; if so, I just hope I'll be joining Dad where he is, because he seems to be happy and in no difficulty. I don't want to go into this attack negative, but I can't help feeling that my time is near. Tomorrow is Valentine's Day, an appropriate day to die?

Our Father, Which art in Heaven, Hallowed be Thy name. Thy kingdom come. Thy will be done on earth as it is in Heaven. Give us this day our daily bread, and forgive us our trespasses as we forgive those who trespass against us. And lead us not into temptation, but deliver us from evil. For Thine is the kingdom, the power, and the glory, for ever and ever. Amen.

With 59 Brigade being regarded as the key to the Fapla defences, it was imperative to attack their position and destroy them, or at least drive them back, along with the Fapla mobile reserve force consisting primarily of 3 Tank Battalion. The close proximity of all the Fapla brigades, after being driven back in previous attacks towards the Tumpo area, meant that there was a real threat of support coming from other brigades once the 59th had been attacked. The primary assault would be launched by 4 SAI, with 61 Mech being deployed in a cut-off position to prevent interference by other brigades. We would also act as a mobile reserve to deal with any counter-attack launched by Fapla and to support 4 SAI in a subsequent attack on 25 Brigade, should they still be in their positions after 59 Brigade had been destroyed. At the time, we did not have access to this kind of detailed information relating to the battle plans – we were given a brief synopsis of the situation, issued with orders and told where to go and what to do. I am only able to provide detailed tactical information now as a result of consulting Helmoed-Romer Heitman's book, *War in Angola – The Final South African Phase*. The bottom line was that we were in for a big fight that would be nothing like the previous attacks.

Both 4 SAI and 61 Mech moved out of their positions on the night of 13 February into their respective forward assembly areas. We reached ours in the early hours, some time between 01h00 and 02h00, and were told to get some rest, as it was going to be a long day. We were the first to move out in the morning and things were going very slowly, thanks to the MiGs. Around midday, some of them actually attacked us – but to no avail. By about 14h00, we had arrived at our designated position and began moving into battle formation (Arrowhead or V). The tanks made up the front of the arrowhead, with a mixture of Bravo Company's infantry Ratels (Ratel 20s) and the anti-tank Ratel 90s forming up on the flanks. I had been transferred to the mortar command Ratel with the call sign 6-0-A (Six-Zero-Alpha) under the command of Lieutenant Saaiman, the mortar platoon commander. Immediately in front of 6-0-A was Commandant Mike Muller's battalion command Ratel with the call sign 0 (Zero).

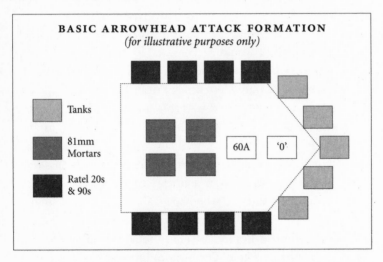

BASIC ARROWHEAD ATTACK FORMATION
(for illustrative purposes only)

Tanks

81mm Mortars

Ratel 20s & 90s

60A   '0'

The radio communication structure was set up so that each platoon (tanks, infantry, mortars and anti-tank) had its own internal communication network through which instructions could be relayed from the respective command vehicles. These vehicles also carried a second radio, which connected them to the battalion command network and the battalion commander (0 in this case). He was linked up to the main command network, which allowed him to

Remains of some of the buildings in and around
Mavinga following Operation Modular

Standard sleeping arrangements involved a shallow trench, groundsheet, sleeping bag and a rucksack for a pillow – no tents. Note the close proximity of the rifle

The traditional foxhole, which later underwent modifications to form a group bunker

Following pages: Propaganda pamphlets distributed by Fapla (front and reverse)

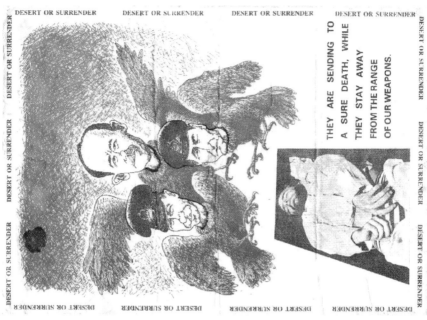

WHERE ARE THOSE WHO SENT YOU TO ANGOLA, WHERE DEATH IS VERY CLOSE TO YOU EVERY — WHERE?

SOUTH AFRICAN OFFICERS, SERGEANTS AND SOLDIERS

HAVE YOU THOUGHT ON WHAT YOU ARE DOING TOO FAR FROM YOUR HOME AND YOUR FAMILY, RISKING YOUR LIFE?

IN THIS WAR YOU HAVE ONLY TWO ALTERNATIVES; TO REMAIN MUTILATED OR TO PERISH.

WHICH IS THE FUTURE OF A MUTILATED MAN?

ABANDON THE BATTLEFIELDS. GO BACK.

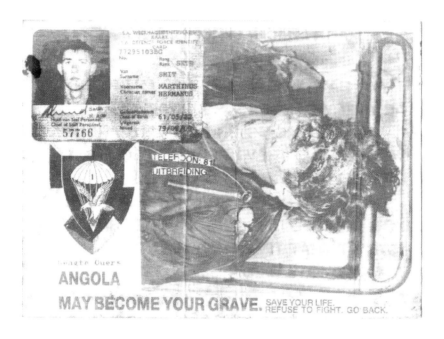

ANGOLA

MAY BECOME YOUR GRAVE. SAVE YOUR LIFE. REFUSE TO FIGHT. GO BACK.

SOUTH AFRICAN OFFICERS, SERGEANTS AND SOLDIERS

YOU HAVE BEEN PUSHED TO AN UNCERTAIN AND VERY DANGEROUS ADVENTURE.

YOU ARE FACING UP MEN WHO ARE WELL TRAINED AND THEY ARE READY TO FIGHT BRAVELY.

THESE MEN DEFEATED YOUR TROOPS WHEN YOU INVADED THE ANGOLAN TERRITORY IN 1975. AT THAT TIME MANY OF YOUR COMPATRIOTS DIED.

REFUSE TO FIGHT. SAVE YOUR OWN LIFE.

Proudly displaying their 'mascot' – a human skull
picked up at an enemy position

Russian-made weapons captured from a vacated enemy position

A Russian-made logistics vehicle burns during an attack on a Fapla position

Looking down into the driver's compartment
of a South African Olifant tank. The tanks formed
the spearhead of all our attacks and the drivers
were often the first to spot the enemy

communicate with other battalion commanders, as well as tactical HQ. An order would come in from tactical HQ to the battalion commanders, who would then relay the message to the platoon commanders, who in turn would relay it to their specific platoons. I was in a position that allowed me to hear all communication between Commandant Muller and the other command Ratels during the attack. Captain Terblanche was the commanding officer of Bravo Company and went by the call sign of 2-0 (Two-Zero).

Everything was set and ready to go, but we had no idea that our confidence from the previous attacks was about to be shattered forever.

It was quite late, coming up for evening, when we made our move. By all accounts, the attack by 4 SAI had gone well, and one of the other Fapla brigades had sent tanks to help 59 Brigade deal with the attack. Suddenly we heard that these tanks had been spotted on the other side of the shona and we were to give chase immediately and engage them. We were on the move when our tanks started firing at the enemy tanks. I don't think they hit anything, so we kept going. We were crossing the shona and feeling very vulnerable, so we tried to get into the bush line on the far side as quickly as possible to avoid being taken out. Our tanks were still firing when we reached the bush line and had obviously done some damage, as there was a burning enemy tank just off to my right – it lit up the evening sky quite nicely.

Things became rather chaotic as the enemy tank crews began jumping out of their vehicles and running away. Our infantry opened up on them with 20mm, machine-gun and rifle fire. We had advanced about another 100m when the mortar platoon was told to stop and prepare to fire. Meanwhile, an enemy tank had broken through our lines and was moving freely among us, apparently stalking Mike Muller's Ratel from behind. This was a popular manoeuvre with the enemy tanks. They would try to fire a round in under the Ratel, knocking out the differential on the rear axle and immobilising it. The tank could then stop, steady itself and destroy the Ratel with a clean shot.

Captain Terblanche saw what was happening but could not engage the tank with his Ratel, as its weapon was defective. There was also the real danger of hitting his own troops, as the tank was moving within our battle formation, so he climbed out of his Ratel, ran towards the enemy tank and shot the Cuban commander in the head with his rifle. There was still some infantry fire going on around us, but nothing too serious, so Lieutenant Saaiman and I were standing up in our hatches and directing the mortar Ratels into position. I noticed something on the ground in front of the Ratel and realised it was a body. It looked as though it could have been a Cuban, but I wasn't sure. One arm was completely gone and the whole abdomen area was just a bloody mess. While standing there, I heard a radio conversation on the command net that made me go absolutely cold and feel quite sick inside.

It was between Captain Terblanche, Bravo Company commander (call sign 2-0) and Commandant Muller, Officer Commanding 61 Mech (call sign 0), and it went something like this:

20: One of my vehicles has been hit, I've got 4 dead.
(Short, silent pause)
0: Sorry to hear it, how are the men?
20: They are still positive.
0: OK, let's keep going.

I can't even begin to describe what it felt like to hear that exchange. I could not believe what I had heard – some of our guys were dead! Just then, while I was still in shock and as if to really ram the point home, heavy direct fire (probably 23mm) came in and smashed some branches off a tree just in front of the Ratel. Things seemed to move into slow motion then, and I saw a line of fire come in from the left flank and go across the nose of our Ratel. We seemed to take forever to react, but it was actually instantaneous. Lieutenant Saaiman and I both sat down in the turret at the same time and, as I reached up to close my hatch, I saw some tracers flash directly above it, exactly where I had been standing only seconds before. It blew my mind to realise that somebody was actually aiming at me with the sole intention of killing me. Welcome to Angola, have a nice day!

We reversed out of there rather quickly, and I remember catching a glimpse of one of the guys in the mortar Ratel next to us (I think it was Deon) holding his rifle over the side of the vehicle with one hand and firing into the bush as the Ratel rushed to get out of there. The adrenalin was pumping and we moved back just far enough to get out of danger (about 50m). Geldenhuys, the driver, told me to have a look at his windscreen – there were bullet marks on it. That was close.

It was about 19h00 and things were beginning to calm down. Orders had been issued for 61 Mech to withdraw for the night, leaving one combat team behind to secure the position and prevent Fapla from reoccupying their old positions. This task was assigned to us. We started to move back to our designated positions, and just when I thought everything was over and nothing worse could happen ... GAS! GAS! GAS! was the message that came across the command net. This was what I had feared most – fucking gas! We went into gas drills immediately, only for me to come to the shock realisation that my gas mask would be useless. I had not shaved since being in Angola, and my beard prevented the mask from sealing onto my face! As I sucked in a breath of air to test the seal, I realised that I was sucking in air from around the edges and not through the filter. Now what? Fortunately, the vapour cloud that had been detected turned out to be from a coloured smoke bomb, and I escaped another close shave.

We finally settled down for the night, but everyone was on edge – understandably so. My nerves were shot and my mind was racing, trying to comprehend what had happened. We had lost four guys. There was a total of 17 casevacs (casualty evacuations), including the dead. My life had been threatened a few times and I was exceptionally tired. But, even though I was exhausted, I didn't get much sleep, as there was still the threat of Fapla coming back to reoccupy their positions through the night. We made damn sure that there were sufficient guards in the area, and it wasn't too long before something happened.

One of the guards reported seeing some movement in a nearby tree – possibly an enemy observer relaying our position to his artillery. We decided not to take any chances and a few of us took our rifles and began to approach the tree, slowly crawling along the ground to avoid detection. I could still not identify any definite shape in the branches but one of the other guys obviously could, and fired off a few rounds. We held our positions for a while, but there was no movement, so we returned to the Ratels and tried to get some sleep.

In the morning, we moved back to our previous laager positions to take stock of damage, replenish ammunition and start planning for the next attack – yes, another one! The scorecard that we received from the previous day's attack was as follows:

- **Fapla losses:** Approximately 520 troops, including 32 Cubans; 17 tanks; 6 BM-21s; 3 M-46s.
- **South African losses:** 4 killed, 13 injured; 3 Ratels damaged.

By now I was seriously beginning to doubt whether we would ever get out of there and see civilisation again. The Ratel that had been shot out had the call sign 2-2-C (Two-Two-Charlie) and had been hauled out by a recovery team. The vehicle was placed away from the main force in an attempt to prevent anyone from seeing it and becoming demoralised. Unfortunately, I saw it. I had to walk to the support echelon and collect some new radios; or something like that, I can't really remember, as my mind was a bit of a mess at that stage. The echelon was about a kilometre away from the main force and 2-2-C was parked between the two. I was walking with two guys from the echelon, and I reckon my mouth must have dropped open when I saw the damaged vehicle.

There were four holes on one side, with bloodstains running all the way down from the hatches on top. I don't know why I wanted a closer look, but I did. I walked up and looked into the back of the Ratel through one of the holes. It was eerie. All the gas masks were still hanging up, there were massive exit holes on the other side and everything was covered with some kind of white powder. There was blood splattered everywhere inside. Just then, the sergeant came walking past and launched into one of his finest deliveries of profanity and verbal abuse. We left immediately, but that vision will remain with me forever.

While doing research for this book, I tried to contact some of the guys who were involved in this conflict with me. I managed to track down only about five of them, one of whom was Hein Groenewald. Hein was driving 2-2-C when it was hit, and kindly agreed to tell the story as he experienced it from the driver's seat on that fateful day. It could not have been easy for him to relive the experience and reopen old wounds, so I am deeply grateful to him for agreeing to do so, and hope that it will somehow help him come to terms with what he went through. This is what Hein wrote:

> We were a well-drilled bunch of guys, the best that you can get, good friends who went through a lot of pain together during

training. The SADF command structure knew of the threats that were coming in Angola and what it would take to combat them, thus we were drilled like no one else before; fucked up on several occasions, over and over again.

We did formations over and over at Lohatla, until everything was perfect.

But we didn't really know what was coming ... told only that we were going to the border.

Even my parents knew nothing; they only knew I was going to the border.

From Bloemfontein, we were flown to Rundu, crossed the border into Angola and acclimatised (drilled again in the mornings).

This to us was a real relaxing time, as we were drilled so hard previously in our training that we appreciated it as one huge holiday.

We grew beards, we got refreshments every day, and to me it was a really nice time.

Then we were flown to Mavinga, where we got our batch of Ratels.

I can still remember that, when we flew into Mavinga, we thought the enemy would be waiting for us just around the first bushes.

We drove in huge trucks to a place where we would take over from the *ou manne* [outgoing troops who had conducted Operation Modular]. I remember pointing my rifle towards the bushes the whole time, as I did not know where the enemy was.

We slept that night under massive trees, close to a beautiful open shona. I thought to myself, what a beautiful country this is.

The previous battle group's *ou manne*, from whom we took over the Ratels, had a massive party that night. They were going home!!! Shooting flares into the air and probably having a few beers as well. The next morning we moved in to take over our Ratels. Those *ou manne* looked terrible, and you could see that they had had bad experiences. They had beards and were dirty as can be. The only thing I remember hearing from a 19-year-old, who looked 40, was 'Good luck.'

My Ratel was so fucked up by the previous battles that they ordered a new one for me. For a few days we were drilled again into formations to familiarise ourselves with the dense bush and new surroundings. After a few days we drove north, closer to the enemy, where we could also see some debris from previous battles. At times we were scared to death when Unita drove past us, as we thought that these were enemy vehicles.

The Bravo Company guys were a brilliant team, and we had become such good buddies, joking the whole time with each other. Close to the enemy lines, we slept together under the 2-2-C Ratel and had many good laughs. By coincidence, there were four Groenewalds in one Ratel – me, JJ, A and PH.

We had been under fire 3–5 times prior to this incident, by regular high-flying MiGs dropping their parachute bombs and artillery. Nothing scared us any more.

At one time, our platoon went to protect the artillery and had to take up a formation in front of their positions. Some of us were too lazy to dig a bunker to sleep in. That day, the enemy bombed us so much that we had to flee to another position. Seeing the trees in front of you being ripped down by artillery was not a nice sight. Have you ever seen three men jumping into a 50cm by 2m bunker?

The next few nights, we fought each other for a shovel to dig bunkers as deep as 2m, while having good laughs in between.

The following few weeks, we awaited some secret code to attack, but weather conditions apparently did not allow this. We were ill-informed, on a need-to-know basis, but I think this might have had to do with the command structure's own inner secrets. Thinking back, prior to the attack, there were three definite signs from above that things were going to go wrong:

1. On the morning of the attack, my Ratel would not start, as the batteries were flat.
2. In attack formation, I got stuck on a tree that the tank ahead of me drove over.
3. In attack formation, 2km from the enemy lines, I *again* had to be 'slaved' [jump-started] just before we entered the open shona.

After so much waiting, adrenalin pumping the whole time, awaiting the secret code to indicate the day of attack, it finally arrived: 14 February 1988.

Early that morning, I got slaved for the first time, as my Ratel would not start.

We went into the attack formation as fired up as can be, psyched up, and some of the guys even opened their hatches and were standing outside. Some of them sang 'La Bamba'. Of course we did not expect what would happen that day. When following the tank in front of me, I had the second sign from above. It knocked over a 30m tree. I got stuck, and the rest of the force continued in formation. A back-up Ratel took my place in the attack formation and Corporal Kleynhans ran to the replacement vehicle, leaving us behind. Totally stuck, we were told via the radio that a recovery truck would come for us. After two failed attempts they sent the recovery tank, and we were lifted out like a bird into fresh air. I raced to catch up with the rest of the force and take my place at the front of the formation. Corporal Kleynhans, amazed to see us again, ran back and jumped back into my Ratel. He was sitting in the small back turret, as Corporal Strauss (section leader) was in the main turret. We were not getting much information over the radio and even went into silent mode a few times to avoid being tracked, I assume, I don't know exactly. The few words we received were instructions on what we had to do and where to drive. We had to carry on, stay 20m behind the tank in front, and wait for further orders.

We were now on the eastern flank of the V-shaped attack formation, mingled in with the tanks. Our tanks would take care of the enemy heavy infantry vehicles and tanks, while the 20mm Ratels would take care of any 'light' enemy armoured vehicles and ground troops. Behind us, on the flanks, were the 90mm Ratels, and in the middle were the command group and medics. Also in the middle, and a little further back, were the 81mm mortar Ratels accompanied by the other 20mm Ratels. We were approaching our target through dense bush, driving approximately 20m behind our tanks, trying to stay in their tracks to avoid hitting any landmines. We approached an open shona, where we remained hidden in the bush, just behind our tanks. I was again slave-started to charge the batteries (third message from above).

We were told at the edge of the shona that we could expect to attack within minutes.

When the tanker in front of me fired the first round across the shona, we started racing towards the other side, firing as we went. We were in full V formation and attacking all out. At this stage, it was reported that we were being attacked by a 23mm anti-aircraft gun (ZU-23-4), and it was firing at will. This gun was supposed to have been taken out by 4 SAI or the Recces beforehand, but this did not happen. We were like sitting ducks racing over the shona. We made it across and again entered dense bush. We were told to turn 90 degrees right, but the tank commander in front of me went straight ahead, probably after another enemy vehicle. I could only follow, so as to stay in his tracks and avoid the mines. We were about 100m into the bush when we got hit from the side.

Suddenly there was a deafening bang. The Ratel pitched from one side to the other; there was smoke everywhere, and then the smell of burning flesh. Then I saw blood on the inside of the windscreen. Corporal Strauss radioed that we had been hit; he was starting to cry as he said he thought we had lost men. He was also injured, and so was the gunner. The gunner, driver (me) and the section leader were in full radio contact – I could hear them groaning in pain. Almost suffocating from the smoke, all of us just wanted to get out of the Ratel. We still did not know the full impact of what just happened and we could see nothing. I started to panic. I had no air and I just wanted to get out. I was shit scared!

I wanted to get out through the driver's turret, but could not, so I opened the side doors. We managed to get out (those of us who were still alive) and lay down on the ground next to the Ratel. Most were badly injured and covered in blood. One buddy, JJ Groenewald, had been hit by shrapnel, opening his throat right up. He almost suffocated in his own blood. The gunner and section leader were also hit by shrapnel in their upper bodies. On the left side of the Ratel were 4 × 23mm holes, cutting right through the vehicle and exiting through the other side. The troops sitting in the back were hit head on. One of our tanks approached us to help out, but I was so rattled that I did not know whose tank it was. I thought it was an enemy tank, so I ran back to the Ratel to get my rifle and shoot this 'enemy'. That was when I saw the full impact inside the battered Ratel, 2-2-C. One of my buddies was still sitting upright and buckled in his seat, but his neck was all I could see. No head. The others were all face down, their seatbelts also still fastened. I knew there was no life left here.

I was totally rattled, and when the recovery vehicle came to collect the injured, I did not want to go with them. I ran about 100m to another Ratel, 2-2-A, and tried to get inside. My buddies inside did not want to open the doors, probably fearing enemy fire and rattled by what they had seen happen to us. I could not climb up onto the vehicle, as I had no strength left. The bullets were flying past me. I ran another 100m to another Ratel, 2-2-B, which picked me up. Once inside, I felt safe again. I carried on throughout the attack and all its bombings later that night.

During the two days when I was waiting to be flown out, I cried a lot and was alone, waiting for the helicopter. I prayed a LOT. When flown out of Angola, I had to sit on top of my buddies' Jiffy bags [body bags], as there was no place left in the helicopter. The stinking Jiffy bags were disgusting. I just wanted to go home.

I was taken to Rundu hospital, where I saw my other friends who had been flown out earlier. They were in a better state than when they left me. We did not talk much; everyone seemed to try to reflect back on what had happened to them. Even in the hospital, I prayed a lot. There, I had a 30-minute talk with the *kopdokters* [directly translated, means head doctors, the psychologists and psychiatrists] and I told them that I found faith in God, and that I was OK. After that, I received no more counselling or support from the SADF.

I was sent back home for a few weeks, to be with my family. This was a quiet and relaxing time. They did not know what to expect from me, and when telling them the full story, it seemed that they could not believe what had happened. I did not want to burden them with details, and did not want them to get worried, so I kept most of this to myself. There would be none who would understand except my buddies who went through it with me, up there.

I was then called back to 1 SAI in Bloemfontein for another few weeks. Thereafter, I was sent to join my company on the border again. Reflecting back, in hospital, I was told by the counsellor that the only proven way to treat post-traumatic stress was to get back into combat as soon as possible. History had proven this to be the best way to handle the Americans in Vietnam. But, above all, God made it happen for me.

So, two months later, I was in contact with Fapla again, on the western side of Angola, close to the Ruacana Dam. This time, I was in the recovery platoon.

A Ratel was hit by Fapla when we were in a head-on surprise attack by the enemy. We had to recover the bodies of the guys who had been hit in the Ratel 90. Back at Ruacana, the MiGs bombed us from everywhere, creating havoc again and killing more of our troops. I think this may have saved me from post-traumatic stress.

I don't really know how this affected me afterwards, as I tried not to think about it. I just wanted to forget about everything I saw and get it out of my mind. I spoke a little bit to my family about it, but they don't understand at all. How do you explain this to them? Will they ever understand? I sometimes experience feelings of loneliness, but then there are also times that I just want to be alone. I have got a short fuse, as my wife will agree. I don't want to have anything to do with death. When someone dies, there is an empty feeling inside. I think the effects of death strike me much later than others, almost a delayed reaction. When my mother died in 1998, I did not go into a state of shock, but wanted to make plans, resolve things, show no feelings, just try to be the strong one in the family!

We were instruments of the SADF, machines that had to do things without thinking about it. We were well drilled (as they knew we would go to Angola). I am proud of what was done, but looking at how we were abandoned by the SADF afterwards, I don't have much respect any more. If you ask me to defend this country again, I will not. I will look after my own family, and that's all.

After all that happened, after *all* that I went through, I did not get a medal (no Pro Patria, absolutely fucking NOTHING) and this, to me, is a shame. I would love to get together with my old company for a huge reunion and just talk about the old days.

I know the impact that this incident had on me, and I was not even in that Ratel at the time. I cannot begin to imagine the effect it had on those who were directly involved, or the families of those who died that day. Even now, I make a point of buying four beers every Valentine's Day and finding a nice, quiet place to drink them on my own. In memory of those who died that day, I have written a poem:

Gone – Never Forgotten (Valentine's Day 1988)

On this day of roses and wine
let us pause for a short time
and remember those who are
not able to smell the roses,
nor savour the wine.

Friends and comrades who walked with us
'til fate's dark hand them did snatch.
We knew not why, and probably never will
but in those split seconds, lives were lost
and families forced to swallow
this bitter pill.

It is said that time heals all wounds,
But what of the wounds that form scars?
Scars not always seen by the eye, but felt in the heart.
Of these scars I have a few
And on this day I say to you,
Join me, brothers in arms
As we salute our fallen friends
And raise a glass, or two
for those who perished this day, 1988.

Our four friends who walk among us no more
yet are with us always
we take this time to remember and honour you
as you crossed the line of selfless sacrifice.
22 Charlie, this one's for you.

6

Rumble in the Jungle: The Battle of Cuito Cuanavale

AFTER THE VALENTINE'S DAY attack, what little remained of my earlier enthusiasm for recording daily events was dampened by the intensity of the contact and the harsh realisation that we were not infallible, after all, and that the threat of death was now a very real prospect. We all knew that our war was not yet over – not by a long shot – and that others would almost certainly be killed in the weeks, possibly months, ahead.

It was like a raffle where there are only 100 tickets and no predetermined date for the draw. Someone's name was going to come up, but no one knew who it would be. The only thing we knew with certainty was that we were all ticket holders.

In the days immediately following the battle, we spent our time reporting and repairing damages, and refilling with ammunition, fuel and food. There was talk of the next attack being just around the corner, and this time, 61 Mech would be the main assault force. The writing was on the wall for this to be the mother of all battles, since the remnants of all the Fapla brigades had regrouped in the Tumpo area, just in front of the Cuito Bridge, and been digging themselves in for some time.

Tumpo was now probably the most strategically important zone in Angola. As long as Fapla occupied and controlled it, they would have access to the entire south-eastern province. The Cuito Bridge could act as a supply line for reinforcements that would enable Fapla to mount increased attacks on Unita. In the meantime, Fidel Castro had sent additional troops and equipment from Cuba to support his Angolan campaign in the hope that it could be concluded without costing him too much more in terms of personnel, equipment and finances.

Tumpo and the Cuito Bridge were going to be defended by Fapla with all they had. The positions around Tumpo were now heavily fortified, with Fapla even clearing away large areas of bush so they would be able to see the South African advance and get a clear shot at us as we came in to attack them. They had also laid extensive minefields in front of their positions to stop any advancing force. Our standard operating procedure was that, when the first mine was detonated, the entire force would stop and wait for the engineers or the 'mine-roller' tank to clear the path ahead so that the attack could resume.

The minefields were laid just inside or in front of thick bush on the far side of an open clearing. The idea was that, when the first vehicle detonated a mine in the bush line, the remainder of the force would have to stop in the open clearing, the coordinates of which had already been registered by Fapla's artillery. Talk about the ultimate sitting duck! They had also taken all of their damaged tanks and dug them in as an additional line of defence. These tanks could not be driven or move out to meet the advancing force, but their weapon systems were still fully functional, so by digging them into the ground, they could take aim at leisure and pick us off as we advanced. All that could be seen of the tanks were the turrets and barrels, making them a more difficult target to acquire and destroy. The odds were heavily stacked against us for taking Tumpo and the Cuito Bridge, but we were going to give it our best shot.

It was probably just as well that we did not know all of this at the time, as morale had taken a definite turn for the worse since Valentine's Day. We had been in Angola for three months, living (and in many instances looking and smelling) like animals, constantly bombarded by MiGs and artillery fire, been involved in some horrendous contacts and experienced at first hand the loss of some of our buddies. This was the true brutality of war – and there was plenty more to come. The officers had clearly been briefed on the situation and would give us little pep talks from time to time, reassuring us of the importance of what we were doing and how our superior fighting skills would allow us to prevail over Fapla and ultimately secure a hard-fought victory over the communist threat. They promised that it would all be over soon and we would get to see our families and loved ones before long.

It became difficult to maintain a positive attitude at times, as the moment someone started speaking slightly negatively, the sentiment became contagious and spread rapidly through our ranks. I had developed a fairly good relationship with Sergeant McDonald (the same guy who had given me the *opfok* in basics that had triggered my asthma attack), and my natural ability to tell good jokes and impersonate a range of accents became an endless source of amusement for him and some of the others. Sergeant McDonald would often come round to my Ratel and ask me to tell him some jokes – particularly anything involving an Australian accent. It was probably just what we needed, as it allowed us to take our minds off the shitty situation we were in and think about something else for a while – until the next bomb fell nearby or a MiG warning came in.

On 16 February, we were told to be on our best behaviour, as the 'top brass' would be visiting us. SADF chief General Jannie Geldenhuys, accompanied by generals Liebenberg and Meyer, flew in for a briefing at the tactical HQ and to discuss plans for the Tumpo attack. General Geldenhuys spent some time talking to a few of the tankers, and I reckon this was his way of trying to boost morale prior to the battle – he obviously knew that we would be pushing shit uphill all the way and did what he could to perk some of the guys up. It worked for a while, as there was a slight upturn in spirits – until later that afternoon.

Lance Corporal Price was approached by a 'Unita' soldier requesting water. He obliged, took the water bottle from the soldier and went to fill it up from his vehicle. The bottle exploded, killing Price instantly.

The 'Unita' soldier was actually a Fapla spy who had infiltrated our position with the booby-trapped water bottle. I can't say for certain what explosive device was inside the bottle, but the general consensus was that it had been a hand grenade. This incident happened about 100m away from my Ratel, and there was immediate activity on the radio as people tried to find out what had happened. About two minutes after the blast, Commandant Mike Muller's voice came over the command net, informing us of what had happened, and issuing orders for all of us to fan out and stop all Unita soldiers, disarm them and bring them to a central point for identification.

His words were not yet cold when two Unita soldiers emerged from the bush right next to the Ratel. Michael was the first to react, and aimed his rifle straight at them, commanding them to halt. They were taken to the assembly point, but unfortunately the Fapla soldier had managed to slip through our net and get away. Our defences had been breached and death was once again among us. General Geldenhuys's attempted morale booster had all but fallen flat within the space of a few hours.

Things were beginning to heat up. The MiGs were flying more regular air strikes and there seemed to be an increased level of urgency about the planning for the next attack. Our artillery was pounding the Tumpo area and effectively softening up the target in preparation for the ground attack. There were even a few air strikes by the South African Air Force (SAAF) in an attempt to disrupt the Fapla supply lines by targeting supply convoys. In one such strike, on 19 February, the SAAF suffered its first casualty of the campaign. A Mirage was shot down by Fapla forces and the pilot, Major Ed Every, was killed.

Two days later, the MiGs attacked a South African convoy but, as was quite common, missed the target. However, their cluster bombs fell into a nearby South African laager, killing three guys and wounding another. We decided to dig our bunker deeper and put some kind of roof over it as protection against any possible air-burst bombs. The result was a 2m deep bunker capable of accommodating about six people, with a roof consisting of logs covered with canvas and sand piled high on top of the tarpaulin. Branches from nearby trees were placed on top of the sand as a form of camouflage against detection from the air.

On 24 February, word came through on the command net that all platoon commanders were to report for orders and be briefed on the next attack plan. Lieutenant Strydom asked me to accompany him to this briefing. What I saw on the whiteboard sent a shiver up my spine. The sketch plan of the Tumpo area looked like the car park outside a rugby stadium on the day of a test match. There were vehicles everywhere, and I counted five enemy brigade positions in all. There was also a massive section in front of this area that indicated the Fapla minefields.

I decided to copy the drawing, in case we had to make reference to it later on or during the battle. The attack had been scheduled for first light on 25 February, and from what we had seen and been told at the briefing, it was going to be pretty hard going. One did not have to be a rocket scientist to figure out that this assault would be at the cost of still more lives. The intention was to effectively rid the Tumpo area of all Fapla and Cuban forces and equipment by either destroying them (the preferred option) or forcing them to retreat across the Cuito River. Once achieved, the Cuito Bridge was to be destroyed, thus securing the entire south-eastern corner of Angola as a Unita stronghold and making it damn near impossible for Fapla to launch any attacks from the town of Cuito Cuanavale. Tumpo was Fapla's last line of defence to the east of the Cuito River. This was going to be one hell of a fight!

As I drew a copy of the battle plan map, I remember thinking: 'Shit, there are a lot of troops and tanks in this area.' We were going to throw everything we had at them (including the kitchen sink) and they were going to do exactly the same to us. It would be the proverbial collision between an unstoppable force and an immovable object.

There was a silver lining to this dark cloud, however – we were told that this would be our final battle before going home on pass! Needless to say, this would undoubtedly increase the motivation and adrenalin of the South African troops, as we knew we had something to look forward to – provided we emerged from the battlefield in one piece.

Diary entry

24/02/88

Tonight we move in to take Tumpo. This is the final fight and it's going to be a big one. In total there are 5 enemy positions to be taken and it will probably last about 4 days – then it's home time!!!

This turned out to be the attack that saw things start to unravel and go horribly wrong for me. It was probably a combination of the stress that had built up over the past few months, coupled with the intensity of the events that took place during the battle. All I know is that after 25 February 1988, I was never the same again.

We moved into our forward assembly areas at about 20h30 on 24 February, and I knew we were in for a long night, with the attack only scheduled for first light the following day. The approach was slow and sometimes difficult, due to the dense bush and 'no lights' policy when driving at night. The Ratels were fitted with small convoy lights on the rear of the vehicle to enable the drivers to follow each other, but most of these had long since stopped working. We relied heavily on moonlight, and on a number of occasions I would end up sitting on top of the turret, holding onto the gun barrel and leaning forward to try to see where we were going so that I could pass this information down to the driver (left a bit, right a bit, slow down, speed up, STOP, it's a tree!!).

Albeit slowly, we managed to reach our designated 'hide' (area from which the attack is launched and, should the need arise, to which one can retreat fairly easily to take cover) at around 01h00. Then we waited for our attack orders. By taking it in turns, all three of our crew managed to get a little sleep, though it wasn't easy under those conditions, knowing what we would be going into within the next few hours and that we were not far from the enemy positions. My mind kept on going back to the map I had seen at the briefing, and I could not help but wonder how we could even think we could win against such odds. I suppose it's in this kind of situation that the word 'faith' takes on a whole new meaning.

There was a sense of uneasy tension among the troops, mixed with a feeling of 'let's just get this over with so we can go home and see our families'. The attack was scheduled to get under way with 32 Battalion making contact with Fapla at about 04h00, which would be about the time we started moving forward again. Things began to heat up at around 06h00, with our artillery launching a barrage of 155mm G5 shells on Fapla's forward positions. The Fapla artillery responded immediately, and then the MiGs joined in to provide air support. The 'big party' had begun and we were heading straight for it – without an invitation.

The force was in formation and moving through the last shona before entering the bush line that concealed the first of the Fapla bases. All was going well until about 07h30, when there was a massive bang just in front of us. The lead tank had detonated a mine. Standard procedure kicked in and the entire force stopped, in the middle of an open plain and totally exposed. This was a bad sign, as our approach route had been given to us by a reconnaissance team the night before and we were told that it was a clear path with no mines. Fapla had obviously found the route markers and mined the approach path some time during the night. Commandant Muller tried twice to turn the force around and look for an alternative approach path, but both times, another tank hit a mine. It became obvious that we were well into the minefield and in pretty serious trouble.

After about an hour, we were ordered to 'backtrack' a couple of hundred metres so that the engineers could clear a path through the minefield. This required us to literally drive backwards, without straying from our original vehicle tracks – not a pleasant experience, as the driver is totally blind and has to rely on instructions from the turret. We managed to complete this manoeuvre and the engineers moved in to do their job. Most of us were still fairly relaxed at this point, until the next air strike came in at around 09h20. The bombs were not far off the mark, and we soon realised that we were about to become the targets of whatever Fapla and the Cubans decided to throw at us. The only thing we could do to avoid detection from the air was to close the anti-reflection flaps over the windscreens on all the Ratels and hope we were not spotted by the last wave of MiGs.

The anti-reflection flaps were plates of armoured steel on a spring-loaded release system that, when triggered from inside the vehicle, covered the windscreen to prevent sunlight being reflected. Once in place, however, the driver could not see anything through the flaps, and the biggest problem was that they could only be removed from the windscreen from outside the Ratel. Somebody would have to climb out of the turret to do this, but we were under 'closed hatch' conditions, which meant nobody was allowed to open the hatch or climb out of the vehicles.

Within a matter of minutes it became obvious that we had been spotted. An artillery bomb landed just behind our Ratel, and from the noise of the explosion, I knew it was close – too bloody close. Lieutenant Saaiman told me to turn the turret so we could get a look at what was going on. One of the recovery vehicles was burning about 100m behind us – a direct hit. Somehow, miraculously, the crew had not been injured and were trying desperately to extinguish their burning vehicle. As we watched, another bomb landed about halfway between the burning wreck and our Ratel. This could mean only one thing: there was an observer in the area who was 'talking in' the artillery fire – and we were his next target. I was still rotating the turret to its forward position when the next bomb landed almost under our arse. It shook the Ratel, pitching it forward. That was too close for comfort, and the lieutenant quickly made an executive decision to move the vehicle, in spite of the fact that we were stalled in a minefield. I fully supported his decision. Two bombs had already landed behind us and it was pretty damn obvious where the next one would land. The problem with this action was that we were still under air raid conditions with the anti-reflective flaps in place, and Geldenhuys, our driver, could not see a fucking thing.

With the incoming artillery fire and MiGs above us, we had our hatches closed and no one could get out to remove the anti-reflection flaps from the windscreen – we were about to drive blind through a minefield under both ground and aerial bombardment. The only vision we had was through my gun-sight periscope and a small viewing slit in front of the turret commander. Between us, we had to talk to Geldenhuys and guide him to the nearest tree, hopefully not hitting a mine in the process.

I know how intense the situation was for me, even with the benefit of limited sight, so I can't even begin to imagine what Geldenhuys was going through – steering a vehicle through a minefield with MiGs flying overhead and unable to see where he was going – but the effects of his experience became manifest a few hours later.

Somehow, we made it to shelter under a small tree without incident. Everyone had been scanning the trees for Fapla observers, and a radio report that one had been spotted was followed by a few bursts of machine-gun fire, which I think was right on target.

The mines that were hindering our advance were eventually cleared by something called a *Plofadder* (an explosive device that detonates all the mines planted in its range), and we were back on track and moving just after midday. The Fapla artillery continued to bombard us, so our hatches remained closed for most of the time. The temperature was more than 40°C and it was like sitting in a sauna inside the Ratel. We had finally gotten through the minefield and I remember looking at the total devastation around us, massive trees lying everywhere, the Fapla bunkers and trenches totally destroyed and deserted. They had evidently left in a hurry, as there were still items of clothing and pieces of equipment lying around.

The Unita soldiers were generally tasked with clearing the Fapla positions, and they would do this by hitching a ride on top of the tanks and Ratels. As we moved into an enemy position, the Unitas would jump off the vehicles and start clearing up, taking all weapons, food and clothing left behind by Fapla – and also looking for wounded Fapla soldiers to capture or kill. The problem with this type of follow-up action was that, in the event of incoming artillery or air strikes, they had no cover. It was not uncommon to see a few Unita soldiers fall off the vehicles as the bombs dropped around them. Others would then jump off, assess the condition of the wounded men and, if they were dead, retrieve their weapons and carry on with the attack.

We successfully linked up with 32 Battalion, but during our advance, one of the Ratel 90s took a direct hit from a 120mm mortar bomb. The force of the explosion ripped off the door of the Ratel, as well as the crew commander's legs. Two crew members also sustained injuries, though I'm not sure to what extent. This incident was mentioned in a debriefing session with the Ops Medic who had performed the 'amputation' – apparently with only a pair of scissors and the patient lying on a groundsheet in the middle of the battlefield. A short while later, one of our tanks took a hit from an enemy rocket, resulting in the driver being decapitated while attempting to close his hatch. This, too, was recounted by an

Ops Medic during debriefing at the end of the operation. He spoke about how he had been sent to recover the body at night and, when he climbed up onto the tank, he could not see anything. The driver's hatch was open, so he reached down into the driver's compartment and his hand went straight into the neck of the decapitated body. The force of the bomb had taken the driver's head off and his body then slumped back into the seat.

There were a couple of reasons for doing after-dark vehicle and body recoveries. First, this could be done without the threat of detection by the enemy and the MiGs did not fly at night. The second reason had to do with the morale of the troops – it was not a good thing for them to see the bodies and the damaged vehicles. Our policy was to leave no one behind, dead or injured, and to recover all vehicles where possible. When a vehicle could not be recovered, it was destroyed in order to prevent it from falling into enemy hands. This was crucial, as the loss of a vehicle to the enemy would give them access to our communications equipment, and we could not afford that – they already had us outnumbered and outgunned and enjoyed total air supremacy.

It was quite late in the afternoon, probably around 16h00, when we were halted by another air raid. The fire had been extremely heavy from both sides, and there was no way of knowing when or where the next bomb would come from or if you were about to hit a mine. We had become accustomed to the constant incoming fire and kept pushing ahead in spite of it. All in all, it had been the most stressful day of my life, and it was about to get even worse.

As we were awaiting orders to move into a new position, Geldenhuys, our driver, put his head down on the steering wheel and said (through his headset microphone): '*Ek kan nie meer nie*' (I can't take any more). This posed an interesting situation, to say the least. We were in the middle of a very intense contact, with artillery shells coming in from all sides, MiGs in the air and uncharted minefields all around us, without a driver. There were only three of us in the command Ratel, so the lieutenant stayed in the turret while I climbed down to get Geldenhuys out of the driver's seat and into the back of the vehicle to try to stabilise him. He appeared to be suffering from extreme heat exhaustion and was pretty dehydrated. By the time I manoeuvred him into the back of the Ratel, he had all but passed out. The lieutenant asked me if I could drive the vehicle and get us out of there, but I had only driven a Ratel once before and did not fancy my chances of getting us through the minefield in one piece. Besides, Geldenhuys was in need of serious medical attention, and quickly. We were stranded in a wide open clearing right in the middle of one hell of a fire-fight, with nowhere to go.

It was probably only a matter of minutes since Geldenhuys had slumped over the steering wheel, but it felt like a lifetime. That slow-motion effect, again. I had just managed to haul the almost unconscious driver into the back of the Ratel when I witnessed what was possibly the most selfless act of bravery on a terrifying day.

One of our mortarists had acquired some experience driving Ratels and he climbed out of his vehicle, ran across to our stranded vehicle and jumped into the driver's seat. His name was Phillip Crouse, and to this day I believe he was responsible for saving at least three lives that day.

We informed 0 of our situation and said we would return to the medical post so that Geldenhuys could receive medical attention. I had him stretched out in the back of the Ratel and was trying to stabilise him and get some fluid into him. His eyes were closed and he kept on mumbling something about his brother. He was becoming delirious and I could not make out anything he was saying, so I just kept on telling him, 'It's all right, we're going home now, it's over.'

Then I heard something I really did not want to hear coming through on the radio. It was 0, informing us that there were some 32 Battalion casualties at the front that we had just exited, and that we had to go and pick them up before heading back to the medical post. 'You can't be fucking serious!' I shouted, to no one in particular. The Ratel turned around to carry out the order, and I knew that whatever I told Geldenhuys from then on would have to be anything but the truth.

No sooner had we turned around and started going forward again, when another shower of artillery came in. These bombs were close – so close that everything seemed to shake. I could actually hear the shrapnel hitting the side of the Ratel; it made a 'ping-ping-ping-ping' sound as it bounced off the armour plating. Geldenhuys started losing it, shouting and screaming and trying to get out of there. He was about 2m tall and had the nickname *Langes* (Long One), and I was finding it increasingly difficult to control him. He had become quite hysterical, and I ended up lying on top of him, struggling to control him. I just kept on reassuring him that everything was fine and we were going home, knowing all the time that it was a lie. It seemed to be working, though, as he began to calm down, but was still mumbling something about his brother. We were almost at the pick-up point and I had to ensure that there was enough space in the back of the Ratel to accommodate the wounded men. I had no idea how many there would be, or the extent of their injuries.

As the door opened at the pick-up point, I was greeted by the face of Captain Emslie, the field doctor with 32 Battalion, and I began helping him load the wounded. The first man was lying on a groundsheet, used as a makeshift stretcher, and although I did not have time to take a good look at his injuries, there was a lot of blood around. We were still in the middle of a contact, so we had to load the casualties as quickly as possible and get out of there. By the time I had helped get the first guy into the back of the Ratel and laid him down on the centre console seat, everyone else was already in the vehicle and we were moving again.

Things were pretty cramped in the back of the Ratel, so I climbed back up into the gunner's seat. Geldenhuys was sitting huddled in the rear corner with a blank expression on his face. I had been feeding him as much water as I could and I think by this stage he was recovering from the heat exhaustion, but that wasn't what I was worried about. He looked as though he was far away and in total shock. On our way to the medical post, I glanced into the back of the Ratel a few times, mainly to keep an eye on my friend, but also to gauge the extent of the injuries sustained by the 32 Battalion troops. It was pretty ugly, and there were more of those blank expressions. One of our passengers had what looked like an entry wound on the front of his thigh, with the exit wound somewhere on his inner thigh. Another was in a far worse state with what appeared to be multiple chest wounds.

The medical post was located with the support echelon just behind the battlefield, and served as the first port of call for any injured troops. There they could be stabilised and, if necessary, moved to the surgical post, located even further back from the firing line. The support echelon was positioned just behind the main attack force so as to be ready to replenish ammunition and fuel at short notice.

We arrived at the medical post somewhere around 18h00 and proceeded to unload the less seriously wounded, before moving on to the surgical post with those who needed more advanced attention. I was standing outside at the door and helping them out when my legs gave way and I toppled over backwards. Heat exhaustion had struck me, too. Things were starting to calm down and I was lying down next to the Ratel, about to have a rehydration drip inserted, when a massive explosion erupted only 100m or so away from us. We frantically climbed back into the Ratel (my drip is still lying there somewhere). The next thing I knew, Malan (our ammunition truck driver) was standing outside our Ratel, looking pretty shaken. '*Hulle het my trok geskiet*' (they bombed my truck) is all I remember him shouting. He was in total panic, and I'm not sure if he climbed into the Ratel with us or if he was picked up by someone else – things were getting a little frantic at that stage.

Something had scored a direct hit (we all concurred that it must have been a piece of artillery, probably an M46, as there were no MiGs overhead at the time), and the truck was burning, sending up a thick column of smoke into the sky. It was only a matter of time before the ammunition started exploding. Sergeant Koekemoer climbed into the cab of the burning truck and tried to drive it away from the rest of the echelon so as not to attract more fire, but he made only a short distance before the ammunition started exploding, turning the whole area into a gigantic fireworks display. Needless to say, there was a 'Victor-Victor' alert on the command net almost immediately, warning that the MiGs had spotted a column of smoke and were heading straight for it.

Our lieutenant requested permission to move, pointing out that we were dangerously close to the smoke, but he was told: '*Negatief, dis Stand Rooi, staan stil!*' (Negative, it's Condition Red, don't move). That is a moment in time that I will never forget. It went painfully quiet inside the Ratel and I heard the badly wounded 32 soldier start gasping for air. All I thought was, 'He's not going to make it.' I also became acutely aware of the smell inside the Ratel. It was a mixture of sweat, blood, diesel and something else I could not quite identify … possibly fear, although no one would admit it at the time.

Another executive decision was about to be made. I was sitting in the gun turret (almost passed out from the heat exhaustion) with my head down on the 20mm cannon's rotation and elevation handles, listening to the conversation on my headset and thinking, 'That's us they have spotted, we are the target!' The lieutenant radioed back and explained our predicament, again requesting permission to move the Ratel immediately in spite of being under air raid conditions. He was again told, 'No, it's Victor-Victor, Condition Red, stand still!'

I was starting to get a bit tetchy by this stage. There we were, right next to this fireworks display, with the MiGs about to bomb the shit out of the whole area, and we had to simply stay put and wait for it to happen – not fucking likely! I remember kicking Crouse (the substitute driver) on the back of his helmet and shouting, 'Drive! Just fucking drive! We need to get out of here!' The lieutenant issued the order and we did just that. We drove away without worrying about following tracks or kicking up dust, so long as we were moving away from the target area and in the opposite direction to Cuito. The more distance between us and the target area, the better. Besides, what was a little bit of dust when there was a nice big target for them to bomb?

I must have passed out at some stage, as I don't remember arriving at the surgical post. I do remember working well into the night, however, assisting the rest of the troops who were coming in with an array of injuries. I had still not been given a rehydration drip, but at the time you just focus on the job at hand and help out where you can. Besides, my condition was nothing compared to some of the injuries that had been sustained. There was one fellow who had absolutely no idea where he was or what he was doing. We were standing in front of his Ratel and I remember the expression on his face as he came into the beam of the headlights. He was far, far away, mumbling about going to the beach the next day. I started talking to him, took him by the arm and walked slowly towards the medical tent. I have no idea what time I went to sleep that night, or if I slept at all. I seemed to be in a dazed, shocked state and functioned without thought or emotion.

The next day, a heavy atmosphere hung over everything and there was little conversation. Geldenhuys had his bag packed and, while waiting for the next chopper, was sitting in the Ratel, aimlessly whittling at a stick. I spoke with him for a while, and what he told me was shocking. About two days prior to the attack on Tumpo, he had received a letter from home telling him that his brother had been killed in a car accident. He decided not to tell anyone, as he felt he could not let the team down and he thought he would be able to deal with it himself. I think the combination of this and the stress of the battle took their toll on him. I have never heard from him since that day when we said goodbye in Angola, but I would like to make contact with him, some time. I don't know if he felt that we somehow held him responsible for what happened, but, if so, he can rest assured that no one blamed him for anything.

As for the rest of us, it was pretty much a case of taking cover and licking our wounds. We knew that the objective of the last attack had not been achieved, so it was very likely that we would be going in again as soon as possible, within days. How much more of this could we take? Everyone was dead tired, physically and emotionally. We had lost more vehicles, with many others damaged or unserviceable.

I was sitting in the back of the Ratel, pondering this situation shortly after Geldenhuys had left, when I noticed there was still some blood on the base of the turret from our wounded 32 Battalion passengers. I cleaned it off and left the doors open to try to get rid of that awful smell. I remember being envious of the fact that Geldenhuys was on his way home. God knows, that was all I wanted to do right then – go home, relax, sleep and forget all about this tour of hell.

A few days later, we heard that some of our observers had done a 'bomb count' (who actually counts incoming bombs during an attack?) and, according to their figures, 972 M-46 artillery shells were thrown at us during this battle – not to mention all the other assorted bombs and direct fire. The MiGs had flown 59 sorties during the fighting and would have unloaded a good few tons of explosives on us. From what I saw and heard that day, I would have to say that I am inclined to agree with these figures.

After the attack, I felt somehow different, empty inside and devoid of all emotion. I had a distinct sense of loss and apprehension about going into another intense contact situation. I went very quiet and did not speak much to anyone. It was almost as if my mind was trying to comprehend the magnitude of the last 24 hours and put everything into some kind of perspective or logical sequence, if there is such a thing in war. I gained a new level of respect for Lieutenant Saaiman, as he had somehow managed to keep a relatively cool head throughout. I don't know if his training had taken over and he just did what he had been taught to do, or if his conduct under fire was a reflection of his strength of character. I just know that he performed well under extreme conditions and did not outwardly display any negativity, fear or doubt at any stage – the mark of a good officer and leader. I often wonder how he coped with things after it was all over. My subsequent research into PTSD indicates that it is often the person who is 'strong' during the traumatic experience who has the greatest difficulty dealing with things later on in life. By all accounts, Lieutenant Saaiman never displayed much emotion at all, and I only hope that the effects of the war did not come home to roost in later years. Perhaps he is one of those people who can handle anything and not have it affect him in any way – I don't know. I have not spoken with him since the war.

My mood was mirrored by the general atmosphere. Everyone seemed to be a lot more reserved and quiet, almost withdrawn and shell-shocked. It was as if the wind had been taken out of our sails and we were just drifting aimlessly without any direction – except forward into another attack, which I don't think many of us were too enthusiastic about at the time. Yes, we had expected it to be one hell of a fight, but I don't honestly think anyone really anticipated the level and volume of resistance we encountered, or the intensity of the artillery and air strikes we had endured. By that stage we had hoped to be celebrating – or at least be well on our way to achieving – victory, and possibly even heading back towards South West Africa to go on pass and see our families for the first time in about four months. But this was not to be. There was unfinished business in Tumpo, and the Cuito Bridge was still standing.

The objective of the second attack was no different from the first: clear the Tumpo area of all Fapla troops and equipment, destroy the Cuito Bridge and then withdraw. The main force would be made up of 61 Mech, 32 Battalion and two Unita infantry battalions, with a second force acting as a decoy to deceive Fapla into believing the attack was coming in on the same route as before. The idea was to allow the main force to get close to the Fapla positions without being detected until the last possible moment, ensuring the element of surprise. The other interesting part of this plan was that the attack would take place at night, with the mortar platoon firing illumination bombs over the target area to allow the attack force to clearly see their targets. A new factor then came into play: lack of serviceable vehicles. By that stage, we had 11 tanks and four Ratel 90s in an unserviceable condition and unable to take part in the attack. Nevertheless, the attack would go ahead as planned.

By early evening on 29 February, we were formed up and ready to proceed. We were told that we had to wait for the tanks with the mine-rollers to catch up, as they had fallen behind by quite some distance and were an important component in ensuring the success of the attack. In the meantime, a few more tanks had developed problems and the force was down to just 11 tanks. A squadron of Ratel 90s was sent to join us to compensate for the lack of tanks. Progress was slow, and at times it felt as though we would never get to Tumpo. Visibility was poor and became even worse when it started to rain in the early hours of the morning. At around 02h00, we were informed that the attack had been delayed until first light, depending on the weather conditions and adequate cloud cover to prevent the MiGs from causing too many problems. Since our anti-aircraft guns had been withdrawn due to difficulties in coping with deployment on the terrain, we would certainly need all the cloud cover we could get. We stopped and tried to catch some sleep.

Before first light, we were up and moving into formation for the attack. Our sole surviving support vehicle would remain camouflaged and ready to replenish ammunition at a position on slight high ground overlooking Tumpo. Just before moving out, I was told that one of the permanent force members (I think it was Sergeant McDonald) wanted to ride in our Ratel for this attack, as he had been with the support echelon for the duration of the operation and had not been directly involved in battle so far. He would occupy the gunner's seat, namely mine.

I'm still not sure of the motivation behind this move. It could have been that the sergeant genuinely wanted to see some action on the front line before leaving Angola (which is the most likely scenario), or it could have been because I looked a bit shaky after the previous attack. My options were to be deployed with the support vehicle on the high ground or to ride in the back of the Ratel during the attack, but based on my last experience in that compartment, I was not keen to do so again. It's one thing to be able to see what is going on around you, but when you have no idea where you are or what is going on, it becomes a different ball game altogether. Besides, I would not really be serving any purpose in the back of the Ratel and, as far as I was concerned, I had seen more than my fair share of this war from a front-row seat. If someone else wanted a close-up look, he was more than welcome. I decided to stay with the support vehicle.

Our position on the high ground had to be well camouflaged, as we were still within range of the Fapla artillery and there would certainly be a few MiGs flying overhead during the course of the battle.

It was not long before the first Fapla artillery barrage began, with the MiGs not far behind, although the low cloud cover would have made things a bit risky for them, as one pilot found out later in the day. I cannot go into much detail about the actual attack, as I was not part of it, and my mind was still in a bit of a mess from the previous one. I caught glimpses of dust and smoke from my position, but, by all accounts, there were not many Fapla troops left in Tumpo. The one concern I had was that there were only three or four of us in the rear position, and should we come under attack by anything other than regular infantry, we would have some serious problems. At times the silence was deafening, just sitting there in the dense bush with no sound around us. There was a distinct lack of any wildlife in the area, and all I can think is that all the game had been killed or gotten the hell out of there when the fighting started. There was not even a bird in a tree. It was like being in the middle of a wasteland totally devoid of life. At one stage I wondered fleetingly what would happen if the main force forgot about us during the withdrawal, but that soon passed as the sound of MiGs filled the air again.

Shortly afterwards, around midday, I heard over the radio that one of the MiGs on the last strike had been shot down and the pilot was Cuban. This type of news was always cause for celebration, as the MiGs enjoyed full air supremacy and gave us a hard time without any of us being able to do anything about it. It was great to hear that one of them had gone down!

Late that afternoon I heard the unmistakable whine of Ratel engines and knew that the force was on the way back. There was a decidedly upbeat mood among the crews as they drove into the forward assembly area, almost as if they knew that Fapla had been defeated and the job was finally done. They were talking about the number of bombs they had thrown at the enemy and how they could see Fapla soldiers retreating across the bridge. The notion of crossing the bridge and taking the town of Cuito Cuanavale was being freely bantered about, and in one conversation we started discussing the possibility of taking Cuito and just continuing on in a northerly direction. How far could we go?

That 'bullet-proof' attitude was returning, and I think that for many of us, it would have been quite easy to have just kept on going. It was like the second wind that athletes get when they feel they can't go on, yet somehow dig a little deeper into their spirit and find the strength to not only continue, but overcome seemingly insurmountable odds. For me, I think the first Tumpo attack was that low point, and somehow I now felt less enthusiastic about going home and having to fit into Civvie Street again. This probably sounds somewhat contradictory, but the human spirit can be raised or come crashing down equally quickly under such extreme conditions.

We had suffered no casualties in this attack, and by all accounts the resistance encountered was not very strong at all. It appeared that the objective had been achieved, so naturally confidence levels would be high again. What I did find slightly disturbing was that, at times, there seemed to be little distinction between our high levels of confidence and a kind of primitive bloodlust to carry on doing what we had been doing, and go as far as we could. It was what Shakespeare meant when he had Macbeth speak of being 'in blood waded in so deep that turning back is as tedious as going forward'.

It was as if a mental junction had been reached and a single decision would determine the outcome. We had been in this situation and living by a new set of rules for so long that there was only a thin strand still connecting us to Civvie Street and our previous lives. Our hair was long, we wore beards and we were dirty. Had we continued, I fear this strand would have snapped and we could have probably stayed there indefinitely, living by these new rules that we had begun to understand and exploit to our own advantage. This second wind would blow in one of two directions – north or south.

Besides the possibility of crossing the bridge and continuing, there were strong rumours flying around about going home within the next few days. As the rumours grew stronger, so too did the sense of relief and achievement. Sanity (what little was left) had prevailed, and conversations were soon being dominated by the prospect of going home and seeing family and loved ones again. The 'pass' rumours were confirmed a few days later, when we were told that we would be withdrawing and going on leave, hopefully by the end of March. Although still deep in enemy territory and in real danger, nobody seemed to care any more – let's just keep heading south and out of here!

The trip back to the border took a few days and I had to drive the Ratel for a fair amount of the way. The other driver was called Smit, and we took it in shifts. I did not care how tired I felt, I knew we were finally heading home, away from all this shit. I remember being in the turret one night and looking at Orion's Belt in the sky. That confirmed that we were heading south, and it was good. Operation Hooper was about to conclude and fresh troops were on the way to take over from us, clean up the Tumpo area and hand it over to Unita. Tumpo and the Cuito Bridge were now someone else's problem.

It seems pertinent, at this point, to record a few facts relating to the completion of Operation Hooper and the subsequent withdrawal of the main force. The Battle of Cuito Cuanavale has been widely referred to as a major turning point in the history of Africa. While this is undoubtedly true, there have been two very distinct and contradictory interpretations of the outcome of this historic battle. On the one hand, Fidel Castro and the ANC claim that 'The forces of apartheid were dealt a crushing defeat at Cuito Cuanavale,' because we did not actually take and occupy the town. On the other hand, the SADF has consistently said that it had never been their intention to occupy Cuito Cuanavale, as it would have been extremely difficult to hold and defend the position with such a small force.

Military occupation of a town in a foreign country would have undoubtedly posed all sorts of political problems that the government was not prepared to deal with, particularly since these operations had been carried out in a clandestine fashion. The other option would have been to take Cuito and hand it over to Unita, but this was not viable either, as Unita alone would have been no match for the Fapla and Cuban armies, not to mention the Angolan Air Force, which could launch air strikes from the nearby Menong airfield almost at will. There was no natural barrier around the town to assist with the defence of the position, unlike the Cuito River, which formed a formidable obstacle between the town of Cuito and the south-eastern Cuando Cubango province of Angola.

The SADF therefore made a strategic decision not to take the town of Cuito Cuanavale, but rather to clear the south-eastern province of all Fapla forces and hand over a defendable position to Unita. The destruction of the Cuito Bridge would certainly make it extremely difficult for Fapla to launch any further attacks on Unita. The situation was probably best summed up by then army chief, Lieutenant General Kat Liebenberg, when he said that the taking of Cuito Cuanavale by the SADF would have been 'like the dog that finally caught the bus' – and could do nothing with it.

While I am not in a position to assess the political ramifications of these operations, I am able to comment on the outcome of the battle itself. I was there, and I witnessed the situation at first hand. The SADF achieved its objective and Fapla and the Cubans sustained heavy losses, both in terms of personnel and equipment. Possibly the best way of putting the whole thing in perspective is to quote official SADF figures published in *Paratus* (an SADF magazine) shortly after the completion of Operation Hooper. These figures reflect the total losses on both sides for the duration of Operations Modular and Hooper between September 1987 and March 1988.

You decide who 'won'.

South African losses

- 31 soldiers killed
- 3 × tanks
- 4 × Ratels
- 1 × fighter aircraft

Fapla losses

- 4 768 soldiers killed
- 94 × tanks
- 4 × MiG 21 fighter aircraft
- 8 × MiG 23 fighter aircraft
- 2 × SU-22 aircraft
- 8 × helicopters
- 32 × BRDM-2s
- 65 × BTR-60s
- 5 × bunker vehicles
- 4 × radio vehicles
- 372 × logistics vehicles
- 5 × radar systems
- 48 × missile systems (SA 8, 9, 13, 14 & 16)
- 21 × mortars (60mm, 82mm & 120mm)
- 20 × ZU-23 guns
- 1 × ZSU-23-4
- 15 × artillery guns (M-46 & D-30)
- 3 × BM-14s
- 33 × BM-21s
- 7 × AGS-17s
- 1 × GRAD 1-P
- 2 × BTS-4s

7

Thirty Minutes to Clear the Mindfield

THE RETURN TRIP TO the border crossing point was pretty uneventful, though rather tiring. Before leaving Angola, we had to go through a demobilisation camp, where we would get cleaned up, shave and possibly even have a few beers. There would also be a psychological debriefing and evaluation session, which none of us was looking forward to.

We had heard all sorts of stories about guys not being allowed to go on pass because they were not quite 'right' in the head. We were told on a few occasions to be wary of the 'koptiffies' (head or mental mechanics), as they would play with our minds and get us to say things that could be misinterpreted. The main thought at this stage was to just get out of Angola and go home and see our families, and nobody was going to take that away, even if it meant shutting up totally or saying the 'right' things to be declared fit to go on pass.

We were not far from the transition camp when we stopped for the night at a river crossing. The mobile pontoon bridge could only carry one vehicle at a time, so it would take a while for the entire force to cross. The bridge was guarded by a few military police (MPs), who had set up camp on the banks of the river. Being a keen fisherman, I headed for their tent to find out if there were any fish in the river and if they had caught any. The ground in front of the tent was littered with large fish scales, and the MPs told me of the massive tiger fish they would catch on a daily basis. I couldn't help but envy them, spending their national service camping next to a beautiful river in the middle of an angler's paradise, under no immediate threat and being paid danger pay just for being in the operational area.

The river was extremely fast flowing, which made swimming rather difficult, so we hung some ropes off the side of the bridge, walked upstream and jumped into the water to be swept down by the current. The idea was to grab hold of a rope as you went under the bridge and pull yourself out of the current. If you missed the rope, you would have to try to get out further downstream. There were rumours of crocodiles in the river, but this didn't seem to bother anyone. It was just nice to be clean again, and have some fun at the same time – something I fear many of us had forgotten how to do over the past four months.

We arrived at the demobilisation camp late on the afternoon of 17 March 1988. Along the way, we had been told to get rid of all ammunition by burying it in the bush, as we could not take live ammunition out of Angola with us. Most of this had been done, but there were still quite a few '1 000ft flares' in the Ratels. These are signal flares that soar about 300m into the air before exploding and then descend really slowly with the aid of a parachute. They were predominantly used for illumination purposes, but were about to become a rather dangerous source of amusement.

It was quite an achievement to smuggle a few of these flares out, so a number of troops had them in their possession. The thing about the 1 000ft flare is that you can prise it open and remove the parachute, transforming it into a rather effective close-range direct weapon. As we were approaching the demob camp, there was a decidedly upbeat mood in the ranks, much like the excitement of a child about to arrive at a holiday destination after a long car trip. There was almost a carnival atmosphere as we began to realise that we had made it through this ordeal and would be heading home within a few days. It was at this point that the flares began to go up. I suppose it was a way of celebrating our survival of this horrific war and announcing our arrival – we were the victorious soldiers returning from a crusade and wanted everyone to know it. The only thing missing was the hero's welcome. It made for quite a spectacular entrance, although we did get into serious shit shortly afterwards.

Some of the guys thought it would be fun to remove the parachutes from the flares and fire them directly at other Ratels, watching turret crews ducking and diving to avoid being hit. In spite of the obvious dangers of doing this, it was very funny at the time, but no sooner had we stopped at the campsite when an officer (I think it was Major Vermeulen) came charging up, shouting the usual profanities common to permanent force personnel, and threatening to cancel our passes. He had a real go at some of the mortarists (and yes, we were guilty as sin), demanding to know who was responsible, but everyone just acted stupid and said they had not seen anyone actually firing the flares. I suppose it was very much a team thing, where we instinctively banded together and refused to 'dob in' our mates, who had all been through the same shit together. There was also a collective tension while the major was threatening to cancel our passes that I felt could quite easily have boiled over and resulted in the group turning on the officer and physically attacking him. We were not in a healthy state of mind just then, and it might not have been the wisest thing to threaten to cancel our passes, the one motivational factor that had kept us going while staring death in the face repeatedly over the past four months.

Fortunately, the dust soon settled and we were shown to our tents, told to unload our kit and get ready to go and listen to the general, who had taken time out of his 'busy' schedule to congratulate us on a job well done. Personally, I didn't care what the general had to say – I just wanted to grab something to eat and have a few beers. Operation Hooper was finally over, and I could have a shower (with soap) and shave off this fucking beard!

We reported to the parade ground, where a big stage had been erected for the general and to accommodate a band for a welcome-home concert the army had so generously laid on for us. General Geldenhuys stood up and congratulated us on what we had done, telling us how proud our country was, and that, in order to commemorate this historic operation, the largest since the Second World War, the SADF had made a special commemorative T-shirt, which we would all be given. It was a really shitty T-shirt, emblazoned with the phrase *Hooper – Ek Was Daar. I Did My Bit*. The text was printed in the colours of the South African flag and, all things considered, it was a rather pathetic gesture for a bunch of guys who had just been through hell and laid their lives on the line for their country.

We were then told that there would be a braai and the SADF would provide each man with a T-bone steak, to be followed by the concert. I cooked my steak, had a few beers and then decided to try to lay my hands on a bottle of whisky – a privilege reserved for permanent force personnel and officers. There were a few of us who agreed to contribute to the cost of the liquor (provided I could get hold of it), and we would then share it among ourselves in the tent. I managed to find Sergeant McDonald and asked him if he would help me out, which he agreed to do. It wasn't long before I had a bottle of White Horse in my hands and, despite the fact that the only mixers available were a few cans of raspberry soda and water, we proceeded to get stuck into our ill-gotten gains while the rest of the guys were listening to the band.

The concert was quite loud, and at one stage the music stopped. I heard someone shitting on the guys for being too rowdy, as a result of which there would be no more music. A few moments later, though, the band struck up again. I believe that Commandant Mike Muller had intervened and insisted that the concert continue. Did they honestly think that a bunch of youngsters just back from the battlefield would sit there quietly and on their best behaviour after what we had been through?

The next day proved quite chaotic, as it seemed they wanted us to move through the demob camp as quickly as possible so that we could get back on the road and drive to the 61 Mech base near Oshivello. At some stage during the day, everyone had to report for a haircut (which we had to pay for), shave, report to the psychologists for debriefing, obtain permits for our Fapla 'souvenirs', ensure all ammunition was handed in and clean up the vehicles. We were allowed to take home a few pieces of Fapla uniform as souvenirs, but no weapons, bayonets, ammunition or a complete set of Fapla uniform. If you had any of these items, or too many pieces of clothing, you had to hand them in. I was in possession of a complete Fapla uniform, consisting of a cap, trousers, shirt, jacket (complete with bloodstains), belt, boots and a groundsheet. I decided to take my chances and hide some of the items instead of declaring them all. I had no idea how I would get my contraband past security at the airport, but I was sure I could figure out a way.

The main concern was that we did not take any foreign weapons or ammunition home, and I was not about to relinquish my souvenirs to someone who had not been anywhere near the fighting. I know of a few guys who had complete AK47 assault rifles that they'd stripped down and hidden among their personal kit. I have no idea whether any of them succeeded in getting their trophies home, but if they did, well done.

The first task of the day was to shave and report for a haircut, so that we would look human again and not be an embarrassment to the SADF. We had to collect our outstanding danger pay from the mobile pay office, and then it was on to the big one – the psychological debriefing.

Barry Fowler was a permanent force clinical psychologist who was assigned to the team responsible for debriefing soldiers returning from Operation Hooper. He had completed a previous tour of border duty at Oshakati, the main SADF base in Ovamboland (Sector 10), which he subsequently documented in a book called *Grensvegter?* (Border Warrior?)

Now living and working in the United Kingdom, Barry also hosts a website called *Sentinel Projects*, which documents the personal accounts of former SADF members, especially national servicemen. He has written extensively on post-traumatic stress disorder and techniques for debriefing traumatised individuals, and kindly agreed to make some of his work available for inclusion in this book, including the following debriefing model that was specifically designed for Angolan War veterans.

DEBRIEFING TRAUMATISED PEOPLE: A Model for the Treatment of Post-Traumatic Stress Disorder
It's all very well talking about proximity, immediacy and expectancy, but how about some clear guidelines on what to do with someone who is plainly suffering from Post-Traumatic Stress Disorder, and is looking at me to ease their suffering?

THE INTRODUCTION STAGE: It is often helpful for a traumatised person if the helping professional uses the phrase 'debriefing', which does not have the possibly threatening

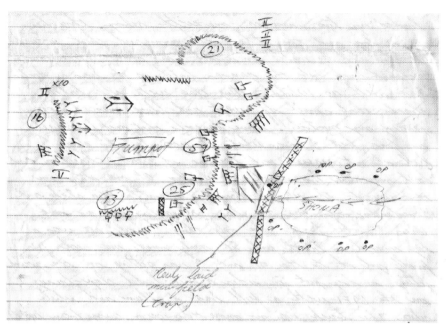

The original map I drew of the first plan of attack on the Tumpo area (25 February 1988) at the pre-attack briefing held the previous evening. The red additions were made after the attack, clearly indicating our approach path and how the newly laid minefield caused so many delays and problems, resulting in loss of life. The circled numbers (13, 16, 21, 25 and 59) each represent a Fapla brigade

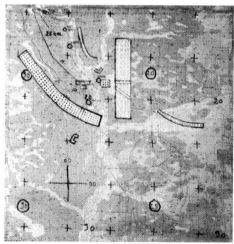

A map that I located on the Internet depicting the minefield around the Tumpo area, presumably drawn by the Fapla field engineers who laid the mines. The blue drawing on the map appears to be that of a heart

South African Olifant tanks in action. Their go-anywhere abilities made
them a formidable force to contend with, even in the unforgiving Angolan bush

The Ratel 20 was well equipped to handle the soft sand in Angola. Armed with a 20mm cannon and a coaxial machine gun in the turret, it also carried an infantry section in the back. Its speed and manoeuvring capabilities meant it could respond to a situation quickly, while being able to deliver immense firepower

Taking stock: The bomb capacity of a Ratel 81; armed with an 81mm mortar and capable of delivering effective medium-range and close support fire against enemy vehicles and personnel

A typical post-battle scene when clearing vanquished enemy positions.
This photo was taken from the turret of a South African tank after
the attack on Fapla's 21 Brigade and quite clearly shows a dead
Fapla soldier lying on the ground

Russian-made T-series tanks typically littered the landscape after every attack. In many instances, the crew would simply abandon the vehicle at the first sign of danger, resulting in many enemy tanks being captured in working order. This particular tank was a casualty of an attack on Fapla's 59 Brigade

A Russian BRDM-2 Armoured Personnel Carrier destroyed during the attack on Fapla's 21 Brigade on 13 January 1988. The same model of vehicle pictured below was captured intact

The battlefield after the Battle of Cuito Cuanavale. Note the total
devastation of what was once dense bush and the destroyed tank

Driving through captured enemy positions
revealed the true extent of the destruction

A BRDM-2 and Multiple Rocket Launcher (Stalin Organ)
destroyed in their positions after the Battle of Cuito Cuanavale

Serviceable enemy equipment being recovered for
intelligence-gathering purposes prior to being handed over to Unita

Souvenirs: The Kwanza was the official
Angolan currency. Although worth
nothing in monetary terms, a complete
set was a sought-after souvenir

The author, sporting a full set of Fapla camouflage.
The jackets were considered a real prize, as they
had the words 'Made in Cuba' printed on
the label. This photo was taken at home
on pass after Operation Hooper

Surveying the damage inflicted on the Calueque Dam
wall after the MiG bombing raid on 27 June 1988

More destruction caused by the parachute-delayed bombs

The water pipelines destroyed in the bombing raid

Fateful vehicle: The Buffel troop carrier destroyed by the bomb that went
'off course' and resulted in the deaths of 11 South African soldiers on 27 June 1988

Medical crew taking off from Ruacana to perform the casevac of the Ratel crew following the contact with the Cuban force on 27 June 1988. Stephen Addison is the Ops Medic in the photo

© Stephen Addison

The sight that greeted the medical crew as they flew into Calueque. The same Ratel crews in this picture were bombed by Cuban MiGs only a few minutes later

© Stephen Addison

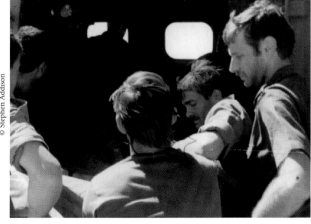

© Stephen Addison

Loading up the injured Ratel crew from the contact with the Cuban force on 27 June 1988

The Ruacana Falls that effectively mark the border between Namibia and Angola

A bomb crater formed during an attack on a
South African base camp just across the Cut Line

connotations to the person's self-concept that use of the words 'counselling' or 'therapy' might conjure up.

It might be necessary to address doubts or reservations, which the person may have, such as 'What is the use of talking about it? It won't bring my friend back.'

Some comfort might be derived for the traumatised person from knowing that the debriefing technique has been used with people who have been similarly traumatised previously, thereby indicating that other people have suffered what he is presently experiencing, and thus that his suffering is not unique or abnormal.

It can also be helpful to inform the person that there is no limit to the time that the session may last, that the process will be followed until it has been concluded, and the person will not suddenly be stopped while he or she is emotionally vulnerable. Confidentiality and the possible limitations of this should be outlined in advance of the debriefing.

THE STORY STAGE: Invite the person to describe the traumatic event which he or she experienced which has led to the referral and presentation for treatment. Many people who suffer from Post-Traumatic Stress Disorder present a history of having coped well with adversity, and often they may try to block out the feelings which might now be overwhelming them. Initially, a traumatised person is likely to produce a very short and factual account of the traumatic event, devoid of any emotional content.

THE BACKGROUND STAGE: Ask the traumatised person to try to describe his or her situation or context before the first hint of the traumatic event. Focus on feelings, mood, and expectations of the immediate future when the traumatic event took place. This may help people to realise how unexpected the trauma was for them, and might help them to accept their lack of preparation in dealing with the trauma, or their initial disorientation during the traumatic event.

THE RETELLING STAGE: Take the person through the story already provided, but ask him to describe his thoughts and feelings during the time of the trauma. The normality of their actions and feelings would be pointed out by the debriefer. Sometimes the traumatised person will, realising what is expected of him, provide a more detailed account of the traumatic event than the one originally presented, but most are likely to try to gloss over the actual emotions experienced at the time, which may be very threatening. The debriefer often has to try to slow the person down, and to ask specific questions about the thoughts and feelings at what he or she might consider to be 'traumatic highlights' noted either during the initial story-telling, or else during this stage.

The most common *emotions* that seem to be expressed are anger and guilt. Anger can either be expressed (often initially) at others: people who should have helped but failed to do so, ambulances taking a long time to arrive, etc.; and (often later) anger directed at themselves: at their lack of preparation, knowledge or skills which might have improved the situation, or saved a life. Guilt may be expressed, often about any actions carried out which might have proved to have been incorrect, and which thereby exacerbated the problem. There may also be guilt about actions, which the person failed to perform, which they, rightly or wrongly, believe that they should have done. People might also blame themselves for not having followed standard procedures, which they might have forgotten in the heat of the moment.

Thoughts remembered from during the traumatic event can sometimes be found to be 'cognitive distortions', and the person can benefit by examining and restructuring them. Common irrational thoughts and beliefs expressed during such debriefings include the idea that it was within the ability of the traumatised person to have saved the life of an injured person who subsequently died. It can be reassuring to a traumatised person to be convinced, if true, that any number of medical specialists in the most modern of intensive care units would not have been able to save the life of that person either.

THE 'GOING BEYOND' STAGE: Ask the traumatised person to continue to narrate the sequence of events that followed the point at which the initial account of the story ended. This might flow on naturally from the above stage. This can provide more information that the person might originally have tried to forget, which might include reactions from others, possibly relatives of the deceased who might blame the traumatised person for not having saved the life of their loved one. This may have reinforced existing feelings of guilt.

Before moving on to the closing stage, and especially if the person has 'warmed up' to the way of exploring his thoughts and feelings, it might be valuable to ask if there are any points which he feels the debriefer might have overlooked. This might enable people who feel that they have to comply with the structure imposed on them by the debriefer, to reveal new relevant material.

THE TERMINATION STAGE: Having worked through the above stages at a pace that has allowed the traumatised person to meaningfully re-evaluate his emotions and thoughts, the following techniques might be useful:

Ask a question along the lines of: 'If you were back in the traumatic situation, but knowing what you know now, what would you do differently?' This may help the person to further clarify how he might have acted differently if more knowledge or skills had been available at the time, had more time to act during the trauma, or fewer distractions. It might also help him, where relevant, to realise that he would not actually have done much differently, which can be used to point out the appropriateness of his actions, even though he might have felt inadequate at the time.

THE 'DEBRIEFING THE DEBRIEFERS' STAGE: Such debriefing sessions, of unpredictable length and involving intense concentration and empathy with much raw emotion to deal with, can be stressful and draining for the debriefer. It is very important for the debriefer to arrange for his or her own debriefing as soon as possible after the debriefing session that they have conducted.

THE FUNCTION OF THE DEMOB CAMP: THE JOB WE WERE THERE TO DO: The purpose of the Demobilisation Camp was to facilitate the termination process of soldiers returning from the Operation Hooper stage of the 1987–1988 war in Angola. The termination process included issuing the soldiers with new uniforms and kit to replace those damaged or lost in Angola. There were also psychological debriefings to identify and treat those likely to develop Post-Traumatic Stress Disorder (which was where the psychologists came in), intelligence debriefings, giving the soldiers a chance to get used to 'wet' rations (fresh food) again after months of living on 'dry' ration packs. Apparently the transition from dry to wet rations resulted in massive outbreaks of 'gippo-guts' (diarrhoea).

That is what should have happened, according to the SADF's own guidelines. This is what did happen.

Special tents had been set up for the debriefing sessions, and we were told to report to them as a group, not individually. I think there were 10 guys in each group. We went into the tent and sat on small benches arranged around the perimeter in a U-shape. The psychologist sat in the middle of the U with a clipboard and some papers. It was about 10h30, and I remember the psychologist saying something about having to be somewhere by 11h00, so the chances of anything meaningful happening were pretty minimal to begin with. I don't remember the psychologist's name, but he was English-speaking, and he began by asking if there was anything that anyone would like to talk about relating to our experiences.

You could have heard a pin drop. Everyone just sat there, shrugged their shoulders and looked at each other as if to say, 'I'm not going to tell this guy a fucking thing. He wasn't there, he won't be able to understand.' It was very much a closing of the ranks, with tacit agreement that the team was not about to let an outsider come in and disrupt things. The one thing I will say is that everyone looked decidedly different. There was something different in our eyes and, in many cases, in the way we spoke. There was one guy in particular, Andrew, who had come into the army as a quiet and deeply religious person. He always did as he was told, never argued, never swore and was generally a nice guy to be around. Something had definitely changed within him. He now swore like the best of us, was very aggressive and had a really wild look in his eyes. The transformation from boy to man had gone a step closer to madman. As for the rest of us, the psychologist eventually managed to drag some information out of us, but the session was over in about 25 minutes and I felt that I had not even begun to get in touch with the emotional and traumatic impact of what I had been through.

Even though I felt relieved that the session was over and that we would all be heading home, I knew there was so much stuff buried so deep inside of me that it would take a long time for it to come out and for me to get to grips with everything that had happened. I felt as though I had been through an entire lifetime in the last four months and seen what most people would never see in their whole life. Yet I felt somehow confident that, at the age of 19, I would be able to cope with all this trauma and life would go on unchanged. How wrong I was.

We left the debriefing tent and went straight back to the tasks we had to complete before leaving. The whole debriefing process was a bit of a rush job and, in my opinion, the army's way of saying 'but we gave you a debriefing session'.

The facts are as described, but you may draw your own conclusions from them.

Barry Fowler's book *Pro Patria*[1] provides good insight into the way the psychologists viewed and coped with the situation. I have selected a few quotations from his work that I feel are both relevant and add credence to an otherwise seemingly unbelievable series of events:

> The soldiers were in well-bonded units that had [mostly!] been together for more than a year. They had been participating in the war for four months by the time we saw them. The psychologists were outsiders – intruders? – and the soldiers were not going to open up and express their feelings to us. It must almost have been an insult to the soldiers: '*You've been in a war, and now you've all got to go and see the shrinks, and we all know that shrinks work with mad people, don't we?*'
>
> We have come across many stories of disinformation, which has had a demoralising effect on our troops. One group was actually airborne, believing that they were being flown to Port Elizabeth to do a course on riot control, when they were told for the first time that they were on their way to Angola. Many of the soldiers did not know they would be going to

---

1 Copies of Barry's books, *Grensvegter?* and *Pro Patria*, can be ordered direct from barryfowler@onetel.net.uk

Angola, and had brought things with them that they would need in an ordinary camp. They spent four months in Angola with things that they would never use. Most had civvie clothes with them, and some had irons with them. [I had mine!] One soldier got so frustrated with his iron that he buried it in the middle of the bush in Angola!

False information was also given to people at home so that soldiers returned from four months in Angola to find letters from their significant others saying: 'So glad you're in Grootfontein. We saw Grootfontein on TV at Christmas and the wonderful Christmas dinner they had laid on for you,' or worse: 'All your letters were posted from Pretoria. Why didn't you phone?'

Friends of a soldier killed by a booby trap believe that his parents were told that he had been killed while 'playing with ammunition'. They were concerned that such false information would also be circulated if anything happened to them.

Soldiers sitting safely at Rundu were given the same danger pay as the people fighting near Cuito Cuanavale – R4,80 per day for national servicemen. Soldiers returning from the battle up north became angry seeing staff who had not ventured further than Rundu wearing 'Ops Hooper' T-shirts. Some complained at having to pay R3,50 for a haircut at the demob camp, and not being treated as *ou manne* [old hands] although they had gone through a lot more than the average *ou man*.

In one debriefing session, the following incident was recounted to one of the psychologists, named Michael:

A Fapla tank burst into South African forces at close range, with a Fapla soldier standing head and shoulders out of the turret. The South Africans opened fire. The first bullet took the fingers off his left hand. The next soldier shot him three times in the right shoulder. The Fapla then put the stump of his left hand to his right shoulder. The third South African then shot him in the forehead, knocking his head back.

'How did you feel about this?' Michael asked.

They looked at him as though this was a stupid question.

'We enjoyed it,' they replied.

A tank(er) was 'taken out', and one person was given the job of removing the body of the driver. The driver had been decapitated. The soldier had to remove the body at night for some reason. The soldier climbed onto the top of the vehicle and looked down through the hatch, but could see nothing. So he put his hand down, and this went into the open neck of the dead driver. The body was trapped so he had to get inside the vehicle to free the legs, and doing so he was surrounded by bits of the driver's head, which also had to be removed.

Neil Tuck spent a long time debriefing an Ops Medic called Sean, who had been traumatised by having to remove the charred remains of a Ratel crew which had been 'taken out'. When Neil tried to trace the man to arrange a follow-up, he was told that no one of that name had been involved in the incident.

I overheard our Major Beatty talking to Chaplain Fred Celliers about what positive religious experiences the guys who had been in Operation Hooper had had [*There are no atheists in foxholes!*][2] and what a difference Christian leader elements had made, with a colonel and a dominee [pastor] fasting and maintaining a prayer vigil on the eve of an attack. They also spoke of a dominee at the front who would hold a prayer service before each attack, and who would go into battle with the troops, and would then hold a thanksgiving service at the end of each battle. The guys relate to him well because he knows

---

2 See Joseph Heller, *Catch 22*, 1961, p. 40.

what they have been through, because he's been through it with them. He would be approached by different combat sections, each asking him to ride with them that day.

One casualty's legs had to be amputated, and the patient was sent down to 1 Mil.[3] A medic had to bury the amputated legs, which was traumatic for him. He had difficulty with the thought that the patient could be recovering in the RSA while his legs lie buried (unmarked) somewhere in the Angolan bush.

I will never forget the day we left Angola. Driving over the pontoon bridge and looking back at the land that had changed me, I felt a distinct sense of relief and satisfaction. Relief that it was all over; satisfaction that I was still alive and in one piece. I had a Walkman cassette player with me and played Chris de Burgh's song 'Say Goodbye to It All' as we drove across the river. I had survived this ordeal and would soon see my family again. Angola was behind me. Or was it?

---

3 1 Military Hospital in Pretoria.

8

Home Alone

THE DREAM HAD FINALLY become reality. We were going home! The trip from Rundu to the 61 Mech base at Oshivello took only a few hours, and it was great to be able to drive on tarred roads without the constant threat of MiGs or artillery bombs. As we drove into the camp, one of the first things I saw was Donald running towards our Ratel. He jumped onto the side step and seemed pleased to see me. He had been sent back to the 61 Mech base after his suicide attempt in Angola and was driving trucks around the campsite.

I don't know what I felt when I saw him. I was happy to see my friend again, but there was also a measure of resentment because he had not had to go through what I had, and envy because he possibly had the foresight to get out of a potentially bad situation before it materialised. *Why the fuck did you make me pull a loaded rifle out of your mouth?*

I knew that Donald wanted to talk about what had happened, but I struggled with this concept, because he had not seen what I had seen and I somehow felt that he should have. How do you explain to someone who was not there about bloodstained Ratels, ducking for your life under fire, being in close contact with dead bodies and generally living like an animal? What do you tell people about the anger you felt when your mates got taken out, or the constant fear that you could be next? I harboured an intense hatred within me that I felt could only be appeased by going back into a combat situation and doing 'better' than I had done before.

Those feelings stayed with me for a long time afterwards, and I often thought about what would have happened if we had just kept on going. We could probably have gone all the way to Cairo, but what did it all mean? Yes, we were the best trained conventional warfare unit the SADF had ever produced, but what would happen when our purpose was served? Did we still have a purpose? By all accounts, the communist threat in Angola had been neutralised, so what more could we do? The answer to this would become clear when we returned from pass.

We had to officially register as members of 61 Mech, and were promptly issued with new equipment and clothing. I heard that all the equipment used in Operation Hooper had been written off by the SADF and that we would all receive brand new kit – what we had in our possession was ours to keep. For most members of the mortar platoon, this was an absolute necessity, as their kit had been destroyed when our supply truck was hit during the first Tumpo attack. Before going home, we had to go back to 1 SAI in Bloemfontein and officially '*klaar-out*' (deregister), as we were to form part of another unit. We would have to go through a security checkpoint at Grootfontein airport, so any contraband items would need to be carefully concealed. I had kept my complete Fapla uniform and now had to figure out a way of smuggling the trousers and boots out.

I simply packed the boots with my SADF pair and decided to wear the Fapla trousers underneath my uniform, thus managing to take my complete set of souvenirs home. None of the Fapla items had been washed and there was a massive bloodstain on the jacket, but this did not worry me. The various pieces of clothing had labels saying 'Made in Cuba', and this seemed to increase their sentimental value, somehow. I don't know how the guys with the stripped-down AK47s fared at airport security, but I managed to smuggle a fair amount of ammunition through, so I hope they succeeded.

The Alpha Company bungalows at 1 SAI had been vacated for us, and the new recruits were given strict orders not to come anywhere near us. We were officially on pass, so there was quite a festive atmosphere, with plenty of loud music and drinking. I caught up with Jaco (who had stayed behind at 1 SAI headquarters) and he was really keen to hear all the gory details and the blood-and-guts war stories. I found this quite disturbing. Here was a guy lapping up every bit of information and wishing that he had been there, while I was not that keen to talk about it and in many ways wished I had been any place *but* there.

This was the first time I really had the chance to sit down and think about what had happened in Angola. It was only a few days since I had left a war zone and, while in it, there had been no time to reflect on the situation, the living conditions, and the overall horrors and brutality of combat. This was also the first time I had been asked to share my experiences with an 'outsider', and in the process I listened to myself and began to reflect on the events I was describing. I left Jaco's room feeling empty and guilty about what had happened over the past four months. I had just lived every young boy's dream of being a soldier, and I was still only 19.

We were flown from Bloemfontein to Pretoria, where I caught a train to Johannesburg. It was strange being back in civilisation. The sights, the sounds, the smells and even the people all seemed unfamiliar. Just about everything in Angola was either green or brown and smelt like diesel, but suddenly I could see and appreciate bright colours and take in pleasant odours. It felt as though I had found paradise.

From Johannesburg station I took a bus home, and there were plenty of university students among the passengers. I wore my uniform and medal with pride and sat quietly on my own. No one even noticed me or spoke to me. I felt like standing up and shouting, 'Don't you know about the war and how close the Cubans are?' But instead, I just sat there and said nothing.

Home felt very different. It was the first time I had really been there since my father's death, and I now had a head filled with other death experiences to try to come to terms with. It was great to see Mom and Gary again, although I had a distinct feeling of isolation because I had not been there to help with the grief and shock of Dad's death. It was almost as if they had formed a deeper bond with each other by sharing that experience. I had formed a similar bond, but it was with my army buddies.

I wanted to speak about my experience and what I had gone through, but it somehow had no place in the overall scheme of things. I would have really appreciated speaking to my father, but instead, I had to deal with his death and put my war aside for the time being. Death had become a part of my everyday life, and I found myself cold and unemotional when speaking or hearing about it, even in relation to my father. It was very much a case of accepting that it had happened and just getting on with doing whatever had to be done next.

Mom and Gary probably thought I was being insensitive, but believe me, I was not. I just did not know how to express all the raw emotion inside of me at the time. In the space of eight months, my father had died, I had fought in a war and celebrated my 19th birthday. I needed to put all of this into perspective in my own mind before knowing where and how to start dealing with or speaking about it.

Something that really stood out on this pass was my feeling of total alienation from the life and friends I had known prior to going to war. I initially thought my friends had changed, but soon realised that I was the one who was different. Society had always been there and kept on going; I just viewed it through different eyes now. I found it difficult to speak to people about what I had seen and done. There was very little public knowledge about the Angolan War, and I got the impression that people thought I was bullshitting when I told them what had happened. I can't blame them for this – they really had no way of confirming anything I said.

National servicemen returning from the border had developed a reputation for embellishing the truth somewhat and making up war stories so as to impress other people, particularly young women. I did not want to fall into this category, so I just shut up and opted not to speak about it. I also felt that so much had happened that I did not know where to start.

We had been praised and congratulated by the chief of the SADF on what a fine job we had done for our country, yet none of us received a hero's welcome. I suppose I had this romantic idea that South Africa would mark our return with some kind of red carpet reception. Instead, what I found was a total lack of appreciation for and understanding of what I had done – because the South African public had been so misinformed (kept in total darkness is more like it) about what had happened in Angola and how serious the communist threat actually was at the time. I felt like a prostitute who had served a purpose and was no longer needed – although prostitutes at least get paid after being screwed.

I spent a lot of my time sitting at home and just relaxing in front of the television. I had always been a sociable person, keen to be part of the crowd and ready for a party at any opportunity. I now felt uncomfortable in crowds of people and preferred solitude to parties. Some of my friends remarked on how 'jumpy' I was.

While walking through a shopping mall one day, someone dropped something that made a loud and sudden bang. Instinctively and instantaneously, I crouched down behind a large pot plant, evoking some rather curious looks from other shoppers.

It was great to be able to watch television again and catch up with what was going on in the rest of the world. I caught glimpses of SADF spokesmen saying something about the recent campaigns in Angola, but they never told the real story. Probably the most memorable event was when I went to the local library to borrow a book. The librarian informed me that I had to become a member first, and gave me a form to complete. I did so, signed the form and handed it back to her. She went through it and said: 'I'm sorry, but you're still under the age of 21. You need to get your parents to sign the form.' I found it deeply ironic that I was old enough to fight for my country and kill people, yet had to get my mom's authorisation to borrow a library book!

Something else I became aware of was how many people, once they knew I'd been in Angola, asked me: 'So, did you kill anyone?' Should any of those curious people read this book, perhaps they will appreciate why that is the most inappropriate question to ask any returning serviceman.

One night, I had arranged to meet my friend, Steve, at a pub for a few beers. On the way, I was involved in a hit-and-run accident when another car slammed into the driver's side of my vehicle. Fortunately, the impact was just behind my door and I was not hurt. Both cars had spun around from the impact of the accident, and then the driver of the Jetta suddenly pulled off and sped away from the accident scene. I gave chase to try to take down his vehicle registration number, but it was too dark and I never drew close enough to read the licence plate. I had almost caught up when the idiot driver started running red lights at intersections.

I decided it wasn't worth the risk of getting injured or killed in a car accident while chasing some prick who obviously has no regard for other people. Besides, I was really pissed off and would probably have killed him if I had caught him. I drove to the police station and reported the accident, which happened in April 1988 at the intersection of Peter Place and William Nicol Drive in Bryanston (just in case the driver of that red Volkswagen Jetta ever reads this book).

The problem was that, with no way of tracking down the other driver, I could not claim against his insurance for the damages. It was my mom's car and her only form of transport. Needless to say, I felt quite bad about it, but Mom seemed to be quite okay and was just relieved that I wasn't injured. I, on the other hand, was really angry that the other driver had gotten away with it. I did not see the potential danger of the accident, but focused instead on pursuing the 'enemy'.

I never made it to the pub that night, and Steve never bothered to phone and find out why I had not turned up. I spoke to him a few days later and he quite casually said something to the effect of 'Where were you the other night, you wanker?' I was quite angry at how fickle Steve was. He had somehow managed to dodge national service, so I had very little respect for him to start with, and he obviously attached no real value to our friendship. My answer was short and sharp: 'In a fucking car accident, you wanker!'

It was probably at this stage of my three-week pass that I began to want to go back to the army and be with guys who truly understood friendship, who supported and looked out for each other and were not preoccupied with their own sense of importance. I wanted to go back to my own team where I had a sense of belonging. I felt I no longer belonged in Civvie Street.

Since my father's death, my mom had been pushing hard to try to get me transferred to a unit closer to home. She was now more determined than ever to do so, and although I would probably have welcomed such a move, I somehow knew that it would never happen. There was unfinished business in Angola, and I knew, deep down inside, that I had not seen the last of that hellhole. The reality of the situation was that the SADF only had a handful of troops capable of dealing with the Cuban threat, and it stood to reason that those who had first-hand combat experience in this type of warfare would be sent in again, should the situation warrant it.

It was with extremely mixed emotions that I returned from pass. Part of me was pleased to be back in familiar surroundings, while another part was concerned about what lay ahead. It felt distinctly like half-time in a rugby match, where both teams have had a break and are about to commence the second phase of the contest. The only difference was that our contest had no rules, and the losers faced death instead of defeat.

9

The Wild West

AFTER REPORTING BACK TO 1 SAI on 20 March 1988, we spent a few days at the base before flying to the operational area again. Back at 61 Mech, there was really nothing for me to do in an administrative role. During Operation Hooper I had effectively learnt how to be a gunner, signaller and Ratel driver. I also knew how to drive trucks, and as there was an apparent shortage of logistic vehicle drivers, I was told to do a quick refresher course in order to get my military driver's licence, a legal requirement for driving military vehicles on public roads. Our next operation would be on the western side of SWA, meaning we would have to travel a few hundred kilometres by road to Ruacana before crossing the Angolan border – again.

Life at 61 Mech was actually quite pleasant. We lived in permanent tents (a standard army tent erected over a concrete base) and soon settled into some kind of daily routine. There was even a chance to take part in sport, which many saw just as a way of getting into town and having contact with civilians – not to mention the chance to ogle the local women. Tsumeb was the nearest town, about an hour's drive from the base. We would occasionally get a day pass, which meant we could spend a whole day in town, but these were few and far between. Not all sports were available at the base, which meant that by choosing carefully, you could pretty much assure yourself of a weekly trip to town. I had been quite a good badminton player early in my school career, so when I heard that badminton was on offer in Tsumeb, I put my hand up straight away.

The person in charge of badminton was a staff sergeant and he was a really nice guy. He ran the kitchen at 61 and lacked the usual arrogant attitude to which most permanent force personnel are prone. Muller Meiring also played badminton, and I came to know him quite well. He was a national service lieutenant with one of our anti-tank platoons (the Ratel 90s), and he had a really pleasant manner about him. If he wanted you to do something, he would *ask*, not shout and scream like most of the platoon commanders.

I enjoyed doing my driving refresher course and it wasn't long before I had my licence. Border life was shaping up to be quite enjoyable, and it looked as though the remainder of my time in the army would be less intense than it had been to date. Unfortunately, this tranquil routine was about to be rudely interrupted by the aspirations of our old foe: Fidel Castro.

I can't remember exactly when it happened, but I became aware of that sense of urgency creeping into everything we did. It was similar to the way things had happened towards the end of our training before we went to Angola. Ratel crews had to ensure that everything was functioning and that they had full quotas of ammunition. Drivers had to do vehicle inspections and ensure that all mechanical problems were fixed, quickly. Communication equipment was being tested and replaced, if necessary. I was given a water bunker and told to familiarise myself with operating its pump system – a motorised pump on the back of the vehicle, with extension pipes, and designed for taking on water from rivers or dams. *Why did I need to know this?*

The water bunker was basically a *Kwêvoël* truck chassis with a 10 000-litre tank on the back. A Kwêvoël is essentially a Samil truck with an armoured cab, designed to protect the driver against landmines and small-arms fire. There was a hatch above the co-driver's seat with a machine-gun mounting bracket, but we very rarely had co-drivers, so we were never issued with guns for logistics vehicles.

The support echelon was made up primarily of Kwêvoël trucks, diesel bunkers, water bunkers and a few recovery vehicles. The command vehicle for the echelon was a Ratel, but it was not really set up for combat. I now formed part of the support echelon and would effectively be one row back from the main firing line, although this had previously proved to be of no consequence when it came to enemy artillery and aircraft. Trucks just made bigger targets and were easier to destroy than Ratels and tanks.

In a way, I felt as though I had been downgraded from the main force to the echelon. Cuito was still fresh in my mind, and I wondered if this had anything to do with my new 'job' in the army. Did they think that I had lost it during the Cuito fight and that it would be better for all concerned if I were a little further back from the front? I was assured that this was not the case and that I would be fulfilling an important role, as well as helping to alleviate the driver shortage. My previous experiences on the front line had been pretty intense, so I was quite okay with the notion of not having a ringside seat for the next fight.

Sometime in early May we were called to the parade ground and told to prepare to mobilise. The order had not yet been given, but we had to be ready to move an entire force at short notice. The order arrived soon afterwards, and we left 61 Mech base late one night en route for Ruacana and the Calueque Dam, which would later become known as the Western Front. Once again, the soldiers on the ground had no knowledge of the big picture or why we were heading for Ruacana. What we did know was that we would almost certainly lock horns at some stage with our old friends: Fapla and the Cubans.

Since the end of Operation Hooper, the SADF had maintained a presence around Cuito Cuanavale and made a few more attempts to breach the minefields, but to no avail. These operations were code-named Packer and Displace and were a further attempt by the SADF to secure the south-eastern corner of Angola as a Unita stronghold. The situation at Cuito, and more precisely at the bridge over the Cuito River and the Tumpo area at the bridgehead, had reached a stalemate. Fapla had laid what was probably the largest minefield in Africa as a means of preventing the SADF from reaching and crossing the bridge, while the SADF had all but cleared the entire Cuando Cubango province of Fapla and Cuban forces. The SADF did launch a few more assaults on the Tumpo area, but were not able to penetrate the minefields, and as soon as they detonated mines, Fapla artillery would rain in on them. Fapla, on the other hand, was unable to launch any more assaults into the Cuando Cubango province, as their own minefield now formed a formidable barrier that they themselves were unable to breach. This posed a serious threat to Castro's objectives of getting his conventional forces into SWA and launching an assault on South Africa.

Being a military man, the Cuban leader had foreseen this problem early on in the campaign. The heavy losses suffered by Fapla during Operation Modular prompted Castro to send his crack 50 Division to Angola in a bid to bolster the forces around Cuito Cuanavale in November 1987. As part of this package came Cuba's top general, Ocha Sanchez, a man who had achieved a number of military successes in Nicaragua, Ethiopia and earlier in Angola. It soon became apparent to Castro that the situation at Cuito Cuanavale was a no-win for both sides, so he needed to find another way into SWA. He turned his attention to the south-western

Cunene province of Angola and commenced deploying his troops in this area.

The primary motivation behind this move was to create a potential threat on the western border of SWA and force South Africa to take appropriate action by redeploying its forces from Cuito to the Western Front. However, Castro was also looking for a way out of his little escapade in Angola, which had almost crippled his country's economy and caused him serious embarrassment. Pressure was being applied by the United Nations for a negotiated settlement that would see all external forces removed from the Angolan conflict. Colonel Jan Breytenbach probably summed it up best in his book, *The Buffalo Soldiers*, when he talked about 'plucking the Cuban sting from the Fapla scorpion' and 'removing the South African fangs from the Unita snake'.

The build-up of Cuban and Fapla forces in the west had not gone unnoticed by the SADF. There was growing concern over the size of the force and its close proximity to the SWA border, which, in that area, was an imaginary line called the Cut Line. South Africa had only a very small force equipped to deal with a conventional assault, and if Fapla and the Cubans decided to advance into SWA, the SADF would have a tough time keeping them out. The SADF could not afford to take the chance that this was nothing more than just a threat, so they sent reconnaissance teams into Angola to get a better idea of what was really going on. At the same time, 61 Mech was mobilised and sent to Ruacana, just in case something happened.

We deployed outside an artillery base near Ruacana and set about creating a camp. As I was now with the support echelon, I had to get to know a whole new group of people, including the sergeant in charge of the echelon, Sergeant Horn. He appeared to be nice enough, but the more I came to know him, the more I disliked him. The first thing Sergeant Horn did when we arrived at our designated camp in the bush was order us to dig a massive hole so that he could make a swimming pool for himself. Fortunately, the sand was fairly soft and it took us only a few hours to complete the task. I could not help thinking that if he had issued this type of order in a combat zone, he probably would have been told to 'Fuck off and dig your own hole!' It was an unwritten code at the front that everyone dug their own foxholes, regardless of rank. Later, in a bid to save time and energy, we would often dig group bunkers for the entire Ratel crew, but everyone would take a turn with the shovel.

I knew all of the guys in the echelon, as they had been in Operation Hooper. We were quite an easy-going bunch and got on well together. Teamwork was something that was firmly entrenched in us through our previous experiences in Angola, and we all knew that the best way for anyone to survive this conflict was for everyone to work together. I doubt whether Sergeant Horn had spent enough – if any – time in a combat zone to appreciate this.

An interesting addition to the support echelon was a coloured NCO, Sergeant Swart (somewhat ironically named, as the word *swart* means black in English). I got on quite well with him and he had a really good sense of humour. I remember that, when he introduced himself to us, we were on the parade ground and he stood up and said: 'I am Sergeant Swart,' to which some wise guy immediately responded, 'Yes, we're not fucking colour blind.' He took most things in his stride, in spite of the obvious racial tension associated with being a coloured person in a traditionally and predominantly white army.

I would often hear permanent force personnel sharing a joke at the expense of Sergeant Swart and wondered if they had ever made any attempt to get to know the man, or if they just lived by their own code of 'black and white shall not mix'. I had a deeper level of respect for this man who had joined the South African army and achieved something despite the extra challenges he would undoubtedly have faced based purely on his skin colour.

Being deployed again meant going back to dry rations (ratpacks), something no one particularly enjoyed, but we were accustomed to it by that stage. Once we had set up camp in the bush, it was back to the old routine of sitting around and waiting for orders to do something. Boredom was probably one of the biggest problems, and we would try to come up with creative ways of overcoming this. Most of us read and would lend each other books in order to have some variety. I heard about some guys in the echelon who had devised a way of distilling their own liquor, using ingredients from ratpacks and some kind of still they had constructed. I wanted to find out how they had done this and see if I could do something similar, so I went to have a chat with them. One of the other drivers came with me, and we had a good look at this rather clever little 'moonshine' operation, making mental notes with the idea of setting up something similar. We decided to make this our next project, and diligently set about constructing our own still. Whenever I think of how we did this, I am amazed at what we achieved with the limited resources at our disposal.

The first step involved making some fermenting liquid that could be processed through the still and form the base for the alcohol. We did this by using a jerry-can (petrol can) and filling it with water. We then added a tin of Marula-flavoured cordial concentrate, as much sugar as we could collect, fruit bars from the ratpacks, dried raisins and apricots. The mixture now needed some yeast to aid the fermentation process, so we threw in a lot of 'dog biscuits' from the ratpacks, put the cap on the jerry-can and left it standing in the harsh African sun for about 10 days.

The next challenge was to make a still for boiling and distilling the liquid. The vessel of choice was a fire extinguisher, the only container that would be able to cope with the heat and pressure of the distillation process. We dismantled one and removed all the chemical powder and the gas detonator device, leaving a perfect cauldron. Then we had to construct some kind of system to cool the steam and condense it back to liquid form, producing the end product. Someone suggested removing a piece of the air-brake piping from one of the trucks and connecting it to the fire extinguisher's outlet pipe. This was done and we spent some time bending the pipe into a coil. Now we had to figure out a way of cooling the pipe to ensure that the steam would condense. A water-filled mortar ammunition case proved to be perfect for this purpose. The entire operation had to be kept secret, as we were not supposed to even think about doing stuff like this – not to mention using the army's equipment for our own amusement or pleasure.

The big day finally arrived and I went to fetch the jerry-can from its hiding place in the bush. The fermentation process had obviously worked well, as the jerry-can was bulging and looked as if it would burst at any moment. The cap had a simple valve for coping with pressure build-up, but it was not designed for this type of treatment. Everything was ready, and we made a bit of a ceremony out of it. We built a fire and, once it had created enough hot coals, the fire extinguisher (containing the fermented liquid) was placed in the middle with hot coals packed around it. The outlet pipe had been connected to the coiled metal pipe, which then ran through the ammunition case, filled with water. No one had any idea if this thing would work or not, but it didn't take long before we had our first batch of home brew dripping into a bottle. It took a few hours to distil all of the liquid, and the end result was a 750ml bottle filled with a rather unpleasant-looking green substance (we concluded that the colour came from the green fruit bars thrown into the original mixture). We shared out our creation and drank it. It tasted horrible, but I was thoroughly impressed that our contraption had worked at all.

From our temporary base, we did a fair bit of driving on the road to Ruacana. On one occasion we went on to the Ruacana Falls, which form part of the border between SWA and Angola. The terrain was dry and arid with sparse vegetation; a semi-desert area, but, as we approached the waterfall, I remember driving over a rise and entering a whole new world.

We found ourselves on the top of an escarpment overlooking some of the most lush, green vegetation I had seen since Cuito. The road ran steeply downhill and all the vehicles had to use their exhaust brakes to avoid going too fast and ending up out of control. It was a fantastic feeling to suddenly go from a dry desert area into what looked like something out of a movie about paradise. I'm still not sure exactly why we went to the Ruacana Falls that day, but it was a really good experience.

The falls themselves were nothing short of spectacular, plunging straight down into a deep gorge. A little way upstream there was a sign marking the official border between Angola and SWA. It became a source of fun to walk into Angola, jump into the river and float down into SWA. The logic behind this little excursion may have been that the SADF wanted to give us a bit of relaxation time before going back to war. I'm not sure, but it was good fun and relaxing, and the scenery was truly spectacular.

Not long after the home-brew adventure, I started feeling ill and feverish. I thought it was just a cold or flu that would clear up within a few days, but this did not happen, and I was in pretty bad shape when Sergeant Horn finally decided to send me for medical treatment. The nearest sickbay was at Ruacana, but I would have to wait for a vehicle, so I spent the best part of two days lying in a sleeping bag under a tree and sweating. Scott and Richard made sure I had enough water and generally kept an eye on me. I was quite delirious and don't recall eating anything during this time – I just wanted to lie there and not move. I eventually got a lift to Ruacana on 7 June, and, on arrival, was immediately diagnosed with malaria, even though I had always taken my anti-malaria tablets without fail.

All I really knew about the disease was that there are two strains, one of which is fatal. Obviously I had contracted the other kind and made a full recovery within a few days. The doctor at Ruacana told me that there was a high likelihood that the malaria would recur over the next few years and that I should be aware of any early warning symptoms. Once these developed, I would need to see a doctor, get some medication and spend a few days in bed. The malaria did recur for about five years after I left the army, but it seems to be totally out of my system now. At the end of our national service, we were given a special card stating that we had recently been in a malaria area and told to carry it with us for the first few months back in Civvie Street, so that if we collapsed or fell ill and were unable to communicate for some reason, medical staff would know to test for malaria.

When I got back to the echelon camp, I was told that we would be relocating to Calueque Dam, just across the Angolan border. There we would set up a logistics base to supply the main force, which would be conducting search patrols higher up into Angola. Calueque Dam also housed a hydroelectric scheme, and the SADF was concerned that this could become a strategic target for Fapla and Swapo forces rumoured to be operating in the area. The logistics base would also serve to occupy and protect the dam.

On arrival at the dam, we promptly got to work setting up the base. We had been told that we were going into a 'hot' area, and we had to start digging foxholes again. One of the first things I noticed at Calueque was how hard the ground was and how long it took to dig a foxhole. I eventually decided to leave my foxhole quite shallow, as I thought there would be no real need for it. The bush was nowhere near as dense as it had been around Cuito, so we had to take extra care with camouflaging our vehicles and foxholes. I decided to park the water bunker under a tree and use part of the camouflage net to conceal my foxhole. No sooner had we set things up than I was informed that the water bunker had to accompany the main force on their patrols to ensure that they had sufficient supplies at all times. So much for being one row back from the action! I was quite comfortable with my role in the echelon and did not really want to go back into the firing line. Now I would not only be doing just that, but I would be doing it in a vehicle that was more vulnerable than a Ratel, and without the capability of returning fire.

On 26 June, we were on a patrol to try to locate a Cuban force reported to be advancing 'in a threatening manner' towards Calueque Dam. We left early in the morning and seemed to drive around aimlessly for hours without finding anything. I began to get that all-too-familiar sense of tense anticipation that all hell could break loose at any stage, constantly alert and on edge, just waiting to hear the first bomb drop or someone shout 'Contact!' over the radio, which would have been pretty useless to me, as my radio worked only intermittently.

The bush was sparse and at times we drove along dirt roads without any available cover in the immediate vicinity. There were frequent stops to check maps and intelligence reports, often resulting in a change of direction, and I sometimes wondered if anybody actually knew where we were or where we were going. As usual, there was not much information communicated to the troops on the ground, so all we knew was that we were looking for Fapla and had no idea when to expect contact or what size force we might find ourselves up against. As it turned out, there were three combined Cuban and Fapla columns advancing, and they were at full strength with tanks, mechanised infantry and regular infantry.

Our search had not revealed anything by late afternoon, so the order came to set up camp for the night and resume the search the next day. I had managed to score a bush shower from the stores at the 61 Mech base that I carried with me in the water bunker, and from time to time I would set it up and take advantage of the opportunity to wash. The shower was a simple contraption consisting of a heavy-duty funnel-shaped PVC (plastic) bag with a shower head at the bottom. The bag would be filled with water and then the whole thing had to be hoisted up into a tree and tied in position, so that bathers could stand underneath and enjoy a shower.

That evening, Lieutenant Meiring asked me to set up the shower for him. He spread his groundsheet under the tree and was standing on it as he washed. I was sitting on top of the water bunker, smoking a cigarette and scouting out a good spot for sleeping. The nights were cold and I would often sleep on the bonnet of the water bunker to take advantage of the lingering engine heat. The alternative, especially when it was windy, was to dig a shallow hole under the vehicle and sleep there.

It was a perfect evening. The sun was setting and there was not a breath of wind. Suddenly, machine-gun fire rang out from the bushes to my right and the radio crackled to life with urgent voices issuing orders. I realised that we had made contact with the enemy and were probably quite unprepared. Images of Cuito came flooding back and the adrenalin began pumping – this war was still alive and well, and once again I found myself in a life-threatening situation in a foreign country, knowing that my family had no idea I was there.

Lieutenant Meiring had to return to his platoon immediately, and asked me to keep his groundsheet and toiletries until he could get them from me the next day. I rolled everything up in the groundsheet and bundled it into the cab of my vehicle, along with the shower. Then I jumped into the cab, grabbed my rifle and tried to get some information over the radio about what was going on and what we had to do next.

Standard operating procedure, when attacked like this, was for everyone to get into their vehicles and be ready to mobilise immediately, either in an attacking or defensive pattern. But things were pretty chaotic and it seemed that nobody really knew what was going on. I heard something about tanks over the radio, then orders came through to evacuate all 'soft-skin' (non-armoured) vehicles back to Calueque Dam immediately until the situation had been stabilised. This attack had taken everyone by surprise, and our commanders had to get a grip on the situation quickly to evaluate the size and capabilities of the attacking force. There were only a few support vehicles to be evacuated and we had to do so under Ratel escort.

The drive back to the dam was about 30km, and I reckon we made it in record time. It's not much fun being in an unprotected vehicle with tanks and mechanised infantry bearing down on you. The Ratels are better equipped to handle rough terrain at high speed, so when they set the pace, you do whatever it takes to keep up. There were quite a few rear-end accidents along the way, due mainly to the excessive dust and lack of visibility. Often, if the vehicle in front of you stopped or slowed down suddenly, you would only become aware of this as you collided with it.

On one trip to the dam, I had a corporal with me as my co-driver and, when the dust suddenly thickened, he realised that the vehicle in front must have stopped. He was obviously used to this, as he went into what looked like some kind of bracing position, anticipating the impact. He didn't have to wait long. Within a matter of seconds we went careering into the truck in front of us (which had stopped) but, fortunately, did not incur any major damage or injury. These vehicles were built to withstand that type of treatment and most accidents resulted in little more than a few dents to the massive protective steel bumpers. Sure, we used to be read the riot act by the echelon commander whenever we had accidents, but it was probably more a case of him doing what the army expected him to do. We were in a war, after all. So what if the vehicles got damaged?

On the night of the attack, we arrived at Calueque Dam after dark and I managed to find my previous position under the tree. The cab of the truck was a mess. Everything had been bundled inside and now lay strewn all over the interior, thanks to the hasty retreat. I was quite tired and feeling a little shaken, but I did not want to go to sleep. I would more than likely be rejoining the main force in the morning, so I really needed to get some rest, but felt as though I could not sleep. At the time, I thought I was just feeling the effects of an adrenalin rush, but, in fact, something far more serious was going on. It felt as though I was back in Operation Hooper. The familiar levels of intensity were back and playing with my mind. I was jumpy and overly alert, listening for any noises in the bush and ready to respond immediately. I finally managed to go to sleep under the truck with my rifle by my side and near the foxhole – just in case.

The next morning was quite calm, and we set about refuelling, checking ammunition stocks, ordering rations and carrying out various other 'housekeeping' tasks. No one could have imagined that this was about to become one of the most significant days in southern Africa's history, which would change the course of events in South Africa forever.

It was around mid-morning when one of the other drivers came up to me and asked, 'Do you know Lieutenant Meiring?' I replied, 'Yes, I've still got his stuff in my truck, does he want it back?' thinking that his platoon had returned to the base some time during the morning. I was anything but prepared for the answer my companion gave, quite casually, really: 'No, he has just been shipped out in a Jiffy bag.'

I felt sick, as though someone had kicked me in the stomach. I could not believe what I was hearing. I asked what had happened, and this guy said that Lieutenant Meiring's Ratel had been hit by an RPG-7 in some kind of ambush. The projectile had apparently scored a direct hit on the turret from close range and there was not much left of the lieutenant. The rest of the crew had also sustained injuries in the attack.

I later found out that the main force had continued looking for the advancing Cuban–Fapla column early that morning, and had driven through a small valley with dense bush. They had no idea that enemy infantry was lying in wait.

Once in the valley, soldiers rose up from the bush and fired RPGs from close range, taking out a Ratel 90 that could not be recovered and had to be blown up to avoid capture. The contact with the ambush party was the signal for the rest of the enemy force to engage. Their tanks and armoured assault vehicles were concealed behind a ridge, but soon appeared to engage 61 Mech. They fought back and inflicted heavy casualties on the enemy, including 302 soldiers killed, two T-55 tanks and two BTR-60s destroyed, along with eight trucks. Lieutenant Meiring's Ratel was shot out by an enemy tank and also had to be destroyed to avoid capture.

Part of me wanted to go and see his body so that I could be convinced in my own mind that he was really dead and that this was not some warped practical joke, but I decided not to. Instead, I went and sat under a tree and spent the next hour or so silently staring blankly into space, trying to get to grips with the death of a friend whom I had been speaking to only a few hours ago and whose personal belongings were still scattered around the cab of my truck. It all came to the surface, then: everything that had happened during Hooper; the incident with Geldenhuys; my dad's death and now Lieutenant Meiring's. I felt as if it was all beginning to close in on me, and for the first time I began to doubt whether I could cope. But who could I turn to, where could I go for help? I was an aggressor in a foreign country and part of a military outfit that had one solitary purpose: to destroy the enemy. Mental health was not high on the agenda, and as long as you could perform your assigned function and not succumb to any physical illness or injury, it was assumed that you were okay and fighting fit – if there's no blood, there's no injury. Never mind the mental injuries that nobody was able to see, like cracks in a foundation that are not evident at first, but have the potential to bring the whole building down in time.

In the army, the last thing you want is to appear weak in front of your fellow soldiers, so the only real option was to shut up, keep your feelings inside and carry on with life. I had done this over and over, and now it felt as if all of the emotion bottled up inside needed to be released somehow.

The guys who did show their emotions were labelled *bossies* (bush mad), and although in most cases the army just turned a blind eye, there was the odd occasion when they would be sent back to South

Africa for psychological evaluation and treatment. The problem was that our training told us this was a definite sign of weakness, and most young men, particularly in a military environment, do not want to be perceived as weak.

I was 19 years old and wholly unequipped with the emotional or psychological maturity to realise that the coping mechanisms I was using were probably the worst kind for dealing with such intense situations, and would result in long-term effects for many years after the war was over. As Barry Fowler pointed out, traumatic events need to be spoken about and dealt with as soon as possible after the event. Even if you feel okay and say that you are over it, these events are still inside your head, and they will come home to roost at some stage in the future unless they are addressed and dealt with in the present.

I continued sitting under the tree for the next few hours, con-templating whether I should go and speak to someone about how I was feeling or whether I should 'crack' and just start shooting wildly into the bush. The latter would certainly attract some attention and more than likely result in me being sent home, but then I would have to bear the failure or 'weakling' label, and there would certainly be something on my medical record about a mental condition. Talking to senior staff about this kind of thing was usually dismissed as someone just trying to 'gyppo' (shirk their duties) and get sent back to base, leaving the rest of the guys to do the job. Let's face it, SADF permanent force personnel had no idea of how to deal with psychological issues and could focus on only one thing: winning the war. To win the war you had to be tough; there was no place for weaklings.

Fair enough, but how many times do you have to stare death in the face to qualify as 'tough'? How many deaths (of your friends) do you have to deal with and how many contacts do you have to go through to earn that badge? I felt that I had already earned mine, yet knew that by speaking to someone about my feelings, I would lose it and have it replaced with that of weakling. 'Fuck it!' I thought. I had not come this far to be sent home with a cloud over my name. I was going to see this thing through and deal with my feelings later.

At about 15h00, someone (I think it was Swannie) came and asked me if I wanted to go fishing with him and a few others. Those of us who had seen the pristine fishing waters in Angola during Hooper had brought some basic fishing gear from home after our last pass. We could not take fishing rods, so we used hand-lines and would fish whenever we had the opportunity. We caught mainly small fish and generally ate them as a source of fresh food – a welcome change from ratpacks. I thought a bit of fishing would be a good way for me to get my mind off what I was thinking about, so I joined the expedition and headed for the water's edge, a few hundred metres from where my truck was parked.

The fishing was going well, and I was beginning to feel a bit better and to accept that what had happened was just another death in this war. I mean no disrespect when I say that; it was the only way I could cope with the situation at the time and remain focused on the job at hand. When you find yourself between a rock and a hard place, neither option is appealing, but you have to choose one. I chose to bury my emotions and put on the proverbial brave face, even though I felt sick to my core.

It was around 16h00 when I heard the familiar sound of fighter jets in the air. At first, none of us reacted, as we assumed it was our air force going in to support the main force, but then we got a visual and it was one of the most frightening things I have ever seen. Four aircraft flew along the opposite side of the dam and then banked sharply towards the dam – and us. As they did so, we all realised they were MiGs and that we were in serious shit. We were in the open, and these MiGs were clearly coming in for a strike, directly at us! We dropped everything and began to run towards the trees for cover.

It all happened so quickly, yet I clearly remember seeing the bombs being released from the wings of one of the MiGs as I started to run. There was a lot of shouting as everyone scattered for cover. I had just made it into the tree line when the first bomb detonated really close by. The noise was incredible, and all I could think of was getting back to my foxhole and away from the dam. There was a hail of machine-gun fire from the MiGs and more bombs exploded as I ran. It felt as though they were right behind me – this was a serious attack. I just kept on running, hoping (and praying) that the next bomb would not hit me. The explosions kept on coming, each one shaking the earth and filling the air with dust and debris. My legs seemed unable to move fast enough, and even though I thought my time on earth was up, I kept on running, fully expecting to be taken out at any second.

I finally made it back to my truck, grabbed my helmet and lay face down in the foxhole. It was fairly shallow, but I hoped it would be deep enough. I had heard stories of how the force of exploding bombs could lift a person out of a shallow foxhole and rip you to pieces, so I kept my head down and continued praying hard. Returning fire with rifles was totally ineffective and would only serve to reveal our positions, so we just had to keep our heads down and hope for the best.

The whole thing lasted mere minutes, but my mind recorded it in slow motion, as usual. It was like having a nightmare in which you can't run fast enough to get away from whatever monster is chasing you. People often talk about your life flashing before your eyes in a situation like this, but all that flashed before my eyes were trees, dust and smoke as I ran like hell to take cover. I just kept on telling myself, 'I'm not going to die today!' until I reached the safety of my foxhole.

It is the sense of self-preservation that takes over in extreme life-and-death situations which I believe drives us to accomplish whatever we have to in order to avoid death. I can only liken it to a mind-over-matter scenario, in which the mind overrides the body's physical constraints and allows it the freedom to perform at a level previously unseen, a level that surpasses what we believe our bodies are capable of achieving. While some may disagree with my reasoning, anyone who has actually faced death and triumphed will know exactly what I am talking about. We make a *decision* not to die and our mind takes over. Yes, there are situations that are beyond our control, but, while we are still breathing, we are still alive, and the choice to remain alive drives us to believe that we will achieve this. We will almost always choose life over death.

The air strike was over and it was time to assess the damage. The target had been the dam wall, and nobody could understand the reasoning behind this. It seemed like a pretty senseless strike, but I later found out that the intention had probably been to prevent us from crossing the wall and launching more land attacks on the Fapla forces. With the road running over the top of the dam wall sufficiently damaged, the only other viable crossing point was Ruacana, and the enemy had quite a large force deployed in that area, waiting for us. Another, more sinister motive for this action was to effectively trap all SADF forces already on the other side of the dam and systematically slaughter them, with no possible escape.

At first it appeared that we had not incurred any loss of life or serious injuries, but then a message came through that one of the bombs had gone slightly off course and landed next to an 8 SAI

Buffel (troop carrier), killing 11 South African soldiers instantly. We lost 12 soldiers as the angel of death roamed freely among us that day.

In a bizarre twist of fate, May 2005 saw me meeting up with Stephen Addison in Melbourne, Australia. He was the Ops Medic who, along with two doctors, performed the Calueque casevacs. Steve and I spoke at length about what had happened that day at the dam and how what had started out as an evacuation, by Puma helicopter, of the wounded and dead crew of Lieutenant Meiring's Ratel during the earlier attack, rapidly deteriorated into something that none of the medical personnel were prepared for.

'Soon after the two Pumas landed at Ruacana to stabilise the patients before flying them back to the surgical base at Ondangwa, the MiGs came screaming overhead,' Steve recalled.

'Within seconds, we heard the earth-shattering noise of the bombs detonating, echoed with fury in the valley below. Within minutes, the Pumas with the medical crew aboard were airborne again and racing back to Calueque at tree-top level.

'We could not believe the sight and smell that hit us as we landed in the same place where we had been only a short while earlier. We frantically began trying to evacuate the wounded men and place the shattered remains of the dead soldiers in body bags, while the pilots and flight engineers watched anxiously for signs of more enemy aircraft.'

Steve also showed me photographs of the casevac operation, one of which finally gave me closure on the death of my friend, Lieutenant Muller Meiring. Of all the casevacs he was involved in during the war, Steve said, the one from Calueque was by far the most distressing – worse than all the others combined. I hope that everyone involved was able to deal with what they witnessed and had to do that day, and I salute all the Ops Medics and doctors who were tasked with what was possibly the most gruesome and sickening part of any war, the casevacs.

Immediately after the air strike, there was still a lot of tension at Calueque. I think we were all concerned that there would be another strike or that the first one had been intended to soften us up for either an artillery strike or ground assault. We had received no early warning of this attack, so who could tell when they were planning the next one? All the feelings and thoughts I'd had during my earlier pondering had returned, and I found myself not wanting to leave my foxhole. I remained there for about an hour, and recall a couple of guys walking past and sniggering to each other. I did not care. I was sweating, my body was shaking and I felt that I could not go through any more of this without something snapping in my mind (if it hadn't already done so).

Shortly afterwards, I wrote to my mother, asking her to please find out if there was any news on the transfer I had applied for after my dad's death. It had been almost a year since I had put in a request to be stationed closer to home, so I knew there was really very little chance of anything happening, especially since I only had about six months of service left. I knew someone who was being flown back to South Africa, and he agreed to mail the letter for me so that it would not have to go through the usual censorship process. My patriotic pride was running low and I just wanted to get out of this fucking war and go home! It was very much like the 80/20 rule in business, where 80 per cent of your income is generated by 20 per cent of your clients, only this was more like 90/10 with 90 per cent of the war being fought by 10 per cent of the army. Surely the SADF could find someone else to have a go?

As we set about tidying up our camp and fortifying our positions against more attacks, we had no idea that the events of 27 June 1988 had been recorded by the media. It took little more than 24 hours for the front pages of all of South Africa's national newspapers to be dominated by reports of the Calueque Dam incident and the 12 soldiers who had lost their lives. This effectively forced the SADF to admit (once again) to its involvement in Angola and paint a realistic (if not frightening) picture of the potential communist threat posed by the Cuban presence.

The SADF took a real beating from the South African media over its lack of information about the situation and the involvement of national servicemen in this conflict. The names of those who had died at Calueque Dam were published, and I think that, for the first time, the South African public realised the extent of SADF involvement in Angola. Obviously, the whole story was not released at the time, but the SADF did go into quite a lot of detail about the operations and why it was conducting them. When you look at the situation in Angola then, it pretty much justifies the SADF's decision to deploy troops around Calueque Dam. The Cuban force had reportedly built up to around 60 000 as a result of reinforcements being sent to protect Cuito Cuanavale earlier in the year. This force was still in Angola, and the bulk of it had been deployed close to Calueque in preparation for a possible large-scale offensive into SWA.

The communist threat was real, but no one knew exactly what their intentions were. It could have been that they in fact planned to invade SWA and link up with Swapo cells there, or it could just have been a sabre-rattling exercise. Either way, the SADF was vastly outnumbered and had to deploy as many conventional warfare-trained troops as possible in this area. Deployment of the combined Cuban and Fapla forces would have allowed a two-wave assault on SWA, consisting of two equally strong forces advancing one behind the other. This strategy allows the first force to penetrate as far as possible into a country, and as soon as it begins to run out of steam, the second force or wave comes in and continues the advance, penetrating even deeper into the country. Besides being very threatening, as pointed out by Colonel Breytenbach in *The Buffalo Soldiers*, this method of waging war was in exact accordance with Soviet doctrine.

The international attention drawn by the Calueque Dam incident prompted the United Nations to bring all parties back to the negotiating table as quickly as possible in a bid to reach a settlement. The South African public was demanding answers as to why their sons were fighting a war in a foreign country, and the SADF could not tell them the full extent of the communist threat without risking massive panic. The only way South Africa would even consider a withdrawal was if the Cubans did the same. Something obviously came from these negotiations, as we were quickly issued with orders to withdraw from Calueque Dam and observe a ceasefire agreement. We vacated our positions and withdrew to a base just south of the border, still ready to fight at the drop of a hat. The initial shock of the air strike on Calueque and the subsequent deaths was soon replaced by anger and aggression among the troops. 'They' had got the better of us at the dam and we wanted a chance to even the score.

The following months saw us on the move most of the time, but never going far from the border. We would set up camp outside other bases in the area, spend a few days at each site and then move on to the next one. I believe one of the objectives of this pattern was to create the illusion that a massive force was present in the area, so as to deter any possible Swapo activity, while still being within striking distance of the border should the Cubans decide to advance. I can't recall the names of all the bases we stayed at during this period, but there were several. On one occasion we even participated in a parade through Oshakati – another show of strength. The whole process became quite tedious, but it was better than having your life threatened on a daily basis and not knowing whether you would actually make it home. This was probably the SADF's way of making sure that we stayed 'sharp' and ready to engage the enemy should the need arise. I don't think any of us had any idea of the enormity of the Cuban force just across the border and the potential slaughter we would have faced had they taken the decision to invade SWA. It was probably just as well.

One day we were sitting outside a base and going through the usual routine of checking equipment, ammunition and supplies when word came that we had to pack up and move again. This time it was different, though. The sense of urgency prompted me to think, 'Fuck! Here we go again!' A base on the SWA side of the Cut Line (I think it was Okalongo) had been attacked by what appeared to be mortar or light artillery fire the night before. We had to go in and take up positions in the bush around the base, wait for another attack and then mobilise and track down the enemy.

The base was about 5km from the Cut Line, and by all accounts a small group of insurgents (probably Swapo) had crossed the border, carried out the attack and fled back across the border to the safety of Angola. The orders that were issued made it quite clear that, should this type of attack happen again, we would not worry about this imaginary line and do whatever was necessary to eliminate the attackers. I filled the bunker with clean drinking water and we were on the road again, heading for another fight.

Upon arrival, we immediately deployed into the bush around the base and saw some decent-sized bomb craters fairly close by. That sense of anxious anticipation was back, although no one really knew what to expect or who we would be up against this time. Reports seemed to indicate that the attack was not the work of the conventional forces we were used to clashing with, but rather smaller groups of foot soldiers, carrying out quick strikes and then retreating immediately. These types of attacks fitted the SADF description of 'terrorist' activity, and were what people in South Africa generally associated with being 'on the border' or in the operational area. I found it somehow ironic that we had been in the operational area for about 10 months and had not yet experienced that type of contact. When comparing this sporadic activity to the kind of fighting we had done at Cuito Cuanavale, the cross-border raids seemed somehow insignificant and rather pathetic. There were no tanks, no MiGs, no artillery and no Cubans. This was a different kind of warfare – guerrilla warfare – with different threats and different rules. This was terrorism, and we would have to change our tactics in order to be effective against it.

Landmines began to pose a different type of threat than in Angola, where they were laid in fields to act as a defensive or early warning system, heralding the advance of an opposing force. In SWA, the landmine assumed a decidedly more offensive role. With nothing but dirt tracks to drive on and plenty of Swapo terrorists in the area, there was always the chance that a mine could be laid on a track you had just driven on, waiting for your return trip. Another rather disturbing story doing the rounds was that Swapo's tactics had been adapted so as to be more effective against mechanised infantry by setting up ambushes on the main roads. The particular type of ambush in the stories doing the rounds involved a trip wire across a road at the height of a Ratel turret. The trip wire was connected to an explosive device (usually a hand grenade) positioned in a tree at the same height as the turret. The whole thing was based on the Claymore ambush strategy, with the idea that the Ratel would hit the trip wire and cause the explosives to detonate, killing or injuring any crew members who might be standing out of their hatches at the time. I never encountered one of these ambushes, so I cannot confirm or deny their existence.

We soon settled into a relaxed daily routine and were quite comfortable with the idea that our job was to sit around waiting for something to happen, and then to respond. The water bunker had been ordered to accompany the main force again and act as their drinking water supply, so I was back in the familiar territory of not knowing when or where to expect the next attack. There was a big bomb crater only a few metres from where I had parked and I could not help thinking that if another one (of whatever made that hole) landed anywhere nearby, I would not have much cover. Without the threat of MiGs and their massive bombs, we did not dig foxholes. Another reason for this was that, in the event of an attack, we would have to mobilise immediately in an attempt to track down and kill our attackers. The preferred sleeping options involved digging shallow trenches and then parking the Ratel over them, so that there was little chance of being hit by flying shrapnel or bullets.

Guard duty suddenly took on a higher level of intensity. We now faced the real threat of being attacked by foot soldiers and had to be more alert and vigilant than ever before. Radio procedures and smoking rules had to be enforced to the letter, as sound and light were dead giveaways at night. At one of our many campsites, a guard heard noises and detected movement coming directly towards him through the bush. He went through all the procedures of 'challenging' the intruder and, getting no response, opened fire, only to find that he had shot a stray cow.

One of the biggest problems during this type of deployment was boredom. Unlike the fighting in Angola, when we knew we would be shot at by something every day, there were now long periods when nothing happened. Reading material was in short supply and you can only check your weapons so many times a day, but, fortunately, we found a new form of entertainment – donkey riding! There were a few wild donkeys wandering around the bush, and it did not take long before someone came up with the idea of catching and riding them. The hardest part was getting onto the animal, which would inevitably bolt and run into the bush. You just had to hang on and hope it did not go too far from the campsite. We had no saddles, so it was pretty uncomfortable riding these animals, which had the cunning habit of running as close to bushes as possible in an attempt to dislodge their riders.

Things were going well and we had almost slipped into 'holiday mode' when the Ratel 20s were ordered to go to the shooting range and 'shoot in' their weapons. At the same time, the support vehicles were ordered to move inside the base perimeter.

The base was manned by troops from the South African Coloured Corps (SACC), and I couldn't help but notice how seriously they had taken the previous attack. They had constructed massive bunkers, using whole trees to form the roof. The bunkers could probably house about 20 people and were positioned at various strategic points within the base. The troops were generally a friendly bunch who took pride in what they were doing, particularly on the parade ground.

We had been assigned a tent and kept pretty much to ourselves, though we were called upon to help out with bunker construction and other tasks around the base. The reaction procedure, in the event of another attack, involved a warning signal, which meant everyone had to get into the nearest bunker and await further instructions. While this was happening, the main force deployed around the base would mobilise and try to locate and destroy the attackers. I was not very comfortable with the fact that massive trees had been used to cover the bunkers. There was a very real chance that this could be to our detriment should the bunker take a direct hit.

So it happened that, when an attack came, I found myself sitting in the bunker contemplating the logic behind surviving the war, only to be crushed by a tree while taking defensive cover. This may sound paranoid, but we had been promised passes some time in October and I really wanted to stay alive so that I could go home and see my family again.

As it turned out, we only had to use the bunker on that one occasion. The attack was quite heavy and involved mortars and rockets, but compared with Calueque Dam, it did not seem as threatening. I don't know if this was a true reflection of the attack or if I had just become a bit blasé after Cuito and Calueque. I somehow felt that nothing could come even close to what I had already gone through. Sure, there were the usual anxious feelings and butterflies in the stomach; being under fire is never easy, you just get used to it, as we had done before.

It was not long after the attack on Okolongo that we received orders to pack up and move again. There was obviously no longer a threat in the immediate area, so we had to move to another base and take part in an exercise. This was probably yet another way of maintaining a presence in the area without being officially deployed. I was informed that the water bunker would be seconded to the tiffies (mechanical maintenance) for the duration of the exercise, and that I would fall under their command. This was possibly the best news I had heard in a long time. The tiffies were Citizen Force members who had been called up to do a camp, and, as a result, they were far more relaxed and a pleasure to be around. They worked hard and sometimes very long hours trying to keep the entire force mobile, but they also partied hard at the slightest opportunity. They had access to as much beer as they wanted, and there was a sort of roster system in place where everyone had a turn to buy a case of beer.

The sergeant in charge of the tiffies, Eddie, was a Portuguese-speaker from Johannesburg, and we got on well. During a serious drinking session, I got really drunk and started going off about Geldenhuys and what had happened during Hooper. I did not recall everything I said, but when I was told the following morning, it disturbed me deeply. Apparently, I told them that I felt guilty about what had happened at Cuito, and the more the other guys tried to reason with me, the more aggressive I became. I do recall that at some point I was lying face down in the dirt, crying and punching the ground.

I withdrew quite a bit after this incident, but felt more embarrassed than anything else. I did not speak about Operation Hooper again. My new buddies had not been there, and I felt there was no way for them to understand what had happened or what I was going through. So I did what I had been doing for the past months – shut up and thought about something else. As anyone who has done any reading or research into the field of PTSD will know, I was starting to show classic warning signs of something I would not recognise for several more years.

I don't recall the official name of the exercise we were engaged in, and I didn't really care at that stage, but it took us to the end of September, which meant our next pass was only weeks away. This stint had lasted almost six months, and there was a real carnival atmosphere when we returned to base and finally went on pass on 6 October 1988.

10

Only the Dead Have Seen the End of War[1]

THIS TIME, GOING HOME was quite different. Perhaps it was because I knew my national service was almost over and that, by the time I returned to base, there would only be about two months left. In addition, the peace talks were continuing and by all accounts it seemed that we would not have to go back into combat again. I felt like celebrating, but with the situation in Angola still poised on a knife-edge, I thought that any premature celebrations might be tempting fate.

The Calueque Dam incident had made the front page of all the major newspapers in South Africa, and my mom had kept them for me. For the first time, I felt that people might start to appreciate what I had been through, because it had become public knowledge. The reality, however, is that unless the event affects someone directly, it is forgotten soon after making the news. Besides, the attack had been in June and it was already October.

While at home, I retrieved the letter I had written to my Mom after Calueque about wanting a transfer. I felt somehow ashamed that I had admitted to genuine fear, so I put the letter away and told myself that it was written in a moment of weakness and that everything would be fine now.

This pass also saw the development of some rather disturbing

---

1 Plato.

behaviour patterns. I found myself having nightmares about Angola and struggling to sleep peacefully. I had not experienced nightmares during the war, so why were they starting now? Battle scenes would play over and over again in my mind and I began to analyse them, thinking that perhaps I could have done things better or been 'braver' in certain situations. I was also starting to remember details that I had previously either blocked out or buried deep in the hope that they would go away forever. My mind was daring to relax for the first time, and I was becoming seriously concerned with the amount of information it had to process and put into perspective. I kept on telling myself that it would all be fine once my military service was over and I could get on with my life.

Unfortunately, the human mind is such that it is always looking for solutions, and, when presented with conflicting information, a state of cognitive dissonance is the result. The mind seeks balance, and when there is none, it works even harder to try to find answers or explanations. Traumatic experiences are not within the mind's perception of normal events and it won't rest until it achieves that balance again.

People often talk about experiencing internal conflict – being torn between two or more options and having to make a decision. The key is to make a decision and then work with the choice you have made. It is the same as the concepts of right and wrong. Neither exists as an absolute – they are merely our perception of an event or information based on our belief systems, morals and values. When something happens, it is just an event. How we view or perceive that event determines whether we label it right or wrong.

At the time, my belief system was telling me that what I had experienced definitely fell into the spectrum of 'wrong', and I was having difficulty distancing myself emotionally from these events in order to process them objectively. It was all becoming rather frustrating, so I resorted to just blocking out these events and focusing on something else. The only problem was that they were still stored in my system, in my subconscious, and my mind was still trying to achieve that elusive state of balance.

It was while on this pass that I began to seriously consider the option of staying in the army by joining the permanent force or taking a short-service contract for a few more years. In a military environment, war was an acceptable part of the package and a way of life, which meant it would fall into the category of 'right' and be easier for my mind to process. I was beginning to feel totally alienated from civilian life, and viewed staying in the army as an easy way out of an increasingly confusing situation.

I did not mention this to my family at the time, because I could see how relieved my mom was to have me home for a while. I can't even begin to imagine the stress she must have endured, not knowing where I was or what I was doing, except that I was in a war. My challenge was that I had been playing by a different and rather extreme set of rules for so long that I was having difficulty reverting back to my original rules, morals and values. Behaviour that was acceptable on the battlefields of Angola had no place in civilian society.

Apart from my sleep disorder, I found myself drinking heavily and fairly frequently. It was almost as though I felt that if I got drunk enough and passed out, I would not have to face the nightmares, and would be able to get a good night's sleep. It also seemed that the only time I would mention anything about Angola to other people was after a few drinks. Perhaps I felt relaxed enough not to care whether they believed me or not, perhaps the alcohol broke down some of my mental defences and allowed certain information to come to the surface. I don't know. What I do know is that I did not like this pattern, yet did nothing to break it. If it is true that we supposedly drink to forget, why do we always end up reminiscing about old times, lost loved ones or broken relationships when we get drunk? Perhaps intoxication offers an immediate way out or an excuse, allowing us to say things like 'I did not mean what I said, I was drunk,' or – even worse – 'The alcohol made me say/do that.'

Towards the end of my pass, I met someone, and we started dating. One night I stayed over at her place, and in the morning she asked me if I had been dreaming about an ex-girlfriend. She said I was talking a lot in my sleep, and it sounded as if I was saying, 'I want you back.' I had actually been dreaming about Cuito, but when I tried to explain this to her, I realised it was simply beyond her comprehension. By then, the nightmares had become quite frequent and I would often wake up in the middle of the night in the proverbial cold sweat, unable to go back to sleep. Once more my thoughts drifted to the short-service contract the army had offered us just before going on pass, and which was starting to look like a very real option. At least I would be around people who had experienced what I had and we could talk about it. There was also a financial incentive to sign up.

My return to base was delayed by two days due to suspected appendicitis, which turned out to be a misdiagnosis, but resulted in my having to wait for the next available flight to Grootfontein. I did not mind, as this gave me more time to spend with my girlfriend, and I did not feel that I would be letting my team down, as with little more than a month of our national service left, there was no real prospect of being deployed in combat again. If anything, the remaining time would be spent preparing to hand over vehicles and equipment to the incoming troops.

The flight from Pretoria to Grootfontein on 2 November 1988 turned out to be a comedy of errors, which resulted in us turning around to make an emergency landing in Pretoria after about two hours. Apparently there was some problem with the aircraft's hydraulics, which meant the landing gear would not engage and the aeroplane had no wheels to land on. The crew had to drop the landing gear manually, using crank handles. This was a fully loaded cargo plane with only about 10 passengers on board, some of whom were journalists on their way to cover SADF activities in SWA. After landing safely, we were told to disembark and wait until another aircraft became available. The journalists were the first out and, as they stepped onto the tarmac, one of them knelt down and kissed the ground, obviously very pleased to be back on terra firma.

I eventually arrived at Grootfontein late that afternoon, only to find that, due to the delay, no transport had been arranged from the airport to 61 Mech (about 200km). I checked in with the local command and was told to go and sleep in the old detention barracks. There were a few guys from other units who also had to sleep over and no arrangements had been made for food, so we pooled what we had and shared it. Dinner was half a tin of spaghetti in tomato sauce and a can of Coke, with breakfast being half a tin of evaporated milk and two biscuits.

I finally made it back to base, only to find it almost deserted. Fortunately the guys had not been deployed, but were out doing another exercise, which did not last long. My last few weeks of national service were spent primarily in the base, performing whatever jobs and tasks were required. Brand new kit was issued to everyone for use in the Citizen Force, and many of us exchanged phone numbers and made plans to stay in touch once back in South Africa. All in all, it was a very uneventful time, and I think we were all preoccupied with counting down the days we had left in the army. I celebrated my 20th birthday during this period, which was just another excuse to get really drunk with my friends.

I also came to a decision about staying in the army, deciding against it. I reasoned that I had still not fully come to terms with my father's death and that my family probably needed me more than the army. I had been feeling a lot more positive since returning to base and thought that I had somehow dealt with all the war issues while on pass and put them behind me. In reality, all I had done was suppress these issues and my emotions even further. At the same time, I decided to break off the relationship with my girlfriend.

When the big day arrived on 6 December, we stood proudly on the hallowed parade ground of 61 Mechanised Infantry Battalion for the last time. Commandant Mike Muller praised us for our actions over the past 14 months and told us to go home and be proud of what we had achieved for our country. There was also mention of additional medals, which we would receive when reporting for camps at our designated Citizen Force commando units (to this day, these medals have never materialised). Then we were dismissed, loaded onto trucks and driven to Grootfontein airport. National service was over.

The atmosphere and excitement on the flight to Johannesburg was similar to that of children about to arrive at a holiday destination. There was also a heightened sense of pride that we had served our country well and were about to be welcomed home. Uniforms were neat and tidy, boots gleamed and each protruding chest bore the unmistakeable gold Pro Patria medal. This would be our finest hour, in which the pain of war is momentarily replaced with patriotic pride. Although no one knew what to expect, I think we were expecting something – after all, we were about to land at Jan Smuts Airport (now called Johannesburg International), South Africa's largest airport, and we had been to hell and back for our country.

The aircraft touched down amid much cheering and jubilation

on board and taxied past the main terminal to the cargo section of the airport. We disembarked and were promptly told to walk about a kilometre to the passenger terminal if we wanted to find a taxi.

David was so pissed off that he stepped into the path of an oncoming utility vehicle and forced the driver to stop. He asked the driver, a black man, if he would 'mind' giving us a lift to the main terminal. The driver agreed. From the main terminal I shared a taxi with three other guys to Johannesburg station (about 20km), where I caught a bus to Randburg (about 35km) and walked home from the bus stop. I dropped my kitbag in my room, got on my motorcycle and headed straight for the pub that my friends used to frequent.

That night, I went to a local club with some friends, and although it felt good to be there, I was also uncomfortable, isolated and out of place. I bumped into Claire, with whom I had shared a brief relationship before going to Angola, and we spent some time talking and catching up. During the course of the evening, one of my friends introduced me to a young girl and promptly told her that I had just returned from Angola. The first words out of her mouth were: 'Wow, so did you kill anyone?'

I put my beer down on the pool table, went outside and sat quietly on my own for a while.

11

Cowboys Do Cry

IT HAS BEEN SAID that bravery is a measure of our ability to mask our fear and appear fearless in a dangerous or life-threatening situation. I find this very interesting because, in the heat of battle or when our lives are threatened, we all feel fear. It makes no difference who we are or how well trained we are to deal with life-threatening situations: fear is ever present. Those who mask their fear are called 'brave', while those who outwardly display it are usually labelled cowards or weaklings, incapable of dealing with the situation.

The truth is that everyone experiences fear in the face of danger, but we mask it for the sake of overcoming the threat or in the interest of self-preservation, which is perceived as bravery by our peers. This is largely due to society and what we are led to believe as being expected of us. The old expression 'Cowboys don't cry' is, in my opinion, absolute bullshit. It is the cowboys who don't cry that end up struggling to cope with things later on in life. This has been documented over and over. The army did a good job of training us not to cry, but conveniently forgot to put any contingency plans in place for dealing with the stress of our prolonged 'act of bravery'.

When a person is placed in a life-threatening situation for extended periods of time, there has to be some kind of debriefing or coping strategy in place. It is inconceivable to think that anyone can endure this level of mental and emotional stress without needing to let off some steam occasionally. Even pressure cookers have release valves!

On completion of my national service, I had bottled up enough traumatic stress for 10 normal lifetimes, with no valve to release the pressure. There were times when I felt like exploding and shouting and screaming at anyone and anything, but couldn't. I was back in civilisation and that was not acceptable behaviour. On other occasions, the pressure would manifest itself in the physical need to get into a fight or act aggressively towards others, in the hope that they would respond and start a fight. I became a very ill-tempered and aggressive person within only a few months of leaving the army. I had never been like that before and it became a major concern for me.

In terms of a career, I had no idea what I wanted to do. Many of my old school friends were already two years into their tertiary studies, but I felt I had spent that time acquiring a degree in war, for which I now had no use. I could not financially afford to go to university, and the prospect of entering yet another system, governed by another set of rules, did not appeal to me. Claire and I had rekindled our relationship, and in January 1989 her father, Keith, offered me a job as a sales representative with his industrial chemical supply company. I accepted because it meant I would spend a lot of time on the road, by myself, and at least be earning an income. Keith and I developed a very special bond, which transcended the usual employer/employee relationship or that between a young man and his girlfriend's father. It soon became apparent to me that I had placed Keith in the father-figure role as a means of filling the void created by my own father's death.

In February, Claire experienced a personal trauma, and I found myself in the support role, helping her through it. This was not an uncommon role for me, as I had gained significant first-hand experience in helping others during my time in Angola. A close friend of mine, Ian, was in a similar situation, having to cope with news that he had failed his final school exams and would have to repeat a year. Ian and I shared many a late-night conversation in which we would try to solve each other's problems, invariably after a night out and quite a few beers. I think at the time we both felt comfortable with the idea of being with another 'victim' and reciting our tales of woe to a sympathetic ear. The 'victim mentality' habit is one that we can so easily fall into and, once in, it is very difficult to break out of.

What do I mean by 'victim mentality'? Have you ever found yourself in a group of people when one of them tells a story about something bad that had happened? All the attention is on this victim, so the rest of the people in the group try to outdo the story by relating their own, far worse accounts, thus making them appear more of a victim than the original storyteller, in an attempt to draw attention to themselves. This leads to a decidedly negative conversation, with everyone focusing on their own level of 'victimness' and enjoying the attention and sympathy of their peers. While it is often painful for the victims to tell their stories, they attach a higher value to the pleasure received from all the attention. That is the victim mentality in which I had totally immersed myself, without even knowing I was doing so.

I spent the rest of the year living somewhere between the new and the old, not wanting to acknowledge that I had issues that needed to be dealt with. It wasn't until New Year's Eve of 1989 that everything came to a head, and the boil finally burst.

We had a party at home, with the whole family, girlfriends and their families, in attendance. Everything went well until midnight, when people started hugging and wishing each other a happy New Year. Mom came up to me with tears in her eyes and said how much she wished Dad could have been with us – and that was when something inside me snapped.

I don't know what triggered my reaction, but I think it was just seeing everyone so happy and feeling that I could not share in their joy. So many thoughts were rushing through my head all at once: my father not being there to celebrate with us; the families of the guys who never made it out of Angola. How would they be 'celebrating'? I pulled away from my mom and ran outside, shouting and swearing. Gary followed me out and tried to calm me down and find out what was going on. I told him to 'just fuck off and leave me alone'. I noticed Mom and Claire standing a short distance away, and I could see that they were too scared to even approach me. I had displayed aggression and violence in front of people who loved me, and it frightened them. It frightened me, too, and I decided to do something about it.

The next day, I apologised to everyone for my actions and asked Mom if I could borrow the caravan for a while. I needed to get away and spend some time trying to figure out what was going on inside my head. Someone suggested seeking psychiatric help, but I already had a major mental block against that, based on my debriefing experience. I felt that it had not helped in the past, so what would be different now? I did not tell anyone where I was going or how long I would be away, and ended up booking into a caravan park near Hartebeespoort Dam, where I spent about a week in deep reflection and solitude.

I decided that the initial step would be to change my environment by looking for a different job. At the same time, I joined a martial arts school as a means of regaining self-control and discipline. I am pleased to say that, since taking that step, I have never been involved in a fight. Whenever a situation appeared to be heading towards physical conflict, I had the discipline to walk away rather than engage. To many people it must have seemed that I was too scared to fight, and they were right. I was reluctant to get into a fight because I would probably perceive my opponent as being the 'enemy', and I had been taught that there was only one way to deal with the enemy: kill him. Physical conflict, at that stage, represented life or death; there was no grey area in between. So I learnt how to avoid it.

My search for a new career brought me into contact with a man called Terry Cohen, who owned a Success Motivation International (SMI) franchise. I went to his presentation on how to start my own SMI business, and was particularly impressed with the way Terry spoke about personal motivation, achieving goals and mastering control over our own lives. I wanted to learn more, so I borrowed money from my mom and enrolled for Terry's course on personal motivation. Attendance was mandatory in order to buy into the business, but I was more interested in the personal growth potential it offered and viewed it as a way of finding possible solutions to my situation. I regarded Terry as a mentor, and his teachings had a significant impact on my life. I became a more positive person and started to learn how to understand some of the conflict that was raging inside me. It was through this process that I became acutely aware of the areas in my life that required immediate attention and ongoing maintenance.

The process of self-evaluation can be extremely intimidating for most people (myself included), as it involves taking a long, hard and honest look at yourself and identifying areas of your life that you are not happy with. It is often easier not to go there, for fear of what we might find. While this process may be challenging, I believe it is the first step in the pursuit of change and ultimate fulfilment. How can we change our lives when we don't know what we want (or need) to change?

During this time I met Alison, who would become my wife, and although we did not become involved in a relationship until almost two years later, we did make a connection on a deeper level. She was studying psychology as part of her degree in speech pathology and we spoke for hours about the power of the mind, motivation, attitudes and the psychology of life in general. Here was a person who operated on a similar level to me and possessed the ability to listen without passing judgement.

The next two years saw me move around a lot and work in many different jobs, ranging from nightclub DJ to bouncer, tool salesman, clothing salesman and even roof painter. I could not settle in one place or one job for any length of time and ultimately found myself back in Johannesburg, broke and living with Mom. During this time of instability my relationship with Claire had ended on a particularly sour note, and I soon embraced victim mentality once again.

The problem with living as a victim is that it can restrict us from moving forward because we spend so much time and energy reliving past (negative) experiences. It can also lead to a very destructive process of self-sabotage, during which we are so surrounded by pain, negativity and failure that we start believing we are not worthy or capable of experiencing success. Ever met those people who say things like, 'Knowing my luck ...' or 'I never win anything' or 'I'll never have that much money/success'? These are the people who, when things actually do start going well for them, do not want to let go of their victim identity – so they do whatever it takes to sabotage the process and remain within their comfort zone. Once this has been achieved, they typically say things like, 'See, I knew it wouldn't work, things never work out for me.'

Once we are able to break free of this victim mentality and start to focus on what we want to achieve, as opposed to all the 'bad' things that have happened to us, the future suddenly becomes a very exciting prospect. Unfortunately, it took me many years to realise just how much time I had spent living in the past.

The past consists of a series of events that have occurred, which we cannot change. What we *can* change is our perception of the events and how we use these experiences to better shape our future. This is not something I have just made up; it is an accepted psychological principle, and I learnt about it through studying the work of people such as Anthony Robbins[1] and Paul Counsel, both of whom are considered leaders in the field of personal development. Change cannot occur without action, and action cannot occur without direction, so it all boils down to making a decision to go out and find the information you need, internalise and apply it.

I was not prepared to settle for what was happening to me, so I went back to Terry's teachings and made a decision to change things on a massive scale. My other option was to continue down the path of self-destruction, which had become unpleasant and painful. As human beings we are driven by only two forces: pain and pleasure. When the pain becomes unbearable, we will do whatever it takes to *avoid* any further pain and, conversely, we will do whatever it takes to *acquire* a certain level of pleasure. It was that level of pain that drove me to make the decision I did. Within a matter of three months I got a full-time job as a photographer, started a relationship with Alison and moved into a rented house with her in February 1992. I was 23 years old and my life seemed to be heading in the right direction.

On 26 June, Alison's brother Greg was killed in a car accident.

I immediately assumed the support role for Alison, yet found myself struggling to display any emotion about Greg's death. There

---

1 www.tonyrobbins.com

was the pain of loss inside me, but not much made it through to the surface. I had begun to get quite close to him, and found myself in the all-too-familiar position of saying goodbye to a friend, so I automatically reverted to my default system of blocking out all emotion and doing whatever had to be done to help Alison and her family through the grieving process. I had only known the family for about six months, and in a way I saw myself as an outsider in the situation. The family had made me most welcome, yet I somehow felt I had no right to be upset or show any emotion. I did not understand why I felt that way.

This was the first time I had been forced to deal with death since leaving Angola, and although I was unaware of it at the time, it had stirred up dormant feelings inside me. I started to have the odd nightmare and occasional flashback. I did not tell anyone about it, as I thought it would soon go away – and things did calm down within a few months. What was disconcerting, though, was that there was obviously still a lot of 'stuff' inside me that I had not dealt with and thought had gone away. There were still monsters lurking in the dark recesses of my mind, and they would have to be faced and vanquished at some stage.

Shortly after Greg's funeral, Alison and I talked about our relationship and where it was going. We had been together for just over six months and things were really good between us, so the inevitable 'M' word crept into the conversation. We knew we loved each other, and Greg's death had reinforced just how suddenly loved ones can be lost. We decided to get married and live our lives to the full. We shared a mutual determination to experience everything life had to offer, because you never know which day might be your last. Our wedding was on 2 October 1993, by which stage we had bought our own home on a luxury housing estate. Achieving this required plenty of hard work, often working two jobs at the same time, but we knew what we wanted and nothing could stand in our way.

Our first five years of marriage were absolutely wonderful, but not without incident. I was still experiencing flashbacks, although the anger and aggression had given way to feelings of guilt. I felt guilty about surviving in Angola, when others had been killed or maimed. I could not come to terms with the brutality of many of the events that had happened during the war and invariably offloaded on Alison, who then assumed the support role for me. A relapse or flashback could occur at any time and it became a matter of trying to pinpoint what had caused it – commonly referred to as 'triggers'.

Triggers come in many shapes and forms and could be something as innocent as the smell of diesel fuel, the sound of an aircraft, a sudden bang, certain words or even songs that somehow remind us of the traumatic event. What happens is that the mind associates particular sounds, smells, words or surroundings with the traumatic event that has been categorised as 'bad' or dangerous, and connects directly to that event, causing it to be recalled and appear real at the time. Anthony Robbins is an authority in this area, which he calls neuro-associative conditioning, and I have found it to be highly beneficial in pinpointing and dealing with triggers.

There were occasions when my flashbacks would occur in front of other people, and I usually ended up feeling embarrassed afterwards. If I felt it happening and was able to identify it in time, I made an effort to excuse myself and would usually go and sit outside, on my own. A common cause was being in a crowded room and suddenly starting to feel that I needed to get out of there and have some space around me. This is called anxiety, and is often accompanied by physical symptoms such as muscle tension, sweating, shortness of breath and uncontrollable shaking. Once you are able to identify and understand the process, it becomes a lot easier to start dealing with the cause.

I am doing no more than scratch the surface of post-traumatic stress disorder and the associated symptoms, reactions and causes. If you are interested in learning more about the subject, I have no hesitation in recommending a book titled *Post-Traumatic Stress Disorder (PTSD) and War-Related Stress*, produced by the National Centre for War-Related Stress in Victoria, Australia. It has provided me with an invaluable understanding of the condition and explains things in layman's terms, so you don't need a degree in psychology to benefit from it.

Another common symptom I displayed was being in a constant state of alertness, keeping an eye on my surroundings in order to detect possible dangers or threats before they materialised. The correct term for this symptom is 'arousal', and it is usually characterised by the person appearing jumpy or constantly on edge. Once again, this is based on my personal experience and research; I am in no way claiming to be qualified in or an authority on the area of PTSD.

Over the years my flashbacks became less frequent, but I knew in the back of my mind that if I were ever going to truly conquer this condition, I would have to reopen the Angola files at some stage. Sometimes I could go for months at a time without anything happening, but then I'd have a sudden relapse. Thankfully, Alison always stood by me when this happened.

On 1 October 1998, the day before our fifth wedding anniversary, I experienced a truly life-changing event when our son, Kynan, was born. The effect this had on me was enormous; it was like a paradigm shift into a whole new world. Besides the usual happiness and pride associated with childbirth and becoming a father, I felt as though I had finally achieved something meaningful by having been involved in the creation of life rather than the destruction of it. My own life now had new purpose, something really positive to focus on. It was as if a massive weight had been lifted off my shoulders and I could let go of my past and devote my attention to my family and their future. We emigrated to Australia 11 months later, and even though this was a particularly stressful time, I did not have any relapses.

We weren't even thinking about relocating at the time, but the decision was made when Alison was recruited for an excellent position while we were still in South Africa. However, leaving South Africa meant more to me than just moving to another country. It was as if I was leaving a haunted house, along with all its ghosts.

I established a consultancy business, and on 2 October 2001, exactly eight years after Alison and I were married, we were blessed with the arrival of our daughter, Courtney. I had not experienced a relapse since arriving in Australia and things were going really well for us.

Sometime in 2002, I received an e-mail about a new website called SAreunited.com, which offered a database of South African schools for the purpose of tracking down old friends with whom contact had been lost over the years. I thought it was a fantastic concept and promptly registered as a member. A short time later, the website added a database of South African military units, through which you could catch up with old army buddies. This started me thinking, and something inside me stirred. I still wanted to get in touch with Geldenhuys, so I posted a message on the notice board in the hope that he would find it and contact me. This did not happen, but I did hear from a few other guys who had been in Angola with me, and this prompted me to float the idea of writing a book on the war. The feedback I received was very positive, as no books had been written on the Angolan War from the perspective of the troops who were involved.

I knew that writing this book would mean opening up old wounds again and running the risk of possible relapses. I also knew that I had grown considerably as a person, and a book was something I had always wanted to do. I could see that Alison was not enthralled by the idea initially, but I think she also realised that this would be my opportunity to revisit Angola in a different frame of mind and approach it from a more objective perspective, and finally deal with it. I had gone through immense personal growth by learning from Paul Counsel, my client and mentor. He had shown me how to get back in touch with who I *really* am and inspired me with the confidence to take on challenges I would normally have shied away from in the past. There is a Zen philosophy that goes something like this: 'When the student is ready, the teacher appears.'

I took a deep breath, and opened my Angolan War diary.

Reflections

THE ANGOLAN WAR AFFECTED my life and the lives of many others in ways we have not even begun to fathom. It was never my intention to produce a historical account of the war; that has already been done. I wanted to write a first-hand account of what it was like to fight in the war, based on my personal experiences and thoughts, which I recorded in my diary.

My experience of PTSD is by no means unique to me, or the guys who fought in the Angolan War. This is a condition that can affect people from any walk of life, both in military and civilian environments. My research into this field was undertaken as a personal project in order to gain a deeper understanding of the symptoms and how to deal with them. By sharing some of this information, it is my sincere hope that other people may identify some of the behaviour patterns I experienced and seek either more information on the subject or professional help on how to deal with PTSD. I have no idea how many people are going through what I have been through, but I hope this book will inspire some of them to take action.

Writing this book has not been without personal challenges, but it has been extremely therapeutic, so perhaps we will see a few more personal accounts of the Angolan War make their way into the public arena before long.

Throughout our lives, there are times when we enter a place of darkness, where the one thing we desire most is light, so that we can navigate our way through the blackness.

In many instances, we are not able to create that light ourselves, yet somehow it seems to appear when we need it most, and usually from an external source.

So we gladly accept the light, often without so much as acknowledging the provider, and continue on our journey through the dark place.

Possibly the most important thing I have learnt during the process of writing this book, and from the healing process that has taken place within me, is that none of us will ever be the only or last person to enter that dark place.

We gladly accept light from others, navigate a path through the darkness and, upon reaching the other side, extinguish the light in most cases and continue on our journey, leaving our path in total darkness.

But what about the others who are going to enter that dark place after us? What if there is no one to provide them with the light they need to find the path?

To accept light from someone when you need it is easy; to pass it on to another in time of need is more difficult. To leave it burning once we have found the path, so that others may find it too, requires giving. And that is why I have written this book: to illuminate a path for others who may still be lost in the darkness.

If we can all give but one thing back throughout our lives, leave one candle burning for the benefit of others, possibly even strangers, then I truly believe we will experience the absolute joy of sharing, giving and helping others.

When I started writing this book, a friend of mine quipped that he knew of at least two words that it would contain: The End. Upon reflection, however, I feel that this is by no means the end. It is my dream to be able to establish a foundation for veterans that will provide them with the support and resources necessary to live a long and happy life. With that in mind, may this be

THE BEGINNING

Roll of Honour

At thy call we DID NOT falter,
Firm and steadfast we stood.
It was your will for some to perish,
Yet you turned your back on those who fought.
An army so proud of its troops …

Or so we thought.
National colours are not awarded in battle,
Yet the soldier's game has higher stakes.
We played not to win but to be victorious,
Defeating more than opposition
And defying death itself.

14 FEBRUARY 1988
A Groenewald
PH Groenewald
J van Niewenhuizen
J Kleynhans

16 FEBRUARY 1988
Price

19 FEBRUARY 1988
Major Ed Every

21 FEBRUARY 1988
J de Lange
Two unnamed soldiers

25 FEBRUARY 1988
Tank driver
Hendricks

27 JUNE 1988
Andries Stefanus Els
Emile Erasmus
Johannes Reinhardt Gerhardus Holder
Evert Phillipus Koorts
Phillipus Rudolph Marx
Muller Meiring
Thomas Benjamin Rudman
Gregory Scott
Noah Tucker
Michael Johan van Heerden
Wynand Albert van Wyk
Johannes Mattheus Strauss Venter

AUTHOR'S NOTE: Where the full names of the deceased soldiers are not given, it is not out of disrespect, but purely because I have been unable to establish them, despite making every effort to do so. My lack of success is yet another reflection on the limited amount of information about the Angolan War that is available, even now.

Glossary

I have written this book on the assumption that readers have little or no knowledge of the SADF structure, equipment and terminology. Here are some of the unfamiliar terms and abbreviations used.

Air-burst – A bomb specially designed to detonate a few metres above the ground, creating massive devastation. Usually delivered by aircraft or artillery.

AK47 – Soviet-made assault rifle used by both Fapla and Unita.

Bossies – Colloquial term for 'bush madness', a condition associated with strange/abnormal behaviour as a result of spending prolonged periods of time in the bush under combat conditions.

Buffel – South African anti-mine troop carrier.

Civvie Street – Term used to refer to non-military life, home, friends and family.

D-30 – Russian medium-range artillery gun that could also fire anti-tank rounds.

Fapla – Angolan Army.

Fiver – Common term for the 300kg bombs dropped by MiG fighter aircraft, derived from '500-pounder'.

Foxhole – A type of bunker that we had to dig whenever the force stopped for longer than one day, to serve as personal protection against air strikes or artillery fire. Ironically, foxholes were expected to be about two metres deep and long enough for a man to lie down in – hence it was like digging your own grave every time you stopped somewhere.

G5 – South African 155mm artillery gun capable of firing a 47kg bomb up to 40km.

Kwêvoël – South African 9-ton anti-mine truck used for transporting ammunition, supplies and spare parts in operational areas.

Laager – A defensive position involving the deployment of vehicles in a circle, with command vehicles in the centre. This strategy dates back to the days of the Great Trek, when the Voortrekkers would arrange their ox-wagons in a laager as a defensive measure against marauding bands.

Log vehicle – Logistics vehicle used for carrying ammunition and supplies.

M-46 – Russian-made long-range artillery gun (similar to South Africa's G5) capable of firing a 33kg bomb up to 27km.

MiG – Refers to the two models of Russian fighter aircraft used in Angola; the MiG 21 and MiG 23. Both were armed with a 23mm cannon, various air-to-air missiles and an assortment of air-to-ground weapons, such as 500-pounder and air-burst bombs.

Olifant – Tank used by the SADF. Essentially a modernised version of the Centurion Mk V, with a 105mm gun and carrying 72 rounds. These tanks formed the point of the arrowhead formation used when attacking enemy positions.

Ops Medic – Derived from 'Operational Medic', highly skilled front-line military paramedics attached to specific units during combat and trained to deal with casualties on the battlefield.

Ou Manne – Outgoing troops who were about to complete their two years of national service.

Platneus – A derogatory term used to describe Fapla soldiers. Directly translated, it means 'flat nose'.

R4/R5 – Assault rifles used by SADF troops.

Ratel 20 – South African mechanised infantry assault vehicle armed with a 20mm cannon and coaxial machine gun. The three-man crew consists of a commander, gunner and driver. It carries a nine-man infantry section in the back.

Ratel 81 – South African mechanised infantry assault vehicle armed with an 81mm mortar mounted on a turntable in the centre of the vehicle. The top of the vehicle opens up when deployed and the mortar is capable of firing an 81mm bomb up to 4 856m. The five-man crews were extremely effective in delivering support fire onto designated targets or being deployed as a cut-off force to prevent the enemy from escaping. The assortment of bombs carried by these vehicles could be applied against either enemy vehicles or personnel.

Ratel 90 – Essentially used in an anti-tank role in Angola, this vehicle is armed with a 90mm low-pressure gun and carries 72 rounds. It accounted for many of the enemy tanks destroyed in Angola.

Ratpacks – Daily food packs consisting of dry rations such as cereal, coffee, tea, high-protein biscuits, flavoured cold drink powder, two small tins of canned food and specially designed (or at least that's what they told us) energy bars that became known as 'Tarzan Bars'.

SADF – South African Defence Force (renamed SA National Defence Force since 1994).

Samil – Range of heavy-duty South African military trucks.

Shona – Open clearing surrounded by bush, characteristic of northern SWA and particularly Angola.

SWATF – South West African Territorial Force.

T-54/T-55/T-62 – Various models of Russian tanks used in Angola.

Tiffies – Nickname for mechanical maintenance crews who had to fix all the vehicles and equipment we broke or that were damaged as a result of enemy fire.

Unita – The movement opposed to the Angolan government and led by Dr Jonas Savimbi.

Vegspan – Combat team, consisting of whatever elements were necessary to carry out an assigned offensive.

Victor-Victor – The call sign to warn troops of an imminent air raid. Victor is radio code for the letter V and the call sign originates from the Afrikaans term *vyandelike vliegtuig*, meaning enemy aircraft.

White phos – Mortar bombs containing white phosphorous.

ZU-23-24 – Traditionally an anti-aircraft weapon, this is a quadruple 23mm gun system capable of firing between 800 to 1 000 armour-piercing and high-explosive rounds per minute out of each of its four barrels. These guns were mounted on a PT-76 amphibious tank chassis and could be easily moved around. They were later used with deadly effect to deliver direct fire on the South African forces and were probably more feared than any other weapon in Fapla's arsenal.

Do you have any comments, suggestions or feedback about this book or any other Zebra Press titles? Contact us at **talkback@zebrapress.co.za**